DOUBLE STANDARDS

DOUBLE STANDARDS

AVIVA HELLMAN

Doubleday & Company, Inc., Garden City, New York
1981

ISBN: 0-385-17358-X
Library of Congress Catalog Card Number 80–1861

This book is dedicated to my husband
Yehuda and my children Dor-Lee,
Jonathan and Pinny—with love.

Contents

DOUBLE STANDARDS

Prologue

TODAY

Beth and Adam Stillman stepped out of the elevator into the lobby of the Roosevelt Hotel. It was teeming with people, and signs of "Adam Stillman for Congress," "New York City Wants Adam Stillman," and "Adam Is STILL Our MAN," covered the walls. Young men and women carrying placards with his picture, and wearing hats and carrying balloons with his name printed on them, were standing around anxiously waiting for their victorious candidate.

As soon as the Stillmans emerged, the air of quiet anticipation turned to shouting frenzy. Strobe lights blazed as television cameras began to roll and photographers started taking pictures. A group of newspapermen rushed over, screaming questions at the Congressman.

Adam flashed a big, hearty smile and threw his arms forward as though wanting to gather everyone to him.

"Have you heard from your opponents?" someone asked.

"The Democrats are far more gracious than my conservative Republican opponents. The former called, the latter sent a telegram conceding defeat."

"Will you be leaving the Republican Party after this campaign, and how do you see your future in the political arena?" someone else asked.

"Adam Stillman could win in New York if he ran without any party behind him," a young admirer shouted.

Adam's smile broadened and its warmth and sincerity were captivating. "We've won tonight, and I think it's time to celebrate the victory," he answered avoiding the question. "The waiting is over, and for everyone's sake I'm glad it's so early in the evening." Then winking at the newsmen, "It means an early night for everyone."

A shout of appreciation rose from the crowd and Beth, watching her husband, marveled at how quickly the fatigue and concern, which had been present in him just minutes before they arrived in the lobby, had vanished.

At that moment the impatient crowd rushed forward and swept Beth and Adam toward the large ballroom where everyone was waiting for the festivities to start.

When they entered the brightly lit auditorium, the band struck up a victory tune and Beth, standing next to her husband, felt exhilarated. This had been the seventh campaign in which she had waited for the results of Adam's efforts in running for the United States Congress, and the feelings of triumph, when the votes were in, was identical to those she had experienced the first time he ran for office. As the shouting and applause grew louder, Adam waved to the crowd and Beth did too. She was aware the homage was for him, but it did not matter. The victory was hers too.

They were standing side by side when Beth suddenly felt Adam's arm encircle her waist, and she was surprised she felt drawn to him physically. It had been a long time since that had happened. Feelings of loss, sadness and controlled passion rushed through her, and she was annoyed. She continued to smile as she withdrew herself gracefully from the public embrace and seated herself at the long table reserved for the dignitaries. Several people came over to congratulate her. She smiled pleasantly, barely listening to the platitudes. She disliked the social end of politicking and whenever possible avoided becoming involved with Adam's colleagues. A political campaign was a moral and intellectual challenge, not a garden party. A waiter poured her a scotch and she reached for it automatically. It was warm. Her hand rested on the glass, waiting for the last well wishers to leave. Finally alone, she looked over at Adam who was talking to an aide. With exaggerated nonchalance, she picked up the drink and started sipping it slowly, but within seconds found herself gulping it down. Adam turned at that moment and saw her place the empty glass down. He smiled briefly, but there was no recrimination in his expression.

Taking a deep breath, Beth tried to absorb herself in the activities around her. The room was crowded with everyone milling around, smiling, chatting animatedly, ignoring the heat under the glaring lights. They were all involved and her exalted feelings of minutes before began to fade. She felt like an outsider in spite of her position.

Sitting on the dais, Beth Stillman, at fifty, was an extremely attractive woman, and some of her former beauty was still very much in evidence. Her skin was taut, her neck smooth, her makeup underdone, but perfect. The reddish-blond hair, pushed back off her face, was fashionably cut to just below the jawbone line and complimented her fair complexion. Aware of fashion and in keeping with her age and position, she was dressed in a simple floor-length, heavy silk, light green gown, which set off the color of her eyes, and a hip-length matching jacket. The double-strand cultured pearl necklace and matching earrings completed the over-all picture of the wealthy debutante from the late forties who was aging gracefully. Poised and elegant, smiling pleasantly, it would have been hard to guess that she was a frightened, lonely and extremely unhappy woman. It was all there in the eyes, which had lost their luster, but she had mastered the art of pretence and, upon meeting her, a coolness and purposefulness of manner dominated.

The crowd was growing restless, and Beth wondered when Adam would make his acceptance speech. Her excitement over the victory was wearing thin, and the inner turmoil she had succeeded in suppressing was rapidly coming to the surface. She wanted the evening to come to an end. She looked over at Adam again. He was surrounded by several young people and was deeply engrossed in conversation with them, oblivious to the noise around him. He was talking and laughing exuberantly, his hands flaying the air, which he did whenever he was making a point in a discussion. The youngsters around seemed hypnotized by what he was saying, and their adulation was obvious. He was old enough to be their father, but they were listening to him as though he were a contemporary. In spite of his age, there was a youthfulness about him which made Beth feel old. More and more she was beginning to wonder about Adam's life when he was not in New York. They had been married for twenty-five years, but still she never felt she knew him as intimately as a wife should know her husband. She turned her head away and feelings of displacement returned more forcefully. She wished her children were with her. She knew why they were not present, still she would have been happier if at least one of them had been able to attend.

The waiter refilled her glass. Beth gulped its contents down and touching the waiter's arm, indicated she wanted a refill. She caught his knowing almost compassionate expression as he poured her a stiffer drink. It angered and embarrassed her, but she could not bother with either emotion. She did, however, wait for him to walk away before picking up the glass. Bringing it to her lips, she took a small sip and held the burning liquid in her mouth before swallowing it. Then, closing her eyes, she waited knowing that in a few minutes she would feel better, more in control. Slowly her mind began to clear and she gave in to the thoughts she had been trying to avoid all evening.

It was exactly twelve years since Adam's first congressional victory. It was also twelve years, to the day, that she had last seen Dan.

Twelve years! At that time she had stood at a crossroad and was in a position to go in one direction rather than the other. She knew everyone could look back and know, too late, that they had had choices. But she was fully aware of the diversified paths. She was in her late thirties then. A young woman, vibrant, resourceful, filled with dreams. Had she stood her ground, taken a firmer stand, been more selfish, everything would have been different. If only she had . . . If. Such a small insignificant word.

"Speech, speech, speech." The crowd in the ballroom was shouting and clapping. It brought Beth back to the present. The memory that had surfaced so vividly was one she had buried years ago. She looked about and realized Adam had come to sit beside her. He was smoking a cigarette, a pleasant smile hovering over his lips. Except for his eyes, which were alert and moving rapidly over the crowd, Beth could have sworn he was oblivious to the events around him. Trying to decide what he was looking for, she too scanned the vast auditorium. Masses of faces peered up at them, imploring Adam to make his speech. Beth looked back at him and saw his eyes focus on the far corner of the room, and she followed his gaze. Sam Ryan was just walking in. Adam rose quickly and raising his hands over his head in a triumphant gesture, walked over to the speaker's podium. Beth felt inexplicably relieved. It was unlike Adam not to respond to a screaming audience. Waiting for Sam Ryan, his mentor, his powerful political backer, made sense.

Adam began to speak and Beth looked over at Sam. There was no love lost between them. After Adam's first campaign, Sam had succeeded in eliminating her from Adam's subsequent bids for office. He had done it subtly, and it was a while before she had become aware of how completely Sam had isolated her from her husband's public life. By the time she became conscious of it, she was out of touch with the political scene and somehow was never able to fight her way back into the picture. She was surprised when she was asked to help out on this race, but never questioned it. She was told she was needed, and that was all that mattered.

Beth was staring at Sam when she saw him lean over and whisper to his companion. The young woman with him was a pretty brunette model, typical of her breed. Beth wondered why Sam would be out with her. She was not Sam's type. He liked the young, blond, all-American girl. She recalled her wedding day when she had met Sam for a drink. She had talked to him as to an older wise man, and he had mentioned his attraction to her. In subsequent years, the girls he brought around were bright, politically savvy females involved in the women's liberation movement. A pretty model was a strange choice for Sam. Beth continued to look at them and saw the girl shake her head and Sam put his hand on her brow. The thought came to Beth slowly before it struck her fully. Adam was not waiting for Sam to come before making his speech, he was waiting for the girl. It staggered her, and she was angry at her reaction. She and Adam had an unspoken agreement that precluded any intimate discussion. She had no idea if Adam had girlfriends. She had never asked and, with time, she did not really care. Was it possible that after all these years Adam had taken a mistress? she wondered. What was even more baffling was the thought that Sam was party to it. Sam, with all his big talk and pretended modern approach to the new era, was quite Victorian.

Adam's voice came back to Beth and she heard several names mentioned in appreciation, and she prayed silently that he would not mention hers. Her need for recognition was in constant conflict with an innate shyness. Being singled out embarrassed her.

"And last, but not least, my appreciation to my wife, Beth, without whom I believe I could not have won as handily as I did. She's a pro in more ways than one, and I would be remiss if I did not mention her."

The spotlight came to rest on Beth and she felt herself blush. Adam should not have done it, she thought furiously. He knew how she felt about being in the spotlight. The glaring light would not leave her, and finally she stood up and bowed. The applause grew louder and there were shouts of appreciation from the crowd. In spite of herself, Beth was pleased, and that annoyed her even more. She was trying to maintain the stance of indifference and not succeeding. The spotlight moved on and Beth sat down, completely confused by her feelings. She wanted to go home. The evening had lasted too long. Suddenly she remembered Sam suggesting they all go to El Morocco after the results were in. At the time it seemed like a good idea; now the thought was outrageous. She wanted another drink, but dared not ask for one. She was already feeling slightly tipsy. One more would cloud her mind, and the anger which was always close to the surface would burst out. Also, if her suspicions about Sam's date proved correct, she had better be in control of her thoughts and her tongue. Pretty as the young woman was, Beth was sure of herself and her position in Adam's life. They had worked too hard together to have it jeopardized by any woman who happened to come along and wanted to get on the bandwagon.

Adam finished his speech and the applause was deafening. The people at the table where Beth was sitting began to leave. A glass of scotch was left untouched by her nearest seating companion. Furtively she reached over, picked it up and gulped it down.

"Is it true, Mrs. Stillman, that your husband intends to run for mayor of the city at the next election?"

Beth looked around and saw a young reporter standing next to her.

"It's news to me." She placed the empty glass on the table and tried to hide her surprise and shock.

"Well, rumor has it that it's all set, and I was wondering how you would feel about it if it were true?" the young man persisted.

"As I said, I haven't heard the rumor, but if it should come to it, I'd say my husband would make a superb mayor." Her smile broadened, but the implication of what she was being told suddenly took on a new meaning. Sam Ryan and Adam had tricked her into helping with the campaign for reasons she could not understand at the time. Now it was becoming obvious. Adam running for Congress all these years, backed by the whole Republican Party machine, was something Sam could control and manage. Adam running for the mayoralty, possibly as an independent, certainly without the backing of the conservative faction of the Republican Party, and possibly without the more liberal one, either, would make it essential for him to have all the reinforcements. A wife, a family portrait worthy of the position would be a must, especially if there was a young mistress in Adam's life. An almost uncontrollable fury exploded in her. For Sam to be so hungry for power was understandable. For Adam to allow Sam to use her so blatantly was degrading.

The crowd began to thin out, and within minutes there were only a few of Adam's aides around and some television camera crews cleaning up. While Adam was putting things into his briefcase, Beth took out a compact and stared at herself. Drinking these days caused her eyes to redden. She snapped the compact shut in disgust and replaced it in her evening bag. Nervously she fondled the glass standing before her. When she saw Adam start toward her, she picked it up and, although empty, raised it to her lips defiantly, as though relishing the remainder of a drink as Adam looked on.

"From the look in your eyes," he whispered, "this is number four or five, right?"

"Well, if we're going to spend the evening with dear Sam and some pretty model, I really feel I should be well fortified." She answered sweetly and stood up. "I'm ready, Adam, whenever you are."

He turned to face her and their eyes met, but Beth felt that Adam was not really looking at her.

"Shall we, Mr. Congressman?" she said pleasantly, trying to hide her mortification.

"Congressperson," Adam answered. "We must keep up with the times." His smile was equally sweet, and they started toward the back of the room where Sam was waiting for them.

"This is Lauri Eddington," Sam said, as Beth and Adam reached the table. He was standing and the young woman stood up as well.

She was pretty from a distance. She was completely stunning up close, Beth thought as she put out her hand in greeting. The girl shook Beth's hand and then looked over at Adam, who was being introduced to her.

Looking at the two of them, Beth knew without a doubt that Lauri Eddington was Adam's mistress. She also knew it was a serious affair. A vein in her forehead began to throb.

"Lauri isn't feeling well," Sam was saying, "and she asked to be ex- cused from joining us this evening."

"That's too bad," Beth said sweetly. "Anything we can do?"

Lauri smiled wanly. "It must have been something I've eaten."

"What a pity," Adam said. "We were going to celebrate my victory." He laughed self-consciously. "Or I should say our victory." He looked at Beth and Sam. "We would have liked to have you share it with us."

"Such gallantry!" Beth exclaimed. She tried to keep her voice light. Her inner reaction was horror. Adam was not even trying to hide his feelings.

"If you'd get me a cab, Sam," Lauri said quickly, "I'll run along."

"We'll drop you," Sam said, and the four walked toward the exit.

Waiting at the curb for Sam's limousine, Beth stared openly at Lauri. The young woman turned and looked directly at Beth. Her gaze was clear and unflinching. The composed aloof manner disturbed Beth. If Lauri was having an affair with Adam, would it not be more in keeping for her to be uncomfortable, embarrassed, self-conscious, in the presence of her lover's wife? The self-assurance was amoral, Beth thought angrily. Yet her rage was daunted by frustration. She felt old-fashioned, out of her depth, out of step with the times. The generation gap was more like an abyss.

At that moment the car arrived and Sam helped Beth in. Adam was about to take Lauri's arm, when the young woman swayed slightly and fell to the sidewalk in a dead heap. Sam bent down and cuddled her head. Jeb, Sam's driver, rushed out from the car while Adam stood by, and a look of disbelief came over his face. Beth, looking at her husband, saw his expression change to deep concern. But it was more than mere concern: He was looking at the young woman as he had not looked at his wife in years.

Beth lowered her eyes. Lauri Eddington was an important person in Adam's life. But more important—Lauri was the present and future whereas she was the past, and Beth felt powerless to compete with her.

Part I

YESTERDAY

1

It was a particularly hot summer evening when Beth Van Ess arrived at the courthouse in lower Manhattan. Stepping out in front of the imposing buildings, her excitement was mingled with discomfort. The street was almost deserted, and except for the occasional siren of a police car, the silence was strangely eerie. The daughter of a judge, Beth had been to the area throughout the years, but she had always seen it during the day through her father's office windows. It looked different now. Looking at the huge structures, she wondered what she was expected to do.

"Miss Van Ess?" She heard someone say her name and she turned around startled.

"I'm David Malloy, assistant district attorney." He held out his hand. "We've met once, but you must have forgotten. I was asked to be your escort for the evening and guide you around." He was pleasant and Beth was relieved.

As they entered one of the buildings, a chill ran through her. It was quite dark, and she hastened her step to keep up with her escort. They waited for the elevator and the silence was disconcerting.

Stepping out of the elevator, the sight that greeted them was startling. The hallway was wide, brightly lit and dirty. It was teeming with people, all talking and gesturing nervously. There were men and women, black and white, yet they all seemed faceless. They looked unsavory, frightened and angry.

"Shall we?" David Malloy touched her elbow and led her into the courtroom, pushing his way through with authority toward the front.

"I'd rather not sit too close up," Beth said. She felt conspicuous enough as it was.

He complied and found her a seat on a bench toward the back of the courtroom.

"I must run now, but I'll be back shortly," he said, and Beth's impulse to ask him not to leave was great, but she restrained herself. Instead she took out her pad and pencil and placed them on her knee and looked around.

Sitting in the overheated criminal courtroom, waiting for the night session to start, she knew she looked out of place. Although dressed in a conservative beige shirtwaist dress, the wide camel-colored belt showed off her waist and emphasized the fullness of her breasts. Instinctively, she fastened the top two buttons of the dress hoping to cover up the cleavage. Her reddish-blond hair, pulled back in a ponytail, the deep, smooth summer tan that accentuated her green eyes, made her wish for anonimity even more difficult. For a brief moment she wished she had not come.

A graduate of Radcliffe with a B.A. in Journalism, Beth had dreamed of finding a job that would lead her toward a career as a newspaper woman. Instead she succeeded in finding work, through her father's connections, as a secretary to Gillian Crane, a noted journalist. The secretarial work was boring, but Beth admired Gillian and the woman kept encouraging her to stay on with the promise that there was a future for her in her chosen field. Now after almost a year of working she had been given her first assignment. Gillian was doing a series about the courts in New York, and Beth had been sent down to cover the night-court session.

The room was beginning to fill up and the noisy hysteria that was evident in the hallways was subdued. Beth watched the people closely as they searched for seats. Fear and anguish was evident in their faces. Unlike herself, they were all participants in the drama that was about to unfold, and she felt like a peeping tom. Her first assignment was turning into a nightmare.

Suddenly a hush fell over the room, and Beth realized the judge had entered. Everyone stood up. When he was seated, everyone took his place and the night court was in session.

She found it hard to follow what was going on. People were being brought up before the judge; some were manacled, others were not. The charges were read by the court clerk and his words were garbled, which infuriated Beth but did not seem to bother anyone else. A conference would then take place between the defense attorney, the DA and the judge, and then, invariably, the offender would plead guilty. A fine would be imposed and then the next lawyer would come up with his client.

David Malloy returned and sat down beside her. Beth was about to ask him a question when she suddenly heard someone arguing with the judge.

"Your honor, my client is pleading not guilty to the charge." The voice was arrogant, the tone almost disrespectful. Beth spun around. She could not see the young man's face, but she noticed he was tall and thin with jet-black hair which was quite long and looked uncombed as it curled around his white collar. Something about him made her pause.

"Young man, I suggest you change your tone when addressing the bench."

"I'm sorry, your honor, but I refuse to have my client put off as all the rest have been. Peter D'Angelo is not guilty of the charge of soliciting on the streets."

"Bail is set at two hundred and fifty dollars," the judge said wearily. "Next."

"My client does not have the money and has no way of getting it," the lawyer persisted.

"What bullshit," David Malloy whispered.

"Then he'll have to spend the time in jail until the case is brought up," the judge said indifferently.

"He can't do that, sir," the lawyer persisted. "He's got an important exam tomorrow at school."

Beth dragged her eyes away from the stiffly poised back of the lawyer and looked over at the accused. Peter D'Angelo was a frail-looking Italian boy in his late teens with a sullen, almost petulant look that was now overshadowed by unbelievable fear.

"Read out the charge," the judge said in an exasperated voice. The clerk reread the charge, which alleged that Peter had gone over to a plain-clothes detective and made a homosexual overture toward him.

The prosecuting attorney was called over, and he reiterated what the orderly had stated. "According to the arresting officer, he was revolted by the obscenity of language and felt this type of scum should be taken off the streets and sent back where he came from."

"Your honor, I object," the young lawyer said vehemently.

"Objection sustained," the judge said, and everyone in the courtroom was suddenly quiet.

"I know Peter, your honor, and I've spoken to him and his family. He tells the story quite differently."

"Would everyone please come to the bench," the judge ordered. The lawyers, the young man and a woman dressed in black, who had been sitting in the first row, rushed forward, with a priest following close behind her. The woman was obviously Peter's mother.

"That son of a gun." David Malloy smiled. "He gets away with it most of the time."

"What happens now?" Beth asked, looking over at her companion. During the interchange Beth had only briefly taken her eyes off the defending attorney.

"Oh, the kid will be allowed to go home tonight on his own recognizance. With a mother and a priest around, he's probably going to show up tomorrow or whenever they set the trial, and then with Stillman defending him, I assure you the charges will be dropped."

"Is Stillman the lawyer?"

"Yes, Adam Stillman," David Malloy said, growing serious. "He's really something. Works for the Legal Aid Society, although God knows why. Bright as a whip and never loses a case. I don't even make an effort when I'm up against him, especially if the accused is an ethnic minority. He really goes to bat for them."

"But he's not Italian."

"Adam Stillman is hardly an Italian name. He's Jewish, but any time we bring in a colored boy, an Italian or a Jew, watch out."

"Do you know him personally?" Beth asked, surprised at her own question.

"Yes, we both went to N.Y.U. law school, although he attended at night. And mind you, he graduated with the highest honors, Phi Beta Kappa and all, and did it while teaching during the day at some school in God knows where—the Bronx, I think. That's why everyone is so surprised that he went into Legal Aid. I'm sure he could have gotten into several top law offices."

"I'd like to meet him," Beth said slowly, aware she was behaving in an unusual manner. The expression on David Malloy's face confirmed her thoughts. She was a prominent judge's daughter and was hardly the type to go slumming.

"I'll introduce you to him when court closes."

It was nearly two in the morning when the court finally adjourned. As the introductions were made, Beth felt an excitement she had never known before. Adam was enormously attractive to her. There was a strength about him and a drive, which she envied. Looking at him she had the feeling that through him she could satisfy many of her own ambitions—ambitions that were not fully defined but which she knew she could not achieve on her own. The feelings she had when first hearing his voice, returned.

"I must run along," David Malloy said. "I've still got some work to finish." He paused briefly. "May I help you find a cab?" he asked.

"Thanks for your help, Mr. Malloy." Beth turned to him, relieved at the opportunity to break the tension she was feeling. She ignored his offer of help as she held out her hand. She watched him walk away. Feeling more composed, she turned back to Adam.

"I'm doing a story on the New York court system, and I was wondering if you could spare me a few minutes."

A slow smile appeared on Adam's face.

"How about a drink?" she suggested, trying to sound professional.

"You really want a drink?" he asked, and the look of amusement deepened.

"As a matter of fact, I don't," she answered candidly, "but you've had a long day, and it occurred to me a drink might help you unwind."

"Okay," he answered, and his smile was now totally captivating. "But suppose you come up to my place and we'll have it there."

She was taken aback but agreed without hesitation.

They went down to the subway, which was a novelty to Beth. She had never been out with a man who took it for granted that subways were a mode of transportation. The noise of the train was deafening and the harsh neon lights made the dreariness around more repugnant. They did not sit, although the train was quite empty. Beth focused her attention on Adam. Even in the unflattering light, he looked tanned. His eyes were almost coal-black and seemed to be mocking her. She had to check the impulse to reach over and touch his face.

"I live on Seventy-second Street," she said tentatively. "Where do you live?"

"Ninety-eighth Street, between Madison and Park avenues."

"Why not come to my place? It's closer."

He looked annoyed for a moment, then he smiled. "I'll never get used to you pushy ladies, but by all means, your place is probably a hell of a lot more comfortable than mine."

Walking along the wide crosstown street toward Beth's apartment, she could hardly contain her excitement.

The doorman opened the door for them.

"Good evening, Miss Van Ess. I have a package for the judge, may I give it to you?"

Handing her a large manila envelope he said good night, and the elevator man whisked them to the penthouse apartment without comment.

"They don't even seem surprised," Adam said as she unlocked the door, "considering the hour."

"Why should they be?" she asked as they entered the apartment. Beth switched on the dim hall sconces hanging on each side of the oval Queen Anne mirror. Fresh flowers stood on the sideboard beneath it. The mail was neatly stacked on a tray, and the marble floors gleamed in the soft light. She led the way into the living room and turned on a tole lamp. The cool luxurious atmosphere was intoxicating. The place reeked of wealth and good taste. By the french doors that led to a terrace, stood several well-cared-for plants, all obviously tended by someone who either cared or knew about potted plants.

"I was right," Adam said, as he looked around.

"Right about what?"

"This is far nicer than my place, by a long, long shot."

"Make yourself comfortable," Beth said pleasantly, "while I get us a drink. What will you have?"

"Anything cold, ginger ale, soda, water, juice, anything," he answered as he loosened his tie and threw himself into a comfortable armchair which faced a huge sofa flanking the unlit fireplace.

When Beth returned to the living room with a tray holding a glass of juice, a highball of scotch and soda, and some biscuits, Adam was asleep. She placed the tray down on the coffee table, picked up her glass and sat down on the sofa, devouring his face with unabashed desire.

He was truly an extraordinary-looking man. It was not that he was handsome; he was too intense looking to fall into that category. He had a high forehead, prominent nose accented by sunken cheeks. His eyebrows were too full, his mouth, even in repose, was thin with an expression of disdain. Yet the animal-like sensuality he exuded seemed to spring from every part of his being.

She was staring at him intently when he opened his eyes and looked at her.

"Who are you?" she asked, when she felt she could control her voice.

"I'm Adam Stillman, born in the Bronx to Hannah and Jacob Stillman. My father died when I was fourteen, and being the older of two children, I helped my mother bring up my sister. I'm a lawyer, as you've noticed, a good lawyer and I'm going . . ." he stopped.

"Where are you going?" she asked quietly.

"Well, tonight I'm going to bed with Judge Van Ess's daughter," he said as he sat up and reached for his juice.

The blood drained from Beth's face. She wanted to be indignant, say something rude and biting, but knew it would be pointless. She had brought it on herself. She was attracted to him from the minute she saw him, and she had invited him up to the apartment, but she had not thought out the complete scenario. Certainly she had not expected such an indelicate proposition.

"Mind you," he continued, "I don't like such aggressiveness on the part of women. I like to do the choosing—the courting, as you would call it. But you secure little wasp ladies really think you can call all the shots, and I guess"—he looked around the room—"you have every right to."

She stood up quickly, confused by what he was saying. He was being insulting. He stood up too and in a minute she was in his arms and his face was close to hers. His eyes were devoid of expression. She pressed her mouth to his trying to blot out her feelings of humiliation.

Suddenly she felt him push her away.

"You little fool." He could barely hide his anger. "Who do you think you're playing around with? Little boys from your dance class?" He paused to regain his composure. "Or are Mommy and Daddy sleeping in one of the bedrooms, and they'll come barging out to protect their precious girl from the bad guys?"

She lowered her eyes. "They're away in Greenwich, Connecticut."

"How convenient," he sneered. "So while Mommy and Daddy are away little Beth Van Ess will play. And with all the brouhaha, I'll bet you're probably still a virgin to boot." His voice softened.

She looked up and he was smiling.

"I'm sorry," she said with relief. "I didn't mean to appear so obvious." She disengaged herself and moved away. "I'm not a virgin, though, if that helps."

"It helps, but it doesn't make any difference. I'm a big boy and I like to play in my ball park where the odds are at least even." He looked around, "This is way out of my league, and you really should be more careful when picking up strange men. You're a beautiful girl. Very desirable. But stick to your own kind. Play with the boys you grew up with. You're less likely to get hurt."

Walking over to her, he lifted her face to his, kissed her gently on the lips, and walked out of the apartment.

2

Beth was convinced Adam would call in spite of what he said. She wanted to call him, but remembering his dislike of aggressive women, she held off. She did, however, rush home from work every evening and sit around waiting for the phone to ring. It was unlike her. A fun-loving young woman, she was extremely popular and sitting home alone was a novel experience. She did not like it. After two weeks of waiting, it finally dawned on her that Adam had meant what he said, and she felt overwhelmed at being so blatantly rejected. It had never happened to her before and she had no idea how to cope with it. To overcome her confusion, she decided to give up the vigil and accept an invitation to a weekend party in Boston. But when Friday came around she realized she could not go. The need to see Adam would not leave her.

Her parents were away for the summer, and the apartment was strangely quiet. Taking a drink, she went into her bedroom and sat down in the darkened room trying to figure out what it was about Adam that attracted her. He was, after all, as foreign to her as any man she had ever met. They had nothing in common, and he was obviously not interested in her—not even physically. She blushed at the memory of being pushed away by him the night they met. Maybe he was right when he said she was less likely to be hurt if she stuck with her own crowd.

But to be hurt, one had to feel, Beth thought nervously.

The phone rang at that moment and Beth picked it up quickly.

"Aren't you coming out?" It was her mother calling from the country.

"No, I'm expected at a late supper party," she lied.

"Will you be coming tomorrow?" Mary Van Ess sounded annoyed.

"I doubt it, Mother. I think I'll spend the weekend in New York. When are you coming back?"

"Not for a couple of weeks, at least. It's lovely out here and everyone is around." There was a pause. "I really don't like you to be alone in the city, Beth. All your friends are asking for you."

Beth smiled to herself. Translated, her mother was commanding her to come out to the country and mingle with the eligible bachelors, settle on one and get married, as befitted a young woman of her age.

"I'll come out soon," Beth said pleasantly and hung up.

She was behaving irrationally. Instead of being in New York, she could be in the country with her parents, waiting to be picked up to go to the club where she would be greeted warmly by everyone and would become the center of attraction the minute she walked in. She grimaced to herself. The center of attraction! What the hell did that mean? She was wealthy, pretty, the daughter of the prominent judge and Mrs. Drew Van Ess, and was a good lay. If she were not a Van Ess, she would never get away with her outrageous behavior. She felt like a phony. She was a phony! The last thought disturbed her. When did she become one? Why was she one? Who was she anyway?

"She's a winner," Drew Van Ess was always saying while she was growing up.

But who was the competition?

Beth stood up and started pacing. As always in moments of stress, Allen came to mind. If only Allen were alive she could ask him these questions. He was more than a brother; he was her friend. Although only two years older, he had wisdom and she loved him more than anyone in the world. But he was dead, and she was tired of being a winner competing with a world she was disinterested in and had no feelings for. Thoughts of Allen plunged her into further depression. Absently she looked at the clock. It was past 11:00 P.M. It had been a long time since she had thought of Allen, and the pain was as alive as ever. Unable to bear the pain, unhappy with the feelings about herself, she picked up the telephone book and looked up Adam's number.

Adam seemed surprised to hear from her. There was no pleasure in his voice.

"Are you staying in town for the weekend?" she asked, not knowing what to say after the opening pleasantries.

He laughed mirthlessly. "*Most* people don't go away for the weekend. They're happy they have a place to live in right here in the city."

The silence which followed grew awkward.

"Would you like to have a nightcap?" she asked.

"Only if you'd like to come up here. I'm bushed."

She wrote down the address, knowing she would have to control the impulse to rush right over to his place.

The block between Madison and Park avenues on Ninety-eighth Street was ugly and dreary. The taxi came to a stop in front of a tenement with naked fire escapes. The building looked hideous. The street was deserted. Beth climbed the steps to the fourth floor landing, hating the dirty hallway, hating the creaky stairs, expecting to hate the apartment. To her surprise, it was quite pleasant. Sparsely furnished, it had a small living room with a skylight, a well-appointed kitchenette and a tiny bedroom. Books and records lined all the walls of both rooms. A framed picture of a woman and a young girl hung over the living room couch. Beth was about to ask who they were, but Adam was standing close to her and within minutes they were in the bedroom and he was making love to her.

Lying beside him, naked, feeling his muscular body pressing against her, having his hands touch her, feeling him enter her, she felt herself losing her self-control for the first time since she started sleeping with men. It was different from any other experience she had ever known. It could hardly be called lovemaking. There were no whispered words of endearment, no tenderness. There was purpose. He was not oblivious to her physical desire or need, but there was a conscious need of his own that he was determined to satisfy. He was in complete control at all times. There was something almost tyrannical about him, and it reminded her of her father.

Beth closed her eyes. Thinking of her father while in bed with a stranger was embarrassing. She shuddered imperceptibly, but his image would not leave her.

Her father was a tyrant and he had destroyed Allen. The thought flashed through her mind, and Beth felt her body go rigid. Somehow she had always known it, but never before had she allowed it to surface so clearly. Drew hated Allen. He was never a father to his son but rather a judge, sitting on a bench meting out punishment, as if determined to break him. And he had succeeded—with her help.

For the first time since his death, Allen's last day of life took form, consciously.

They had gone to the Paramount Theater to see the movie and stage show. She was twelve and Allen was fourteen. They were in Southampton for the summer, and she persuaded him to go into the city without permission. When they came out of the theater it was dark out. Unaccustomed to being downtown, alone, at that hour, they decided to go to their house on Sixty-third Street before venturing back to the Hamptons. Neither had a key, but Allen opened the back garden door with ease and led them into the downstairs dining room. The house was in complete darkness and very quiet. It was disconcerting.

"Dad isn't home yet," Allen said with relief, and was about to turn on the lights when they heard a woman's low husky laughter coming from their parent's bedroom on the second floor. They both froze. Then a silence, more ominous than before, fell again.

Cautiously, Allen took Beth's hand, and they started climbing the stairs, feeling their way in the darkness.

The door to the bedroom was open. Allen edged his way toward the room with Beth close behind.

"Oh, God," she heard Allen say hoarsely, and within seconds total confusion broke loose. The lights went on and Beth saw her father standing in the doorway, glaring at them. Allen grabbed her hand and ran down the stairs dragging her behind him.

Sitting opposite Allen on the train back to Southampton, Beth's mind was numb. She peered at her brother and was frightened by his pallor. He was staring out the window, his eyes dancing in agitation from side to side. He was breathing heavily. Suddenly, she saw tears begin to stream down his cheeks and he started sobbing.

"What happened, Allen?" Beth asked, although she did not really want to hear the answer.

"He's a liar, a cheat, a hypocrite. He's a dirty old bastard," the boy hissed through clenched teeth. "I hate him. I hate his guts. I wish he were dead."

Beth wanted to protest. She knew something was wrong, but she did not want her father to die.

Getting up, she crossed over to where Allen sat and, putting her arms through his, pressed close to him. She felt him shudder as he put his head up against the window pane.

Mary Van Ess was hysterical when they finally arrived at the house.

"Your father called and told me you were in New York," she screamed when they walked in. "He's on his way out here, and you'll get it when he gets here." She was speaking to Allen rather than to Beth.

"He can't give me anything ever again." He spoke quietly and without a trace of fear. Then, turning around, he walked out the front door.

"Get back in here!" Mary ran after him. Beth walked over to the open front door and realized it was dark outside, and she wondered where Allen would go.

It was nearly midnight when Drew Van Ess arrived home. Beth was in bed pretending to be asleep. She did not want to see her father. She felt frightened and confused. Her mother was unable to catch up with Allen, who was still not back. Beth wondered if her parents would come into her room. To her relief, they did not.

Allen's naked body was washed ashore the next day. The police report said he had been caught in a whirlpool.

Everyone was solicitous. Her mother wept bitterly, her father sat ashen, silent and brooding.

Beth stood between her father and mother at the grave site. She wondered why no tears came. She wanted to cry. Her eyes were burning with the unshed tears. She felt an icy chill envelop her. It started with her toes, creeping slowly up her legs, up her back to the nape of her neck and finally she felt it settling in her eyes. For a minute she thought her pupils would freeze as she stared at the simple oak coffin standing next to the open grave. When the coffin was finally lowered into the ground, she felt no pain. Instead, an overwhelming desire to laugh gurgled in her throat. She tore her eyes away from the partially covered casket and looked up at the clear blue sky, wondering where Allen's soul was. When she felt her father's arm squeeze her shoulder, she moved away instinctively and looked at him. He was staring down at her. For a minute he seemed to be pleading with her, but then his gaze turned inward. Sounds of her mother's sobbing came to her, and then everyone was gathered around whispering their condolences.

Walking away from the cemetery, Beth knew a part of her had died with Allen. Certainly the part of her that generated emotions seemed to have disappeared.

The next few years were blurred. From a lively, fun-loving prankster, Beth turned into a withdrawn, quiet girl. She devoted all of her time to her studies and was obsessively attached to her parents. Feelings of love or hate, happiness or sadness were nowhere in evidence. She moved from day to day as in a trance. The blankness in her, the void she lived with, was so complete that she could never recall moving from the house in the Sixties to the apartment on Park Avenue, just as she could not remember the move from Southampton to Greenwich. Allen became a dreamlike figure.

The street lights coming through the shutters in Adam's bedroom caught her attention, and Beth closed her eyes and dared not move, fearful of losing the thread of her vague memories. She had turned her mind away from the past, and it made her an incomplete person. Now she wanted to relive it, face it, come to terms with it, and maybe understand who she really was. Was it possible that having had a complete experience with Adam, she would finally pry open the closed doors, allowing her a glimpse at those years? Years which were sealed away and which she suddenly missed.

Her next clear memory was being at Jody Carmichael's sweet-sixteen birthday party in Southampton. They had not been back there since Allen's death, and had it not been her closest friend's party, Beth would not have gone. Jody, a plain girl, with mousy blond hair, faded blue eyes and a small pug nose, looked up to Beth as the most glamorous person she knew. It would have been shattering to her if Beth had not turned up. Mary Van Ess was exhilarated at the idea of spending the weekend in Southampton, and it annoyed Beth. To Beth, the trip was a torturous reminder of her brother and happier days, yet her mother did not seem to associate any of it with Allen.

The party was in full swing when Beth overheard someone ask her mother when she planned on reopening the Southampton house. She listened intently and discovered that her parents had not sold the house after Allen's death, but had merely rented it out for the past few years. The shock overwhelmed her. She looked at her mother talking excitedly about her plans for the summer, telling everyone how much she had missed coming out to the Hamptons and how she planned on resuming her lovely summers which she had longed for.

Unable to control the tears, Beth ran out of the house toward the waterfront, memories of Allen hammering away at her.

It was dark and she removed her shoes. The warm sand, the sound of the soft waves hitting up against the shore were soothing. She leaned down and felt the water. It was still quite cold, but as she washed her face with it she began to feel better. Walking more slowly she could feel Allen's presence. She could almost hear his voice. She looked out at the dark waters and wondered what his thoughts were that night when he swam out to his death. For the first time she wondered if she could have prevented it.

"Hi," someone said, and Beth looked around startled. A young man whom she noticed at the party was sitting near the water's edge. He was smoking and had a paper mug in his hand.

"Want some?" he asked as he offered her the cup. It was straight vodka. It burned her throat, but she liked the sensation.

"Can I have a cigarette?" she asked.

He lit it for her and in the flicker of the flame she saw his face. He was good looking, very fair and quite young.

"I'm Bill," he said.

"I'm Beth."

"I know. I asked who you were."

"Dull party isn't it?"

"They usually are." His laugh was pleasant.

Beth lay back and inhaled deeply, letting the smoke out slowly and watching it rise toward the darkened sky. When Bill lay down beside her and started caressing her body, she began to undress automatically. Within minutes they were both naked. Beth felt his fingers grope clumsily down her body and a small shiver ran through her. As she felt his hand touch her pubic hair, she held her breath. She and Allen used to play this game years back. She had never dared touch him as he had touched her. The temptation to touch Bill now was overwhelming. Suddenly he was on top of her, pulling her legs apart and was pressing his body between her thighs. She felt the hardness of his penis push into her but felt no pain, although she had heard it did hurt when girls first had intercourse. She also felt no pleasure. She lay beneath him, her eyes wide open, and recalled the times Allen had pressed himself on her, made motions similar to the ones Bill was making, although he never fully entered her. The other difference was that Allen's organ was soft and damp, whereas Bill's was like a sharp dagger. She lay motionless waiting, although what it was she was waiting for she did not know. He seemed angry and that, too, puzzled her. His breathing grew labored and he started to sweat. Suddenly he let out a long, soft wail and rolled over beside her. She looked over at him fascinated. He was crumbled into a limp, dead mass. Beth sat up slowly and her eyes wandered down his naked body and came to rest on his penis. It was damp, red, small and wrinkled. It, too, looked lifeless. She averted her eyes quickly. Lying on the white sand, he looked as Allen must have looked when dragged out of the water the day he died. The thought made her sick.

She arrived home from Jody's at 5:00 A.M. Her parents were waiting up for her. Mary was wailing, much as she had at Allen's funeral, concerned with what people would say. Her father was white with rage. Suddenly a missing link from the night Allen died fell into place. Just before Allen grabbed her and they ran down the stairs, she glimpsed her father standing in the middle of the room. Now she remembered—he was naked. The picture streaked through her mind and disappeared. As she walked away from her parents she felt strangely content.

Sleeping with the boys she went out with became a way of life for Beth. She never enjoyed sexual intercourse, but was elated when she knew her partner was spent and she was still fully in control of her faculties. The need to be in control of every situation, the overwhelming compulsion to have things go her way, dominated her every action. Every affair was a triumph. Her father had said she was a winner, and now she was proving him to be right.

A deep sigh escaped her. The journey into the past solved nothing. It only reaffirmed her conviction that her father was responsible for Allen's death and her mother was a heartless frivolous woman.

Adam moved beside her. She looked over at him and suddenly it did not matter. When he reached over to touch her, all thoughts were wiped away. She was in his arms and he was making love to her. The physical pleasure was as great as before. Adam inside her, deep and probing, slowly exploring every part of her, made her cry out with joy. She felt him come, but still he did not withdraw from her. She opened her eyes and stared at him. His face was serious, his eyes deep and tender, his lips brushing against her brow and his body continued to press against hers.

It was dark when Beth woke up. She had no idea what time it was. She was exhausted, but her desire for Adam had not abated. His for her seemed as strong as ever. Their bodies were fused to each other and he was as firm inside her as he had been when they first started making love.

"My mouth is dry," Beth whispered, her tongue feeling heavy as she spoke. He withdrew from her but his erection, as he walked out of the room, was visible. When he returned with a glass of water he crawled in beside her, took her in his arms and held her close. She felt relaxed and protected. When his breathing grew steady and she knew he was asleep, she moved away and scanned his face. He was sleeping peacefully, but there was a dignity about him she had never seen in any of her former lovers. Was it possible that Adam Stillman was someone she could not dominate, someone she could not crush? Someone her father could not destroy? She had felt like a phony before coming to his apartment because she was pretending to be a winner when she did not feel like one. With Adam by her side, she could be one.

She was staring at him when he opened his eyes. It was a clear and unemotional look which met hers. In a minute he was wide awake.

"I think it's time you went home, Beth," he said as he stood up. "I've got work to do." He started dressing. "You'd better dress, and I'll go down and help you find a cab."

"Don't you offer a lady a cup of coffee before kicking her out?" she asked lightly, although deeply offended at being asked to leave. She wanted to stay on and be made love to again.

"Sorry about that. You dress while I put the water on to boil." He smiled sheepishly.

They drank their coffee in silence, and Beth wondered if he would ask to see her again. The invitation was not forthcoming. Sitting in the taxi on her way home, Beth wondered how she could force the relationship to continue.

3

Thanksgiving was over and the mad rush toward Christmas was on. Everyone was planning the holiday season with extra ferocity. Nineteen-fifty, the half-century mark was coming. Invitations to parties were piling up. New Year's Eve was set for a big celebration at the Greenwich Country Club. A couple of men asked Beth to accompany them. Neither date was particularly appealing. Since meeting Adam, she had curtailed her dating to the point where her availability was in question. As usual, her parents expected her to spend Christmas Eve with them, and it was that prospect that bothered her most. The thought of spending it with them was depressing. It was Jody Carmichael who saved the day. She called one day and asked Beth if she would go to St. Moritz, Switzerland, with her.

She had remained friends with Jody through the years. They had gone to Radcliffe together, and Beth was still the most cherished friend Jody had. And, in a way, Jody was her best and only friend. She was simple, pleasant, adoring and not demanding.

"How the hell are we going to get a hotel reservation at this late date?" Beth asked, her excitement rising.

"Oh, all arrangements have been made. There is a little chalet we can use for two whole weeks," Jody answered. "It's small, but it'll accommodate us."

"Us meaning you and me?" Beth asked, aware that Jody was itching to tell her something she did not want to hear. She hated being a confidante, feeling it was an unnecessary imposition.

"Us meaning you, me and one other person."

Beth raised her brows in spite of herself. Jody was engaged to be married to Johnny Blake, a childhood sweetheart. She tried to remember what Johnny looked like, but he was one of those nondescript people whom Beth had known most of her life, and she could not conjure up his features. The idea that Jody had a lover was amusing.

"Tell you what," Beth said, knowing that Jody was about to plunge into a long explanation. "I'll go along on one condition. You leave me alone while we're there, and I'll leave you alone until the day we're ready to come back."

Jody let out a deep sigh of relief. "I told my parents I'm going with you, and that was the only condition on which they considered the idea."

"How did you know I'd go?" Beth asked in surprise.

"You're a free soul," Jody said simply, "and I knew you wouldn't let me down."

Sitting through the long plane ride, while Jody slept, Beth recalled the conversation. A "free soul" indeed, she thought wryly. She was so free she was floating in space, wanted by no one, wanting nothing, except Adam, who did not know she existed. She hadn't even called to tell him she was going away. She was sure he would never know the difference.

The trip was endless. When they finally reached Zürich, it was cold and crisp. Jody and Beth stepped into a car that had been waiting for them, and they were off to St. Moritz, where they were deposited in front of a small house with a sloping roof and framed windows. It looked warm and inviting—a romantic little castle. Beth felt a twinge of envy as a houseman rushed out to greet them. She missed Adam desperately. Suddenly Beth knew she could not spend the time with Jody and whoever it was she was coming to be with.

"Jody, you run along in and I'll try my luck at the Palace Hotel."

"You'll never get in at this late date," Jody said with concern, although she had a hard time hiding her joy at the thought of Beth's departure.

To Beth's relief, the concierge remembered her family from the time they had spent their vacations there in the past, and although the hotel was full, a small room was found for her. It was quite late by the time she was unpacked and settled. After calling Jody and reassuring her that all was well, she took a luxurious bath and went to bed.

An expert skier since childhood, Beth returned from her first full day of skiing and had a brandy at the bar. It was very crowded, but she noticed few Americans among the guests. She could not decide if she was pleased or unhappy about the discovery. Once in her room she washed up and started dressing for dinner. With all the bravado, she felt embarrassed about being alone. The prospect of dinner in the dining room filled with people she did not know was uncomfortable. She went through her wardrobe and realized she had not brought any elegant clothes. Somehow she visualized herself skiing, reading and doing nothing else while chaperoning Jody. She was angry at having agreed to come, annoyed that Jody had not called her. She also knew that if the positions were reversed and she was with someone like Adam, she would not have called Jody. Unhappily, she got into a bathrobe and ordered a simple dinner and a bottle of wine to her room.

It was nearly 1:00 A.M. when she woke up. She lit a cigarette and tried to decide what to do. She could hardly return to New York. She would be letting Jody down dreadfully if the Carmichaels got wind of it. She had no choice but to stay. The bleakness of the next two weeks loomed lonely and unpleasant. Unable to fall asleep again, she kept glancing at the little portable clock she had brought along. By 1:45, she knew it was hopeless, and dressing in her ski clothes, she decided to take a walk.

As she was passing the Stubli Room, which was usually reserved for private parties, she decided to walk in. She was quite sure they would not turn her away. She seated herself on a small leather sofa, ordered a brandy and looked with pleasure on the pine-wood paneling which made the room feel cozy and intimate.

"May I offer you a drink?" a deep voice said, and Beth looked up. A man with closely cropped curly gray hair, and light blue eyes was standing at her table smiling down at her, two drinks of brandy in his hand. She looked at her almost empty brandy glass and smiled her thanks. "May I sit with you?" He lowered himself beside her. "I'm Jean Paul de Langue."

"I'm Beth Van Ess," she answered, with amusement. The man was extremely attractive and young, in spite of the gray hair. He was charming and there was a gaity in his manner which cheered her up.

"You come here often?" he asked.

"We used to before the war. Which means we haven't been here for quite a while."

"We?"

"My mother, my father and, long ago, my brother. We'd come every season."

"But you are alone." It wasn't a question, it was a statement. The implication was obvious, but she did not react. "In any event, I'm pleased you decided to come."

"So am I," she said, and meant it. She had eaten little of her dinner but had drunk the wine, and the two brandies had gone to her head, although she was still fully aware of what was going on around her.

He waved to the waiter for another round and Beth sat back and looked at the crowded room.

"I understand this is a private party," she said, watching the elegant women, the suave, charming men. The atmosphere was completely removed from the reality of post-war Europe.

"Yes, as a matter of fact, it is in honor of my wife, Dominique," he said, pointing toward a diminutive, dark-haired beauty who was dancing with a tall, blond young man. She was looking up at the man with extraordinary intimacy, and Beth wondered if Jean Paul was as aware of it as she was. She glanced sideways at him. He was watching his wife and her dancing companion with affection.

"My lovely Dominique is infatuated with Gino," he said, and the merriment that characterized his way of speaking did not change. "He's an Italian prince and she loves titles. I'm only a Marquis, and she doesn't quite feel important enough with it, although our family title goes back much farther than his," he said with pride.

The waiter brought their drinks and his manner was an exhibition of extreme discretion, which made Beth want to laugh.

"Why is he being so secretive?" Beth asked as the man moved away.

"He does not want to disturb my courtship of a beautiful young woman."

They drank in silence and finally Beth stood up. "I think I'll turn in," she said. Jean Paul stood up too.

"May I invite you to ski with me tomorrow?"

They made a date, and Beth went up to her room feeling relaxed. She undressed and got into bed. It was all so simple, so smooth, so civilized. She fell into a deep sleep almost immediately.

Jean Paul was waiting for her at the ski lift.

He was a superb skier, and they took the slopes together for a couple of hours. He knew the terrain and she followed him without hesitation. They stopped several times to chat and have a cigarette. They had lunch in a small restuarant, and Beth found herself laughing gaily at the stories he related.

"I have a small lodge farther down the mountain," he said as they resumed skiing. "May I invite you in for a drink?"

"After you, Marquis de Langue," she laughed happily.

"Madam," he bowed, and she followed him down.

Lying naked in front of the huge burning fireplace, the peace and well-being that Beth felt was jarred only by the sudden memory of Adam. For a brief moment she hated him. She looked around the rustic room furnished simply but with exquisite taste and could not help but compare it to Adam's ugly little apartment in New York. Jean Paul was every bit as good a lover as Adam, she thought furiously, but there was a difference. He gave of himself, he allowed his feelings to surface. The idea that this was simply an affair was immaterial. After all, as far as Adam was concerned, theirs, too, was a passing affair, yet he found it necessary to hold on to his indifference, his control, causing tensions that were totally unnecessary.

"You are truly a most outrageously beautiful young woman," Jean Paul interrupted her thoughts, and she looked up at him. He, too, was naked and Beth could not help but marvel at his physical beauty. His legs were muscular, the legs of an athlete, his hips narrow, his waist tapered, his shoulders broad. He was endowed with a massive sex organ and, impulsively, she rose and kissed it, running her hands along his legs, his thighs and finally touching his testicles. They were firm. The lovemaking, as he lowered himself toward her, was more passionate, but Beth knew it was no longer Jean Paul she was making love to but Adam. His image kept hammering away at her brain as she reached her climax.

When she woke up, she was covered by a furry blanket. The fire was still burning and the room was very quiet. Jean Paul was sitting in a chair reading.

"Doesn't your wife wonder where you are?" she asked sleepily. She did not really care, but it seemed strange that he could be so calm and indifferent to the passage of time.

"Dominique is probably at Gino's, and I doubt that I will see her until lunchtime, when the children will be coming from Paris."

Beth sat up. "She's with Gino, you and she have children and you will all have lunch together later?" It was unbelievable. "How many children do you have?"

"Three lovely boys," Jean Paul said proudly. "Seven, five and three."

"Forgive my naïveté," Beth said, anger and amusement fighting for dominance. "But does Dominique know where you are too?"

"But of course," he answered seriously.

"You mean she knows you are with me, here, now?" She felt uncomfortable.

"Oh, you dear American hypocrites," he said sadly. When he noticed her face grow tense, he stood up quickly and rushed over to her. "No, my dear Beth, I did not mean to sound harsh or unkind." He took her in his arms. "Dominique and I are married for ten years. We love each other very much, we will always be married, we will always love each other, but we will love others as well, and we shall not interfere with each other's attempts to snatch the moments of happiness either of us can find."

"Does she know it's me, Beth Van Ess, who is the current moment of happiness as you put it?"

"I have not discussed it with her. She would not expect me to, just as I do not discuss Gino with her. She probably knows it's you because the night you walked into the Stubli Room and she saw you, she smiled with pleasure and pointed out the beautiful American lady. After ten years, she knows my taste, as I know hers."

It was all said in a most civilized manner and seemed completely logical, except that to Beth it sounded sordid and ugly. Not wanting, however, to show her lack of sophistication, she stood up slowly and started to dress.

Dawn was breaking through as they skied down to the lift that took them to the hotel. Beth was wondering how she could leave St. Moritz gracefully. Somehow she would have to get hold of Jody and explain.

Jean Paul kissed her hand when he left her at the hotel. "Shall I see you later?"

"How can you? The little marquises are coming, remember?" She had a hard time keeping the sarcasm out of her voice.

"You are upset, Beth," he sounded sad. "I have upset you and I'm sorry." He hesitated. "Please have dinner with me this evening."

"Call me," she said, and walked into the lobby of the hotel.

Exhausted from the skiing, the lovemaking, the memories of Adam, she lay in bed trying to understand the world of the de Langues. Somehow what Jean Paul described as a life-style made sense, but she was sure it was all wrong. Certainly if she were married and in love with her husband and they had children . . . She fell asleep without finishing the thought.

The relationship with Jean Paul took on a marvelous quasi-serious tone. As hard as it was for Beth to adjust to the way he thought, the manner in which he did things, the momentary honestly spoken declarations of love, she knew it was all temporary. She even found herself telling him she loved him and knew she meant it as seriously as he did, and that the life-span of their love was to last between Christmas and New Year's Eve.

"Will I ever see you again?" Beth asked one evening as they lay side by side in his lodge. Her flighty mood was gone. Jean Paul had entered her barren life, and in spite of her determination to keep the affair light and free of deep emotion, she felt a need for continuity. Her feelings for him were not serious or in any way resembled her feelings for Adam, but at the moment, being gently caressed by Jean Paul, feeling his lips on her body, tempting, wanting to arouse her, she needed to make believe, to pretend a future. Marquessa Beth de Langue, the thought crossed her mind briefly.

Jean Paul looked over at her and his eyes were troubled.

"I love you, Beth," he said seriously. "I wish we had met years ago."

"Do you really?" She wanted to cry. He was lying. He'd been married for ten years.

"Of course I do. But I'm Catholic and so is Dominique." He paused, and somehow Beth felt sorry she had brought such a serious mood down on them.

"But I'm not talking of marriage," she said trying to lighten the sudden strain that was engulfing them. "Can't we just live together for a while when this vacation is over?"

He brightened immediately. "I'd like that."

"Well, what's to prevent it?" she asked, surprised at herself for being so persistent. She closed her eyes. It would be nice not to have to go back to New York. Not to have to see her mother. Writing the letter about living in sin with a married, Catholic, titled man, was delicious. Not seeing Adam! The last thought was painful.

"I'll meet you in February in Bermuda." Jean Paul's voice came back to her. He sounded excited. "I've got a business meeting there. We can be together for two months. My yacht is anchored there, and we can cruise the Caribbean . . ." His voice trailed off in reverie.

"And then?" Beth was trying to keep up the fantasy for both their sakes. February was a long way off. Jean Paul was misunderstanding her suggestion, but she wanted to hear the fairy tale to the end.

"We'll cruise toward St. Tropez," Jean Paul said, but he sounded uncertain.

"Jean Paul, I want to have your child," she said impulsively, and knew she did not mean it.

The silence which followed was total. He lay motionless beside her.

"Did you hear me?" she asked, her voice soft, but the dreamlike quality was gone.

"Yes, I heard you, and you know it's impossible. You also know you don't mean it."

She began to laugh. And it was not out of unhappiness. It was a laugh which exorcised her attempt to buy a slice of make-believe with someone who could accept it without recriminations.

"I do love you, Jean Paul," she said, and kissed him affectionately. "I shall always love you, and I only wish my true love could be someone like you."

He sat up and smiled at her. "You shall always be a precious part of my memories."

Beth had not spoken to Jody except once when Jody called to ask if all was well. She sounded ecstatic and was effusive in her gratitude to Beth for having given her the time with whomever it was she wanted to be with. Beth could not help but ponder Jody Carmichael's future, who would soon marry Johnny Blake and settle down to a life of fidelity, loyalty and hypocrisy.

When the invitation for the New Year's Eve dinner-dance came from the Marquessa Dominique Louisa Teressa de Langue, Beth accepted without hesitation. She had met the Marquessa several times on the slopes and found her to be a charming French woman who spoke little English, but whose grace and vivacity were infectious.

It was to be a masquerade party and everyone was to dress in a period costume. Beth was quite sure she would be the only American there and she had a sudden need to make a statement about who she was. It took a great effort, but she succeeded in putting together a costume and she went as an American pilgrim from the eighteenth century.

It was an enchanted evening, with Jean Paul being openly attentive. Dominique was charming and everyone marveled at Beth's costume and her almost flawless French. At midnight, Jean Paul kissed his wife with great passion, kissed several other guests, and came over to her. He was completely at ease as he kissed her, and she knew, without pain, that the affair was coming to an end. It did not matter. It had been a lovely experience, and 1950 was a reality with which she would have to contend when she returned to New York.

4

Beth spotted Jody immediately upon entering the Zürich airport. She was standing alone next to her suitcases looking like a forlorn waif. In contrast to Beth who was properly dressed in a smart black-and-white herringbone traveling suit, black fur-lined boots and a Burberry raincoat draped over her shoulders, Jody was wearing a camel hair tuxedo coat, penny loafers, an outmoded sloppy-joe sweater and a pleated skirt. The sight jarred Beth. She had not consciously thought of Jody since meeting Jean Paul, but somehow she had assumed Jody was involved with someone glamorous and worldly, an older man, perhaps, who had swept Jody off her feet. The Jody Carmichael who looked lost and confused was hardly the person who would have attracted the man Beth had conjured up as the debonnaire lover.

Walking over to Jody, Beth put her arm protectively around her shoulder. Jody looked up startled. Her eyes were red from crying, and although she was trying to control herself, the tears started streaming down her cheeks the minute she saw Beth.

"Give me your ticket and go have a coffee while I attend to everything," Beth said with authority.

"Where?" Jody seemed unable to move.

Beth looked around and spied a small coffee shop. Pointing Jody in its direction, she pushed her gently toward it. She watched the girl walk away dragging her feet, her shoulders stooped.

Thank God for Johnny Blake, Beth thought busying herself with the travel arrangements. Jody was sweet but pale and dull in both appearance and personality. Waiting for the luggage to be weighed, Beth wondered if she would have to listen to the details of Jody's affair. She sighed audibly. It was bound to be a bore. To Beth's relief, they were asked to board just as she finished all the arrangements and was spared talking to Jody until the plane took off.

They ordered drinks and Beth watched Jody gulp hers down quickly. The tears never stopped flowing and Beth felt sorry for her.

After Jody ordered her second drink and drank it, she relaxed and leaned back staring into space.

"Want to tell me about it?" Beth asked, hoping to snap Jody out of her misery.

"Oh, I couldn't," Jody whispered and her face grew red with embarrassment. "I couldn't and I mustn't." Sitting up her eyes began to move about frantically. "No one must ever know. Ever." She sucked her breath in. "Beth you must swear you'll never tell anyone about it." Her voice was edged with hysteria.

"Of course I won't," Beth said solemnly, although she wanted to laugh. "I wouldn't dream of it, and I think you're being very wise."

Jody sat back again, putting her hand on Beth's arm. "I know you won't, Beth." She closed her eyes. "You're my dearest friend and I can trust you. But more than that, I'll never forget how much of a friend you've really been. No matter what happens, you've made it possible for me to have the most wonderful experience of life."

Beth held her breath, wondering if Jody would, after all, plunge into details of her affair.

"I wish I didn't have to go home—ever," Jody said through clenched teeth.

"What about Johnny?"

Jody shuddered imperceptibly. "Johnny, indeed." The tone of disdain puzzled Beth.

"Did you have a miserable time?" Jody said suddenly, and she sounded like herself for the first time since they met at the airport. "I feel so selfish. Dragging you away from home and then leaving you on your own." There was almost a note of pity in her voice.

It infuriated Beth. "I had a wonderful time, Jody," she answered, trying to keep the irritation in check. "I met the most divine people, ate the most delicious food, drank the finest wines, skied endlessly during the day and had the most heavenly affair with a gorgeous man."

"Where did you meet him?" Jody sat up and looked at Beth with unabashed amazement.

"I picked him up at a bar."

"You went to bed with someone you picked up . . ."

"No, actually, he picked me up," Beth said frivolously, enjoying the words and pleased with Jody's reaction.

"You didn't go to bed with a man you met just like that." Jody's faded blue eyes grew large with shock.

Beth's anger returned. "He was a lovely man. Rich, suave, intelligent, worldly and the best lover." She emphasized the last words. She resented Jody's implication and narrow-minded hypocrisy.

"Weren't you terrified?" Jody gasped.

"Of what?"

"Well, a stranger. He could have killed you. He may have had a disease."

"Come off it, Jody," Beth snapped. "I don't want to know who you were with, but whoever he was, he too could have been a maniac or whatever."

"Don't be silly. I know him. Knew him from before," Jody said feebly.

"Well, after meeting this man, I knew him too." Beth began to laugh softly. "This conversation is too stupid," she said finally. "Why don't we have another drink and forget it all."

They changed planes in Paris, taking a Pan American sleeper for the long transatlantic flight, and to Beth's relief, Jody finally fell asleep in her berth and Beth could relax and think of her experience in St. Moritz.

Saying good-bye to Jean Paul was not difficult. He had driven her to the airport and was warm, gentle and flattering and during the drive succeeded in turning their charming love affair into a friendship she knew would last for as long as she wanted it to. She also knew she would never go back to St. Moritz. It would be a fool's attempt to repeat something that could not be duplicated.

"We shall be landing in New York within a short time." The pilot's voice woke her and she sat upright with a start.

New York! Home! Adam! Her mother and father! Gillian! Work! Career! The sequence of thoughts flashed through her brain with such rapidity she could not catch any of them. All she knew was that she was facing a life which was troubled with uncertainty. The temptation to get off the plane in New York and take another one to somewhere far away, rather than face her living reality in the city, was whirling through her mind. She could go to Colorado, California, Utah. No one would know who she was and she would start over. She would change her name and work as a salesgirl in Woolworth's.

"I feel sick." Jody's voice was weak and she sounded ill.

"Well, sit down and we'll get you some juice and coffee. We'll be landing in a few minutes and you'd better put some makeup on," Beth said as she rang for the stewardess.

Colorado, Arizona, California, Utah were all dismissed as the plane came to a screeching halt and everyone on the plane began to file out.

Joseph was waiting at the airport with the car, ready to take her to Greenwich. They dropped Jody off at her parents' home on Beekman Place and were on their way to the West Side Highway when Beth asked him to turn around and take her to the Park Avenue apartment in New York.

She called her mother, who was cool, her displeasure evident. Beth's impulsive trip to Switzerland had upset her and she was not going to let it pass too quickly. Beth listened indifferently, knowing the pattern. Mary would maintain that attitude through the next couple of weeks or so, and then they'd return, for a brief period, to a normal relationship, until the next time Beth displeased her.

It was late evening and Beth felt extraordinarily lonely. She walked over to the window and looked down at the Avenue, wondering what it was she had accomplished by her trip to St. Moritz. She tried to think of Jean Paul, and it gave her neither pleasure nor unhappiness. It was a charming interlude. It was over. Jean Paul's itinerary for February was tucked away in her makeup case. She knew she would not bother with it. The feeling of emptiness grew. She took a stiff scotch and drank it down. Refilling her glass, she went into her bedroom and started unpacking. She finished her second drink. The house was quiet and she felt restless. She went back to the library and took another drink. She wanted to get drunk, although she could not decide why. Picking up the phone she called Gillian. There was no answer. She tried to think of whom she could call. She did not want to be alone. She looked at her watch. It was just 11:00 P.M. She was not tired and she wanted to talk to someone. Jody was the likeliest candidate.

Jody, Mrs. Carmichael announced, was not feeling well enough to come to the phone. She sounded distressed.

"I think it's the flu, Beth, and she's violently ill, throwing up and crying all the time. She won't allow Johnny to come over and see her in this condition and, frankly, I don't blame her. She looks ghastly." The woman's voice took on an irritated tone. "What in heaven's name did you two girls do on this vacation, anyway?" The reprimand was clear and it was not directed at Jody. "I know your parents have indulged you mercilessly, but I won't have you messing up Jody's life."

Beth felt the blood drain from her face and knew her temper was about to flare up. She swallowed hard before speaking. "I'm sorry, Mrs. Carmichael, that Jody is ill. The food in St. Moritz was very rich, and I must admit it's upset my tummy, too. Please tell Jody I called and have her call me when she feels better." She hung up the phone carefully after saying a pleasant good-bye, but her hand was shaking.

Defiantly she took another drink and sat down in an armchair and turned the lights low. She would think of Jean Paul, she decided. But her mind refused to focus in on him. Instead, Adam pushed his way into her mental view. She had been trying to avoid thinking of him since she got on the plane to come back to New York. Now she was alone, quite drunk, and her defenses were down. She picked up the phone and had a hard time focusing on the numbers of the dial.

He answered on the first ring.

"Adam?" She spoke slowly, wanting to sound calm and controlled. "It's Beth."

"Hi, Beth." His voice was strangely restrained.

"It's been a long time."

"I guess so," he said noncommittally.

"It's been two weeks, two days and some hours."

"Time does fly, doesn't it?"

"May I come over?" she asked, and she felt her speech slur slightly.

"Not tonight, Beth."

"You're not alone." Her voice rose in accusation. "You've got a woman there."

"There is no one here, but if it helps you to think there is, that's really your problem."

"I'm coming over," she continued threateningly.

"Beth, you're drunk. You're hysterical and you're making a fool of yourself. Go to sleep and I'll see you around." He hung up.

She picked up the phone furiously and was about to dial again, but the feeling of nausea overcame her and she ran to the bathroom and threw up. Walking back into her bedroom the temptation to call Adam again was overwhelming, but suddenly she thought of her mother. Mary always called back after a scene. Instead, she undressed quickly and lay down on her bed. The room began to reel as soon as she closed her eyes. She felt as though she was floating in space and the sensation was pleasant.

When she woke up it was early afternoon. She showered, put on a pair of dungarees, a white silk shirt, a V-necked cashmere sweater and loafers and pulled her hair back into a ponytail. Feeling refreshed, if still a bit wobbly, she walked into the library determined to reach Adam. There was no more pretense. She wanted him. He was the only person she wanted to see, be with, talk to. The idea made her pause. They had never really talked. They made love because she chased him. Then he'd put her in a cab and send her home.

She picked up the phone and dialed his number. Their relationship would be different from now on.

"I'm cold sober and I'd like to come over," she said when he picked up the phone. "May I?"

Adam turned away from the window and walked over to where Beth was sleeping. She had slept over for the first time since he'd known her, and it was a big concession on his part. He stood for a long time staring down at her and was furious at himself. Until Beth came into his life he had planned his future carefully. He knew exactly where he was going. He had a career as a lawyer which would eventually lead him into politics. Beth had no place in that plan. From the minute he met her, he felt she was someone who could suck him dry. Yet he had allowed her to walk into his life as though walking through a revolving door. Calling, coming over, getting laid and leaving. She made no demands, other than physical ones, and she satisfied him as no other woman had. She was different from anyone he had ever met, and he was sure the difference would ultimately prevail and he would be rid of her. He felt relieved that he had not heard from her during the holidays. Although he missed her desperately at first, the feeling began to diminish and he was coming back to himself. He was determined to ignore her if she ever called him again. Yet in spite of his resolutions, in spite of knowing she was wrong for him, he felt helpless when she finally did call.

Beth stirred in her sleep and Adam turned quickly and walked into the living room. Lighting a cigarette, he noticed his hand was trembling and he felt defeated. Theirs was not merely a physical attraction. He wanted to marry Beth. He wanted to spend his life with her. He wanted them to have children and grow old together. It was a ridiculous thought. He knew he would marry one day, but he always assumed she would be a woman with a background similar to his. They would have the same values, the same needs, and they would be in love. It would happen when he was ready to undertake the responsibility. Well, he was in love with Beth and she was in love with him, but she belonged to a world that was alien to him. It was a world he did not belong to, did not want any part of. Yet it was also a world that could open up unlimited possibilities for him, and he hated himself for being conscious of it. Squashing out his cigarette, he resolved again to put an end to this impossible destructive affair. He could not afford to let Beth compromise his very existence. Somehow he would explain it to her and she would simply have to accept what he was saying.

"Good morning, Adam." Beth was standing in the doorway. Even in the dim, early light of morning, without makeup, her hair uncombed, her eyes still bleary with sleep, she was beautiful. Adam had a hard time controlling the impulse to walk over and take her in his arms.

"I didn't hear you get up." Her voice was caressing.

"I've made coffee," he said gruffly, busying himself with the preparations.

She sat down on the sofa, her legs curled under her. He handed her the cup and settled himself in a chair at the far end of the room.

"Adam, did you miss me?" she asked softly.

"I've thought about you," he answered, "but I'm not one to miss people. I guess it's a matter of out of sight, out of mind." He hoped he sounded convincing.

Beth paled. "I'm usually like that," she said sadly, "but it didn't work this time." Leaning forward, she touched his face. "Out of sight did not make you out of mind."

He stood up and started clearing away the dishes. "I've got to get to work, Beth."

"When will I see you?" she asked as she stood up, too.

"I don't know," he said firmly, and turned to her. "Beth," he started with determination. She looked at him anxiously. "I'm over my head with work and I really can't make plans," he finished feebly. With her staring at him he found it impossible to say what he had planned.

They walked out of the apartment together. Beth hailed a taxi automatically. She got in, expecting Adam to follow her.

"I take the subway to work," he said pointedly, slamming the door shut.

Beth lowered the cab window. "I could drop you at the station." She tried to smile. He looked so austere, so indifferent. "Have a good day, Adam," she said quietly as she sat back and gave the driver her home address.

5

The affair between Adam and Beth was perpetuated by Beth. Adam never called her or made any overtures toward her. She knew little about his life when she was not with him. He rarely spoke of his family, his background, his frustrations or elations. Often she would try to question him about his life, draw him into conversations that would reveal something about himself which would give her a clue as to how to break through the shell he had built around him. It never worked. He never came to her home, never accepted her invitations to parties, small or large, never cared to meet her friends and indicated a revulsion at the thought of meeting her family. As the weeks went by she began to wonder when the affair would come to an end. There seemed to be no bond between them other than the physical attraction. Still, she would find herself staying up late at night, calling him sometime after midnight, wondering where he was if he did not answer. And when she did reach him, the inevitable, almost bored invitation would be forthcoming, and she would meekly throw on a pair of slacks and rush up to the dreary apartment building which Adam called home.

Things changed the night the phone rang while they were lying side by side, exhausted from their lovemaking, smoking a cigarette in silence. Adam leaned over her to answer the phone which was on the nightstand next to the bed. As always, his body touching hers sent a thrill through her and she was not really listening to the conversation as she started running her hand over his naked back. Suddenly she felt him go taut.

"I'll be right over." He hung up the phone and jumped out of bed.

Beth sat up and although the room was almost in complete darkness she could see the outline of his body as he started to dress frantically. His hands were shaking as he tied the laces of his sneakers.

"What happened?" she asked.

"One of my kids was badly hurt in a street brawl."

"Your kids?" Beth gasped. The thought that Adam might be married never entered her head.

"From the club I run for the boys on St. Luke's Place."

"Oh," she whispered, hiding her relief.

"Those fucking white kids who gang up on my youngsters. They really think they can bully us out of existence." His voice was hoarse, and she was reminded of the first time she heard him speak in night court.

"I still don't understand what happened," she whispered.

"They came armed to the teeth with bats and knives and started slashing around. They hurt one kid badly. That was the police on the phone. They want me to go down to the hospital. The cops say the white kids were provoked."

"Maybe they were," she said quietly.

"Oh, fuck you too," he answered as he ran out of the apartment.

Raising herself up on her elbow, Beth leaned over and picked up the half empty pack of cigarettes lying on the floor, took one out and lit it. Inhaling deeply, she glanced around. Although she had been to the apartment many times, she had never been in it alone. It looked dreary and she wondered what she was actually doing there. Who was the man she was having an affair with? What was her strange need to pursue someone who was so totally different from anyone she had ever known and who seemed so disinterested in her? She had never been one to give up what she wanted, but in Adam's case she was fighting a losing battle. Slowly she got out of bed and started pulling on her slacks which were lying on the edge of the bed. She found her bra lying on a chair in the far corner of the room. Her shirt was flung carelessly on top of a pile of papers on the desk. Her feelings of discomfort grew to embarrassment. Here she was, an extremely desirable, beautiful, young woman, who could have a relationship with most of the eligible men in the city, and she was chasing someone who barely knew she existed. She had been behaving like a spoilt child. In her pursuit of Adam she had lost all dignity.

She was buttoning her blouse when her eyes caught sight of some notes lying on the desk. Self-consciously she began to sift through the papers. An envelope addressed to Sam Ryan caught her eye. The idea that Adam was in touch with someone like Sam baffled her. She had known Sam most of her life. A political adversary of her father's, he had succeeded at a relatively young age in becoming a powerful factor in the New York political arena, and was feared and respected by everyone. She knew that Sam Ryan would not bother with anyone who was not an ambitious political animal. Beth picked up the envelope and was itching to know what the letter said, but reading someone's mail was hardly something she could do. Replacing the envelope on the desk, she looked at her watch. It was 2:00 A.M. The thought of going down into the empty street at that hour was disconcerting, but she had little choice. For the first time in her life she felt sorry for herself. She did not know what she wanted from Adam. Obviously, he wanted nothing from her. Hard as it was for her to face, she knew she would have to give up the useless pursuit.

Fully dressed, she was about to open the front door when the phone rang. Haltingly she picked up the receiver. It was Adam.

"I don't want you going out alone at this hour, so stay put until I get there. I'll be there in an hour," he said hurriedly.

Her feelings of rejection were quickly dispelled. Adam was worried about her. He did care!

Beth walked back into the living room and put the kettle on the stove. While waiting for the water to boil, she knew that something wonderful was happening to her. Someone she cared about cared for her. Adam was not indifferent. Not to her and not to the world around him. His concern for his boys club, his correspondence with Sam Ryan, indicated an awareness of what was happening. There was a lot to Adam. He was a dedicated human being with purpose and drive. Yet he maintained his independence, his distance, his sense of self. She could have a full and exciting life with him. Married to someone like her, he could go anywhere. She could and would become involved in his work and help push him toward his goals.

She was deep in thought when she heard the front door open and Adam came in. She smiled sheepishly. "You did ask me to wait."

"It's a lousy neighborhood for you to walk around in at this hour," he answered gruffly.

She stood up and walked over to him. "I think you were worried about me."

Without answering, he put his arms around her and kissed her.

"But why, Adam?" she whispered, her head resting on his chest. "All those months of seeming indifference."

"I kept hoping you'd get tired of the game," he said, still holding her close.

"It's not a game. It never was."

Pushing her away from him, he turned his back to her. "Beth, it's hopeless. There's no future in this for you."

"No future?" She started to laugh. "Of course there's a future. This is just the beginning."

"For Christ sake." He turned around, his eyes troubled. "I can't offer you anything. Not emotionally, not financially, not socially."

"What are you talking about?" Beth became indignant. "I want you. You're everything I've ever dreamed about. Why, I'd go to the end of the world for you and with you."

"Yes. I know you would go to the end of the world for me, but would you live with me here? In this apartment, on what I earn? I have obligations to my mother and sister." He watched her closely. "And remember, I'm Jewish."

"Oh, for heaven's sake," Beth said impatiently. "Of course I'll live here with you, and I'll work and you'll work and we'll build a life. I'll even convert if that's important."

"I wouldn't ask you to do that," he said, but he was still tense. "How would your father take it?"

"Daddy will take it because I won't ask him."

"And your mother?"

"She'll make a scene, I guess, but then she's always making scenes. She thrives on them."

He laughed a strange little laugh. "What have they done to make you want to hurt them so?"

The question made Beth nervous. "I don't know that they've done anything. I'm just different than they are, I guess." Then, changing the mood, she walked over to him. "Are we engaged?" she asked coyly.

Adam pulled her toward him and pressed her head against his shoulder, so she could not see his face.

"Beth, I am hopelessly in love with you. I've been in love with you from the minute I met you in that crazy courtroom. I've never been in love before. I've had no time for emotional entanglements. Then you come along and all the best laid plans got confused." His voice was very low. Beth felt his body grow tense with emotion. "You don't know what a strain this relationship has been. Seeing you, making love to you, not calling you, hoping you'd call, and hoping you would just go away."

Beth pushed her head back and looked up at him. "Do you mean you would not have called me if I would have suddenly stopped calling?"

"No, I wouldn't have called you, Beth. Just as I am now going to say that I can't think of marriage at this time."

"But Adam, I won't just leave. I'm in love with you and I won't go away."

"Beth, if you insist, we can continue as we have for as long as it lasts."

She lowered her eyes, hiding her frustration. Finally, looking up, she smiled. "Okay, if that's what you want."

As the cab pulled away from Adam's house, Beth sat back and remembered she had not asked Adam about Sam Ryan. It was just as well, she decided. She would call Sam one day, and for the time being she would take it from day to day. She also knew she was going to marry Adam Stillman.

The change in Beth was subtle, but there was a change. She was more devoted to her work than ever. She still went out with other men, but would try to be in before midnight so she could call Adam. Externally the change was more obvious. From the haute couture suits and expensive outfits she always wore, she turned to the simple blouses, sweaters and skirts which she knew most office girls wore. The high-heeled pumps were replaced by simple low-heeled shoes. Fur coats were discarded and replaced by camel-hair tuxedos and alpaca-lined raincoats. Gillian was the first to make a comment about what was happening.

"New man?" she asked one day while Beth was eating a sandwich at her desk.

Beth looked up and smiled. "What makes you ask?"

"There's a new girl in you, and I wondered what brought it about. If it were me, it would have to be a man."

"It is a man," Beth confessed shyly. "I think he's *the* man."

"Anybody I should know?"

"Adam Stillman," Beth said, with pride.

"Never heard of him. What does he do?"

"He's a lawyer who works for the Legal Aid Society. He was a teacher when he got out of the Army and went to night school for his law degree. His main interests are kids who are in trouble."

"Does he also live with his mother?" Gillian asked, amused.

"No, but he supports her and his sister." Beth looked surprised. "What makes you ask?"

"I know the type," Gillian stopped smiling. "They usually go very far when they finally decide where they're going."

"I don't know that you're right. He seems so unambitious," Beth sighed.

"They are the best kind," Gillian said philosophically. "It's just a matter of finding the button that pushes them." She looked at Beth for a long moment. "You might be the best thing that ever happened to him if you play it right, or the worst thing that ever happened to him if you don't."

"How?"

"I don't know exactly. It's just a feeling. But give me time and I'll figure it out. My brilliance sometimes does carry me away."

"I want to marry him," Beth said quietly.

"Then go ahead and do it."

"How? He won't hear of it."

"Get involved in his work. Bone up on what interests him. Start being active in the projects he cares about and make yourself indispensible. Then discuss marriage. I haven't met him, but from what you tell me, a definite statement following positive actions will get results."

"I wish I knew what you were talking about," Beth said helplessly.

"For starters, why don't you move out of that luxury apartment you call home. You're a big girl now and you live a very independent life, and Park Avenue is a far cry from what I imagine Adam comes from." She thought for a minute. "You say he's interested in kids. Well, start working with young wayward girls. I'll give you assignments that will blow your mind when you see what's really happening in this city. That will give a better understanding about who your man is, and what you can do for him."

Beth looked lost, and Gillian started to laugh. "You still don't know what I'm talking about, do you?"

"No I don't, but goddamn it all, I'm going to find out."

Gillian looked at her closely. "I know you will."

"Adam's also worried about my family."

"It's not your family he's marrying, Beth. And when he's a success, your mother will be delighted at her choice of a husband for you."

Beth was taken aback by the woman's insight.

"And my father?"

Gillian's face grew serious. "I'm sure he'll come around. He's a fair man, a good judge—and, frankly, between the little boys you've been screwing around with, Adam certainly seems to be an improvement."

Beth moved out of the Park Avenue apartment after finding a studio in Greenwich Village. The rent was reasonable, and the furniture bearable. The neighborhood was lower middle class, surrounded by great poverty. There were several social centers in the area, and through Gillian's contacts, Beth was permitted to accompany some social workers on their rounds to the families who were in need.

Her mother was dismayed; her father impassive. She never mentioned the move to Adam.

Beth had read about poverty, knew it existed, but seeing it up close was shattering. The ailing mothers, the feeble aged who could not keep warm, the infants dying from lack of proper medication and nutrition, the young teenagers who were angry and frightened. She started inviting some of the young girls up to her studio for a coffee or a soda, hoping to reach them, find out what they were thinking and how they could be helped. Her reports to Gillian took on a new life, a new meaning. Helpless as she was by what she was witnessing, she had faith and hope for these wretched creatures. She also felt she was coming closer to Adam, understanding him better.

In her spare time, she browsed through the stalls on the Lower East Side looking for accessories with which to make her apartment pleasant. She painted the walls herself, bought inexpensive shades and curtains, lamps and ashtrays. She was touched when some of the kids from the neighborhood came in to help her.

After six weeks of living in the Village she was actually learning to enjoy her surroundings, and couldn't wait to invite Adam to dinner. She had it all planned. The next time he appeared at night court she would go down and bring him to her new home.

It turned out to be on a Wednesday. She spent the whole afternoon preparing the meal, setting the table, arranging the flowers. Around five in the afternoon she discovered she did not have candles. She rushed over to the 5 and 10 on Sixth Avenue. When she arrived back at the apartment she found it had been ransacked. The sight of everything she had put together lying around, in shambles, shattered her. She felt as though she had been raped.

Tears of frustration welled up in her eyes, and it was some time before she was able to compose herself. It was not that anything of value was taken or destroyed, but rather the feeling of futility that engulfed her.

That night at his apartment, she told Adam about her life for the last few weeks.

"How does it feel?" he asked disdainfully.

"How does what feel?"

"Pretending to be poor."

"I wasn't pretending. I lived there. I've not taken a penny from my family. I haven't touched the allowance I get from my father." She began to cry again. "It feels terrible," she concluded, when she could finally control herself.

"Honey, move back home." Adam's voice softened. "Whatever it is you're trying to prove, you've done it. I've been reading Gillian Crane's articles and they're damn good. I didn't know you were doing the research, and I take my hat off to you. But stop trying to be something you're not."

"I'm not moving out of that place," Beth said seriously. "The only time I'll move will be when you marry me and I can move into this rat hole rather than live in that one. This one at least has a bedroom."

"I'll marry you on one condition," Adam said suddenly. "That the day we get married you go back to being the elegant, sophisticated girl I first knew."

"Adam, you noticed?" Beth squealed with joy, forgetting her misery.

"Of course I've noticed, but I thought you were just putting it on for my sake."

It was nearly dawn when Beth left Adam's apartment. He was exhausted, both physically and emotionally. He had fought the inevitable and had lost. Somewhere in his facade, built over the years, there was a flaw. He knew he was going to marry Beth, and they were locking horns for a battle, which he was aware of but Beth was oblivious to. It would be a long drawn-out struggle, and he could not predict the outcome.

6

Beth and Adam were married on a wet Monday in early May. The dreariness of the weather did not dampen Beth's excitement. She dressed carefully, wondering if it would be appropriate to wear the mink stole her mother had given her for Christmas. She decided against it. She was going to be Adam Stillman's wife, and furs would be out of place. Instead, she borrowed one of her mother's loose-fitting raincoats, and wore a green jade pin, inherited from her grandmother, at the nape of her neck. In her handbag she carried the wedding ring she had purchased, convinced that Adam would never remember to buy one. She wrapped it in a blue handkerchief. She left the apartment relieved that her mother and father were still out in the country.

She met Adam at the courthouse where a civil-court judge was going to perform the ceremony. Adam was waiting for her in front of the courthouse, and Beth was taken aback. He was clean-shaven, his hair cut short and his navy blue suit, slightly shiny from age, was ill-fitting. His attempt at elegance bothered her, but she kissed him warmly and allowed him to hold her close. She could not afford any doubts at this late stage. The only witnesses to the ceremony were two clerks whom neither Adam nor Beth knew. It was over quickly, and when the judge asked for the ring to be placed on her finger, Beth was pleased and surprised to see Adam fumble in his pocket and produce a simple gold band. All her trepidations were gone. She was marrying the man she loved. She was marrying a man who loved her.

They had a simple breakfast at a corner coffee shop and Adam promised to meet her at the apartment at six o'clock.

"It's our first formal date," Beth said as she kissed him good-bye.

"That's the way it should be." He looked at her for a long moment. "And remember that I love you more than anything in the world." Then turning away, he walked into the courthouse.

Beth was about to hail a cab, but decided to take the subway. She was now Mrs. Adam Stillman on her way to work; cabs were an unnecessary luxury. Waiting on the noisy subway platform, she felt good. They were plunging into their life together without superficial fanfare.

It was early when Beth let herself into Gillian's apartment, which was also used as an office, and shut the door carefully behind her. Unless they were working on a special assignment, Gillian rarely woke before noon. Still, Beth wanted to be around when her boss got up so that she could share her happiness with someone who cared.

The apartment, located on West Seventy-seventh Street off Central Park West, was an enormous floor-through duplex with a wrap-around terrace. The front of the apartment served as Gillian's living quarters. It consisted of a two-story-high living room with a domed ceiling, a stairway leading to a large dining room, kitchen and a couple of bedrooms. The rear had several rooms which made up her offices.

Beth smiled at the huge black porcelain statue, which stood close to the entrance, of an African native boy, draped in colorful garb, holding a tray. It was indicative of the decor in the rest of the apartment which was filled with endless oriental carpets, numerous crystal and Tiffany lamps, roccoco furniture, art-deco paintings and bric-a-brac collected from all over the world. It was a decorator's nightmare, but it reflected Gillian's personality and in a strange way was quite inviting.

Beth went directly to her office and made some coffee. Suddenly she thought of Sam Ryan. She had put off calling him. Now she wanted to talk to him. Perhaps he could be of some help to Adam.

He took her call promptly and invited her to lunch at the Harvard Club. Gillian walked in just as she was hanging up. Without a word, Beth raised her left hand with pride.

"I've done it," she called out triumphantly.

Gillian kissed her warmly and there were tears in her eyes. "Now, you get out of here and I don't want you back here for a week or so," she said in a voice filled with emotion. "Then I want to meet the man. He's got to be something really special for you to have gone to all that trouble."

"He is." Beth smiled with happiness.

Gillian walked over to a calendar. "How about lunch at the '21' next Monday at one?" she asked.

Beth laughed gaily. "You are determined, aren't you?"

"I want to make sure you're in good hands, pet."

Beth spent the morning buying some Beluga caviar and paper-thin wafers. She called the Sherry liquor store and ordered a magnum of their most expensive champagne, which she instructed be kept on ice until she picked it up. On her way down to the Harvard Club, she stopped off at Saks Fifth Avenue and bought Adam a cashmere sweater and a white silk bathrobe.

Sam Ryan was waiting for her when she arrived at the club. After ordering a drink, Beth told him the news of her marriage.

"Well, I'll be a son of a gun." Sam smiled. "Boy, this should shake up your father if nothing else will." When he saw Beth's face change color, he quickly elaborated. "I mean it as a compliment. There aren't enough young people who can take on someone like Judge Van Ess. Adam Stillman might give him a run for his money."

"Tell me what you know about Adam," Beth asked when she regained her composure.

It turned out Sam had never met Adam but knew all about him through his work for the Legal Aid Society. Sam had a high opinion of Adam and had been trying to meet him about some state legislation concerning urban juvenile delinquency. Somehow the meeting had never taken place. Adam, although devoted to the cause, was still not ready to commit himself to a program he felt had little chance of passage through the slow state government channels.

"He's right, of course," Sam concluded, "but when I hear about people like Adam, I like to keep in touch with them. So we correspond. And one day, when he does decide to move, he'll be in touch with me and we'll work together."

Beth felt relieved and elated. She had been right. Adam was very much aware of the world around him. He was simply biding his time.

"So would you say I married well?" she asked facitiously.

"Beth, you could prove to be the greatest thing that ever happened to him—or the greatest catastrophe."

Beth was amused. It was almost the identical sentiment Gillian had voiced when Beth first mentioned Adam to her.

"Now for a glass of champagne in honor of the beautiful bride." He waved a waiter over. "The only thing I'm sorry about," Sam said as they waited for the drink, "is that I shan't have the opportunity of making the pass at you, which I've wanted to do since the time you were sixteen."

Beth felt herself blush. Sam was almost old enough to be her father. She looked at him for a long moment. He was an extremely attractive man and before meeting Adam she would have been thrilled to go to bed with him.

"I wish you had," she said candidly.

They drank a toast in silence.

It was four o'clock when she arrived at the liquor store to pick up the champagne. She was feeling giddy from the liquor she had drunk at lunch and happier than she had ever felt in her whole life. Hailing a cab she gave the driver the Ninety-eighth Street address. Once there, she paused to look at the building. Since meeting Adam this house had symbolized a love nest, a hide-away from the phony world she had grown up with. Now staring at it, it dawned on her that it was to be her permanent home. The prospect was disconcerting. Quickly she entered the building and ran up the stairs. She wanted to be ready when Adam came home. She had bought some flowers, as well, and was quite laden down with packages. She was out of breath when she reached the fourth floor landing and was surprised to hear quiet music coming from the apartment. Hesitantly she opened the door. Except for a couple of lit candles which were placed on the coffee table, the room was almost in complete darkness. Adam was sitting in the large leather chair smoking. She threw herself into his arms and he held her close.

It was the most glorious night Beth had ever spent in her life. They drank the champagne, ate the caviar, made love and for the first time Adam spoke about his mother and sister, his hopes and dreams and their future together.

It was 7:00 A.M. and Beth was still in bed when Adam came out of the shower, a towel wrapped around his lower body.

"I've got a present for you," Beth said as she pointed to the box with the robe.

Adam opened the box, took out the silk robe and began to laugh. "You don't expect me to wear this, do you?"

"Well, that's why I brought it." She was hurt.

"Honey, it's returnable, isn't it?"

"Of course it is, but why would I want to return it?"

"Beth, look around you. Silk robes in this place are a mockery."

"Will you wear a cashmere sweater?" Beth asked, feeling foolish. She jumped out of bed and tore open the second package.

Adam took it from her hand and felt it. "It is soft, isn't it?" He sounded like a little boy.

"Please try it on, Adam, for my sake."

He slipped into a pair of trousers and put on the sweater. It was a plum-colored turtleneck and it fit him to perfection. "Please Adam, I'll return the robe, but you will keep the sweater."

He came over to her and took her in his arms. "Thank you, Beth. It's the first cashmere sweater I ever had, or ever hoped to own. Thank you."

She looked up at him and they stared at each other for a long time. "I think you'd better call your family and tell them the tragic news," Adam said, bringing them back to reality.

"At this hour? My mother is still asleep." Beth gasped.

"But your father isn't, and when he hears what you've got to say, he'll wake her up."

"I'll do it later," she promised.

"No you won't, honey. You'll do it now. Then I'll call my mother. She has to be at her dress shop by 8:30, and I want to get her before she leaves for work."

Drew answered the phone. A man of habit, he always woke at 6:00, showered and Beth knew that at that precise moment he was having his morning coffee in the little sitting room off the master bedroom—the room in which he also slept. The master bedroom was her mother's room.

"I wondered when you would call," he said quietly, taking the sting out of her defiance. "The judge who married you called me late yesterday afternoon."

There was a long silence and Beth was convinced he had hung up.

"He's all wrong for you, Beth," he said finally. "This rebellion of yours will backfire, you know."

"You don't even know him," Beth's voice rose in protest.

"That's true."

"Well, don't you think you should meet him?" It was not what she meant to say. By marrying Adam, she was determined to cut herself off from her family, her friends, their friends, their values.

"We're leaving for the country this afternoon." Judge Van Ess sounded tired. "When we come back I suggest you come to dinner with your mother and me. I'll have my secretary call you at the office to confirm the day." The formality of the invitation was offensive. Beth wanted to protest, but before she could say anything the phone went dead.

Hannah Stillman took the news calmly. She asked to speak to Beth. The conversation, although reserved, was pleasant, and she extended an invitation to Friday night dinner. The voice was soft, and Beth could not place the slight accent.

Beth dreaded the dinner with Adam's mother. She knew the evening was important. Throughout the time she had known Adam, he always ate the Friday meal with his mother and sister, and he would meet her afterward. Until now, it never dawned on her that Adam had never asked her to join him.

It was arranged that Adam would pick her up at 7:00, and they would go up to the Riverside Drive apartment together. As the hour approached, Beth became more apprehensive. She changed her clothes several times, finally settling on a simple black dress, a string of pearls, black pumps and a black tafetta raincoat. She had had her hair cut shoulder length and it curled richly around her face. She was careful with her makeup, using as little as possible. She was ready at 6:30, and taking a glass of wine she sat down to wait for Adam. At 6:45 the phone rang. It was Adam.

"Honey, I'm tied up for at least another half hour. Grab a cab and get up to my mother's on your own. I'll be there as soon as I can." He gave her the address. "It's on 149th Street, just off Riverside Drive. Apartment 6B."

Picking up her coat, she took the flowers she had bought earlier in the day and went out of the apartment.

Entering the building on 149th Street, Beth's feelings of discomfort rose. The hallway was dimly lit, the self-service elevator took forever to arrive. Once on the sixth floor, she had to grope her way to find the correct apartment. Holding the bouquet of flowers in her hand, she started to ring the doorbell, but remembered Adam mentioning that it was improper to do so because of the Sabbath. She knocked gently on the door.

Debbie Stillman, aged fifteen, opened the door and peered at Beth with huge deep-set brown eyes. Beth was struck by the alabaster whiteness of the girl's skin, which contrasted with the thick black hair parted in the center and braided down to her waist. For a moment she felt as though she was looking at a magnificent painting of a biblical character.

"I'm Beth," she smiled self-consciously. "I think Adam and I got our wires crossed. Is he here yet?"

A small, cold smile appeared on the girl's face, exposing unusually white teeth. "Adam is late, as usual," she said flatly and the expression on her face was filled with hostility. "I'm Debbie." Then she waved Beth into the apartment.

At that instant an older woman appeared at the far end of the hallway. She was obviously Adam's mother. The resemblence was unmistakable.

"Come in," she said, and the accent Beth had detected when they had spoken on the phone was more pronounced. Beth placed it as German in origin. As the woman came closer, Beth put her hand out and they shook hands formally.

"That was thoughtful," she said, letting go of Beth's hand. "Adam is always late, and you were kind to try to excuse him. I like that." She smiled for the first time.

The three women walked the length of the hall which led into a small over-furnished living room. The Sabbath candles were lit on the dining table which stood in the far corner of the room. The table was covered with a crisp white cloth and was set for four. Cooking odors were strong and unfamiliar.

Removing her coat, Beth looked around wondering where to put it. She was still holding the flowers. Debbie made no move toward her. Mrs. Stillman, who was staring at Beth, regained her composure and took the flowers, graciously thanking her and helping her with her coat.

"If you'll just make yourself comfortable, I'll go put these in a vase," the older woman said and rushed out of the room.

Beth seated herself in an overstuffed armchair and looked around. The furnishings consisted of two identical armchairs and a sofa, all too large for the room and obviously bought for more spacious quarters.

"Adam's habit of being late comes from his father," Mrs. Stillman said pleasantly, coming back into the room holding the flowers in a vase. "In Germany, where I come from, punctuality was the rule. In Hungary, where Adam's father comes from, the Talmud was the rule." She smiled briefly. "So he knows the Talmud and, as for punctuality, somehow he always does show up." She looked at the small clock that stood on a large dark oak buffet. "He'll be here shortly, so I'd better get everything ready." She placed the vase on the dinner table.

"Do you want me to help, Mama?" Debbie asked.

"No, you sit with your new sister and keep her company."

The word "sister" caught Beth off guard. This was her new family. The thought of having Hannah Stillman to dinner with Judge and Mrs. Van Ess struck her as ludicrous.

"Adam said you were beautiful," Debbie interrupted her thoughts. The phrase, although complimentary, sounded resentful.

"Did Adam really say that?" Beth was pleased, but could not escape the feeling of discomfort that Debbie aroused in her.

"I wish they would let me cut my hair, like yours," Debbie continued seriously. "Do you think you could persuade Mama and Adam to let me cut off these stupid braids?"

Beth smiled and looked at the girl more closely. Despite the old-fashioned appearance, she was an angry child, and it was disturbing.

"What grade are you in?" Beth tried to think of something neutral to talk about.

"Tenth," the girl answered, and slid down in her seat on the sofa. "I've got two more years before I graduate."

"What school are you in?"

"George Washington High."

"Do you like it?" Beth could not place it. "It's quite far uptown, isn't it?"

"Oh, the neighborhood is okay. It's the kids I hate. They're mean."

"Do you have a boyfriend?" Beth asked, hoping to get some reaction other than reserved petulance.

Before Debbie could answer they heard the door open and in a second Adam stood in the doorway. He was clean shaven and dressed much as he was the day they were married. It occurred to Beth it was the only suit he had. He walked over to her, leaned down and kissed her on the lips. She returned the kiss with passion, and the sad thought left her. Moving away from her, he walked over to Debbie, pulled her up and hugged her warmly.

"Where's my other best girl?" he called out, and Hannah Stillman, in the process of removing her apron, came rushing in. Flinging her arms around her son, the full impact of the pure love that existed between them was in that gesture. Then, overcome by emotion, the older woman pushed him away almost roughly and wiped her eyes on the apron she was still holding.

"You're late," she said gruffly, but when he smiled down at her, she sheepishly discarded the reprimand and led him to a chair.

"Bring your brother a schnapps," Hannah ordered Debbie, "before we sit down to eat."

"That's cognac," Adam explained to Beth. "Would you like some?"

Beth shook her head. She felt excluded. She was a stranger sitting in on a family get-together, and she wanted to escape. Nervously she opened her purse and took out a pack of cigarettes.

"Oh God, no." Adam jumped up from his seat. "You can't smoke here tonight." He did not say it unkindly, but Beth felt as though she had committed an unforgivable crime.

Placing the cigarettes back in her bag, Adam winked at her. "If I can do it, so can you." Then, turning to his mother, who seemed not to have noticed the faux pas, he smiled. "Isn't she exactly the way I described her?"

When they sat down to dinner, Adam donned a skull cap and intoned a prayer in Hebrew before the food was served. Looking at him, Beth could barely recognize him. The food was heavy and different than anything Beth had ever tasted. The evening seemed to go on forever, and she felt as though she had entered a foreign land.

"Do we go through this routine every Friday?" Beth asked, trying to keep calm when they finally walked out of the apartment and were looking for a taxi on Broadway.

"You don't have to, Beth," Adam answered soberly. "I go through it because it gives my mother and sister a sense of family. I'm all they've got. I'm the link to the past which died when my father passed away."

His voice had grown cold and impersonal. "What you saw tonight is me, Beth. Sure I smoke when I leave her house. I eat pork and shrimp and I love it, but I respect my mother's need for tradition and, goddamn it all, for as long as she's around and I come to her home, I behave as she wants me to."

Once in the cab, Beth took out her cigarettes, offered Adam one and they smoked in silence, each preoccupied with their own thoughts.

"You've got a very hostile little sister, Adam." Beth said after a while, trying not to sound belligerent.

"I know," Adam said, and a worried expression crossed his face. "She's changed since we moved away from the Bronx. The neighborhood there was awful, but she was used to it. Besides, I was teaching in her school, and of course, I was living at home."

"And now, to top it all off, a strange lady comes along and takes her brother even farther away from her," Beth said, her voice filled with compassion.

Adam pulled her toward him and kissed her hair. "You'll get along fine, eventually. I'm sure of it."

Beth rested her head on his shoulder.

"Well, that's one down and two to go." Beth said, without looking at Adam.

"Two?"

"My parents and Gillian."

"Gillian Crane?"

"She's sort of my surrogate mother," Beth said haltingly. "Somehow it's important to me that you meet her and that you two hit it off."

"I'm sure we will." Adam tried to sound convincing.

"As a matter of fact, we're meeting her for lunch at the '21' on Monday." Beth said slowly.

"We are?"

"I forgot to mention it," Beth confessed. "It's all right, isn't it?" She looked at him imploringly.

"I don't know, Beth. Remember, I work for a living. I'll have to see if I'm free."

All the pent up tension that had been mounting throughout the evening came to the fore and Beth lowered her eyes and bit her lip. "Adam, please make it." She whispered, choking back the tears.

"Okay, honey," Adam said quickly, stroking her hair. "I'll make it. I promise. Just don't cry."

Beth looked at him gratefully. "You'll love her, I know you will."

"I'm sure of it," he answered, lifting her face to his and kissing her tenderly on the mouth.

7

Gillian walked into "21" as though she owned the place. Her presence seemed to send electric vibrations through the room and everyone reacted to it, rushing up to say hello. Finally seated at her favorite table, Gillian looked around with satisfaction. She was in her milieu, recognized and appreciated.

Nearing forty, Gillian appeared ageless. Never having been pretty, she made little effort where her appearance was concerned. She had looked the same when she was in her twenties and would look the same in her sixties. A big-boned woman with shoulder-length thick black hair streaked with gray, she had large, warm, brown eyes, a fleshy, shapeless nose and full lips. She did not care for fashion. Colorful scarves, endless strands of beads over smocklike dresses, or an ill-fitting jumpsuit were her idea of being dressed. Yet in spite of all the external flaws she exuded a sensuality that was felt by all who came in contact with her. Men were drawn to her; women were on guard in her presence. She prided herself on being completely liberated and lived her life indifferent to the opinions of society and its moral codes. She never married, stating she was too much woman for one man to handle. Her affairs were numerous, and it was rumored she slept with both men and women.

Born in Brooklyn, she grew up with gangs and thugs. From an early age she learned to defend herself and what she believed in. Her father was a policeman who was killed in the line of duty, her mother a barmaid who had little time for her only child. Sheer determination made Gillian graduate from high school and get a degree in philosophy and political science from Hunter College. Fighting every day of her life to survive, she grew into a highly opinionated woman, and it was unwise to be on her hate list. Her loyalty to her friends, however, was total. When Beth first went to work for her, everyone was surprised at the kindness she showered on the younger woman. They were as unalike as two women could be.

Gillian was about to order a drink when she saw Beth and Adam come walking toward her table. Several people greeted Beth, and Gillian watched her introducing Adam. She appeared nervous and insecure. Adam seemed aloof.

"You're certainly handsome." Gillian said when they reached her table. "Beth never mentioned that. She only praised your brains."

Adam smiled pleasantly. Beth slipped in beside Gillian and Adam sat down opposite them.

"Beth and I usually have a martini," Gillian said with authority, "How about you?"

"A soda would be fine," Adam said politely. "I've got to appear in court this afternoon."

The drinks ordered, Gillian turned back to Adam. "So, young man, I hear you're with Legal Aid."

"Yes, I am."

"Why?"

"I beg your pardon?" Adam stiffened visibly.

"Isn't it sort of a dead end?"

"Depends on your destination."

"Well, what is yours?"

The drinks arrived at that moment and Adam picked his glass up, took a sip and looked at his watch. "In one hour I shall go down to civil court to defend a woman who is being evicted from her apartment. She has five children ranging in age from two months to eight years old, and she has nowhere to go."

"Why is she being evicted?"

Adam smiled wryly. "Because the landlord is doing something illegal, inhuman and immoral."

"Will you win the case?"

"Probably. She's overpaying for a rathole in Harlem, and her rent has just been raised for no reason."

"If it's that simple, anyone can do it from Legal Aid. Why waste your talents and energies on it?"

"I'm the anyone," Adam said impatiently. "Have you ever been evicted?"

"Yes, I have," Gillian answered and smiled. "I was nineteen and the marshal put my meager belongings on the sidewalk." The smile disappeared. "Have you?"

"I was fourteen. My father had just died and we had no money."

"What happened?"

"An Italian grocer I was working for after school introduced me to a lawyer who, I later discovered, worked for a political club, and he saw to it that we were not thrown out on the street. That man did for me what I'm trying to do this afternoon." He paused briefly. "I learned the lesson of my life that day."

"What was that?"

"It's not what you know but whom you know, and that timing is the most important factor in anyone's life."

"That's not a lesson. That's common sense," Gillian said. "But you're really too bright not to know that the man who helped you was doing the most obvious trade off. He was probably after the Italian vote in the neighborhood." She laughed out loud. "And he probably got it. The lady you're defending today wouldn't have the time to vote. Not with five children around. And her kids are a long way off from casting their ballots."

"At the moment I'd like to see them survive."

"I don't buy all that altruism," Gillian snapped.

"I'm not really selling," Adam said, looking directly at Gillian. She glared back at him. Suddenly his manner changed and he smiled. "What have you got against Legal Aid, anyway?"

"I don't believe it's a stepping stone toward a fruitful career," Gillian said with finality.

"What career?"

Gillian burst out laughing, breaking the tension. "You win," she conceded graciously. "Shall we order?" she asked, waving to the waiter, who rushed over and handed them the menus.

"Not for me," Adam said. "I told Beth I could only stay for a short while."

"What a shame." Gillian became absorbed in the menu.

Beth was relieved by the interruption. She had been sitting on the sideline watching and listening, aware she was completely excluded from the conversation and feeling more like an outsider than she had at Hannah Stillman's table. She was hurt at being ignored, but she was even more upset by the rapport and—yes—the intimacy between Adam and Gillian in spite of the sharp words and abrasive manner. They came from the same mold, spoke the same language, had mutual points of reference. She had been married to Adam for a week, had known him for almost a year and yet in the brief exchange between the two, Gillian had discovered more about Adam than she had. Beth threw a sidelong glance at Gillian, who was involved in ordering lunch, as though seeing her for the first time, and felt unaccountably jealous.

"I'll be running along," Adam said, and Beth looked up at him. He was talking to her and his smile was warm and reassuring. "I'll see you this evening, honey." He leaned over and cupping her chin in his hand, kissed her on the mouth. "Love you," he whispered and straightened up. Turning to Gillian, he put his hand out. "Thanks for the drink, and it was my pleasure."

"You didn't like him, did you?" Beth asked, watching Adam walk away and disappear in the crowd.

"Like him?" Gillian exclaimed. "I adored him. It was love at first sight and goddamn it all, I could kill him."

Beth looked around puzzled.

"That sonofabitch is going to take the longest route possible to get to where he's going. He won't let anyone near him who might possibly help him. He'll fight like a guttersnipe if anyone tries, and it's such a terrible waste of time and energy." She caught her breath with emotion. "That's the way I made it, and let me tell you, if I had it all to do over again I'd let anyone and everyone help me."

"Is there anything I can do?" Beth asked in a low voice.

Gillian reached over and took Beth's hand in hers. "Honey, you've got two choices. One, you continue working, setting your goals for a career of your own and enjoy your life with Adam when he's around. Or you can take all of your abilities and put them to work for Adam."

"How?"

"Look around." Gillian waved her arm toward the crowded dining room. It was packed with the political, financial and social powers of the country. "They can either help you achieve your goals, or they can help Adam."

"I wouldn't begin to know how to approach them," Beth said nervously.

"Don't be a child. You know everyone of these people as well as I do. At the moment you are the judge's daughter, but it should not be difficult for you to make them take notice of you as Adam's wife. Take advantage of who you are. There's nothing wrong with using the monocle you were born with for advancing yourself or your husband." She paused, "But first of all you must find out what it is he really wants."

"Does it have to be my career or his?" Beth asked tentatively.

"Beth, let me tell you something about Adam. If you want to help him at this point, you'll be a very frustrated little lady. He doesn't want help. Not yours; not anyone's. People like Adam, who ask for nothing, are usually very ungrateful."

"But he said that knowing the right people was important . . ."

"He also spoke about timing," Gillian interrupted. "At this time Adam is going it alone. You're his wife, and if you really want to be of use you must do it on your own, without expecting him to help you, guide you or thank you."

"What do you suggest?"

"Concentrate on your career," Gillian said soberly. "Maybe somewhere along the line Adam will come to his senses and realize how lucky he is to have you and your connections at his fingertips."

"There's got to be a way for me to convince him of it now," Beth insisted.

Gillian smiled a warm, almost sad smile. "How romantic." Then seeing Beth's hurt look, she rushed on. "I didn't mean to sound patronizing. But you two have to deal with a big gap in your background. You're miles apart. But I have full faith in you, and I'm sure you'll find a way."

8

Beth could not understand her parents' silence. It was not that she was looking forward to the encounter between her family and Adam, but secretly she did hope that they would meet and hit it off. She knew her father was angry with her, but he had said he would call, and he always kept his promises. It was therefore, a surprise when a month after she was married her mother called.

"I'm sorry we haven't been in touch before now," Mary said pleasantly, "but your father has been very busy and now I wonder . . ." She began to sound fluttery and breathless, which annoyed Beth. "I wondered if you would have lunch with me. You know, sort of a wedding luncheon." A forced laugh followed the invitation.

Beth was tempted to turn it down, but some deep-seated need to look at the world she came from overcame her. Mary suggested the Palm Court of the Plaza.

Beth arrived early and ordered a martini. She had to be well fortified for the encounter. Her mother was impossible under the best of circumstances. Today she was bound to be unbearable.

She was stirring the ice in her glass listlessly when she saw her mother enter the tree encircled restaurant. Mary Van Ess, years not withstanding, had a way of making an entrance. She was a tall, fairhaired lady whose carriage and manner of dress, although conservative, was eye-catching. On this day she was dressed in a magnificent navy Chanel suit with a matching coat flung carelessly around her shoulders, but Beth realized that no one seemed to pay attention to her as they would have in the past. It was also clear that Mary was unaware of the indifference. It occurred to Beth that her mother was probably the same age as Hannah Stillman. The idea was shocking. Hannah Stillman was an elderly woman, whereas Mary Van Ess . . . Beth's thought stopped short. Had anyone ever stopped to look at Hannah when she was young, she wondered. Did Hannah ever expect it? Certainly her mother had always expected it, was probably still convinced she was the center of attraction wherever she went. For a brief moment Beth felt sorry for her, but the feeling disappeared when she saw the maître d' rush over and, after an effusive greeting started leading her toward Beth's table. En route, Mary stopped to talk to an acquaintance, ignoring the waiting maître d'.

Beth watched the chatting women and tried to pinpoint her feelings for her mother. The first emotion which came was anger; the second was dislike. The anger had been there since Allen's death. As far as Beth was concerned her mother recovered too quickly from the tragic death of her son. She played the bereaved mother for a while, dressing in black and looking wan and pale, but within what appeared to Beth like a relatively short time, Mrs. Van Ess resumed her former life-style. As for the dislike —it was due to the fact that her mother seemed to have no inner values, no inner resources, no inner life. She was simply the socially prominent Mrs. Drew Van Ess, wife of an important judge. Nothing else. Beth continued to stare at her mother, who was now laughing gaily.

Who was this woman who was able to go through life seemingly indifferent to any of the realities around her; this woman who could go into a fit of hysteria over a badly manicured nail, but forget she had had a son who had been swept so tragically away at such a young age? Was it possible that she was truly incapable of understanding that her family wanted more of her? That her husband might want more than a good hostess, and in her stupidity and insensitivity had driven him to look for a life outside their home? Was it possible she was unaware of Drew's meanderings?

Beth shuddered as these thoughts crossed her mind. If there was one thing she had resolved a long time ago, it was that in no way would she be like her mother.

At that moment Mary came to the table.

"You're very pale," were the first words out of her mouth after scrutinizing her daughter for a second, "and that lipstick is all wrong."

"Mother," Beth clenched her teeth, "if that's why you wanted to have lunch with me, I'll get up and leave right now."

"Sweetheart, don't be so touchy. You know how I am about what one should look like. And I can't help it if I have an exaggerated sense of color. When you wear that shade of green, the lipstick shouldn't have any pink in it." She smiled. "But never mind that, darling, how are you?"

"I'm fine, Mother." Beth tried to relax, picking up her martini nervously. "And you?"

"Oh, sweetheart, how can I be?" She put on a distressed look. "Everything has fallen apart since your dreadful announcement about your marriage." She stopped and stared at her daughter briefly. Suddenly her eyes grew wide. "You've gained weight!" It was an announcement of dismay mingled with relief. "You *have* gained weight," she repeated with assurance.

"Mother, I'm not pregnant, if that's what you're thinking." Beth wanted to laugh. The woman was so obvious. "Mother, I got married because I fell in love. Is that so strange?"

"Well, your choice is certainly a strange one, and considering the rush . . ."

"Mother, you wanted us to have lunch, and I'm really pleased about it, but don't make it a bore."

"All right," Mary said as she waved the waiter over. "I'll have a daiquiri and my daughter will have"—she looked over at Beth's empty glass—"was it a martini?" Beth nodded. "A martini." She finished the order and made a face. "How you and your father can take that dreadful drink is beyond me."

"How is Dad?" Beth asked, trying to sound casual.

"Oh, my sweet, you broke his heart with what you did. Literally broke his heart. He had such hopes for you."

"What hopes did he have?" Beth asked surprised.

"Well, since dear Allen died, you know his world sort of came to an end."

"He helped bring it to an end." The words were out of her mouth before she could stop herself. Her mother seemed not to have heard.

"He wanted Allen to be a man, and he may have gone about it a bit harshly, but he meant the best, believe me."

Beth stared at her mother. "Mother, do you know anything about Father? Did you know Allen? Do you know me?"

For the first time in Beth's life she saw a glimmer of pain in her mother's face. Hurt. Hurt which accentuated the creases around the eyes, the slight downward sweep of the perfectly colored lips, the sagging of the chin. The moment was over quickly, and Beth wondered if it had really been there or if she had imagined it. Mary Van Ess's smile reappeared and she leaned over and pressed her daughter's hand. "I know you all better than you know yourself." Then, taking a deep breath, she continued. "Now to the real problems. Dad's upset, deeply hurt, but we've had a long talk about it and both of us would like you and your husband"—she paused briefly—"Adam, right? You and Adam to come to dinner next Tuesday night. Is that all right?"

"I thought Dad was going to have his office call and give us an appointment," Beth said sarcastically.

"That was rather gauche, I agree," Mary said, "and I told him so when I finally recovered from the shock."

The waiter came over with the drinks. "Shall we order?" Mary asked as she proceeded to order her carefully planned diet.

Beth felt confused. The conversation with her mother was strangely out of kilter. She could have sworn that her father never consulted her mother about anything. She ordered a turkey sandwich and another martini. Then looking up, she waited to hear the rest of the speech which appeared to have been well rehearsed.

"Oh, before I forget, darling, your husband isn't Orthodox or anything like that? I mean, I don't have to buy special food for him, do I?"

Beth shook her head.

"That's a relief," she said with satisfaction. "Now, what I have to say is this: First of all, if you're not happy just come home. We can arrange an annulment without any difficulty." She smiled. "Being pregnant would have made it more difficult."

Beth sat silently. She was sorry she had come.

"But, if you persist in going on with this marriage, then you can expect little help from us. We're not old-fashioned enough to disown you, and all that nonsense, but your father refuses to continue the allowance you've been getting. However, if your husband wants your father to help him get into a law firm, that would be something he would consider. You can understand that, can't you?"

Beth swallowed hard trying to keep from screaming.

"Mother, if you want to continue this idiotic conversation I shall get up and leave and even make a scene on the way out. If for once in your life you want to talk intelligently I'll stay." She was breathing with difficulty and could not understand the anger that was choking her. She had waited to hear from her father, secretly hoped that he might even help Adam. Now that her mother was saying it quite plainly, she was furious.

"Well, I've done it again," Mary Van Ess said lightly. "Will you come to dinner on Tuesday?"

"We'll come to dinner, but there are certain conditions. You are not to discuss money with Adam. Dad is not to mention that he'll consider helping him get into a law firm, since that is the last thing Adam wants. And if Adam should want help he's a big boy and he'll talk directly to Dad. But most important, you are to treat me as Adam's wife, not only as your daughter."

The food arrived and they ate in silence. Another of Mary's friends stopped by and Beth noticed her mother never mentioned the marriage, which offended her.

As they stood up to leave, Mary took Beth's arm and led her toward the front entrance of the hotel. Joseph, the chauffeur, was waiting. Mrs. Van Ess paused briefly before entering the car. "Beth, there is one other thing. We shan't be able to invite you and your husband to the country. You know . . ." she seemed uncomfortable, "the club doesn't allow people of the Jewish faith."

Beth turned on her heel and walked away, a clenched fist pressing against her mouth. An invitation to dinner through her father's secretary would have been easier to take.

To Beth's great relief, Adam met her in front of her parents' house at 7:00 sharp. They rode up the elevator in silence, Beth clinging to Adam's arm for fear of faltering and deciding against going through with the evening. She had not told Adam about her luncheon conversation with her mother and was praying her mother would not somehow forget what Beth had asked of her.

Martha, the housekeeper who had worked for the Van Ess family for many years, opened the door and nearly fell over Beth with hugs and kisses. Beth was touched.

"Martha is the only civilized person in this house," Beth said under her breath, and Adam smiled and pressed her arm.

They were ushered into the oak-paneled library, and Beth noticed the martini shaker was filled in readiness. Neither her father nor her mother were in the room. Martha offered to pour the drinks.

"I'll do it, Martha," Beth said, and poured herself a martini and gave Adam a soda. They toasted each other silently and Beth looked around. The library was her favorite room in the house. Quite small by comparison to the other rooms in the apartment, it had a coziness and warmth that gave her a sense of security. The furniture was comfortable, the lights properly modulated. The walls lined with books gave off a pleasant aroma. She walked over to a small original Rockwell painting she had always loved and stared at it. Then turning around again it occurred to her that with all of the feelings she had about the room, she felt no nostalgia. This was no longer her home. Her apartment with Adam was home. Some day they would move, but for now she would start furnishing it and making it livable. She was in the midst of thinking of a color scheme for their living room when her parents entered.

Judge Van Ess walked over to Beth, kissed her lightly on the cheek and then, turning to Adam, shook his hand. Mrs. Van Ess waited her turn and shook Adam's hand as the judge poured the drinks for himself and his wife, after noting that Beth and Adam had theirs.

"God bless," the older man said and Beth noticed her father looked pale.

Pleasantries were exchanged about the weather, and Adam made a comment about some book that was lying on the coffee table.

"Shall we go into dinner?" Mary suggested when she noticed that everyone had finished their drinks.

They walked past the huge living room and entered the dining room, which was at the other end of the apartment.

Although Beth had eaten there most of her life, she could not help but react to its beauty. When it came to elegant living, her mother was a master. In contrast to the wood-paneled library, the dining-room walls were covered from ceiling to floor in an expensive damask fabric. The heavy drapes were of the same fabric, which was repeated on the tall-back seats of the dining-room chairs. The indirect lighting was discreet, and one got the feeling that the only illumination in the room came from the long, white, tapered candles which were placed in their crystal holders on the round mahogany table. The white hand-embroidered dining mats with matching napkins contrasted with the darkness of the gleaming wood. The Spode dishes and Georgian silver made the table setting look like a picture in a magazine. The long-stemmed crystal wine glasses shimmered and sparkled in the fluttering light of the candles. The center piece was a spray of fresh-cut pink rose buds.

Beth glanced over at Adam. He, too, was taken in by the beauty of the room.

The atmosphere around the table was strained. Beth seated across from Adam was acutely aware that he was inappropriately dressed. His hair was in need of a trim, he needed a shave and his tie was too loud. It occurred to her that he had made a special effort when they ate at his mother's house and wondered if his neglect this evening was rebellious statement directed at her parents. In a way she understood his feelings, but was embarrassed nevertheless. She knew her mother was displeased, and she was furious at herself for noticing and caring.

The food arrived. On all special occasions, Joseph was called in to help serve. It amused Beth. They were being treated like strangers. When the soup plates were removed and Joseph came in with the small suckling pig, trimmings and all, Beth nearly burst out laughing. She looked over at Adam, his face was somber and she could not tell what he was thinking.

The conversation was dominated by Judge Van Ess, with Adam participating pleasantly. The topic centered around courtroom procedures and general legal matters. Beth relaxed. She knew Adam was on familiar ground. Still, she was acutely aware of the differences between her father and her husband. If there was a social-ethnic gap between herself and Adam, there was an abyss between Drew Van Ess and Adam Stillman.

They were having coffee in the living room when Beth suddenly heard her father say something about Republican Party politics. Her ears perked up and she looked at Adam. His face was white with controlled fury.

"Yes, sir, I'm a registered Republican," Adam said.

Beth nearly dropped her cup. She had never given a thought to what political party Adam belonged to. That he was a Republican was the far-thest thing from her mind.

"A strange choice for someone with your views," Drew Van Ess was saying.

"I don't really think you know my views, sir," Adam said respectfully, but Beth's discomfort grew.

"Oh, I think I do," Drew said, with a smile. "But that's neither here nor there. I'm truly curious what made you join the Republican Party?"

"I voted for the first time when Truman ran for President. I was hardly going to vote for a party that agreed to drop the atom bomb."

"You were old enough to vote when Roosevelt ran in forty-four."

"I was wounded and in a hospital, sir." Adam's voice was low, and Beth knew something was infuriating him and he was having a hard time disguising it.

"But why join a party?" the older man asked. "You could have simply voted without further commitment."

"I agree, but I believe that even the Republican Party can use some liberal-thinking young people." It was not said rudely, but Beth saw her father's face grow red.

"You want to overthrow us from within?" He succeeded in regaining his composure.

"Not overthrow, sir. Bring in new blood."

"Have you any political aspirations?"

"None that are defined at this time."

"Do you expect help from old fogies like me?"

"Not really, sir," Adam said impassively. "But I know one thing. You're a fair man, and I don't believe you'll hold a vendetta against any-one who comes up with something that is just."

"You're overestimating me, Adam." It was the first time he had used Adam's name, and Beth could not tell if she was relieved or frightened by it. Turning to Beth, Drew asked to speak to her privately.

Alone in the library, Drew poured himself a brandy, not offering her one.

"All right, Beth, you've made your bed, as they say, and you're going to have to lie in it," he said quietly.

Beth did not react.

"It's not what I had hoped for you, you know."

"What did you hope for?"

"You were always a winner in my eyes," the older man continued, not hearing her, "and somehow this young man you've chosen to live with . . ."

"Marry, Dad. I'm married to him."

"Marry then. I just don't think he's up to your standards. He's a good lawyer. A good debater. Decent, honest, poor as a roach and, as far as I can see, going nowhere." He paused for a long time. Then looking directly at her he continued. "And I won't lift a finger to help him. More than that, I'll fight him tooth and nail if he starts making waves in the party I helped build and make into a force in this country."

"I didn't notice his asking you to help," Beth kept calm.

"To think I wanted you to marry someone who could be like a son to me, who could carry . . ."

Beth stood up pushing her chair back and it went crashing down. "You had a son once, Dad, and you destroyed him. You'll never destroy Adam. Never." She rushed out of the room confused by what she had said. She heard her father call her name but ignored it.

She found Adam talking to her mother.

"Adam tells me his mother and sister live in New York, dear. Did you know that?" Mary asked.

Beth bit her lip. "Yes, Mother. I've met them. They're charming."

"Well, we must have Mrs. Stillman and her daughter to dinner some time. Don't you think that would be nice?"

"Lovely, Mother. Just call us, and we'll make a date." She went over to her mother and kissed her lightly on the cheek. "Dad asked to be excused and I know the way out, so don't bother."

Smiling pleasantly, Adam shook Mrs. Van Ess's hand and they left.

The night was cool but pleasant.

"It'll be summer before you know it," Adam said, taking her arm. "Shall we walk home?"

Walking up Park Avenue, Beth was deep in thought. She knew she had succeeded in hurting her father and, in a strange way, she was not happy about it. Vaguely she wondered why she had done it that evening. Was it to avenge Allen's death? Or was she afraid for Adam. She looked up at Adam and thought of telling him about Allen and her father, but he did not look as though he would be quite receptive at that moment.

"What are you thinking?" Beth asked, breaking the silence.

"That I've still got a legal brief to go through when we get home." It was as though the events of the evening had never happened.

"Adam, what made you so angry while we were at dinner?" she asked tentatively.

He did not look at her. "Beth, I don't like being spied on. For your father to have discovered that I'm a registered Republican means he had gone to a great deal of trouble to find out about me. There's something degrading about it." He was angry again. "Followed by that 'you were old enough to vote in forty-four.' What crap. He knew everything about me. He must have known I was wounded and hospitalized. I wouldn't be surprised if he knows what portion of the Torah I read at my Bar Mitzvah."

He was probably right, Beth thought. Her father was just the man who would do his homework fully before meeting Adam.

"He shouldn't have done it, but frankly, it is rather strange that you are a Republican. I don't condone what my father did, but the hell with that. Tell me why you're a Republican," Beth said haltingly.

Adam smiled a funny little smile and looked down at her. "I don't really know for sure. As I said, I wouldn't vote for Truman. I had a great deal of respect for Dewey, although I wasn't overwhelmed with disappointment when he lost."

"Well, as my father said, there was no reason to register as a Republican because of one election."

"Okay, let's put it this way. I hate the Democratic machine that runs this city. I find it corrupt, and there's little place for me there. It'd crush me like a peanut if I should ever decide to go into politics."

Beth was listening intently, excited that Adam was sharing his plans —however unformed—for a future in politics.

"As for the Liberal Party," Adam continued, "I'm not enchanted with them either. Henry Wallace was a good man, but somehow they don't seem to be able to get their act together. So although I have no immediate plans for running for anything, I figured I'd register with a party where the likes of me are few and far between."

"Isn't that a bit Machiavellian?" Beth asked.

Adam laughed. "Why does that word always sound like an accusation? There's nothing wrong with being practical. I probably joined the Republican Party out of pique, but I must confess that as time goes by it makes more and more sense to me. There are two political parties in this country. I've looked over their platforms, listened to the various candidates and frankly the differences are not that great. Certainly when they get into office, the differences become miniscule. But more than that, when I'm in that poll booth, I vote as I want."

"Adam," Beth said slowly, "when are you going to start getting involved in what you really want to do?"

"But I am doing what I want to do," Adam answered, looking at her intently.

"You mean, you'll just go on working for Legal Aid, earning next to nothing, living without some plan for a better future?"

Adam swallowed hard. "Beth, I told you all along that what you see is what I am." He paused. "What exactly did you think I was planning on doing?"

"Well, it does seem to me that with all the plans you have for making this a better world for the people you care about, that you start taking a

stand." She stopped walking and he did too. "Why aren't you more involved in party politics?" Her voice rose in frustration.

"I'm as involved as I want to be."

"It's a peripheral involvement. There's nothing concrete or practical
about what you're doing. It's all slogans—nothing down to earth."

"You sound like Gillian," Adam said through clenched teeth.

"What's wrong with that?" Beth shot back. "I thought you liked her."

"She's sensational, but I wouldn't want to be married to her. And, incidentally, I hate the influence she has over you. It's Svengali-like."

"Don't be ridiculous." Beth started walking again. Adam caught up
with her.

"Beth, did you think you were marrying an aspiring politician?" His
voice was filled with mockery.

"I married a man I'm in love with, but that does not preclude my
wanting that man to realize his potential and aim for the top. You've got
everything going for you. Every one of your thoughts, every one of your
dreams should be heard not only in a night court defending some little
kid who's in trouble. You're the one who keeps talking about that world
out there that's crying to be helped."

"Beth, I couldn't begin to think about a political career at this point
in my life. I've got too many things to attend to which make that
thought ridiculous at this time."

"There might always be too many things, Adam," Beth answered
quietly.

"Maybe so."

"Adam, I thought . . ." she stopped, aware that she had pushed too
hard, too soon. "I guess you know best," she said, suppressing a sigh.

When they reached their house Beth looked up at the building that
was now her home with Adam. It looked shabbier than ever.

Once in the apartment, Beth went directly into the bedroom. She
showered quickly and got into bed. She fell asleep immediately and was
only vaguely aware when Adam came to bed. She felt him beside her
but did not react. It was the first time since they had met that she had
no desire to have Adam make love to her. Her sleep was filled with
dreams of a beach, and a man was making love to her. Beth awoke once
during the night damp with perspiration. She could not place the face of
the man in her dream. She was sure it was not Allen; it certainly was not
Adam.

When she next woke up the phone was ringing. She glanced at the
clock and realized it was past 9:00 A.M. The room was drenched with
sunlight. Adam was nowhere around, having obviously gotten up and
gone to work without waking her. It was the first time since they were
married that they did not have breakfast together. The phone's persistent

ringing annoyed her. She was tempted not to answer it, but thinking it may be Adam, she picked it up.

"Well," Mary said disdainfully, "thank heavens he's listed in the phone book. You never gave me your number, and now that I see where he lives, I'm not surprised."

"Mother, I'm rushing to get to work."

Mary ignored Beth's comment. "I'm truly shocked. I knew you married a man I would not approve of, being Jewish and all. But my heavens, he looks dirty. And that suit and shirt." She caught her breath for a moment. "And that tie! Have you lost your mind? It's got nothing to do with anti-Semitism. As a matter of fact, I've met very nice Jewish men through the years. Some are really quite presentable and many of them are very rich. And you go and pick someone I'm embarrassed to have at my table."

"Then you just don't have to have us at your table, Mother," Beth screamed and slammed the phone down.

While she was dressing the phone started ringing again. Beth did not bother to answer it, knowing it was Mary calling back. She was also late for work, and her job was suddenly more important than ever. The conversation with Adam the night before was further proof that he would not allow her to participate in his life outside their home. They were in love with each other, but if she was to survive as his wife, she would have to pursue her own career.

9

Beth had never spent a summer in the city, but in spite of the unbearable heat, she enjoyed it. Adam's schedule was less frantic and they spent a great deal of time together. They would start their day by having breakfast in a small coffee shop along Lexington Avenue, and then he would walk her to the Seventy-ninth Street crosstown bus and he would take a subway down to work. Gillian was involved in writing a book and gave some article assignments to Beth with a promise to give her a by-line when they appeared. Beth was excited by the challenge.

In early September Beth's first article appeared in a national magazine. She had waited for it with growing excitement, but when Gillian showed it to her, she was strangely deflated. Gillian looked like a proud peacock, and Beth wondered why she could not rise to the occasion with the same enthusiasm. She called Adam and told him about it. He too was thrilled for her, but still the feeling of pride and satisfaction would not bubble forth. She felt alone, and knew with great certainty that she did not want to do things alone. She wanted to do things with Adam. They were a team, and she had been lulled into forgetting it. Her career could wait. Adam's had to be established, worked on, nurtured.

Using the publication of her article as an excuse, Beth suggested they give a party.

"I'd love to invite some friends over to celebrate, and I'd also like them to meet you," Beth announced that evening, "and I thought it would be nice if you could give me a list of your friends and we'll have them over as well."

"How many people are you planning on inviting?" he asked.

They were sitting on the sofa in their living room, Beth curled up in the crook of Adam's arm. The dinner dishes were on the coffee table, the beeswax candles still burning, Adam's favorite concerto filled the room.

"About thirty. I'll invite fifteen and you can invite fifteen."

"I don't know fifteen people I'd want to invite." Adam laughed. "I don't know five. As a matter of fact, I don't know one."

"Oh, you must have friends you'd like me to meet." Beth looked up in surprise. She had seen Adam in court, had seen the ease with which he related to people. People were constantly calling him up at home, and she had assumed they were his friends.

"I know lots of people, but none I'd particularly like or need to invite to my home."

"What about guys you went to school with, fellows you were in the Army with, people you work with?"

"Sorry, sweetheart. I can't help you out with a guest list," he said lightly. "I've never been much for the buddy-buddy relationships."

"Don't you mind not having friends?" She was genuinely shocked.

"Not one bit. I have my colleagues whom I work with and we get along famously. They'd bore you to death, and I suspect they would bore me socially as well. Then I have my kids whom I love, but they're hardly candidates for a party. And then there are people whom I would someday like to get to know on a social level, but it would be foolish for me to attempt it at this point." He was silent for a minute. "Besides, where would you put that many people in this place?"

"I wasn't planning on having it here," Beth said. "I wanted to use my parents' apartment. They won't be back in town for a while, and I'm sure they wouldn't mind."

She felt Adam stiffen. "It could turn into a rather expensive affair," he said quietly.

The statement shook her. She had overdrawn her bank account a couple of times over the summer but had not mentioned it to Adam. "You mean we can't afford it?" she asked.

"I don't really know. I give you everything I earn, except for what my mother gets." Adam said solemnly. "I barely keep anything for myself. You'd have to be the judge of that."

Beth stood up and started clearing the table.

"Well, can we afford it?" he asked.

"I hadn't thought of it."

"Beth, I've never asked, but what do you do with your salary?"

She stopped and looked at him. "Adam, my salary covers the clothes I buy, lunches and carfare." She paused, trying to think it out. "The wine I get for dinner, cigarettes and odds and ends." She could not think of any extravagances on her part.

"Honey, those lovely flowers you buy every other day, the expensive wine we have for dinner, the clothes you buy me, the endless books and magazines you keep bringing home, the records, the brandy glasses you bought my mother, the outfit you bought Debbie. Those beeswax candles, they're a perfect example of what you do. It's done instinctively because you've always done it, but it can't be done on what we earn. Just as we probably can't afford a party."

"Will we ever be able to afford anything?"

"We're not hungry. We're not out in the cold," he said gently.

"If I can pull it off financially, may I have the party, anyway?" Beth asked cautiously.

He shrugged his shoulders helplessly. "If you really want it."

Beth's first call was to Jody Carmichael, who was now Mrs. John Blake. They had not spoken since their trip to Switzerland, but Beth was not worried. They were friends and she was sure Jody would understand. Beth knew Jody had gotten married and recalled feeling hurt at not being invited to the wedding, but attributed the snub to Jody's mother, not Jody.

Jody was cool when Beth finally reached her.

"What's going on?" Beth asked, unwilling to be put off. "It's me, Beth Van Ess."

"I know," Jody said stiffly. "How are you?"

"I'm fine." Beth's initial exuberance was fading quickly. "I got married." She continued pretending not to notice the coldness in her friend's voice.

"Yes, I heard."

"Jody, what the hell is the matter with you?" Beth exploded. "Are you ill, or something?"

"No, I'm quite well, thank you."

"Jody, you're behaving very strangely." She hesitated, "Have I offended you?"

There was a long pause before Jody answered. "Beth, I'm awfully busy and I've got to run." She sounded uncomfortable.

Beth refused to accept what she was hearing.

"What's the matter, honey?" she asked, forgetting her hurt and feeling real concern for Jody.

"It's John, Beth," Jody said haltingly. "He doesn't want me to see you." The words were blurted out.

"You have got to be kidding." Beth wanted to laugh. "But why for heaven's sake?"

"He thinks you've been a bad influence in my life."

"And you're buying it?" Beth could not believe her ears.

"I've got to run, Beth," Jody said firmly. "Was there anything special you wanted?"

"Not from you." Beth could barely speak. "Not from you." She slammed the phone down choking back the tears.

She was more hesitant when making the other calls, but when everyone accepted her invitation and was actually delighted to hear from her, she pushed Jody's rejection to the back of her mind.

The party turned out disastrously. Adam came late. He had dressed in the clothes Beth had laid out for him; but he looked disheveled. But worst of all, he behaved like an uncomfortable guest, rather than a host.

Several women complimented Beth on Adam's good looks, but that was not what she wanted. She had hoped they might want to get to know him. She wanted to broaden their social circle, to reinstate herself and bring Adam into the world she had always shunned but now believed was important to Adam and his future.

The party produced several reciprocal invitations, most of which Adam could not attend. Invariably when he arrived to pick her up her friends would become uncomfortable. It wasn't anything specific. It was, rather, his indifference, which bordered on disdain for them. He made no effort to ingratiate himself. If anything, he seemed to enjoy antagonizing them by bringing up subjects which they either had no interest in or did not understand. Often as not, the evenings would end up in heated arguments.

"Adam, these people can't help it if they're not colored, Italian, Hispanic or Jewish. All you do is make them defensive about who they are," Beth cried out after a particularly unpleasant evening.

"Beth, they're your friends and I'm sure they're the nicest people in the world, but they bore the shit out of me. Can I help it?"

"Yes, you can," Beth answered furiously. "I agree that they're dull and unimaginative, but they make up a majority of the people whom you will eventually need to help you with your plans, your dreams."

"Is that why you've been seeing them?" Adam was incredulous.

"I see them because I've known them all my life. I don't want to trade places with them, but I want them on our side."

"On *our* side?" Adam's voice was mocking.

"Adam, someday you're going to get fed up with Ninety-eighth Street, living hand to mouth, scrounging around for the underdog. Someday you're going to face up to the fact that there are people out there willing to help make things better and that you can't do it alone."

A look of disdain came over his face as he stood up and went into the bedroom, slamming the door behind him.

Beth sat in the living room for a long time thinking. Since the day she met Adam she had been so preoccupied with wanting to marry him that she had never really thought out what their daily lives would be like. Their summer had been a honeymoon. Now, reality was taking over, and she had no idea how to cope with it. The thought that she might lose Adam terrified her.

She got up quickly and walked toward the bedroom. Adam was lying on the bed smoking a cigarette. She lay down beside him.

"I do love you very much, Adam."

"And I love you," he answered, taking her in his arms and holding her close.

Beth continued working for Gillian but as the months went by the job which she had loved and which was leading her toward an independent career, became a chore, a time filler between breakfast with Adam and the time he came home from work. Thoughts of her career still flitted through her mind from time to time, but they no longer took root. More and more her life revolved around Adam. Watching him appear in night court, her feelings of frustration would be overwhelming. He was a superb orator, a brilliant lawyer. His charisma and good looks were outstanding, his appeal to people evident, and yet he seemed to be wasting it all.

She tried to keep her social contacts, going without Adam, when she knew he was busy, convinced that someday he would benefit from her efforts. She began to drink a little more heavily. It made her feel gayer, more alive, more charming. But she also knew they were both compromising, although she refused to accept how deeply the compromise was actually hurting them.

It was at Christmas that they had the fight that truly shook the feeble foundation of their marriage.

Beth had gone out and bought a Christmas tree. It was huge and took up a sizable part of their tiny living room. She was in the process of decorating it when Adam walked in. She jumped off the chair and ran to kiss him, but was stopped by the expression on his face.

"What the hell is that doing here?" he asked in an incredulous voice.

"Why Adam, it's Christmas."

"Get that damn tree out of here, right now."

"Adam, I don't understand." She had never known a Christmas without one.

"Beth, for a bright person you do show an awfully dense mind. I am Jewish. I don't impose it on you, as you well know, but don't impose your religious symbols on me."

"It's not a religious symbol," she cried out in dismay. "Christmas is a lovely holiday, just as I know Jewish people have a holiday in which they light candles." She stopped trying to remember the name of the Jewish holiday.

Adam started to laugh, but it was not a pleasant laugh. The ludicrousness of the situation struck him as never before. "The Jewish holiday is called Hanukkah," he said bitterly, and walked out of the apartment.

Settled at a table in a neighborhood bar, Adam ordered a double scotch. He gulped it down and ordered another and mulled over their marriage. He was fully aware of the struggle Beth was having being married to him. He had known the differences in their background and approach to life before they were married, but there was a strong physical bond between them, and although it had not abated, it no longer compensated for what was essential for a successful marriage. He knew she was trying to understand what he was doing, but she was impatient. Married to someone from her world who had his qualifications she would have by now been deeply involved in helping that person build a political base for their future. Adam knew she was waiting for him to take the plunge, but he was not ready. He had to build his own base, make his own decisions, pick up an independent constituency before he could start trading for positions in any political scene.

He also felt her loneliness. She was hiding from it, not allowing the full impact to hit her, for fear of losing what they did have. For a brief moment he wished he were a youngster again and could call his mother for help. And what would he say, he wondered. That he did not want to be married to Beth? It was not so. He was more in love with her than ever.

Their marriage had not worked out, he thought sadly. It had started to crumble after the party Beth had given. He knew it then, but hoped that some miracle would occur and Beth would succeed in integrating her life with her friends along with his. But she was not strong enough to carry on the two diverse roles, and he was still not ready to give up the course he had mapped out for himself. He was going to start working with the Republican clubs of the area and would be even more involved, without Beth being able to participate in what he was doing. She was his wife, but it was quite obvious that there was no bridge that could reconcile their worlds.

It was past midnight when Adam walked into the apartment. The tree was gone and Beth was curled up in the armchair sleeping. He lifted her gently and carried her into the bedroom. She snuggled up to him, and Adam felt as though his heart would break. They had so much, but it was not enough.

In the following weeks both Adam and Beth tried to gloss over the scene that had taken place over the holiday, but the glue that held the marriage together was growing thin. Beth could not understand how it had happened or why. Physically, Adam was still as exciting to her as ever. Intellectually, he was the most stimulating man she knew. Yet they were drifting apart and there was nothing she could do about it. Her resentment grew and they argued constantly. The arguments turned into full-blown fights, and the marriage would have come to an end if Beth had not discovered she was pregnant.

10

Panic was Beth's first reaction when the doctor informed her of her condition. Postponed decisions about her marriage took on a new urgency.

Beth left the doctor's office, depressed. She was going to meet her mother for lunch at the Plaza. They had begun to have their weekly lunches again, and although difficult, they were her sole contact with her family. On this day, however, she wished she could cancel the date. She looked at her watch. It was too late for that.

Her mother was waiting for her and within minutes Beth found herself telling her about the pregnancy, although she had vowed to herself that she would not mention it.

Mary Van Ess looked horrified but quickly regained her composure. She ordered her usual lunch, waited for Beth to order hers, and when the waiter left she turned seriously to her daughter.

"I think the only thing to do is have an abortion." The last word was said in a whisper. "Of course, it'll be a problem to find a doctor, but I'm sure we'll manage."

Beth could not decide if she wanted to laugh or cry. Her prim and proper mother, the wife of the honorable Judge Van Ess, was suggesting an illegal operation.

"Have you ever had one, Mother?" Beth asked, surprised at her question. Suddenly she wondered if her mother had ever been unfaithful to her father. The thought was strangely disturbing.

"No, dear, I haven't. Your father and I would have liked to have more children, but unfortunately . . ." She never finished the sentence, leaving Beth more bewildered than ever. "But that's not the issue. You must not have this child. Your marriage is a farce. Everyone knows it. You made a silly mistake, and there is no reason to perpetuate it by dragging an innocent life into it. Also, there is the problem of money. You can barely keep body and soul together on what your husband earns, and a child needs things. I don't know what these operations cost, but I'll get the money."

Beth listened carefully. Her marriage was a farce! Everyone knew it! Adam couldn't support her!

"Who the hell are you to talk about marriages that are farces?" Beth lashed our furiously. Several people turned around to stare at them and Beth lowered her voice. "I don't need your money to support a child." The tears started streaming down her cheeks. "My marriage may have its problems, but I love Adam and he's my husband, and don't you dare say any of the things you've just said again." With as much dignity as she could muster, she got up from her seat and rushed out of the restaurant.

Riding up to their apartment, Beth tried to figure out what had made her lash out at her mother the way she did. It had nothing to do with the baby or the suggested abortion. It was the fact that her mother had dared slur Adam. She could not wait to see him.

Adam's reaction did not help.

"It's really your decision, Beth," he said, after a lengthy pause. "After all, you'll be carrying the child and you'll be the one giving birth." He was trying desperately to keep his emotions in check. The prospect of Beth having his baby filled him with inexplicable joy, but he knew how precarious their marriage had become, and he dared not show his true feelings.

"Don't you want us to have a child?" she asked, hoping he would make a definitive statement.

"Well, frankly, until this minute, I haven't thought about it," he said slowly, never taking his eyes off her. She was so beautiful, so desirable, so vulnerable. "As a matter of fact, it would be nice to have a baby," he continued cautiously, "but, Beth, it's a huge responsibility."

"Adam, don't you care? I'm your wife. I wanted so much for us when we got married. I still do, but you keep shutting me out. I want to be part of your life. If only you'd come toward me." She found it hard to keep the plea out of her voice.

Adam lowered his eyes. "Beth, I'm not going to take the short cuts you're offering. I know you mean well. I know you want things for me, for us. I do, too, but they'll have to be achieved my way. I'm not going to change. I'd love us to have a baby, but I can't make that decision for you."

For a brief moment she felt a great loathing for him. Then, without a word she got up and walked out of the apartment.

Night had fallen but Beth was oblivious to the darkness as she headed aimlessly down Madison Avenue. She felt betrayed and deserted and wondered what to do. She thought of going into a bar and having a drink. Looking around for an appropriate place where a woman alone could have one, she realized she was on Seventy-ninth Street. Gillian came to mind immediately. She knew Gillian was having a party, but it did not matter. She would simply slip into the apartment, go to the office and wait for the guests to leave.

Gillian was saying good-bye to some people when the elevator door opened and she saw Beth. The expression on the younger woman's face frightened her. Taking Beth's hand, she continued to wave to the departing guests until the elevator door closed. Then, without a word, she pulled Beth into the apartment, past the hoards of people, toward a small library. As soon as the door was shut, she turned to Beth.

"Okay, what's the story?" she started right in.

"I'm going to have a baby," Beth whispered, looking nervously at Gillian. The reactions from her mother and Adam had made her cautious.

"Hey, that's great," Gillian cried out with genuine joy.

Beth gulped in shock. "You're the first one who's said a nice word about it."

Gillian ignored the remark, got up and walked over to the bar and started opening a bottle of champagne. "This calls for a celebration."

"You think it's a good idea?" Beth asked haltingly.

Gillian turned around slowly. "It's not an idea, Beth. Having a baby, being pregnant is not an idea. It's a fact."

"My mother thinks I should have an abortion."

"And what does Adam say?"

"He feels it's my decision."

"A born politician, that one," Gillian said, pouring their drinks, "although in a way he's right." She handed Beth a glass of champagne.

"What do you think?"

"Beth, I've had an abortion," she said seriously. "It's a simple operation. It costs money, but that's the least of it. I've got four gynecologists out there," she pointed to the room where the party was taking place, "and each would do it for a price, if that's what you want." She paused briefly, letting the words sink in. "The question is, do you want the baby or don't you?"

"I don't know," Beth cried out. "Abortions are illegal. My choices are not that clear cut."

"To think that in the nineteen fifties we're still making women go through this routine." Gillian's voice was filled with sadness. Then clearing her throat, she continued, "Honey, even if it were not illegal, an abortion leaves its scars, and if there is a regret in my life, it's that I gave into the dictates of our crummy society and did not have that child."

Beth was speechless. Gillian was the most exciting woman she knew; her life was full of glamour and untold achievements. Yet when she spoke of having a baby, her voice was filled with longing.

"Have you ever been in love?" Beth asked, forgetting her own misery.

"Once," Gillian answered, and laughed self-consciously.

"Was he in love with you?" Beth was totally caught up in the fairy-tale-like quality that had descended on the room.

"We were in love with each other, madly, passionately." Gillian said, staring into space, seemingly reliving a painful moment in her life.

"Then why didn't you get married?" Beth asked softly.

"For starters, he was married."

"Oh, and that's why you had the abortion?"

"Don't be silly. He never knew about it." She stopped abruptly, and seemed confused by what she was saying.

"What was he like?" Beth was completely immersed in what Gillian was saying.

"He was the exact opposite of me, just as Adam is the opposite of you," she said seriously. "The difference was that I didn't have enough faith in myself and didn't believe I could change him."

"Will I change Adam?"

"You'll both change," Gillian said soberly. "That's what I didn't know then. Or maybe that's what I was afraid of."

"Do you ever see him?" Beth asked, wanting to avoid thinking about herself.

"Rarely. But we talk occasionally."

"Are you sorry you didn't marry him?"

Gillian thought for a minute. "No," she said, with finality.

"Well, my marriage isn't a marriage anymore." Beth, too, returned to the present. "Someday Adam may change. Someday, I might change. But at this moment Adam doesn't seem to care anymore."

"Bullshit. He's working his ass off and is actually making headway with the people who count. But you're being impatient. You're unwilling to simply be a wife to a young lawyer who is struggling to get ahead—you know, a young woman who works at being married."

"I've tried," Beth said angrily.

"No, you wanted to do it your way or no way." Gillian was equally angry. "You want him to cave in and come hat in hand to you and ask for help. He should, but he won't."

"We can't afford to have a baby," Beth said tentatively, remembering her fury when her mother had said it. "We're broke. I'll have to stop working, and Adam doesn't earn enough."

"It's a problem." Gillian nodded thoughtfully. "But not insurmountable. You're bright and you're a good writer, an excellent researcher and you're ambitious. All admirable qualities, but you're young and are confusing the quick now with the long run. Adam is taking the longest route possible to get to where you want him to go, but he'll get there and between the two of you, you'll manage until then." She stopped and lifted Beth's face to hers. "Don't rush it, and for God's sake, don't break him."

The last phrase upset Beth. It was Adam's independence that had attracted her most when she first met him.

"But enough with the lecturing." Gillian's mood changed. "You can be sure you'll get as many research assignments from me as I can give you while you're pregnant, so on your end of the earning spectrum, you have no worry. But let me tell you, my little love, problems will probably keep the juices of your kind of marriage flowing." She smiled a strange little smile. "Your real problems will start when there are no more obvious problems."

Beth was too tired to figure out what the statement meant.

"To the baby." Gillian lifted her glass.

Beth did likewise. "To the baby." She smiled for the first time, and a feeling of relief flooded her whole being.

11

Once the decision to have the baby was made, everything changed. For Beth the next few months were pleasant. Her mother, when informed of the decision, refused to see or speak to her. Her father wrote her a note in which he informed her that if she needed help she could count on him. His congratulations on the forthcoming birth were extended to Adam as well.

As the birth date grew closer though, Beth discovered she missed her mother. The thought troubled her. After shunning the mother-daughter relationship for so many years, she suddenly wanted her.

On impulse she called her. Martha answered and her joy at hearing from Beth was touching. When Beth asked to speak to her mother, Martha became evasive.

"Is everything all right?" Beth asked.

"Yes, except I have to see if she's taking calls."

"Taking calls?" Beth was puzzled. Her mother lived on taking calls from anyone and everyone. It was her *raison d'être* for living. She waited a few minutes and then she heard her mother's voice. It sounded muffled.

"Mother," Beth started, ignoring what she assumed was her mother's "hurt" tone, "I want to see you. I know we've had a rotten time, but I"—she faltered briefly—"I miss you."

"Why Beth dear, how sweet." The voice was still indistinct. "I want to see you, too, but you see, darling, I've just come home from the hospital, and I simply refuse to be seen by anyone for at least another couple of weeks."

"Hospital?" Beth's concern was real. "What happened?"

"Well, darling"—she paused—"it wasn't anything serious. What I mean . . ." and she seemed lost for words.

"Mother, did you have a hysterectomy?" Beth asked bluntly, knowing her mother's prudishness when it came to anything dealing with any part of the human anatomy.

"Oh, heavens, no," Mary gasped. "I've had . . . a face-lift," she whispered the words and then began to giggle. "It's really a simple operation, and as far as the doctor is concerned, I can go out right now, but I wouldn't dream of it. No one must ever know about it, Beth. You must swear to me you won't tell anyone. Martha has been sworn to secrecy and you must do the same."

Beth held the phone away from her ear. She had called her mother to ask for—her love and concern.

"I understand, Mother. I hope it all works out for the best. I'm sure you'll be more ravishing than ever, and I know it will make you very happy."

"Oh, I'm as happy as a lark about it." The voice was now stronger. Mary Van Ess was ready for a lengthy conversation. Beth listened for a minute and brought the conversation to an end as soon as she could without offending.

Walking over to a chair, she lowered herself into it. She was starting her eighth month of the pregnancy and had suddenly gained weight which was making her actions awkward. Her back had begun to ache and her legs had swelled. Absently she looked at the clock. It was four in the afternoon and she remembered she had to shop for food. The thought of the four flights was exhausting, but there was little choice.

The grocery bag was heavy. Beth turned the corner from Madison Avenue into Ninety-eighth Street, heading east. She noted the street lights were just being turned on and it occurred to her that fall was coming to an end and winter was setting in. Vaguely she noticed someone walking toward her, his hands outstretched as though offering to help with the grocery bag.

The events that followed were blurred. The bag was taken from her and she was pushed down to the pavement and struck on the head. She started to cry out, but a fist was shoved into her face and she felt a trickle of warm liquid running down her chin. Her instinct was to protect her baby and she clasped her arms around her stomach. The thought of the baby dominated all else. Then she passed out.

The noises around were loud. People were moaning and there was an unpleasant stench surrounding her. Beth lay very still, her eyes shut. Feeling around beneath a blanket with her hands, she realized she was in a bed. Instinctively, she reached up and touched her stomach. It was sore—and nearly flat. She was no longer pregnant! Her baby was dead! Tears started down the side of her face.

"Beth?" She heard her name and recognized Hannah Stillman's voice. "Beth, are you awake?" It was gentle and soothing.

Beth opened her eyes. The face of her mother-in-law was leaning close to hers and she was wiping the tears away from her cheek. Beth took in the room. It was a large, ugly room painted in a hideous shade of green. The ceiling was peeling. Fluorescent lights were strung along the center of it. The moaning she had heard grew louder and she looked around slowly. There was a row of beds alongside hers and another row on the opposite side. All were occupied.

"The baby?" she whispered finally.

"It's a little girl." Hannah tried to smile.

"Is she all right?"

"She's in an incubator, but she'll be all right." There was little conviction in the statement.

"What happened?"

"They found you in a hallway down the street from where you live and rushed you over here. The baby was delivered by caesarean. It was an emergency."

"Where's Adam?"

"He's outside talking to the police. They're looking for the man who attacked you."

"Well, if they catch him, Adam can defend the bastard," she hissed, and suddenly she began to tremble. She put her hand to her mouth, trying to stifle a scream.

"Let me call Adam," Mrs. Stillman said helplessly, and rushed away.

She didn't want Adam. She wanted her mother and father. Her father would know how to attend to everything.

"Beth?" Adam took her hand and kissed it. He looked grim and tired.

"I want my mother." The words tumbled out involuntarily. Then she saw Hannah and she felt sorry for being so insensitive. The woman had obviously been by her side since the minute she heard about what had happened. Her mother must have been informed as well, but she was nowhere around.

"Will the baby live, Adam?" Beth turned back to Adam. "Will she be all right or will what happened deform her?"

"How could anyone as beautiful as you have a deformed baby?" Adam tried to smile.

Without warning, she started crying, which turned to sobbing and then uncontrollable hysteria. A nurse came in and gave her an injection. Within minutes she was asleep.

Walking out of the room, Hannah looked anxiously at her son. "You're all in, Adam," she said.

"It's not surprising, Mama," he answered, turning to her.

"Adam," Hannah said gently, "you haven't talked to me in a long time."

He threw his head back and stared at the ceiling.

"Mama, I've made a mess of it all," he sounded desperate. "I married a girl I worship, who's given me a child, and I can no more afford one of them, much less both of them."

"Affording them is only part of the problem," Hannah said quietly, and waited for him to continue.

Adam came back to himself. "Well, it's a good part of it, right now. This whole thing is costing a fortune, and I've had to ask Beth's father to undertake all medical expenses." He walked over to the window. "I'll say this for the old man, he called me rather than wait for me to come to him. I'm also considering his offer of the use of their Park Avenue apartment."

"Not pleasant, I agree," Hannah said, nodding, "but that's still not the whole story."

"I feel like a loser, Mama." Adam's voice grew hoarse. "For the first time in my life I feel like a hopeless failure. Sure it's not just the money. It's everything. My work—it's crap. The people I try to help are a drop in the bucket compared to what is really needed to make some sense out of their miserable lives. And what's worse, they aren't even grateful for the effort." His frustration was mounting. It had been a long time since he had talked to anyone about his true feelings. "I seem to have lost my convictions. Everything seems so pointless suddenly. Being married to Beth, seeing a world I never really cared about, or thought I didn't, made me lose perspective." He took a deep breath. He was saying things he had never dared think about, much less word. "Mama, that world is so seductive. It lures you, it grabs you and shakes everything out of proportion."

"That's what happens, Adam, when you go outside the boundaries of who you are," Hannah said soberly. "Had you been younger and had I been able to dictate to you, I wouldn't have allowed you to marry her."

"I thought you liked Beth."

"I love her." Hannah smiled sadly. "She's smart and kind and considerate. She also loves you, but it's all wrong anyway. One of you will have to change, and now it's two against one."

"What does that mean?" Adam asked, "two against one. The baby is mine, too."

"Yes, but she's more Van Ess than Stillman."

"That's ridiculous," Adam exploded.

"Adam, for you to be Beth's husband and the baby's father, you'll have to make yourself over into a different human being."

"Meaning?"

"I don't know because I only know you as you are, and I don't know the people they are."

Adam lowered his head into his hands. "Everything was always so clear to me. Ever since I was little I knew who I was. I always knew what my obligations were. I was a survivor, and I was going to help others survive. Time was on my side. Now it's all rushing at me and I don't know that I want to change, that I *can* change." His agitation mounted and he started pacing.

"There's something you're not telling me," Hannah said pointedly.

Adam stopped pacing. "Mr. Van Ess offered me a job in his law firm."

"I think that's wonderful," Hannah said slowly. "If you think of what you've always wanted, deep down inside, you'll see that events are simply pushing you to make decisions you were putting off."

"It would mean giving up my work with my kids."

"Not necessarily. If anything, it might make your work easier," Hannah said.

"Can you see me working with them in a gray-flannel suit, white shirt with a starched collar?"

"You may be able to be of greater help to them."

Adam did not answer.

"What did you say to Mr. Van Ess?" Hannah asked tentatively.

"I didn't turn him down, if that's what you're asking."

Walking toward his apartment, Adam felt dazed, but relieved. He had said things to his mother which, once spoken, were actually quite exciting. Thoughts of Beth and the baby crowded in and hastened his step. Somehow he would work it out. He had to.

It was almost two weeks after Allena was born that the nurse brought the infant into Beth's room. Hannah Stillman walked in at that moment, and the look of adoration in her eyes for Beth and the baby, was gratifying. Beth was smiling through her tears when suddenly Mary Van Ess appeared behind Hannah. She towered over Mrs. Stillman. The little, heavy-set lady dressed in an old black coat, her face red and raw from the cold, was in sharp contrast to Mary Van Ess in her mink-lined raincoat with matching mink hat. Her face was made up to perfection, and she looked years younger than when Beth had last seen her. She pushed past Hannah, leaned over and kissed her daughter, never bothering to see whom she had pushed aside.

"Darling, you look wonderful, and look at that baby. Why she's the exact image of you. I've always adored blond children. They look so clean and fresh."

"Mother, this is Mrs. Stillman, Adam's mother," Beth said forcefully, and Mary looked around.

"Oh, Mrs. Stillman, what a pleasure. I can't imagine why we have not met before, but this is as good an occasion as any." She looked back at Beth. "Although, heaven knows, I don't feel like a grandmother." And she laughed lightly, taking her coat off and throwing it on the side of the bed. "We must get another chair in here, darling," she said seating herself in the armchair which Hannah Stillman had sat in since the day Beth was moved to a private room in the hospital.

Beth rang for the nurse, who came running in, and within seconds, a chair was delivered for Hannah Stillman.

"Now," Mrs. Van Ess said pleasantly, "I've spoken to Dr. Collins and you will be able to come home in four days. I've arranged for Joseph to bring the limousine in, and we'll get you and the baby to Greenwich. Martha is out of her head with excitement, although I've made it clear that Miss Hicks will be in charge of the baby for at least several weeks."

"Miss Hicks? Where did you find her?" She had been Beth and Allen's nurse and nanny for many years, and both she and her brother hated her.

"Beth, you underestimate your mother." Mary smiled and looked over at Hannah. "Miss Hicks is stern, but without doubt the best nurse you could hope for."

"Mother, I'm not going to allow Miss Hicks near the baby. And I know Adam would forbid it."

"But why?" she asked in amazement. "Have you ever heard anything so insane as to jeopardize a baby's life by refusing to give it the best when it's offered?"

"It's not being offered, Mother," Beth said coldly. "It is being ordained, and the answer is no."

"But darling, why?" Mary repeated, genuinely distressed.

"Mother, do you honestly believe I could move to Greenwich where Adam was not wanted? Where Jews are not accepted?" Beth was determined to hold her temper in check. Although she had no intention of ever going back to the Ninety-eighth Street apartment, going to Greenwich was not the answer.

"Well, Beth, it's only the club which has these silly regulations. We just won't go to the club while you're . . ."

"Mother," Beth said slowly, but her voice rose, "this is one of the happiest days of my life and you're succeeding in ruining it, and I won't let you do it."

The baby began to cry, Mrs. Van Ess stood up and looked around, confused. Hannah walked over to Beth, picked the baby up gently and walked out of the room.

"You are a dreadful woman, Mother. You really are an insensitive, stupid, vain woman."

Mary looked as though she was about to say something but changed her mind, and picking up her coat she stormed out of the room.

12

The atmosphere in the apartment was oppressive. Beth was in a deep state of depression and accepted Adam's decision that they move into her parents' apartment on Park Avenue, just as she accepted Miss Hicks as the baby's nurse. She sat around most of the day staring into space. She was overweight, never dressed, her hair grew long and stringy, her eyes were dull and lifeless, her pallor ashen. Nothing mattered but the baby. Her guilt at having considered an abortion loomed in her mind every waking moment.

Adam stood by quietly, trying not to upset her. He seemed to be waiting. In her more rational moments she saw that he looked haggard and worried, but she was too involved with herself to be concerned with his problems. His suggestion that she see an analyst were rejected out of hand.

"There's nothing abstract about my state of mind," she kept repeating. "I've lived through a dreadful experience. I've had a baby who might have died because of what happened. What the hell do you expect? I'll get over it with time. It's time I need."

Although six months had gone by since Allena was born, Adam, sitting in the library looked at her quietly, tried not to contradict her. Suddenly he became aware that she was downing her medication with brandy.

"It's not wise to combine pills with liquor, honey," he got up quickly and tried to take the glass out of her hand. She pushed his hand away harshly and gulped down the drink.

"Well, maybe if you were home more often I wouldn't be so tense and wouldn't need medication or drinks," she said viciously.

Adam turned away and poured himself a soda. "I've got work to do."

"Defending your little nigger boys?" she asked in a taunting voice. "Who do simple things like attack a pregnant woman on the street?" She was being irrational, but could not stop. "And you explain it away as being the environment that causes them to commit these misdemeanors?"

"You never told me the boy who attacked you was black."

"What difference does it make?" she snapped.

"No difference to me—but your assumption is interesting."

Beth poured herself another brandy and gulped it down. She was shaken by Adam's question.

"Well, was he?" Adam asked pointedly.

"I don't want to think about it," Beth became defensive.

"I think you should. Not what his color was, but what happened. Face it and come to terms with it."

She began to shake visibly. "I can't, Adam. It's too terrible."

"Hiding from it won't make it go away. Facing it, flushing it out and realizing that you're safe and the baby is well, might bring you back to yourself."

"Leave me alone." Beth started crying, and within minutes she was sobbing as she had not done since the day she gave birth and thought her child would die or be deformed. When the sobs subsided, Adam got up and took her in his arms.

The following days were easier. Beth began to take notice of her surroundings and became aware that Adam was in a dreadful state. She also realized that Hannah was rarely around. Although they spoke daily, Hannah sounded remote and preoccupied.

"Is everything all right with your mother and Debbie?" Beth asked one evening shortly after her recovery.

Adam became agitated.

"Did Debbie graduate?" Beth asked, aware that she had been too ill to attend Debbie's high-school graduation.

"Beth," Adam spoke carefully. "Debbie got married a couple of months ago. She eloped."

"Whom did she marry?" Beth asked cautiously. It was obviously not a happy situation.

"A young medical student named Jimmy Faulkner."

"That sounds nice. Why the long face?"

"He's a colored boy from Virginia."

The color drained from Beth's face.

"We didn't want to tell you about it because you were so preoccupied with the idea of . . ."

"I understand," Beth managed to say. Then pulling herself together she put her hand out and pressed Adam's arm. He was being torn to shreds. "How is Hannah taking it?" she asked after a moment.

"You know Hannah. If that's what Debbie wants and he makes Debbie happy, that's all that counts. Although God knows it would not have been her choice for her baby."

"Is Debbie happy?"

"I think so, although I doubt if they'll make it in the States as things are today."

"Where could they go?"

"Jimmy wants to move to Sweden when he graduates, and I think he's right." Adam answered seriously.

"Where are they now?"

"They're staying at my apartment until he graduates."

"The apartment on Ninety-eighth Street?" Beth gasped. The nightmare was closing in on her. She got up quickly and ran to the bedroom and flung herself on the bed. Adam rushed in after her and came over to the bed.

"How could you?" she sobbed. "How could you ever go back there?"

"It's my home, Beth."

"*This* is your home."

"No, honey, this is *your* home. This is Allena's home. This is the place where my family lives. I'm a guest who's trying to figure out how the hell to pay for it so that my family does not get molested in hallways."

Beth sat up and wiped her eyes.

"Well, keeping two households running must cost . . ." She stopped. She had not thought of how they were managing financially until that moment.

"One or two apartments don't make the difference." He laughed bitterly. "You don't really believe I could afford any of this?" He waved his arm around in frustration.

"Well, don't you think you should have discussed it with me?"

"The condition you were in, honey, was hardly conducive to intelligent conversation. And remember that along with everything else, I was seriously considering how to pay for psychiatric treatment."

"Well, what happens now?" She was fully composed.

"We go on for a while, and as soon as possible I'll get us out of this mess."

"But I can't live this way."

Adam lit a cigarette and sat down on the chaise lounge at the far corner of the room.

"Did you hear me?" she asked.

"I heard you, Beth, and all I can say is, I know what I'm doing and you must trust me."

"That's not good enough." She felt shut out. "Adam talk to me. I want to know what you're planning.

"Stop trying to carve me up," he said coldly.

"Adam, I can't go on living on vague plans that you won't discuss with me."

"In that case, maybe we should try living apart for a while."

Beth's heart sank.

"It will be a while before everything falls into place, and if the strain is too great for you, I think it best if we separate." His face was set with determination and his lips barely moved as he spoke. He reminded her of the proud young man she had first seen in the courtroom four years earlier, and she knew he meant what he was saying. She got up and ran over to him, and knelt beside him. He did not react.

"Make love to me," she whispered. "Adam, let's forget everything for now. Just let's make love."

He looked down at her, "Oh, my poor Beth, you really think that making love will solve it all. The bills will go away. Jimmy Faulkner will become white. I'll become a gentile, and we'll all move to Greenwich or Southampton and live happily ever after."

Beth rested her head on Adam's chest. She was totally exhausted.

Just before she fell asleep she wondered if the doorman would let Jimmy Faulkner in the front elevator if he ever came to visit them.

13

In spite of Beth's protestations, Adam prevailed and she and the baby went to spend the summer in Southampton with her parents. On the surface it was simply a vacation, but both Beth and Adam knew it was to be a trial separation.

Beth was shocked at how quickly she fell into the role of being Drew and Mary Van Ess's daughter again. Being Adam's wife, Allena's mother, and a working woman who had been on her own were quickly forgotten. She found herself automatically taking her old place at the dining-room table, aware of her mother's displeasure at any form of misconduct on her part, and being constantly criticized about how she looked, dressed or what she said. Within days, she was reduced to being a child.

The deep-rooted feelings of anger toward her mother and what she represented gained unbearable proportions. Desperate as she was to escape, there was nothing she could do about it.

Adam came out once a week in the evening with her father, but always took the last train back to town. On Saturdays, he came out for the day. At first Beth looked forward to his coming, but as time wore on they had less and less to say to each other, and Beth began to wonder if her marriage would last.

As the summer grew to a close, Beth knew it was time for a showdown. It would at least bring to an end the impossible situation in which she was living. Allena was almost a year old and she barely knew her father. She was beginning to make sounds which Beth understood but which were mere cooing noises to Adam. Also, Beth was lonely and needed love and companionship. She was young and she wanted to start rebuilding her life. She had the money to go it alone. It was Adam's pride that made it impossible for her to live in New York. Between her income from her grandmother's estate and a job, which she was sure she could get once she was back in the city, she could manage. It was also not a crime to accept money from her father. It only appeared so as long as she was married to Adam, who felt it was demeaning.

She called Gillian and made a date with her for lunch in the city on

Saturday so she could leave Allena with Hannah while she was busy, and asked her to inform Adam of her plans.

Beth arrived at the Algonquin Hotel early and went into the restaurant to wait for Gillian. The restaurant was crowded and Beth felt the admiring glances that followed her as she was led to her table. She realized how sorely she had missed that attention. Since marrying Adam she had not thought of herself in relationship to other men, and she did not miss it. But if Adam did not want her, if her marriage was over, there was a whole world of people whom she could meet and enjoy. Her anger at Adam rose. She needed him on so many levels. Allena needed him even more than she did, but he seemed not to need them at all.

The humming voices around her grew louder and Beth looked up and saw Gillian Crane walk in. She was wearing a multi-colored tentlike dress, a colorful scarf around her shoulders, and enormous gold loop earrings. Her makeup was quite bright and, although the over-all appearance had an almost burlesquelike quality, she got away with it. Boisterous as ever, she stopped to say hello and chat with various people, laughing and joking as she was led toward Beth's table. Beth envied her joy of life.

"You're more gorgeous than ever," Gillian said as she sat down beside Beth and leaned over and kissed her on the cheek. "Life of leisure and wealth agrees with you, obviously."

"This whole lunch is to talk about me," Beth said, with a smile, "so why don't you tell me about yourself first, so I don't feel too guilty about my side of the story."

"Okay," Gillian started, "life is glorious, I have the greatest book coming out in a couple of months, and it will be a best seller. I've decided to blow the whistle on all the ladies who claim they went liberation but are only talking about it, and, as you can well imagine, I'm angry at you and women like you." She paused for a second. "I've been to Europe twice since I've last seen you, and I've been to Indo-China once." She made a face. "I hold out little hope for the world as we're now going, but I intend to go on speaking out. As for the personal, I've got several divine men in my life. They're all gorgeous and I adore them and they adore me. Some are a little young for me, but what the hell. I make out well, and as fucks go on the score of one to ten most of them rate about seven, which in today's marketplace is not bad. I've bought a house in Darien, Connecticut, a little farmhouse which I'm having done in early Altman's by some idiotic decorator so I can go ahead and demolish everything she's done and brag about my talents. But she's going to make it livable for the first few months until I get my destructive claws into it."

Beth watched Gillian as she talked. She did not look well. Her dark hair was long, more strands of gray were evident. Her eyes were slightly puffed, and her jowls were beginning to sag. Beth almost felt sorry for her.

At that moment a man stopped by and Gillian raised her face to be kissed by him.

"Dan Bradbury, I want you to meet one of my favorite ladies, Beth Stillman."

Beth put her hand out and the man smiled warmly at her. He was tall, fair-skinned and had clear blue eyes. He was handsome but seemed to know it, which bothered Beth. He looked directly at her for just a second and returned his gaze to Gillian. For a few minutes they exchanged some words about the Indo-China situation and other world affairs. Beth was not really listening. She was anxious for him to leave. There was so much she had to talk to Gillian about. When he finally left, Beth watched the departing figure absently.

"Isn't he heavenly?" Gillian asked. "He's a brilliant political analyst. Bright as a whip, and we traveled together."

"How does he rate on the scale of one to ten?" Beth asked, and was shocked at her question.

Gillian smiled. "I never give out ratings on mutual friends."

"I don't even remember his name." Beth laughed uncomfortably.

"But you might meet him again, and that would be unfair." Gillian smiled briefly and then grew serious. "Now, to go on with what we were talking about. I've been asked to do a fifteen-minute radio show five times a week, in the afternoon. The idea is appealing and will give me the exposure I'm looking for." She stopped to catch her breath. "I'm as happy as a lark and don't have a care in the world except for the world." She leaned back and smiled. "I think that about covers it, and I would like a drink." She waved to the waiter, who rushed over, and she ordered a vodka on the rocks, looking inquiringly at Beth, who shook her head. She was still nursing her martini. "Now what about you?"

"I want a job," Beth said simply. "A job from nine to five or ten to six, or whatever the hours are that people work in this town. I don't know where to turn, since you're actually the only person I've ever worked for, and you know my capabilities."

"Plan on commuting?"

"No, I'm moving back into town. I'm going back to our apartment on Park Avenue. I'm sure my mother will lend me Martha to take care of Allena until I find someone to care for her."

"And Adam?"

"He can move in with us if he wants to. I want him to, but somehow I get the feeling he doesn't really care." Beth tried not to show her pain as she said the words. She had not dared word the thought to herself, much less say it out loud. Now spoken, she wondered about her feelings.

"You mean you want a divorce?"

"I don't really know. Certainly the way we're living now is neither here nor there. I think it would be better if we got some semblance of order in our lives." She paused. "Why do you ask?"

"I've seen him several times while you've been away. I can assure you, the last thing he's thinking of is a divorce, a separation or anything other than how to bring you and the baby back to New York and live with him in a style that at least has a semblance of what you want and what he wants for you."

"He's putting on a good act of hiding it from me," Beth said. "Why did you get together?" The thought that Gillian might be having an affair with Adam struck her briefly, but she dismissed it.

"Discussing different job possibilities that may work out financially for him. God knows he's not asking for the moon salary-wise. The question is what he should take that will lead him to where he's heading."

"Where's that?" Beth asked curiously.

"Don't you ever talk to each other?" Gillian asked incredulously.

"Not very much. We hold hands a lot, and he keeps looking at the baby all the time. She seems to fascinate him."

"Adam is going to run for public office at one point. State Congress, U. S. Congress, Senate, or something like that. I told you that from the start. He's a natural."

"And what are his immediate prospects?" Beth asked.

"Ask him. I'm sure he's not going to hide anything from you if you ask him."

"Do you know?"

"I'm not sure, and I'd rather not speculate."

"That's all well and fine, but I still want a job," Beth persisted.

"Honey, you know you've always got one with me. And now that I've got this radio show, you're a godsend."

"Would you have called me had I not called you?" Beth asked.

"Nope," Gillian answered as she downed her drink and picked up the menu. "I have a theory: I believe in hungry people. They're the only dependable ones."

The rest of the lunch was pleasant. Beth felt better, more relaxed, and could pay attention to what was going on around her. Several people came up to the table. It was obvious that a couple of men came over specifically to be introduced to her and she was flattered. She did not really care if Adam wanted her back in the city or not. She was coming back to New York with her child. Vaguely she wondered if it would not be a relief if Adam did ask for a divorce. She knew she would not. He was too down and out at this moment, and it seemed unfair.

Beth left Gillian and arrived back at Hannah's to find the baby sleeping in her portable crib. The house was peaceful with Hannah sitting in the living room talking to Adam, who was lounging on the sofa looking quite agitated. When she walked in, he got up immediately and walked over to kiss her. She almost shrank from him, her anger suddenly rekindled. He noticed it and she regretted the action and quickly threw her arms around him.

"What brought you into town?" he asked, moving away.

"I had lunch with Gillian, and I think she has a job for me."

Adam did not react.

"That's wonderful," Hannah said, fully aware of the tension in the room. "I think this calls for a celebration for the two of you." She got up and brought out a bottle of wine. "You can each have one drink, and then I want you to go out and have a nice time. I'll take care of the baby."

Beth looked inquiringly at Adam.

"Sounds like a super idea." He poured their drinks. Beth wanted a cigarette, but knew it was still Sabbath and refrained from taking one.

"How are Debbie and Jimmy?" Beth asked as she seated herself next to Adam. She was interested in her sister-in-law, but was very conscious of Adam's physical presence. She knew he was equally aware of her. Her anger had evaporated completely.

"They've gone to Virginia to see his parents," Hannah said, and tried to suppress the sigh which followed the comment.

"Anything wrong, Mom?" Beth asked, sensing Hannah's unhappiness.

"Jimmy's father wants him to go back home when he finishes his studies and do his residency there. Jimmy refuses."

"How does Debbie feel about it?" Beth asked.

"Debbie agrees with his father."

"How do you feel about it?" Beth asked.

"I'm frightened for her. I'm frightened for him. I understand him, I understand her, and I'm frightened."

Beth looked over at Adam. "What do you think?"

"I can understand his father, but it will be awfully hard on Debbie."

"On Debbie?" Beth asked in surprise.

"White people don't have a monopoly on bigotry and prejudice, Beth."

"But what are his chances there compared to staying here or going abroad as he first planned?"

"Chances?" Adam raised his brow. "In the long run, he's better off in Virginia, I think. But he's young and wants it now."

He doesn't have your stomach and stamina, Beth wanted to say but knew she'd better not.

"In any event, I don't think their problems should be yours right now," Hannah interjected. "I want you out of my house now, so I can bathe the baby and put her to sleep."

How different she was from Mary, Beth thought. In all the time she had been out in the Hamptons her mother had never once so much as fed the baby, much less given her a bath.

Sitting next to Adam in a small Italian restaurant on West Seventy-ninth Street, Beth felt tense. She was not hungry. She ordered a martini, but Adam suggested they have a bottle of wine instead. It seemed like a good idea. She had had two martinis at lunch and her head was throbbing. Adam was hungry and ordered a full dinner, while Beth nibbled on an antipasto.

"Beth, the apartment is empty. Why don't we go there?" Adam said as they were having their coffee.

"Ninety-eighth Street?" she asked, and the thought was not unappealing. She smiled sheepishly. "I'd love it." Then, remembering the baby, her face clouded over. "What about Allena?"

"My mother is fully capable of taking care of her, I assure you."

"Let me call her."

Adam was fondling her breast in the taxi as they approached the apartment. Beth was almost unaware of where they were when she got out of the cab. All she wanted was to get up to the fourth floor of the building and get into bed with Adam.

Making love to Adam obliterated everything from her mind. There was no thought, no talk, no questions, no answers. They were entwined in each other, her whole body was given over to making love and being made love to.

Beth was resting peacefully in Adam's arms when she heard him saying something. She looked up at him. He was staring at the ceiling.

"What did you say?" she asked, coming out of her state of mindless euphoria.

"I said, I've accepted the job in your father's firm," Adam repeated, not looking at her.

"When did this come about?" Beth whispered, still unable to shake the dreamlike quality.

"Well, we've been talking about it for quite a while," Adam said soberly.

"What took you so long to decide?" She found her voice.

"Various reasons, none of which are relevant. I called him yesterday and told him about it."

Beth lay very still. "When do you start?"

"God willing, on the first of January."

"What had God to do with it?" Beth could not keep the sarcasm out of her voice.

"It's just an expression," Adam answered, ignoring her tone.

"Does that mean you expect me to stay with my parents till then?" Beth asked, getting angry.

"Of course not. You're coming to live at my mother's, and if we can make some arrangement for the baby, you can start working for Gillian. It will do you good, and we will need whatever income you make until I start bringing in a salary. We'll also have to find an apartment."

"But we have one," Beth said slowly.

"Honey, with what I earn from the law and what you earn from Gillian we will manage nicely, but not living on Park Avenue. Certainly not in *that* apartment."

"I bet you the rent we'll have to pay on any apartment would be as high as the maintenance on the Park Avenue one." Beth's mind was racing furiously. She did not want to give up the lovely home, and she was trying to think of some way of saving it.

"You may be right, but there is a certain aura that goes with living on Park Avenue that drags with it all sorts of expenses."

Beth was about to answer that she liked that aura, that she wanted that atmosphere for them, for herself, her husband and her child, but knew she could not put those thoughts into words.

Adam was running his hand over her body and within minutes he was making love to her again, his lips caressing her neck, and she felt him enter her with the passion which she always aroused in him. She accepted him as willingly as ever, but suddenly she felt hot, burning tears running down her cheeks and she could not explain why she was crying.

14

Allena, who was now called Ali by everyone but grand-mother Mary, was three years old when her sister Sarah was born. Beth lay in her hospital bed looking with wonder and awe at the newborn infant lying in the bassinet beside her. She was as different from Ali as though they were not related. Sarah, although only two days old, was clear skinned, had a perfect, heart-shaped face and a shock of fine black hair. Her eyebrows were delicately outlined, the dark lashes unusually long and in sharp contrast to the pale skin. To Beth she appeared to be the most beautiful creature she had ever seen. Not only were the baby's looks different from Ali, the whole circumstance around her birth was. Beth and Adam had planned on having the second child. Their apartment on Riverside Drive in the Eighties, although not as luxurious as the one on Park Avenue, was large and Beth had all the time to prepare the nursery as she wanted it to be. It was done in a pale mint-color with aquamarine accents which proved to be prophetic, since Sarah had, at this point, eyes almost identical in color. Ali was settled in nursery school. Beth's work on Gillian's radio show was fulfilling, Adam seemed satisfied with his work for Drew Van Ess and, although there was a lack of excitement in their lives, Beth was busy and avoided pondering over that fact. They knew the baby would be due in September, and when the doctor told them that it might happen on the last weekend of the month, Ali was sent to Greenwich where Lydia, Mary's Connecticut cleaning lady, took care of the child. Beth went into labor early Sunday morning and Adam called the doctor, got a taxi and took her to the hospital. It was an unusually easy delivery and Adam was waiting for her when she was wheeled in from the recovery room. The memory of him sitting beside her bed, holding her hand, saying nothing, but looking at her with warmth and love, made her feel completely fulfilled.

She shifted her gaze to the window and the unusually bright blue sky was enhanced by the wintery sun which lit up the room. Beth's feelings of happiness caused her eyes to mist.

"Well, you couldn't expect to have two beautiful children, could you, Beth?" Mary's voice startled Beth. She looked around and saw her mother standing by the baby's crib.

"Mother, she's gorgeous," Beth said without rancor, but the blissful moment she was experiencing began to fade. "I can't compare her to Ali, they're so different, but I think she's the most magnificent-looking baby I've ever seen, except for . . ." And she stopped, unable to finish the sentence as a tragic reality in her recent life returned too abruptly.

"Except who?" Mary said as she walked over and sat down in the armchair, her hand moving restlessly over her perfectly coiffed hair.

"Except for Jimmy Jay Faulkner," Beth whispered, almost to herself.

"Oh, the colored child," Mary said in an almost disinterested voice as she proceeded to take out her compact and stare at herself.

"Debbie and Jimmy's little boy, yes," Beth said slowly.

"How is he, anyway?" Mary asked, putting the compact away and looking at her daughter with sudden interest.

"Well, he's not quite two years old now, and since Debbie and Jimmy were killed, he's been with Hannah," Beth said, and her voice was strained. She was also surprised at her mother's interest. In the past, she had avoided mentioning the subject.

"Wouldn't it make more sense for him to be living with his paternal grandparents?" Mary persisted, oblivious to Beth's reaction. "After all, he is colored and they're colored, and it does seem like such an imposition on poor Mrs. Stillman."

"Mother, Debbie and Jimmy were killed by a bomb because the colored and white communities in Virginia refused to accept Debbie. I know you hate the gory details, but she was white and everyone resented her and were furious when Jimmy brought her to his home town. It wouldn't make much sense to have her child living with Jimmy's parents. Who knows what they'd do to him or them."

"Is he very dark?" Mary asked, and she wiped the edge of her mouth with her thumb and forefinger. Beth knew it was a gesture which indicated her mother was nervous.

"He is without doubt the most stunning child you've ever seen."

"Well, they do say that the mixed-blood thing does produce interesting-looking children." She laughed briefly. "Unfortunately, they change as they grow older. But that wasn't my question. I asked if he's very dark skinned."

"No. As a matter of fact, he has a mulatto-colored skin, amber eyes and except for the curly hair, he looks just like Debbie." As she said the words, her eyes shifted over to the sleeping infant beside her and she saw the uncanny resemblance the child bore to Debbie and, therefore, to Jimmy Jay. Beth's mind began to whirl. The past had a way of creeping in at every turn. Sarah, Debbie, Jimmy Jay, Ali, Allen.

"Allena doesn't seem to like him," Mary's voice interrupted Beth's train of thought.

"Allena doesn't seem to like him?" Beth repeated slowly, swallowing hard. "I can't imagine where you got that impression. She's three years old, and at that age I don't really see her talking to you about liking or not liking Jimmy Jay."

"I think it's his skin color she dislikes," Mary said, trying to sound nonchalant.

"Mother, no three-year-old is aware of the color of people's skin. Certainly not the color of a two-year-old infant." She paused for a minute, then more deliberately, "Except, of course, if it's brought to their attention." She looked at her mother and waited for her reaction. When Mary did not answer, Beth's eyes widened in horror. "You didn't!" she whispered in disbelief. "You didn't instill in a little three-year-old child your prejudice, your awful narrow-minded bigotry, did you?" She could not help the pleading tone that had crept into her voice, hoping for a denial, knowing that none would be forthcoming.

"Well, my dear Beth, Allena is not color blind, you know. While she's been with us in Greenwich, she's been playing with Lydia's little girl, Suzanne, and since that child is obviously much darker than Allena, the question did come up."

"How democratic of you to allow Lydia to bring her little girl over," Beth said sarcastically.

"Not at all, Beth, and you needn't be so snotty. She's a sweet child and Allena gets along very well with her."

Beth was suddenly very tired and lowered herself on the bed.

"I'm sorry, Beth," Mary stood up and walked over to her. "I really didn't mean to upset you." She put her hand out to touch her daughter's face. It was icy, and if Mary noticed Beth's imperceptibly shrinking away from her touch, she ignored it. "I will run along now, so you can rest." She threw a glance at Sarah as she was leaving the room trying to restrain her feelings of annoyance that Beth had given birth to a child who looked so much like the Stillmans.

A young nurse walked in and took the baby out, leaving Beth alone with a feeling of emptiness and deep sadness. She closed her eyes and within seconds the picture of the flaming car in which Debbie and Jimmy were killed came into focus.

Beth had received the call a short while before Gillian was to go on the air. The production assistant was unaware of Debbie's relationship to Beth. It was simply a news flash that he felt would interest Miss Crane. The horror of what was being said paralyzed her, and her reaction recalled that strange calm she had felt when Allen was buried.

"Anything wrong?" Gillian asked looking up from the prepared text of her weekly broadcast.

"Adam's sister, Debbie, and her husband, Dr. James Faulkner, were just killed by a bomb in Virginia," Beth said in an almost matter-of-fact voice.

Gillian reacted immediately. She picked up the phone and dialed. Beth listened with detached interest at the brilliance with which Gillian got the details of what seemed to have happened. It was not clear who had placed the bomb in the car. There were conflicting rumors that it was the whites who resented Debbie or that it was possibly the blacks who were angry that she was living among them.

"The baby," Beth heard herself say. "Gillian, ask if the baby was with them."

"No he wasn't," Gillian said, replacing the receiver in its cradle. Her face was white with rage as she put aside her script and settled herself in front of the microphone.

"What are you going to say?" Beth asked absently. Jimmy Jay was so young, she thought. She also wondered what Debbie's last thoughts were.

"I'm not sure," Gillian said, "but it will come to me." For the first time since Beth had known Gillian, she heard her voice crack. "All I know is that there is so much to say."

"Five minutes, Miss Crane," Beth heard the director call from the booth.

"My God!" Beth came back to herself. "I'd better call Adam. He may not know and he listens to your show. And so does Hannah."

Frantically she called Adam's office. He had gotten the news and was rushing up to his mother's house, the secretary informed her.

"Does his mother know?"

"I don't know. I don't think so." The girl was sobbing.

"Okay, get on the phone and call her," Beth commanded. "Talk to her until Adam gets there. I don't want her to hear it on the radio when she's alone."

"Talk about what?" The secretary's sobbing grew louder.

"Stop that sniveling," Beth said evenly. "Just get on that phone and talk. Talk about the weather, talk about gifts for the children for the upcoming holidays. Ask her advice about how to prepare fish for Friday night. But keep talking." She slammed the phone down just as the show announcer started the introduction to the "Gillian Crane Show."

The next few weeks were completely garbled in Beth's mind. The elder Faulkners were in shock, which gave way to recriminations. Jimmy Jay was in their house when the deaths occurred and they felt the child should stay with them. It took Adam weeks of pleading, threatening and trying to be reasonable, until they got Jimmy Jay to New York. The idea was that he would live with Beth and Adam, but then they discovered

Beth was pregnant so it fell to Hannah to take care of him. As in the past, Hannah Stillman's stoic ability to face and cope with tragedies was evident. She took her grandson into her home and started reorganizing her life around him.

Beth's work, Allena, her home and spending more time with Hannah, gave her little time for sharp or clear thoughts. But it was the pregnancy that seemed to insulate her from the horror of what truly happened.

Poor Debbie, Beth thought as she lay back and tried to conjure up the image of her sister-in-law. Her short life was plagued by so much unhappiness.

"White men do not have a monopoly on bigotry." Beth recalled the phrase worded by Adam shortly after Debbie married. And it turned out to be prophetic. Debbie never found a place for herself. She was barely accepted by her in-laws, was completely rejected by the black community and ignored by the whites. Why she insisted on living in Virginia, never ceased to amaze Beth.

They spoke often after Debbie gave birth to Jimmy Jay and returned to Virginia. Beth called at least once a week, and Debbie's grateful tone at hearing from her was always touching. She wanted desperately to persuade Debbie to leave the South—give in to Jimmy's wishes to be in New York—but Debbie felt it was wrong, and so they stayed.

"Well, for a new mother, the expression is not exactly as the books tell it." Gillian walked into Beth's hospital room. She was wrapped in a bizarre-looking fur, her hair flying in disarray, her makeup splashed on with obvious disinterest.

"Gillian!" Beth was honestly pleased to see her. "How sweet of you to come."

Gillian leaned over and kissed her warmly.

"You missed my mother by a hair," Beth said, and wondered why she mentioned it.

"I went over and looked at that little thing you gave birth to. I'm not much for infants, but I do believe she's quite unusual. Am I right, or am I asking the wrong person?" Her voice was filled with emotion.

"You're right, and you're asking the right person, even if my mother doesn't agree. She thinks I've given birth to someone unattractive."

"Thank God there are two grandmothers around." Gillian laughed lightly, took her coat off and flung it on the armchair and came to sit on the edge of Beth's bed.

"Have you ever met my mother?" Beth asked suddenly.

"No," she answered quickly.

"But you know my father," Beth persisted.

"Yes, I do." She was obviously not interested in pursuing the conversation. "Incidentally, when do I get my producer back?" Gillian changed the subject.

"Well, I've decided to breast feed this baby. I couldn't do it with Ali, and I'd like to do it now. So, since I'm for the demand-feeding routine, it will be a while. I wasn't sure I'd feel this way—that's why I never mentioned it—but once I saw her I knew that it's what I want and what I think is right."

"Oh, dear," Gillian said unhappily. "I've just been offered a television interviewing show and I know as much about it as you do, and I figured that between the two of us we could get into that monstrous new media together and work it out."

"I'd adore it, Gillian, but I honestly can't commit myself to a time. When do they want you to start?"

"In two weeks," Gillian said thoughtfully.

"It's probably just as well. We can wing it up to a point, but you would need someone who really knows what the hell it's all about."

"We've got that. Dan Bradbury is going to direct and produce the thing until I get the hang of it. I wanted you to get the guests, prepare the material, do the research."

"Dan Bradbury?" The name sounded familiar, but Beth could not place it.

"You met him with me at lunch several years back." Gillian reminded her. "He got into television quite early and is rising rapidly as one of the experts on visual news, and all the networks are after him. Everyone wants him, and he wants me, which shows you what a genius he really is."

Beth listened and tried to recall what Dan Bradbury looked like. The image eluded her. She was also faltering in her decision about not going back to work.

"Won't you be bored just being a housefrau?" Gillian asked, as though reading Beth's thoughts.

"It won't be forever," Beth said with determination. "I will definitely go back to work, it's just that I really feel I should spend time with the girls until everything settles down."

"How's Adam?" Gillian asked.

"He's fine. I think he likes working with my father, which is amazing to me." She paused, thinking about her last statement. "You know, they're so different, and yet somehow I see a strange similarity between them."

"Has it ever occurred to you that you never really knew your father, and in a way never really knew Adam?"

"Good God, Gillian, they're two ends of a pole in point of view." She said it forcefully, but there was little conviction in her voice.

"But it's the same pole," Gillian said sagely.

"Did you know my father well?" Beth asked, and was amazed to see Gillian grow flustered.

"Yes, but that was many years ago."

"You never told me."

"It's ancient history, and it didn't really seem important." She regained her composure. "I'd rather talk about now. Since you're not coming back to work, will you at least be on the other end of the phone for a while until I get my head together on this new show?"

"Of course I will," Beth answered slowly, unable to understand why the conversation about her father upset Gillian.

"May I come in?" Drew Van Ess was standing in the doorway. Both women looked around, and Beth's eyes instinctively went to her boss's face. It was red with embarrassment. Beth shifted her eyes to her father. He looked briefly at her then turned to look at Gillian.

"Dad," Beth said, breaking the awkward silence. "I didn't know you were coming by. And it's such a coincidence, Gillian just told me she met you years back. I never knew that."

Drew came into the room, kissed Beth lightly on the cheek and then stood seemingly helplessly staring at Gillian, who was unable to divert her eyes from him.

"It's been a long time," Drew finally said to Gillian.

"A very long time, Drew."

Beth watching them, felt caught in a scene from which she wanted to escape. With a clarity that astounded her she knew that theirs was a long-standing intimate relationship.

"I've been following your career, listening to your radio broadcasts, and I must admit I read most of your books and articles," Drew was saying.

"And I bet you hate them all," Gillian replied.

"Not really. I disagree with many of the things you say, but I like an honest point of view. It gives me, as a lawyer, something to work with."

"Know thine enemy, what." Gillian's husky laughter reverberated through the room, and Beth felt herself grow cold. Vividly she recalled hearing it years back, on a hot summer night when she and Allen . . .

"I think I'll run along, Beth," Gillian said, dragging Beth back to the present. "When do you expect to be going home?"

"In about three days." Beth could barely utter the words.

"I'll call you over the weekend." Gillian was unaware of Beth's stiffness in manner. Then turning to Drew she put out her hand. "I really enjoyed seeing you again, Drew. Very much."

"I've more than enjoyed it." He took her hand and held it for a fraction longer than necessary.

Left alone with her father, Beth tried to wipe out the memory that had reappeared so clearly just minutes before. She observed him closely. He looked old and tired, and she felt concern for him rather than anger. Somehow the sting of her fury, which she had always associated with that night, seemed to have abated, and she found it hard to associate this old man with that dreadful event.

"You seem to have known Gillian well," she said, as he came to stand by her bed.

"She was important in my life many years ago." He tried to smile.

"And you haven't seen her in a long time?"

"Not for many years." He sounded more at ease.

"How come?"

"Different world, different time, different circumstances." He took her hand and pressed it with affection.

"Have you seen the baby?" Beth asked, determined to recapture the moments of pure joy that had been hers when the day first started.

"She's unbelievably beautiful," Drew said with more emotion than Beth had ever seen in him.

"Oh, I agree, Dad," Beth answered enthusiastically, and all thoughts of Gillian evaporated. "I'm really so happy."

He leaned over and kissed her brow. She felt closer to him than she had in many years.

When her father left, Beth looked toward the window. Dusk had fallen, and the last rays of the sunlight were barely visible, and somehow the peace which had been shattered several times during the day, gave way to a new contentment. She had her two little girls. She had Adam. She had a lovely home and a pleasant life. She would not go back to work. The money she earned would be missed, but she would dismiss the maid and they would manage.

When Adam arrived, he found Beth sleeping contentedly. He did not wake her. Instead he went to the window and stared down at the streaming traffic on Fifth Avenue. Then his eyes wandered over to the park which was now shrouded in darkness. Had it been worth it, he wondered in a brooding manner which often struck him at that hour of the day. He had given up so many of his dreams to stay married to Beth. He rarely spoke of them anymore, although they still roused his passion. He wondered if Beth knew how hard it was for him to cover up his true emotions when they were with the people he now had to associate with, how difficult it really was to acquiesce to views that still infuriated him, but which he had come to understand. It was becoming easier; he even enjoyed the work he was doing. It was hard-nosed law, cold, impersonal, black and white. And he knew it would eventually come in handy. Someday he would be the better man for having taken the time to do it. Gillian Crane had been the one to persuade him to take the job Drew offered him, and she was right.

"So you won't be the youngest Congressman ever elected to office," she had said, "but young brilliance can be like dry straw—catches on fire and burns out quickly. Drew can teach you a great deal. You don't have to agree with everything he says, but believe me, there are many things about him too many of you hotshots never learn because you're all in such a rush."

But most important, it made it possible for him to hold on to his family. Beth, Ali, Jimmy Jay, and now the youngest baby, Sarah. He stopped with wonder at having considered Jimmy Jay as his child along with his two daughters. It would have been nice if Sarah had been a boy . . .

"Adam," he heard Beth call his name and he turned. She was smiling. He rushed over to her.

"You okay?" he asked as he leaned over and kissed her lightly on the lips.

"I'm more than that. I'm wonderful."

"You won't get any arguments from me on that one," he answered, and sat down beside her holding her close.

15

The front doorbell rang and Beth could hear the children screaming outside. She was on her way to open it when the phone started ringing as well.

Breathlessly, she picked up the phone and without asking who the caller was she asked them to wait as she rushed to let the children in. Jimmy Jay was crying, Ali looked beguilingly innocent, Sarah looked bewildered.

"Go into the kitchen and get your milk and cookies," Beth said as she rushed back to the library and picked up the phone.

"I'm sorry to have kept you waiting," she said into the receiver.

"Mrs. Stillman?" The woman's voice was unfamiliar, "Miss Crane would like to talk to you." The phone went dead for a minute.

Gillian Crane, Beth mused as she picked up a cigarette and lit it. It had been quite a while since she'd spoken to her. The children's loud voices distracted her and she looked toward the kitchen with concern. Since Jimmy Jay had started coming home from school with the girls, there was an inordinate amount of fighting going on between them.

"Hi, my little housefrau," she heard Gillian's deep voice, and it clashed furiously with the high-pitched sounds of the children, who were now thundering through the house.

"Hi, Gillian," Beth said, and could not help but be embarrassed by the greeting which the noise around her reaffirmed. "How are you?" She tried to shut out the commotion with little success.

"I'm well, Beth, very well. And you?"

"I'm alive, if that's an answer." Beth tried to laugh lightly.

"What the hell is going on there?" Gillian asked.

"It's the children. They're having the usual coffee klatch after school."

"It sounds like a political caucus room brawl." Gillian laughed heartily. "How do you stand the noise?"

"I don't," Beth answered honestly. "My nerves are totally shattered. As a matter of fact, if you'll excuse me for a minute, I'll go and shut the door."

She put the phone down and rushed to the kitchen. Jimmy Jay was sitting on the floor weeping, Sarah was beside him offering him a cookie, and Ali was sitting demurely on a stool drinking her milk. It was pointless to ask what was happening while she had Gillian on the phone. "Could you kids bring it down to a low college roar while I finish my phone conversation?" she said as she shut the door and walked back into the library.

"One thing about those old West Side apartment houses, they're soundproof," Beth said with relief.

"That's true," Gillian answered. "And of course, there's another solution. Get out of the house and you'll never hear it at all."

"Fat chance." Beth tried to suppress a sigh. "They're too young to be left alone, and the help these days is too unreliable—if you can get it."

"Pay enough and you'll get it," Gillian answered.

"For that, Gillian, you need a lot of money, which we don't have."

"Bullshit," Gillian said in her old manner.

"Oh, I'm not complaining." Beth became defensive. "Adam is doing very, very well, but . . ." She stopped, wondering why she felt a need to explain. "The truth is, it's a difficult time. We've now got Jimmy Jay with us every afternoon, since Hannah is growing old and needs the rest, and the apartment is big." She wished Gillian had not called. "But all of that is a big bore. Tell me about you and your world, which is a hell of a lot more interesting than mine."

"Okay, I'll tell you right out." Gillian became serious. "I need you. I need someone I know and trust to help me with a campaign I'm about to get involved in." There was a brief pause. "I'm going into political public relations for a man named John F. Kennedy, and what with my television show, the writing, the interviews and every other thing I'm doing, I wondered if you'd help me out. I like Kennedy and I want to work for him."

"The Senator?" Beth asked, trying to conjure up the image of the man.

"Yes, he's going to make a run for the nomination, and I have faith in him."

Beth felt foolish. It had been so long since anything political was discussed in their home or with their friends at their homes. She wondered how Adam felt about John Kennedy and was annoyed at the thought.

"Gillian, I'd like nothing better, believe me, although I know nothing about him. But as I told you, I'm up to my neck with the house and the kids."

"Beth, stop it," Gillian commanded. "I've left you alone for a long time, but you're being wasted and I feel you should get out—plus the fact that you've always been my good luck charm. Remember the radio show?"

"I sure do," Beth said, with nostalgia.

"How old is your little one now?" Gillian asked.

"She's four and Ali is seven."

"And I gather they go to school?"

"Kindergarten and second grade."

"Well, I don't know much about that stuff, but they're obviously out of diapers, and they don't come home until whenever." She laughed self-consciously. "When do they come home?"

"At three-thirty."

"There you are," Gillian said rationally. "You could send them off to wherever it is they go, come to the office and get someone to come in before they come home. It's not really that difficult." She paused for a moment. "And I'll pay you good money so you can cover whoever it is you hire."

"It's tempting," Beth admitted. "When do you need an answer?"

"Sleep on it for a couple of days, but call me back by the end of the week." She stopped again and then continued. "Beth, I really want you to come to work for me." It was sincerely said.

Beth hung up the phone slowly. Going back to work! She had thought of it almost constantly since Sarah started going to kindergarten. The apartment, the cleaning, the cooking, the occasional entertaining of all the dull people Adam brought home were getting to her. She walked over to the liquor cabinet and took out a bottle of scotch and poured herself a drink. As she sipped it, her eyes caught sight of the clock on the desk—3:45 P.M. She looked back at the glass in her hand. Early for a drink, she thought absentmindedly, but did not put the glass down. Instead, she gulped the drink down and walked out of the library.

As she opened the kitchen door, Ali's voice came to her. "You can't help it if you're a colored boy," the child was saying in a shockingly superior tone.

With a blind rage Beth stormed in, grabbed Ali and began to slap her across the face. She seemed unable to stop, even as Ali became hysterical.

"Colored boy?" she screamed, "colored boy? What are you saying, you little horror, you little monster."

"Mommy, Mommy, Mommy," Sarah's voice finally reached her, and Beth looked around dazed. Ali was pale except for the red marks which her hand had left on her cheeks. Both Sarah and Jimmy Jay were pulling at her skirt, and she came back to herself.

Ali's whimpering was the only sound to be heard. Beth turned toward the sink, picked up a damp cloth and went over to her eldest child and started wiping her face. Then, gently, she picked her up in her arms and hugged her.

"I'm sorry, baby," she said softly. "Mommy is sorry." Sitting down on a chair, she held Ali close and looked over at the two other children who were standing terrified in the corner. "Why don't you children go into the bedroom and play. I want to talk to Ali."

"Honey," she said softly, when the children were gone, as Ali snuggled up to her sniffling quietly. "Mommy should not have hit you, but what you said to Jimmy Jay was pretty awful." Did Ali know or understand that she was insulting? Then she remembered the tone in which the words were said. She paused, unable to figure out what it was she could say to make her point to a seven-year-old child.

"Kids at school say it all the time," Ali whispered.

"Well, that doesn't make it right. As a matter of fact, I should think that as his cousin you should make them stop." Her words sounded hollow. "I'll talk to the teachers about it," Beth said, as she pushed Ali away from her gently. "What I do want from you, though, is a promise that you'll never again say anything like that to Jimmy Jay. Baby, it's wrong to refer to anyone in terms of . . . call them names." Her frustration was mounting. "Ali, honey, Jimmy Jay is like your brother. Some people have blond hair, some have dark hair. Look at Sarah, she's got dark eyes, dark hair, and you've got blond hair and blue eyes." The look of bewilderment in Ali's face only made Beth's words seem more meaningless. "Now, you run along and ask Jimmy Jay to forgive you, and we'll forget the whole thing, okay?"

The child slipped off her lap and ran out of the kitchen, leaving Beth completely shaken. She picked up the phone to call the school, but changed her mind. What would she say to them? Instead, she went over to the kitchen cabinet and poured herself another scotch. Then, she picked up the phone and called Adam.

He listened to her tale of woe and was silent for a long time.

"Did she know what she was saying?" Adam asked finally.

"That's the point. It wasn't what she said, it was the way she said it."

"I'll come home early and talk to her," he said, and he sounded deeply concerned.

Beth hung up and sipped her drink slowly. She had not really eaten anything during the day and the liquor made her dizzy. Gillian's offer came back to her.

"I'll pay you good money," Gillian had said. How pleasant it would be to leave all the burdens of daily household chores and be back in the world where things were happening, where people occupied themselves with real issues, important problems. She *had* wanted a career once. That was the whole idea from the start.

Beth started preparing dinner, but her mind was now married to the idea of going back to work. She could get Lydia, her mother's Greenwich maid who had moved to New York, to come in. She would even offer to get her little girl into The New Lincoln School, and the child could come home with the children. The thought began to excite her. It would do Ali and Jimmy Jay good to have little Suzanne as a friend. At least it would be two against one. She smiled wryly as the last thought crossed her mind.

In spite of his promise, Adam arrived home after the children were bathed and fed and were ready for bed.

Beth was unaccountably tired and was convinced that it was mental exhaustion rather than physical. The prospect of going back to work and the inner conflict depleted her.

"Adam, would you do me a big favor and get the girls into bed as soon as Hannah picks up Jimmy Jay?" She was almost embarrassed as she made the request. It was unlike her.

"No problem, honey," Adam assured her, looking at her anxiously. "Are you all right?"

"I'm fine, just exhausted."

As she got into bed, she knew she would go to work for Gillian. Somehow she would work it out. She had paid her dues to her family. The girls were still young, but she had given them a solid foundation and they were ready to have someone unemotionally involved take care of their daily needs. She would probably be a better mother and certainly a more rational one if she were not constantly with them.

16

Gillian's new offices were on Fifth Avenue and Fifty-ninth Street. Beth was given the title of Executive Assistant and within weeks of starting her job, fell into it as though she had never been away.

"Once a bicycle rider always a bicycle rider," Gillian said one evening when Beth was getting ready to leave for the day. "You're doing a super job, Beth, as I knew you would, and I'm really grateful." She was standing in the doorway, a martini shaker in one hand and two glasses in the other. "How about a drink before you leave?" she asked, throwing herself into an armchair.

"Why not?" Beth answered, feeling content.

"I'll be going to the convention in a couple of days," Gillian said after pouring the drinks, "and I want you to do some news releases for me."

"No problem." Beth sipped her drink and watched Gillian as she started scribbling some notes on a pad.

It had all worked out for the best, she thought. Whatever trepidations she had had about going to work in general and going to work for Gillian in particular were dissipated on the very first day. Although they had talked on the phone occasionally since the day Beth discovered the relationship between her father and Gillian, they had not seen each other. Beth could not help but wonder if her feelings at the hospital over four years ago would crop up when they finally met again. Within hours after arriving at the office, she had forgotten all about it. There was a great deal they had to talk about relating to work, details Gillian had to impart and many important routines to be established for the running of the new operation.

"This is a rough idea of what I'm talking about." Gillian handed Beth some notes, bringing her out of her revery.

"Is this a private party or is it open to the public?" A man was standing in the office doorway. Beth and Gillian looked up. He looked familiar to Beth, but she could not place him.

"Dan," Gillian cried out with joy, "Dan Bradbury," she repeated, putting out her arms as he walked toward her. "It's been ages."

He kissed her passionately on the mouth, slapping her backside affectionately. "That's an ass," he said laughingly, and looked over at

Beth. "And you're the red-headed vision I met once while you were lunching with Gillian at the Algonquin."

"How clever of you to remember," Gillian said happily. Looking over at Beth with pride she smiled, "She is a vision, isn't she?"

"I'm flattered." Beth felt herself blush. "I must assume you're both experts, and I thank you for the compliment."

"When did you get back?" Gillian asked Dan, pouring him a drink.

"Last night," he answered, taking his eyes off Beth and looking over at Gillian.

"Where were you?"

"Indo-China," he answered, and shuddered. "What a mess."

"I want to hear all about it." Gillian became serious.

"How about both you gorgeous ladies having a coming home drink with me at the Plaza?"

Beth started to protest, but Gillian interrupted. "Oh, come on. Your Lydia is a gem, and she can bloody well be a gem for another hour."

Beth smiled. "Okay, just let me call Adam and find out what his plans are."

When she hung up the phone after speaking to Adam's secretary, she felt foolish. Adam had told her he was going to Rochester for a meeting and she had forgotten.

They had three drinks each in the Oak Room and Beth listened without participating in Gillian's and Dan's discussion of foreign policy and the campaign front. She tried to follow what they were saying, but found her mind wandering. Her life, until she started working again, had been so insulated, so limited, so dull. Sitting in the bar, listening to the hum of voices around, watching the animated faces of the people—talking, arguing, laughing, seeming to care about what they were saying or being told—made her life with Adam, for the last few years, appear wasted. Adam, working as a lawyer, doing it with the seriousness with which he did everything he touched; with the same single-mindedness he had once applied to his dreams and hopes. Adam, dressing properly, looking the part he was playing—and she was sure he considered it a game—behaving and talking as was expected of a junior partner of the prestigious Van Ess law firm. She did not fault him. If anything, she respected his discipline, his ability to dedicate himself to the work, but she knew that in the process of becoming the up-and-coming legal mind of the firm he had lost the spark that had attracted her so desperately when they first met. But their marriage was a good one, she thought defensively. They were respected, accepted and were in demand socially, except by her mother, although that exception had ceased to be important. If Beth was bored she could not blame Adam. Adam never stopped her from doing anything she wanted. When she told him she had decided to go back to work for Gillian, he was pleased.

"Are you still with us?" Dan asked and Beth came back to herself.

"I'm having a wonderful time," she smiled sincerely.

"Children," Gillian said, "I must run, but don't let me break up this lovely party."

"I should go, too," Beth said quickly. She was suddenly embarrassed. The thought of staying alone with Dan was disconcerting. It was like being on a date and she was quite out of practice.

Both women stood up.

"I'll stick around awhile," Dan said, standing up, too. "I'll see you at noon tomorrow." He directed his statement to Gillian. Then, turning to Beth, he smiled. "And I'll be seeing you, I'm sure."

Sitting in the taxi Gillian gave the driver her home address. "You can drop me," she said to Beth, and a sigh of relief escaped her. "What a coup," she said after a minute. "What an unbelievable coup. To think I'll have Dan as a partner." Her excitement mounted. "If I had planned it, I couldn't have done better."

"What are you talking about?" Beth asked.

"Weren't you listening?"

"I'm afraid not," Beth admitted.

"Dan will be in town for at least the next six months and is willing to work with me on the campaign. He's one of the best political writers around and knows all the media people. And since I'm convinced Kennedy will get the nomination, I'll have someone as expert as Dan to work with me."

"That's great," Beth said, and for no reason she recalled her conversation with Gillian about Dan at the Algonquin and wondered, as she did then, if Dan was Gillian's lover. The thought of working with Dan made her uncomfortable. He was an extraordinarily attractive man and she realized she was attracted to him. It frightened her, and she quickly turned her thoughts to Adam, wondering if he would be home when she got there.

The work load at the office was tremendous, and Beth found herself involved and enjoying it thoroughly. As election day grew closer the excitement reached an almost hysterical pitch, and Beth became completely committed to Kennedy's election. Adam was noncommittal, but it did not dampen her enthusiasm.

When Gillian invited them to the inauguration in Washington and some pre-inaugural parties, Adam bowed out gracefully but encouraged Beth to go.

She and Gillian registered at the Mayflower in a three-room suite. Within minutes after their arrival, Gillian was on the phone and Beth took a leisurely bath and lay down to rest. She was alone without a husband or children, and she relished every minute of it.

"I'm going out to a cocktail party," Gillian stood in the doorway. "Want to join me?"

"Wild horses couldn't get me to move at this moment," Beth said lazily. "Tell me when and where to meet you."

Beth joined Gillian around 11:00 P.M. at the home of people in Georgetown who were all quite high celebrating their candidate's victory. Gillian was completely drunk by the time Beth arrived and kept encouraging Beth to catch up. Beth watched her boss and felt uncomfortable. She was suddenly aware that Gillian was drinking too much. Their after-work martini in New York had become a habit, but Beth knew that after she left the office there were still several drinks left in the pitcher.

"She's really whooping it up, isn't she?" Beth heard someone say, and she looked around to find Dan Bradbury standing beside her. Beth was surprised to see him, and felt excited by his presence.

"When did you come to Washington?" Beth asked politely.

"About an hour ago."

"Well, I'm surprised you're not as excited as Gillian. I agree that she's almost over the rainbow, but it's been an exhilarating experience and she did work hard."

"I'm pleased he won because I always like to be on the winner's side." The cynicism was unmistakable. "But now I want to see him perform." He smiled. "That's where it really sits."

"You mean there was no great conviction, or whatever it's called, when you joined up with Gillian?"

"Me? Conviction?" He laughed out loud. "No, the only conviction I had was that I didn't want Nixon elected."

Beth wanted to say something bright but could think of nothing.

"How about having a drink with me away from here? This enthusiasm is a fucking bore and actually quite insincere. Everybody bought a cat in a bag and is now trying to pretend it's what they really wanted."

Beth was not enjoying herself. She knew none of the people in the room, and Gillian was too far gone to miss her. "Who'll take Gillian home?" she asked as she allowed Dan to lead her out of the house.

"I assure you, there are enough ass-lickers in that room who will see that she gets home safely. I don't think you understand how important Gillian really is."

They walked along the street in the drizzle and Beth shivered. She was not dressed for walking in the rain. She felt Dan's arm encircle her shoulder.

"Cold?"

"Afraid so."

"I live right down the street at the Georgetown Inn. We can go in there."

The bar was dimly lit and the waiter greeted Dan warmly as he led them to a corner table.

The bottle of champagne was delivered without Dan's ordering it.

"Do they do that by rote?" she asked, after the waiter left.

"Whenever I come in with a beautiful woman, they know I insist on champagne, and according to the broad, they bring the vintage." He picked up the bottle. "And you are some broad." He laughed looking at the label. "Dom Pérignon '63. That's the highest compliment you can get."

Being referred to as a broad amused her.

"To the future of President Kennedy," Dan said seriously, as he lifted his glass to hers. "May he live up to our expectations." They drank in silence and for a minute Beth felt he had forgotten she was there.

"Are you staying in the States for a while?" Beth asked, feeling quite deflated by his mood.

"I don't know."

The silence became more pronounced.

She settled down in her seat, leaned her head on the backrest of the small settee and closed her eyes. The champagne was good and she felt peaceful.

"Are you happily married?" Dan asked suddenly.

She opened her eyes and rolled her head toward him without changing her position. "Why, yes," she said. "Why do you ask?"

"I've never met or seen your husband. You come to work every day. You're serious about it. You seem terribly independent and efficient, and I just wondered who takes care of you."

"Takes care of me?" Beth asked in surprise. "Why, I take care of my family, and so does my husband."

"Yes, I know that, but who takes care of *you?*" he emphasized the last word. "You, Beth Stillman."

"I don't really know how to answer that," she admitted, but the question bothered her. "I certainly don't support myself. I'm part of a unit called the Stillmans, which consists of Adam, my husband, Ali and Sarah, my daughters, and we also have a little nephew named Jimmy Jay, who's like a son to us. So that who takes care of me, per se, is hardly relevant."

He poured them another drink and was again silent.

"Do you love your husband?" he asked, after finishing his second glass of champagne.

She resented the question. "Of course, I do," she said, too forcefully. "And he loves me and we love our children and they love us."

"Now, now," he said, as though talking to an insolent child. "Don't get excited."

"And you?" Beth asked, almost angrily. "Who takes care of you? Who do you love, who loves you?"

He smiled, "Nobody."

She felt foolish and sat up. "I'm sorry, that was silly." She, too, finished her drink. He emptied the bottle into their glasses and snapped his fingers for another.

"Do you have a lady friend?" she asked conversationally.

"No. I know a great number of ladies, but I don't really go in for that lady friend bit. They're all too clawing, demanding and frightened."

"What's your type? Maybe I could find one for you who would not be frightened, demanding or clawing." She was struggling not to show her irritation at his personal questions.

"You're my type," he said, without looking at her.

Beth was surprised. In all the months she'd been working at Gillian's there was never the slightest indication on his part that he was aware of her, except as part of the office staff. He had a way of looking through her, whenever she was in his presence, which offended her, since he was the first man who genuinely attracted her since she married Adam. Suddenly she felt unaccountably excited, as the idea of having an affair with Dan began to perk in her head. Vaguely she wondered if it would be unfair to Gillian. She smiled inwardly. She could not compete with Gillian on a work level; would never even try. But as women . . .

"Is there any more champagne?" she asked, leaning over to look at the bottle sitting in a silver bucket next to Dan. His arm encircled her shoulder and she was conscious of the aroma of his pipe tobacco clinging to his clothes. She did not move away.

They were nearly through the second bottle of champagne and Beth was feeling quite high. There was little conversation between them, but it did not seem to matter. She felt him kiss her hair and was aware of his hand caressing her thigh. It did not shock or upset her. When he lifted her head toward him and kissed her on the mouth she responded with unrestrained passion.

"Come up to my room," he whispered.

"You're just saying it because I'm the broad who happens to be sitting next to you," she said hoarsely.

"Oh, I don't know about that," he answered, as he took her hand and placed it on his genitals. She could feel the hardness and her excitement rose. "You think any broad could make it that hard?"

His face was close to hers and he pressed his lips to hers and pushed his tongue deep into her mouth. She began to fumble with the zipper of his trousers. Worming her hand in, she felt the warmth of his penis and began sucking on his tongue. Then she felt his hand pushing her skirt back.

"We'd better go up to my room, or I'll fuck you right here," he whispered.

He stood up unsteadily.

"I think you'd better zip up your fly, sir," Beth said quietly, although the merriment was in her voice.

"Don't be silly. I don't intend to waste a minute when I get you upstairs."

There were two other people in the elevator but Dan ignored them as he pushed Beth up against the side and pressed his body to hers. She was equally oblivious to them, returning his kisses, conscious only of his desire for her and hers for him.

By the time they reached his room, they were nearly undressed. Within seconds, they were on the bed and Dan was pressing himself into her. Her mind was completely preoccupied with the lovemaking. She felt Dan slip into her, reaching deep inside until it almost hurt, but the pain was pleasurable. When they both reached their climax he pulled himself out slowly, and the pleasure of his withdrawal was as great as it was when he entered her.

"More," she whispered. "Oh, Dan, more, please, I want more."

"Honey, we've got two days to screw, and as much as you want, you're going to get," he answered as he pressed his head between her legs and started making love to her with his tongue. She put her hands to each side of his head and pressed him closer, as her legs held him firmly. She felt herself come again and with a quick motion he twisted his body so that his genital was in her mouth as he continued to suck her vagina.

A small clock rang out the hour and Dan reached up and threw it across the room and continued making love to her. At one point Beth found herself mumbling words she rarely uttered, and Dan's obscenities did not offend her. Never a prude, she was still surprised at herself.

"Want a drink?" he asked when they were both spent and Dan was still lying on top of her, resting inside her.

"Only if it's not far away and you come right back and we can drink while you're inside me." She barely recognized her voice. It was low and hoarse with emotion.

"I wouldn't dream of moving away from that warm cunt." He laughed quietly, as he reached over and opened the door of a small refrigerator that stood by the bed. Taking a small bottle of champagne out, he uncorked it without changing his position. It popped and some of it spilled over her breasts. Taking a big swallow, Dan put his mouth to hers and she drank the champagne from him. They fell asleep with Beth's back to Dan with him inside her.

Beth woke up to find Dan kneeling by the bed, the tip of her breast in his mouth and his hand caressing her body.

"You are truly a gorgeous hunk of woman," he said, but the veiled contempt which had been present earlier was gone. Instead, she heard a tenderness in his voice and she moved over so he could lie beside her. She took his organ in her hand and caressed it, while his fingers fondled her clitoris. Then separating the lips of her vagina, his fingers pressed deeper into her.

"I wonder what Gillian is thinking?" Beth said dreamily.

"She's not thinking, honey. She knows I'm balling you and is getting a vicarious thrill from it."

"I thought you were making love to me," Beth said mockingly.

"Isn't it the same?"

She thought for a minute. "*I* was making love to you."

He was silent, and she felt his fingers withdraw from her.

She did not stop massaging him, but lifted herself on her elbow. "You're a conceited ass," she said seriously. "I may be a broad, and you may be balling me, or whatever it is you want to call it, but remember one thing, Dan, I'm neither frightened nor clawing, even if, at the moment, I am demanding." She paused to let the words sink in. "I'm the happily married lady who enjoyed last night to the hilt, am enjoying being here right now, and have no intention of leaving. I'm having too good a time. But believe me, it's animal sexual gratification which we're enjoying, and if I want to call it lovemaking, it doesn't mean that a ball and chain are the order of the day."

She was looking directly at him, and suddenly he put his arms around her and kissed her tenderly.

"You're magnificent, Beth," he whispered. "The most magnificent woman I've ever made love to."

She lay very still and a feeling of happiness crept into her being. It had been a long time since she had been made love to by anyone other than Adam. She had thought of it on occasion while sitting on a park bench in New York, watching Sarah play in the sandbox, looking at the young women talking animatedly about diapers and baby diets. She had even fantasized affairs with various men she met socially. The idea of being unfaithful to Adam, however, had never occurred to her. What surprised her was that she felt no guilt.

"What time is it?" she asked sleepily.

Dan looked at his wristwatch. "Lunchtime," he said, as he kissed her and got out of bed. "Why don't you take a shower and I'll order food."

Coming out of the bathroom in the hotel terry-cloth robe, her hair wrapped in a towel, Beth found herself alone in the room. The bed was rumpled and wet from the lovemaking. Quickly she pulled the blanket over the damp sheets and looked around. The shades were up and a wintry sun was shining. She wondered where Dan was and for a minute she was frightened. Then, hearing sounds from an adjoining room, she haltingly opened the door and found him sitting watching television. He did not hear her come in and she had a minute to observe him. Dressed in gray Daks, a white turtleneck sweater and a loose, light blue cardigan he was more attractive and desirable than ever. Unable to contain herself, she rushed up to him and threw herself into his arms.

"I thought you left me," she whispered.

He held her close, but she knew he was not quite aware of her or what she was saying. His eyes were glued to the small screen and she realized John Kennedy was making his inaugural speech.

Sitting on Dan's lap, she too began to listen. Although she had worked along with Gillian on the campaign, it was not until that moment that the full impact of the young new President struck her. She became completely absorbed in what he was saying and the excitement of the event registered. Memories of what she had hoped for when she married Adam returned. Her eyes wandered over to the beautiful First Lady and a feeling of frustration overtook her. She had never thought in terms of Adam running for President, but she had seen him as a contender for public office, a man involved in the lives and events of the country. Years back, she was sure they were going to be somebodies. Together they were going to climb to heights of recognition and importance. A great part of her fascination with Adam, when they first met, was her conviction that he was heading somewhere. Being the wife of a lawyer, even a good, successful lawyer, was not what she had bargained for.

"Damn good speech," Dan said when it was over, and he got up to turn off the set. Then, as though she was back in focus, he smiled. "You're good looking even in broad daylight, without makeup and all bundled up in that robe and towel." Still he seemed preoccupied. "How about some juice and coffee?" he asked, walking over to the table. "I didn't know what you ate for breakfast, so I ordered everything they had. Eggs, cereal, cold and hot, bacon, ham, toast, buns, marmalade and jam."

"I have only juice and coffee, thank you," Beth said quietly. Her thoughts while listening to the inaugural speech shook her. "And I think I'd better call home."

She dialed the apartment in New York. Lydia answered and assured her all was well. The kids were off to school, her mother had called upset by the results of the election and furious that Beth was in Washington. There were several other messages, none of which were important.

"I'll be back later this evening," Beth said, and hung up. Then she dialed Adam's office.

"Hi," he said when he heard her voice. "You must have had some time. I called you until two in the morning, but neither you nor Gillian were in the room."

"Oh, it was fine," Beth answered in a strained voice. "Have you heard the inauguration speech?"

"Good speech," Adam said impassively. "Now let's see him perform."

It was what Dan had said, and Beth wanted to laugh. "I'll be back this evening. Will you be home for dinner?"

"I'm not sure. Your father asked me to have a drink with him at the club, and it may take some time. So don't rush on my account."

"See you later, then," she said, and felt foolish. She had hoped he had missed her, even if she had not really thought of him.

"Is he coming home to dinner?" Dan asked, sipping his coffee.

"Probably not," Beth said angrily.

"Does he have a mistress?"

Beth looked around slowly. "You've got to be kidding."

"I wouldn't kid about a thing like that," Dan said innocently. "It happens all the time."

"Not in our family," she answered vehemently, and then realizing where she was she began to smile in spite of herself.

"Would you have dinner with me?" He, too, was smiling.

"I'd love to."

They were back in bed making love when Gillian called. Dan assured her that Beth had left him at dawn, after they had taken a midnight cruise up the Potomac River, driven to Arlington Cemetery, which was closed, and had breakfast at a small coffee shop around the corner from the Mayflower.

"She said she had some shopping to do for her children," he concluded seriously as he pressed Beth closer to him. Her head was resting on his chest and she could hear the vibrations of his voice and the steady sound of his heartbeat. She wanted the conversation to end.

"Dinner?" Beth heard him ask, obviously repeating Gillian's question. "I'd love it. As a matter of fact, why don't you both join me," he continued as he caressed Beth's back. "Seven is fine." He hung up and turned his attention back to Beth.

"Is there a midnight cruise up the Potomac?" Beth asked.

"Probably not."

"Would you have driven to Arlington Cemetery in the middle of the night?"

"Of course not."

"So Gillian knows you were lying."

"Sure she does."

"Why did you then?"

"Because it's none of her business, and as long as I don't tell her about what I really do, and if you don't either, she may suspect, but will never be sure." He was quite serious. "And more than that, you'd better remember to buy something for your little girls, if you want to keep up the charade. Remember, you're the happily married woman, not me."

"Will I see you when you come to New York?" Beth asked, feeling suddenly uncomfortable.

"I'm leaving for the Middle East in a few days, and I wasn't planning on going through New York. But if you'll spend an evening with me, I'll make a point of it."

"Where do you stay when you're in New York?"

"I've got an apartment at the Pierre."

She looked at him for a long time. He was a handsome man. His hair was still quite blond, but there a great deal of gray as well. His eyes were icy blue, his lips thin and his face lined, especially around the mouth. He was probably not much older than Adam, but he looked older. It occurred to her that he was unhappy, in spite of all the talk, and lonely. She leaned over and kissed him with great tenderness.

"I hope I don't frighten you, but I could love you," she whispered, and smiled.

"I could love you too," he answered seriously.

"I'm going to leave now," Beth got out of bed. "I've got some shopping to do for the children, and I don't think I'll have dinner with you and Gillian." She hesitated for a moment. "I'm not very experienced with this sort of thing, and I may not be able to pull it off."

17

Beth was surprised that she resumed her daily routine, after returning from Washington, with ease. She waited the first week to hear from Dan. When he did not call, she assumed he had gone off on his trip and she tried to put him out of her conscious mind.

The campaign over, Gillian's office went into low gear. Most of the staff was laid off, except for Beth, who came in daily, but her hours were determined by the amount of work at hand.

Winter passed quickly. Adam was busier than ever, taking on more responsibilities at the office. Hannah had a mild heart attack and Jimmy Jay was spending more time with them. Drew and Mary were now rarely in New York. Beth saw clearly that her father was aging rapidly. He seemed less able to control his rages and they were directed, overtly, at Mary. More and more, Mary hid behind assumed ailments, and Beth felt sorry for her. She had been accustomed to the role of lady of the manor, and it was being pulled out from under. The tearful conversations, which lasted hours, indifferent to whether Beth had time or not, came too frequently. Beth said little, fearful of adding to the unhappiness. The only times friction erupted were when Mary would invite them up to Greenwich for the weekend and would tactlessly announce that they could not bring the little colored child with them. Beth would lose her temper and the fights were similar to the ones they had years back. Adam always offered to stay in town with Jimmy Jay, but Beth would not hear of it.

"He's like a son to me," she'd snap, "and my mother may as well get used to it."

But even that situation was resolved. Sarah did not like going up to Greenwich, and as a result Ali would be picked up on a Friday by Joseph, and Beth, Adam, Jimmy Jay and Sarah would spend their time in the city.

The problem came to a head when the children's summer vacation came up. They were too young for camp, and Mary insisted they come and stay with her in Southampton. Beth was torn by the offer. In a way, she, too, needed a vacation, and the idea of spending a couple of months away from the city was enticing. Gillian was perfectly willing to have the office running with only a receptionist, since she was planning a trip to Australia and New Zealand.

It was a clear, warm day, and Beth was sitting in her office staring out the window, marveling at the loveliness of Central Park and the majestic Plaza Hotel, trying to absorb herself in the sight and avoid thinking about how to resolve her summer plans, when the phone rang.

"I'm looking at the trees in the park and the beauty of the Plaza," Dan said, as though they had spoken a few minutes earlier rather than six months ago.

"I wish they'd clean the building up a bit. It looks old and worn," Beth answered, although she had a hard time keeping the excitement out of her voice.

"It gives it character," Dan answered, and Beth could hear the echo of her own feelings in his voice, in spite of the flippant words.

"I'm glad to hear you think age has character," she answered.

"Feeling old?"

"Aged."

"If you come over, I'll prove to you that, like good wine, age is an asset."

"Where are you?"

"You know damn well I'm at the Pierre," he answered mockingly.

He was right. She had gone by the hotel almost daily and now she realized she had thought of him every time she passed it. She looked at her watch. It was three o'clock in the afternoon.

"I don't know if I can leave the office just now," she hedged.

"Bullshit. Gillian is out of town for the next forty-eight hours, and there is little going on there."

"How did you know Gillian was out of town?" She was annoyed at herself for asking.

"I had dinner with her last night."

"When did you get in?" she asked, unable to restrain herself.

"A couple of days ago."

Beth was quiet for a moment. "Frankly, I don't think I can make it," she said finally. "I have a hairdressing appointment at four."

"It's only three o'clock. We can have a drink and talk for an hour."

Her face grew red with embarrassment. The minute she heard his voice she wanted to go to bed with him.

"You are a dirty old bastard," Beth said, and started laughing.

"No, I'm not. You're a nymphomaniac and you're hot for my body, which is understandable," he answered, with mock seriousness.

"I'll be over in a few minutes." She hung up and felt her hand wet with perspiration.

She arrived home at 11:00 P.M. that night. The children were asleep and Adam was reading in the library. He looked up when she walked in.

"Honey, you look all in," he said with concern. Beth walked over and kissed him lightly on the forehead, trying to avoid looking directly at him. Her guilt at having been with Dan since three, making love to him, not wanting to leave, were all over her, and she was sure Adam would notice.

"One of Gillian's co-workers came back from overseas, and since she's away, I had to spend time with him and take all sorts of notes," she said, and started to leave the room.

"Anybody I know?" Adam asked conversationally.

She looked around with surprise. Adam never showed any interest in who she saw and what she did.

"Dan Bradbury. Do you know him?"

"I've heard the name. He writes for several magazines and is damn perceptive about foreign affairs."

"Yes, that's him." She almost ran out of the room.

The thought of leaving the city for Southampton was out of the question, now that Dan was back. She decided to send Ali and Sarah to her mother's, and keep Jimmy Jay at home.

"I would have liked you to get some rest," Adam said. "You're terribly nervous and high strung these days, and I should have thought a vacation would have done you good."

"I don't want a vacation." Her voice rose. "I don't need a vacation. I just told you, I have work to do."

"Okay," Adam said in a resigned voice. "You know best."

"Do you want me to go away?" Beth asked suspiciously. The conversation about Adam possibly having a mistress, when she was in Washington with Dan months before, came back to her.

"I want you to get hold of yourself," he answered sincerely. "You're driving yourself too hard and I thought a rest would do you good."

Summer slipped by too quickly. Dan was in town throughout, and the strain of emotions and the constant deceit on Beth's part were wearing her out.

She was spending less and less time at the office, rushing to work early in the morning, but stopping over at the Pierre to have breakfast with Dan. The morning hours spent away from him, doing work for Gillian, were an intrusion on her. Lunch would last for hours and she would find herself waiting for the time when she could leave the office and return to him before going home.

Dan gave her life a new dimension. He brought a glamour into it which she was sorely lacking, opening up a whole new world of thoughts and ideas. She felt alive when she was with him. The contrast between Adam and Dan became more evident daily. She hated herself for making the comparison, but it was unavoidable.

"Why don't you spend the night here?" Dan asked one evening as they were sitting around having a drink.

She looked up with shock. Dan was sipping his drink slowly, looking at her over the rim of his glass. He was wearing a dark brown velvet robe which she had bought him as a gift a few days earlier, and the richness of the color set off his blond Nordic looks to perfection. Instead of answering, she rushed to him and put her arms around him.

"Beth," Dan held her close. "This has gone way out of hand." His voice was barely audible. "I can't seem to sluff you off as I can other women. You're getting to me and I hate you for it, but I can't let you go."

She lifted her head and looked squarely at him. "You got to me a long time ago. I'm hopelessly in love with you, Dan, and I don't know what to do about it." The words spoken out loud sounded strange in her ears. She had not dared say them before, and she felt helpless.

The silence following her impulsive declaration made Beth lower her eyes.

"Leave Adam and come live with me," Dan said finally.

Her laughter was slightly hysterical. "You've got to be kidding. I'm an old married woman with children. I have responsibilities I can't walk away from."

"You're more away from them now than you would be if you were honest with them and yourself."

"Please stop it, Dan. I couldn't possibly do it."

"I'm going off on a cross-country lecture tour, and you could come with me. It would be great fun. Then we could take a long vacation in Bermuda." He stopped briefly waiting for her answer. "Have you ever been there?"

Jean Paul de Langue came back to her. He, too, had offered her a trip to Bermuda. It seemed as though it had happened to a different person in a different world.

"Dan, I couldn't possibly divorce Adam and go with you," she said finally.

"Who's talking about divorce?" he said roughly.

Beth caught her breath. Dan was offering her the same arrangement Jean Paul had offered, but then she was single. She suddenly remembered her thoughts concerning fidelity. She was convinced she could never have an affair with a man if she were married and had children. She closed her eyes, trying to shut out the memory.

"I'm sorry," she heard Dan say more softly.

"It's okay." She found her voice and tried to smile. "I was just remembering something that happened centuries ago to a very young, romantic girl."

Dan stood up nervously and poured them another drink. "Well, what are my chances of convincing you to come with me?"

"You've convinced me," she answered, "but I can't do it."

"Would you have considered it if I asked you to marry me?"

"But you didn't."

Turning his back to her, he walked over to the window. "I do love you, Beth. I love you very much." He spoke with great emotion, but she could not see his expression. "Unfortunately, I cannot be tied down to one woman, so I can't offer you marriage. I *am* asking you to come and live with me."

"What about my children, my home? Adam would be lost . . ."

"Oh, what crap," Dan interrupted her, and turned around. "The vanity of women will never cease to amaze me. Adam would be lost without you, was that what you were about to say? Well, I've got news for you. I adore you, love you as I never thought I could love a woman. I want you, I want to be with you, but I'll tell you right now, you're dispensable. To Adam and to me." He paused briefly. "I know it sounds cruel, which is not what I want to be at this romantic moment, but Beth, the world goes on even when a man leaves a woman or a woman leaves a man. It hurts for a while, but that hurt gets diffused with time. Other things, other people, other events come along and the void gets filled up."

Beth was confused by what Dan was saying. She was listening, but her mind was still ringing with the words, "I love you." She got up nervously.

"At least spend the night here," Dan said gently. "I miss you so when I wake up in the morning and you're not here."

"I can't, Dan. Don't you understand? I can't." The temptation was tugging at her better judgment and she was terrified. Impulsively, she grabbed her bag and ran out of the apartment.

When she arrived home she found a message from Adam. He had tried reaching her to tell her he would be out of town for the night. He had to fly to Chicago on urgent business. He would call her late the next day. Beth burst out crying and ran to her bedroom.

"Are you all right Aunt Beth?" Jimmy Jay was standing in the doorway looking at her with fear and concern.

She was startled to see him. She had forgotten he was sleeping over at their house in recent days.

Beth wiped her eyes and opened her arms to him. He ran to her and she held him close.

"Lydia invited me to sleep over at her home tonight and go to the beach tomorrow," she heard him say. "May I, Aunt Beth, and could you ask Gramma if it's all right?"

Beth pushed him away and looked at him carefully. He was more beautiful than ever. His features were perfect, his mulatto coloring exciting and his gentle, sorrowful eyes probing and intelligent. There was a quality about him which broke her heart.

"Would you really like that?"

"Oh, yes, Aunt Beth. Please." The sadness was gone and a bright glow replaced the forlorn expression.

"Let's talk to Lydia and find out if the invitation is still open."

Taking him by the hand, they walked together toward the kitchen.

Left alone Beth took a drink and settled herself in the library. What was Adam doing in Chicago? she wondered for the first time. Until that moment, it never occurred to her that the trip was too sudden, too unplanned. It was not like Adam. Was it possible that Adam really had a mistress? Dan had made it sound as though it were a fact of life when he mentioned it, and she had dismissed it as a joke. She looked at her watch. It was nearly 8:00 P.M. There was no way of finding out where Adam was staying by calling the office, and she did not know his secretary's home number. Pouring herself another drink, Beth picked up the phone to call her father. She replaced the receiver promptly. What would she say to him? She wondered if Hannah would know. She dismissed the idea.

Where was Adam? The thought was more frantic. What right did he have to leave without notifying her first? She would never do a thing like that to him. She felt alone and desperate. "Who takes care of you?" Dan had asked her when they were in Washington. Well, it certainly was not Adam.

Suddenly it dawned on her that if Adam could stay away all night, so could she. And she would not be hurting anyone. She would also not be missed. With great determination, she picked up the phone and called Dan. It rang several times but there was no answer. He must have gone out to eat, she thought, and decided to call him a little later. After all she had the whole night to herself.

Beth continued to call Dan every half hour after taking a bath. By 1:30 in the morning she could not decide whom she was angrier with, Dan or Adam. Both had deserted her. With a sense of doom, she called the reception desk at the Pierre. After several rings, a sleepy porter answered. Mr. Bradbury was not in, he said after trying the apartment. She hung up and the feeling of desperation returned.

She slept late and arrived at the office at noon. She did not stop off at the hotel. Instead, she attended to the mail and made some business calls. Then, with exaggerated composure, she dialed Dan's number. She leaned back in her swivel chair feeling virtuous. It was just as well that she did not find Dan in last night, she thought as she stared out the window. He was wrong to ask her to leave her family. But even as these thoughts crossed her mind, she became aware that he was not in. Dan rarely left the house during the day unless he had an assignment. Cocktail hour was his usual time for going anywhere. She redialed the number. Still no answer. She hung up and called the hotel switchboard.

"Mr. Dan Bradbury, please." She tried to sound officious.

"Who's calling?"

"Mrs. Stillman."

The operator went off the line and returned after an inordinately long time. "I'm afraid he's not in," she said. "May I leave a message?"

"That won't be necessary." She hung up convinced the operator had reached him. She busied herself with some work, but after fifteen minutes walked over to the receptionist.

"Joyce, could you ring up Mr. Bradbury at the Pierre. Miss Crane wants me to give him a message. And if he's not in, ask him to call her back."

"Is Miss Crane coming back today?"

"No, but if I'm not here, he'll at least know she's trying to reach him."

She stood while the girl dialed the number, pretending to be absorbed in a pamphlet lying on the desk.

"It's Miss Crane calling," Joyce said and waited.

"Oh, when did he leave?" Joyce asked after a while. Beth's heart sank. "Can you hold it a minute?" she said and turned to Beth. "He's left for California. Should I leave a message anyway?"

"No," Beth tried to sound nonchalant. "Just find out when he's coming back." Turning away, she walked slowly toward her office.

"They don't know," she heard Joyce call out after her.

Beth sat in her office for a long time staring into space. The full-blown hangover with which she had awakened was returning as a dull throbbing at her temples. She was exhausted and thought of going home, but being alone in the apartment was unappealing. Instead, she lay down on the little sofa in her office and, as her body relaxed, she permitted herself to face what had actually happened. It was over. Her affair with Dan had ended, and she was strangely relieved. Like her affair with Jean Paul, the episode with Dan, although far more serious, could have jeopardized her whole life. She had been behaving strangely at home, and if Adam had found companionship elsewhere, it was because she had not been a complete wife to him. Now it would all change. She had come back to her senses. Whatever feelings of loss she had, now that Dan was gone, would eventually diminish. She would miss him, she knew that. She would miss talking to him, listening to him, being with him. But most of all, she would miss the physical passion which he had reawakened in her. She tried to hold on to the last thought. After all, their relationship was purely physical. For a brief period they had both mistaken it for love. Now it was over and she had to pick up her real life, which she had neglected too long. The image of Adam and the children emerged. They were her life. Dan could make it alone. Her family could not.

A tear trickled down her cheek and she wiped it away viciously. There was nothing to cry about, she thought angrily. She had so much and she was being ungrateful.

Adam was unpacking when Beth arrived home. When she first opened the front door and the silence of the apartment greeted her, she felt lost. Then she saw the light from the bedroom.

An overnight bag was sitting on the dresser and the tag on the handle clearly read O'Hare Airport.

Adam did not hear her come in and she had a minute to observe him. He looked exhausted. He was terribly thin and his fingers tugging at the straps of the suitcase reflected his agitation. He was unusually pale, and his dark hair falling over his forehead was streaked with gray. Beth was stunned. She had not noticed it before.

"Adam?" she said softly.

He looked up, and his face brightened immediately.

She ran to him and began to kiss his face, his eyes, his lips.

"Hey, hey," he said, as he held her, "I've only been gone one night."

"I missed you. I missed you more than I can tell you," she whispered. "Oh, Adam, I love you. I'll always love you. Please don't ever go away again without telling me about it beforehand."

He lifted her off her feet and placed her gently on the bed. "You're overwrought, honey, overwrought and overworked." He lay down beside her and pulled her toward him.

"I am," she whispered and snuggled up to him. It felt good to be home. Adam began to massage her back and she relaxed. He turned off the light and, within minutes, she fell into a deep sleep.

It was dark when she woke up, and for a moment she was startled, wondering where she was. She looked over at Adam. He was sleeping peacefully beside her. The house was quiet and she remembered that the children were away.

"Adam," she whispered. "Adam, we're alone in the house for the first time since Ali was born."

He opened his eyes, and dark as it was she could see the white around the pupils of his eyes. She leaned over and turned on the light.

"We're actually by ourselves in this huge apartment, without children, without a maid, no deliveries expected, no groceries, no cleaners or anything. We don't even have to answer the phone if we don't want to."

"Beth, I have a feeling you're making an indecent proposal to a defenseless man."

She laughed almost gaily. "I certainly am, and I do wish you'd take me up on it."

Satisfied from their lovemaking, Beth ran her fingers over Adam's body. She knew it so well. She knew its warmth, its every curve, its every reaction. He was different from Dan. Her hand stopped moving. She had not thought of him since walking into the apartment hours ago. Sex with Dan was possibly more exciting, but that was because they both knew it was a passing phase. With Adam there was a lifetime, past, present and future.

She lifted herself on her elbow and stared at her husband, feeling an overwhelming tenderness toward him. He had aged. The lines in his face were becoming more pronounced. Again she noticed the gray streaks in his hair and saw the start of graying temples. He was going to be a distinguished looking man as he grew older. What a pity he gave up his dreams of a political life, she thought sadly. He had the looks, the talent, the ability. He had wanted it so, and he gave it all up for her and their life together. She leaned over and kissed him on the corner of his mouth. His eyes flickered open.

"You're as beautiful as ever," he said simply.

She settled back in the crook of his arm.

"Adam, do you have a mistress?" she asked dreamily.

"Lots of them." His voice was tinged with amusement.

She persisted. "Have you ever been unfaithful to me?"

"Beth, my love, I don't like the conversation, and I won't answer the question because we should not be having it." He began to stroke her hair absently. "I would never ask you whether you had a lover, and I hope you'll have the good sense not to feel you must confide in me, if you should. You're my wife and I love you. Every thought, every waking minute of my life is devoted to you and this home. My loyalty to it is complete." He pulled her toward him and kissed her brow.

His little speech made Beth uncomfortable. "Adam, whatever happened to the little apartment on Ninety-eighth Street?" she said, after a while.

"I still have it."

She sat up like a bolt. "What did you say?"

"I still have it."

"But why?"

"It's a place I cherish. It's a corner of a world which I've put aside but which I go back to, on occasion, just to feel that I'm still in touch with it." He reached over and took a cigarette from the nightstand and lit it. "You see, Beth, I love where we live, I love what you've done with the place. I'm happy here. I even like my work. But I miss the atmosphere of Ninety-eighth Street. The smelly stores, the poverty that cries out to be wiped away, the people who live there with little hope of ever getting away. I don't want to forget them just because I was luckier than they are."

"Do you still have the same telephone number and all that awful furniture?" she asked disdainfully, trying to drag him away from the memory that was his and did not include her.

"It's all there. Dusty, moldy, but there."

She was deeply disturbed. Adam had a life independent of her. Somehow he had succeeded in blending his past and their life together, while she was totally committed and involved in existing from day to day. Throughout the years of their marriage, when she felt sorry for him, pained that he had given up everything for her and the children, abandoned his ambitions, he had actually held on to a part of his life that had existed before he knew her. The idea was difficult to digest.

"Adam, I am tired," she said suddenly. "Can we go on a vacation together, just you and I?"

"When would you like to go?" he asked.

"As far as I'm concerned, we can leave this Friday."

"I've got a case starting in the morning. I could try and wrap it up quickly, but even so, it will take a week to ten days."

"We've never been away together." She became petulant.

He did not answer.

"Do you realize you've never been to Europe?" She tried not to sound condescending.

She felt him grow tense. "True, but the fact is, I've never really been able to afford it."

She squirmed, uncomfortable. She had taken the children skiing several times in the last couple of years.

"Have you ever been to Bermuda?" she asked, and was surprised at herself.

"No."

She knew she was playing a bizarre game, was mocking Adam, trying to diminish him, but there was no satisfaction in it.

"Neither have I," she said angrily, and the anger was directed at herself.

The whole conversation was an exercise in futility. They could not go away on vacation. The girls would be coming home soon. Jimmy Jay could not be left alone. Hannah would be unbearably disappointed if they did not show up for their Friday night dinners. She was ill and lonely, and they were all she had.

Beth got out of bed, careful not to wake Adam, who was again fast asleep. Pulling on her robe, she went into the library and poured herself a brandy.

Dawn was coming up and Beth walked over to the window and stared down at the river. It looked peaceful and it soothed her. In all the time they had lived in the apartment, she had never really looked at it. She never seemed to have the time. It would be different from now on, she decided. She would begin to enjoy what she had. This was her life, and all the flights of fancy were just that. She had chosen what she had and there was no way she could change it or leave it.

18

Beth quit her job within days of Dan's departure and decided to devote her time to her family. The kids were delighted and Adam seemed pleased. Getting up in the morning and seeing the children off to school, being able to get back into bed and sleep for a while longer was a luxury she had not allowed herself in a long time. She began to redecorate her home, go to auctions, galleries, have lunch with her mother and made an overt gesture toward the wives of the people who were important to Adam in his law practice. But she was relieved when Gillian called her a few months later and asked her to come in and help out with a new campaign. Boredom was setting in and she took the assignment.

Following her success with the Kennedy election, Gillian Crane's office became one of the most sought after in the city, and Beth loved being involved again.

At first it was easy. Her views and Gillian's were almost identical on most issues, and the satisfaction of being able to mold and promote hopeful political figures was exciting. But as time went by Gillian's political convictions began to run more and more to the far left, and the candidates she agreed to work for usually annoyed Beth. Gillian was away most of the time and Beth found herself involved in work she no longer believed in. At the end of each campaign, she would vow not to accept the next offer from Gillian, but somehow she was always persuaded to return.

Beth had been with Gillian on a free-lance basis for three years, and she knew she could not go on working for Gillian's candidates. She glanced at the papers on her desk. This, she thought furiously, is the end.

The phone on her desk rang out at that moment.

"Yes," she said unceremoniously.

"Beth, it's Maggie Jackson. Do you have Joe Sabian's speech and press release ready?"

Beth tried to remember which of the girls working in the office was Maggie Jackson and what she looked like. Each campaign saw new faces whom Gillian hired, giving them impressive titles and little pay, who were to become her disciples and follow in her footsteps. They were in their late twenties or early thirties. All attractive, well-dressed, bright, with degrees from various Ivy League colleges around the country, and very aggressive. They made Beth uncomfortable. Although not much older than they were, she lacked their confidence and could not compete with their self-assured manner.

"Yes, Maggie," Beth answered, annoyed by the young woman's patronizing tone, "they're right here."

"Could you bring them to me?" Maggie asked.

"Come get them yourself," Beth said, and slammed the phone down. Her face was flushed with anger.

Within minutes Maggie walked in. She was a tall, dark-haired girl with a bouffant hairdo. Jackie Kennedy reincarnate, Beth thought with disdain.

"You're in a vicious mood, aren't you?" Maggie said, picking up the papers from Beth's desk. "I'm just trying to compile all the material for the Sabian rally in Buffalo."

Several biting remarks went through Beth's mind, but they were all petty and out of place.

"I'm just tired," she said instead, and got up. "I think I'll call it a day."

"Are you sure this speech is okay?" Maggie asked.

"Every speech I write is more than okay," Beth said, and picked up her bag. "I can assure you, if your little candidate gets any votes at all, it will be because of that speech." She stormed out of the office.

Gillian called her that night. "I hear you're on the war path," she said, and laughed her raucous laughter, which Beth came to know as Gillian's armor when she was upset.

"Not really," Beth said, taking her drink over to a new armchair which had been delivered that day.

"You had a run-in with Maggie."

"Which one is she, the dark-haired one with the bouffant look, or the blond with the bouffant look?"

"Beth, what's gotten into you?"

"I don't know, Gillian," she said, and her tone softened. "I think I'd better quit for good. I don't really enjoy the work anymore. I certainly don't like most of the people we work for."

"You're too rigid," Gillian said cautiously. "Times are changing. There's a whole new young group of voters and we've got to consider them, keep up with them. There's the black movement which you seem unwilling to face or understand."

Beth's laughter rang out. "*I* don't understand the black movement? What do you think Jimmy Jay is, Scandinavian?" She caught her breath.

"I live with it. I talk to his grandparents in Virginia at least twice a week. They come up and visit me and we discuss the racial problems from the inside, and we don't exchange slogans." She stopped, aware she was hitting below the belt.

"Will you at least finish the Joe Sabian campaign?" Gillian's voice changed. It was cold, almost impersonal.

"You know I will," Beth answered, and hung up.

"If that was Gillian you were talking to," Adam said and Beth swung around. She had not heard him come in. "I would say you two ladies are on the verge of breaking up a long and fast friendship."

"Was it that bad?" Beth asked.

"It was worse than bad. You were downright cruel."

"Well, I'm sorry about it, but something's happened to her. She's not what she used to be. I think she's frightened of growing old and, in the process, is working too hard at being 'with it,' as the kids say." She paused before continuing. "I know she drinks too much, but I think she's also into drugs."

"Don't, Beth," Adam said pleasantly, but it was clear he would not have her elaborate. Gossip, as far as Adam was concerned, was taboo at all times.

"Would you like a drink?" Beth changed the subject.

"I'll have a soda." Adam sat down in the new chair. "It's comfortable, all right, but does it go with the rest of the stuff in here?"

"I can always give it back, if you don't like it."

"No, if you think it's suitable, it's fine with me."

She handed him his drink and went to refill her martini glass.

"You could retire," Adam said in mock seriousness.

"I know I can, but I like being involved."

"What about finding a job somewhere else?"

"Good God, no," Beth answered automatically. "I'm too old to go work for anybody. I wouldn't know how to take orders from some stranger. At least with Gillian I have free reign, make my own schedule, am my own master." She laughed self-consciously. "Besides, I don't think I could stomach the young working women who are just starting out and who are tuned into the work scene."

"What about opening your own office?" Adam suggested. "You could do it with your hands tied behind your back, and you could choose whomever you wanted to work with, instead of taking what Gillian offers."

"I couldn't," Beth answered quickly. "I couldn't do it to Gillian."

What she did not say was that she was scared, and very insecure about herself. "Besides, no one knows me. I do the work, but it's Gillian who gets the people. It's her name, her fame, her personality." A bitterness she was trying to keep in check seeped through. In spite of knowing the work, doing most of it, running every aspect of the campaigns, Gillian and her young brood of career girls were getting the credit and she was still a nobody. No one knew she existed. Gillian had the knack of attracting attention, as did the young woman who kept passing through the office. She did not have it and she envied them desperately. She also had no idea how to change it.

"I'd hire you like a shot," Adam said, and Beth smiled in spite of herself.

"Running for anything in particular?" she asked.

"Not this week, but maybe someday."

"You couldn't afford me."

"How much do you charge?"

"Nothing. And that, my love, is very expensive."

"I'll keep that in mind." He laughed pleasantly.

Beth drank down her martini and poured herself a refill. The fact was, she thought as she gulped down the drink, she was a housewife, not a career woman. Someday, when the kids were all grown up, on their own, she'd make a stab at it. For now, she had little choice but to continue as she was.

Beth made a point to get to the office early. She wanted to make amends for her words with Gillian. She was absorbed in the mail when Gillian came in.

"It's a masterpiece," Gillian said, walking in and throwing a book on the desk. "It's going to make all the best-seller lists or my name isn't Gillian Crane."

Beth looked down and a picture of Dan was staring up at her from the jacket of a shiny book cover. She dared not pick it up. Instead, she smiled pleasantly at Gillian. "Yes, so I hear. Everyone is talking about it, and they say it's a smash." She knew she sounded strained, and she tried to relax. "I didn't know it was actually out."

"It's out, but not officially," Gillian said, and sat down opposite Beth. "The pub date is tomorrow," she continued, and Beth marveled at the ease with which Gillian seemed to have forgotten their conversation of the night before. "You must know that, though." She stopped and looked surprised. "Don't tell me you didn't get an invitation to his publication party?"

"No, I didn't," Beth was trying to speak naturally but was having a difficult time. "Why should I?"

"I thought you were quite involved with him at one point."

Beth looked blankly at Gillian, and the older woman returned her look. "I can't imagine what gave you that idea," she said simply. A look of uncertainty came over Gillian's face, and Beth wanted to laugh. Dan had told her the first night they slept together in Washington that as long as no one said it, Gillian would suspect but would never be sure. After all this time, Gillian was not sure.

"I'll talk to him and have him invite both you and Adam. I know they'll have a great deal in common."

Beth could not decide if there was hidden sarcasm in the statement, but decided to ignore it.

"Sounds lovely," was all she said, and turned back to her typewriter.

"It's at the Pierre." Gillian did not move. "He lives there, you know."

Beth stopped typing.

"The party is from five to seven, and I really think you should come. Everyone who's anyone will be there." Gillian stood up and Beth was forced to turn around. Their eyes met and Beth knew Gillian had not forgotten their angry exchange of the night before and was getting even with her.

Left alone, Beth picked up a pencil and broke it in half. She looked down and was shocked at her action.

She had known Dan was in town. She always knew when he arrived. She had not heard from him since the day he left for California three years ago. But she was aware of his whereabouts and his actions, since he had become quite famous and the newspapers reported his comings and goings in great detail. She had called him once, and hung up without saying a word when he came on the line. He sounded like a stranger, and she could think of nothing to say.

Now he was back in New York and Gillian was playing a mean little game because she was angry. Well, Beth thought almost calmly, she would not fall into the trap. If an invitation came, she would not go.

It was Adam, however, who received the invitation, not Beth. It was mid-afternoon and she was finishing some work when Adam called.

"Honey, Gillian phoned and asked if we'd join her at the press party for Dan Bradbury. You remember him, don't you?"

"Yes, of course I do," Beth answered impassively.

"Well, you know his book is coming out, and frankly, I'd like to meet the guy. I think he's one of the finest minds we've got around these days, and it would be nice to hear what he has to say."

Beth spent an inordinate amount of time trying to figure out what to wear. It was a hot July afternoon, and she finally settled on a shocking pink, two-piece dress, consisting of a loose, sleeveless, high-necked overblouse and slim skirt. The hem was just above her knees and her long slim legs were shown to great advantage. She wore no jewelry, in an attempt to keep up the pretense that she had come from the office. While applying her mascara, she noticed the little lines around her eyes, and they were not laugh lines, she thought wryly. The grooves around her upper lip were deeper and her forehead was not as smooth as she would have liked it, but her jaw line was still firm and her neck uncreased. She chose the color of her lipstick carefully so it did not clash with the outfit. Slipping into a pair of patent leather black sandals, she picked up a patent leather clutch bag and looked at herself. The overall appearance was pleasing. She felt she looked youthful and attractive. Her red hair, which she was tinting every few weeks to keep the rich color, was cut just below her earlobes and parted to one side. Blown dry, it gave her a carefree air. By the time she was ready to leave the house, she was flushed with excitement. She was also quite late.

She arrived at the Pierre just past 6:00 P.M. Adam was nowhere in sight. They had planned on meeting at 5:30 in the lobby, and she decided he must have gone up without her. She wished he had waited.

Dan's living room was crowded and noisy.

"The bar is through that door, miss." A waiter pointed the way. She wanted to tell him she knew where the bar was, where the bedroom was, where the bathroom was. She bit her lip.

Winding her way through the crowd, Beth recognized several of the girls who worked for Gillian. They were laughing and chatting and seemed at ease, as if they belonged.

Beth's self-assurance began to fade. She felt matronly and dawdy.

"Beth," Gillian called out over the din of voices, "we're right here."

Gillian, Adam and Dan were standing talking in a corner.

"I'll just get a drink and join you," she called back, and hurried toward the bar.

With a double martini in hand, she approached them.

"Beth, how nice to see you," Dan said and leaned over and kissed her on the cheek. "You look younger every day, or should I say every year." He smiled pleasantly at Gillian. "It has been years. Kennedy's election, right?"

Gillian's eyes narrowed with suspicion. Adam put his arm around Beth's shoulders. "Isn't she gorgeous?" he said with pride.

"You can say that again. And she has brains to boot." Gillian decided to play the game.

Standing between Adam and Dan, Beth felt hot and perspired. The exuberance she felt when she left her house was gone. She should not have placed herself in the position of being in the presence of the two men who meant so much to her, she thought unhappily. She also felt that she was making a fool of Adam in front of Dan, and that was unforgivable. Disengaging herself from Adam's embrace she moved away and tried to evaluate the men objectively, to see if she could somehow understand what had attracted her to each. Adam, she noted, was far better looking than Dan. He was taller, younger and there was an eagerness about him that was exciting. His eyes sparkled and his face was flushed, giving his olive skin a glow. He was talking politics, which he did rarely with their friends or his business associates. For a brief moment she was angry with him. He should not have given up his dreams for her. He had too much going for him to have abandoned everything for a life of boredom and frustration. Her feelings were quickly replaced by a surge of love. He knew what he was doing, and she had no right to fault him.

She turned her attention to Dan, and her heart lurched with desire. She adored her husband, but she wanted Dan. Cynical, cold, impersonal, his eyes mocking, his thin lips smiling, barely moving as he spoke, he still excited her, and Beth had to restrain the urge to walk over and touch him. Suddenly his expression changed, and Beth became aware of a magnificent, diminutive Eurasian girl approaching the group. Dan put his arm around her shoulder.

"Tanya Wam, I want you to meet the Stillmans," he waved Beth over.

They all shook hands.

"How about having dinner with us?" Dan asked, putting his other arm around Gillian.

"Beth?" Adam turned to her.

"I don't think we can." She tried to smile. "I really must get home and finish up some work I have to do."

Gillian raised her brow. "You take work home?"

"Gillian, my love, that Joe Sabian has to be worked on night and day if there's any hope of getting him elected." Her tone was pleasant, but she saw Gillian wince. It was her way of getting back at Gillian. It also marked an end to their working together, and it pleased her.

19

Within a very short time, the triumph of Beth's last statement to Gillian at Dan's party turned sour. They had not spoken since that day, and the loss of Gillian's support and friendship caused her great unhappiness. Her life was emptier than ever, and Dan took on a greater importance in her thoughts. A picture of him appeared in a newspaper with a story that he was being considered for a very high official post in Europe. The idea that she could have been part of his life abroad and that she turned it down was upsetting. She missed him desperately and wondered if she would ever see him again. Her thoughts took on an eroticism which embarrassed and frightened her. She would find herself conjuring up sexual fantasies that would leave her weak with desire. Adam became the substitute for Dan and she felt great self-loathing. She drank a little more than she should, but it gave her a hazy glow which somewhat diminished her desperate feelings of loss now that Dan was out of her life.

Turning her attention to her family, she tried to involve herself in the daily routine of the household, hoping to reestablish herself within that framework.

In September the Jewish New Year was ushered in, and Beth spent time helping Hannah prepare for the holiday. Being with Hannah, listening to her stories about her childhood in Europe, hearing her relate her life with Adam's father, soothed her and fortified her determination to make her marriage to Adam a better one, make the bond stronger. Right after the holiday Adam was promoted to full partner, and the firm name was changed to Van Ess and Stillman. It meant a great deal of prestige and a hefty boost in their income. It also meant that Adam had to be away a great deal of the time, since the office was opening a branch on the West Coast.

October started badly for Beth. Drew had a mild stroke and Beth had to spend time in Greenwich. Added to that, Jimmy Jay, who was going regularly to Hebrew school, became morose and fretful. Fearful that he would stop going, Beth made a point of waiting for him in the synagogue so she could walk him home.

"I hate that place," Jimmy Jay announced one day when Beth picked him up. "The kids make fun of me and I have no friends."

"You're imagining it." Beth tried to make light of his complaint.

"I know I'm Jewish, but I'm the wrong color." He ignored her statement.

"Why don't you wait to talk to Uncle Adam before you make your final decision? I'm sure he'll figure something out." She felt unable to cope with the situation. "I'll talk to him as well, I promise."

That night, Beth waited until the children were in bed before broaching the subject to Adam.

"The fucking little bastards," Adam exploded. "I'll talk to the rabbi as soon as I get back from the Coast," he said, trying to calm down. "But until then, could you talk to him?"

"No, I can't," Beth said coldly. "There are just so many things I can cope with. Jimmy Jay's religious upbringing is something you have to take responsibility for."

He looked at her with surprise. She too was amazed at her statement. Always in the past she would have agreed without hesitation.

"Well, maybe we should just take him out of the school and get him a tutor," Adam suggested.

"Adam," Beth started haltingly, "why does Jimmy Jay have to go through this whole routine?"

"He's Jewish, and Jewish kids must study for their Bar Mitzvah," Adam answered vehemently.

"What makes him Jewish?" Beth persisted.

Adam looked at her bewildered. "But he is," he answered, and became flustered. "Debbie was Jewish and that alone makes him Jewish, and he's been brought up as a Jew, has lived with Hannah as a Jewish child, was bred on Jewish law, and will always see himself as a Jew." His face was red, and Beth felt momentarily sorry for him.

Walking over to the bar, she poured herself a drink and without turning around, said, "But he will always be perceived as a black."

"How he is perceived is one thing. How he feels is another, and that's why this Bar Mitzvah is important," Adam snapped back.

"Why burden him further?" Beth turned and looked directly at her husband. "He's bound to have a hard enough time as it is, freedom-riders notwithstanding. Why not leave him alone?"

"Because difficult as it is to be black, it is more difficult when you don't have a religious identification to fall back on. Jimmy Jay was given to my mother by the Faulkners, and she brought him up the only way she knew."

He walked out of the room, leaving Beth feeling strangely lonely. They never discussed religion, they did not attend any religious services, yet Adam was Jewish, felt Jewish, was always conscious of his heritage and was very proud of it. Hannah and Jimmy Jay were on his team, but she, Ali and Sarah were not included. Who was she anyway? The old thought returned. Who were her daughters? How would Ali and Sarah be perceived? But, more important, how would they perceive themselves? They needed as much guidance as any child, male or female.

She took another drink and lit a cigarette nervously.

Adam came back into the room, but before she could say what was on her mind she realized he was laughing. It was not a happy laugh.

"What a great big funny game we play." He walked over to the bar and poured himself a stiff drink and downed it in one gulp.

Beth was staggered. Adam rarely drank. "What happened?"

"I just finished talking to the rabbi," he said seriously. "And do you know what the problem is? It had nothing to do with Jimmy Jay's color. He was an outsider for a brief time when he started classes, but it was forgotten by everyone until you started going there and sitting around waiting for him."

"I went up there because Jimmy Jay seemed unhappy. He told me so." She could not keep the shock out of her voice.

"Honey, I'm not blaming you," Adam said. "I swear I'm not. But the fact is that most children go through periods when they don't want to go to school—Hebrew school or any other school. But if he was not black, you would have gone up to the school, talked to the teacher and worked out whatever the problem was, without becoming so overprotective." He came over to her and put his hands on her shoulders. "Beth, we, the liberated grown-ups, the intelligent ones, insist on bringing our values, logic, standard, thinking and feelings into situations that could best be solved by the children on their level."

Beth lowered her eyes. Adam was right. She had overreacted and felt foolish. She also knew it was an inopportune moment to bring up Ali and Sarah's religious education. There was no way she could make her point convincingly.

The incident rekindled Beth's feelings of separateness, of feeling detached, of not belonging. She wanted to get away and found herself wondering what her life would have been like had she accepted Dan's offer.

When Dan suddenly called in early November Beth felt shaken. It was as though her prayers had been answered. In the flippant manner of the past, he asked her to meet him at the Laurent Bar on East Fifty-sixth Street in half an hour.

She dressed carefully, trying to achieve a look of casual elegance, and was conscious of the need to look as young as possible. She realized she had not paid much attention to her appearance in the last few months and was aware of every line on her face, every weakened muscle in her body.

She was nervous when she walked into the dimly lit bar. Dan was sitting in a round booth, and got up the minute he saw her. As Beth sat down beside him, she felt alive for the first time in months.

Neither spoke for a long time.

"I liked Adam," Dan finally broke the silence.

"I love him," Beth answered.

"For the first time in my life I feel like a heel." He laughed. "I actually feel guilty."

"I don't understand why, but I don't," Beth answered, and was surprised at her statement.

"And they say that women are more emotional than men." Dan laughed again.

"How long are you staying in New York?" Beth asked, changing the subject.

"As long as you want me to."

"Forever?"

"That's not very long."

"It's a start." Beth sighed with contentment.

20

It was the beginning of a life filled with turmoil for Beth. In spite of what she had said, she felt the pressure every minute of her day. She spent a great deal of time in Dan's apartment at the Pierre. It was ridiculously indiscreet. The elevator men knew her by sight, the front desk staff greeted her by name. How they knew it, she never found out. She always used the Sixty-first Street entrance, fearful of meeting Gillian on Fifth Avenue. She would arrive in the morning and Dan would still be sleeping. It did not bother her. Just being in the same apartment with him was enough. When he woke up, they would have something to eat, make love and Beth would watch him work. She knew she was neglecting her home and her children, but she could not help it. Dan was everything to her.

It was a week before Thanksgiving and Beth finished with her morning chores at home and was getting ready to meet Dan when he called to find out when she was coming. She was surprised. He knew she would arrive as soon as she could.

When she walked in Dan was sitting at his typewriter working. He got up quickly and rushed over to her. Taking her in his arms, she felt an excitement in him which thrilled and baffled her. Removing herself from the embrace, she took off her coat, not taking her eyes off him. She noted he was dressed in gray Daks, a white turtleneck sweater, and a loose, light blue cardigan. That was how he was dressed the morning after she had slept with him in Washington. He was looking at her with an amused glint in his eyes.

"You're dressed as you were the morning after we first made love in Washington," she said, and walked toward him, feeling the desire he always evoked in her, but it was mingled with trepidation.

He pulled her toward him and pressed her lower body to him, and kissed her with great tenderness. She returned his kisses and, as had happened to them throughout the times they spent together, all thoughts evaporated. Dan unbuttoned the top of her shirt and slipped his hand beneath her bra. She could feel his fingers massaging her breast and her nipples hardened with desire and she slipped her hand toward his groin. He still wanted her as much as she wanted him. He lowered his head and she felt his lips sucking at her breast. They were moving toward the bedroom, when there was a tap at the door.

"Shit," Dan said, moving away from her.

It was the waiter rolling in a table laden with food and a bottle of champagne. When he was gone, Dan seemed to have gotten control of himself and he smiled sheepishly at her. "I wanted it all to be ready when you got here. Then, when you walked in, I forgot that they were late."

Beth looked over at the table. The oysters were huge, the caviar beautifully gray, the little necks, the salad, the black, thin slices of bread and the champagne was Dom Pérignon '63.

"Dan, I love you. I love you now more than I did when we first met."

"I didn't know you loved me then," he chuckled. "As I recall, you specifically said you were not clawing or frightened, only demanding."

She walked over and clawed his hand gently. "So, now I'm clawing, but trying to do it gently. I'm demanding, still, and I am frightened . . ." She stopped. "Oh, damn it." She moved her hand away.

"What are you frightened of, Beth?"

"Every time I leave you, a feeling of panic sets in. I'm terrified that you won't be here when I come back. And now this feast. Is it the condemned man's last supper?"

"Beth, will you marry me?"

His face was somber and she could see he meant it.

"You're serious," she whispered.

"I am." He began to grin. "I never thought the words would cross my lips, but now that I've said them, you bet I'm serious."

She could not speak.

"I've been appointed permanent news correspondent to the Voice of America in France, and put in charge of all of the Western Hemisphere. I want you to come with me, Beth. I don't think I want to do it alone."

Beth continued to stare at him. Thoughts of Adam and the children flashed through her mind. She loved them very much, but her life was also important. She had a right to have an exuberant, carefree, exciting life, filled with glamour, travel, being involved with important people. As Mrs. Dan Bradbury she could have it all. She could work beside Dan, make something of herself while helping him. Adam didn't really need her anymore. She had laid it all out for him and the children. He was going to be a top legal mind, make a great deal of money, but he did not need her for that. A decent housekeeper, plus Lydia, would do the job. She would be around, she would not be more than a phone call away. She would even continue to see Adam. They would be friends like two civilized people who had known each other intimately, but who had grown apart. Eventually, Adam would find a new, more suitable love who would be getting a successful man, whom she could admire, respect and be proud of. Whoever she was, she would not have to go through the struggling years.

"Well," Dan said, "have you figured it out?"

She smiled. Dan knew her so well. He understood and appreciated her.

"I would love to marry you, Dan," she said, and fell into his arms.

"Thank you, Beth," he whispered. "I know we'll be very happy."

Then, moving away, Dan led her toward the table. "I had a feeling we would be celebrating. And, as I recall, the waiter at the Georgetown Inn rated you as Dom Pérignon '63."

She smiled, recalling his statement then.

"A broad rated that high by my favorite waiter should have been a warning to me," Dan said, as though reading her thoughts. "And not wanting to be outdone by a wise-guy waiter, I figured I'd repeat the compliment in honor of the future Mrs. Bradbury."

Finished with the meal, and the champagne, Dan went to the phone to order a second bottle. Beth leaned back in her armchair and gazed out the window. The sky was extraordinarily clear, although it was November, and her eyes were following the small puffs of clouds that were speeding by the window. She could hear Dan having a hard time getting the operator, but she was too content to concern herself with it. For the first time, in many years, she did not want a drink. It pleased her.

"Sweetheart, would you go into the bedroom and use my private phone to get the goddamned operator at the switchboard to answer, and if she does ask her to get the restaurant on the phone?"

Beth walked into the bedroom. She felt gay and young. A new life was starting for her. She was going to have another chance to make something of herself with a man she loved, adored, worshipped.

The hotel lines were busy. She looked around for a cigarette and was in the process of lighting it when Dan appeared in the doorway. He was deathly pale.

"He's been shot," he said hoarsely. "Kennedy has been shot."

Beth could not figure out what he was saying. The words refused to form a comprehensive sentence. Suddenly, she saw Dan cross himself, and the act of faith brought it all into focus.

Dan went over the television set and turned it on. The newscasters were hysterical, sirens and shouting blared forth. Beth turned her eyes toward the window. The sun was still shining, the sky was bright, the clouds were racing by. The screaming voices from the TV set were louder, and she heard Dan talking on the phone. His voice was cold and crisp. He was giving orders, making arrangements. He was totally preoccupied.

Adam, Beth thought frantically. She had to call Adam.

She ran into the living room and picked up the house phone. It took a while, but finally she got the operator and called Adam.

"Have you heard?" she asked.

"Yes," he answered, in full control. "I've heard. Where are you?"

"I was having lunch with Dan Bradbury when we heard it."

"Have you called the children?"

"No, I called you first."

"I'll be home in a little while. You call home and I'll call Hannah. She'll be very upset, and it's bad for her. I might even go up and bring her over. She shouldn't be alone."

"Adam, what happens now?"

"I don't know." His composure did not crack. "I don't know." He hung up.

Beth replaced the receiver, picked it up again and tried to reach her house. She could still hear Dan's voice coming from the bedroom.

Finished with her conversation with Lydia, who was crying, Beth went in to see Dan. He was just replacing the receiver in its cradle. He was still very pale, and his eyes were shaded over.

"What happens now?" she asked him, as she had asked Adam.

"It's one of the greatest tragedies that could have happened to us as a people, but we'll survive. Now the question is, who did it. That's important."

"I've got to go home," she said quietly.

"Of course you do," he said, but Beth felt as though she had ceased to exist for him.

"When will I see you?"

"I don't know."

"I told Adam I was having lunch with you," she said, for no reason. The phone rang at that moment and Dan picked it up and, within seconds, began to dictate a statement.

Beth turned away and walked out of the apartment.

21

The weekend passed slowly. The children were nervous and Adam was either on the phone or was out. He was not home when the shooting of Oswald by Jack Ruby was shown on television while the children were watching. Ali did not react, Jimmy Jay was stunned and Sarah burst out crying. Beth felt their world was coming to an end and was deeply disturbed that Adam was not there to help her cope. For the first time she took note that in recent weeks Adam was rarely home evenings or on weekends, and when he did spend time with the family he was ill-tempered and preoccupied. She had been so involved with Dan, she had not been conscious of him or his moods. Now she wondered where he was, and it crossed her mind, as it had years back, that he had a mistress. But unlike her feelings in the past, she almost felt relieved. It would make leaving him easier. Not being able to contact Dan was far more distressing. She had called him several times since leaving him on Friday, but the phone was either busy or no one answered.

Mary telephoned on Monday evening to remind them she was expecting them to come for Thanksgiving dinner, and asked Beth to go by the Park Avenue apartment and get some of Drew's favorite brandy from the wine room. The invitation was stated as a *fait accompli*, and Beth was surprised. They had never spent Thanksgiving with her parents since Jimmy Jay was excluded. She hung up without voicing her reservations and turned to Adam.

"What's this about going to Greenwich for Thanksgiving?" she asked. "What happens to Hannah and Jimmy Jay?"

"I've accepted the invitation," he said firmly.

"Adam, Hannah and Jimmy Jay will be alone and that's unfair." She was upset for them. She also wanted to spend some time on Thursday with Dan. She assumed he too was alone, and she wanted to see him.

"The Faulkners are coming up from Virginia to spend the day with them," Adam said, almost angrily.

"You never mentioned it to me." It was unlike Adam to make arrangements of that sort without consulting her.

"I forgot."

"Does Hannah know about it?"

Adam raised his brows. "Obviously."

"Then I'd better go out and do some shopping and prepare the dinner. Hannah can hardly be expected to make the meal." Preparing a Kosher Thanksgiving dinner was not simple, she thought with annoyance.

"I've ordered the whole kit and kaboodle from my mother's butcher, and all the trimmings will be brought to the house by one of Mama's friends," he said impatiently.

"Adam, stop snapping at me," Beth said angrily. "We're all tense and upset and your behavior is not helping."

"I've got a great deal on my mind." He sounded apologetic.

"Is anything wrong?" she asked automatically.

"Nothing is wrong and nothing is right."

The phone rang and Adam picked it up. Beth watched him and saw his eyes dart about nervously. He said little and hung up after a few minutes. She could not figure out whom he had talked to.

"Who was that?" she asked, in spite of herself.

"Sam Ryan," Adam answered, and started pacing. "I've got to go meet him at his club."

"That's a name from the past," Beth mused. She did not believe him. "When did you start seeing him again?"

"I've never stopped seeing him. He's a great man." He looked around nervously.

"You look like a trapped animal," Beth said slowly.

"I feel like one." For a minute it appeared as though he wanted to say something but changed his mind. "I've got to run now," he said instead, and tried to smile. "I'll see you later."

The minute she heard the front door shut, she rushed into the kitchen and told Lydia she was going out. She had to see Dan and talk to him. She felt she was losing control, and needed reassurance.

Beth arrived at the Pierre and was on her way to the elevator when the front desk clerk called her over. "I've got a letter for you from Mr. Bradbury." He handed her an envelope.

Beth tore it open. "My dearest," it read, "I had to go to Washington and I didn't dare call you. Paris is out for now, and I'll be working out of Washington for the next few months. I'll be in touch as soon as I can. I love you. Dan."

Her first reaction was relief. Dan still loved her. The second was that staying in the United States would facilitate her divorce from Adam and would make things easier for the children.

It was still early and not wanting to go home, Beth wondered what to do, when she remembered her mother's request for the brandy and decided to go up to the Park Avenue apartment.

Heading eastward on Sixty-first Street, Beth was preoccupied with how she would break the news of her plans to Adam. She was convinced she was doing the right thing. She did not know if Adam had a mistress, but she was sure he would never ask for a divorce. He was too set in his ways, too comfortable. They had their daughters, their home, his career and their dull little existence. Her future with Adam was predestined. If she did not leave now, the years would pass and she would never be a person in her own right. With Dan it would be different. His work was interesting and glamorous, and he would share it with her. They would travel and meet people, see new places, do things together. They could even have a child. She was still young enough to have children. The last idea reaffirmed her decision. It would never have occurred to her to have another child with Adam.

Beth was about to cross the street, heading uptown, when she noticed a crowd gathered in front of a church. Edging her way over she saw a newly wed couple emerge from within. The bride was very young, no more than eighteen or nineteen years old. She was quite lovely, standing close to the bridegroom, smiling up at him. Her youth, purity, happiness were openly displayed. She was wearing an ankle-length, cream-colored wedding dress and a little pillbox hat was perched on her head with the veil falling away from her face. Beth's sense of identity with the girl was overwhelming. At that moment an older woman appeared beside the bride. She was tall, graceful, beautifully groomed and elegant and was obviously the girl's mother. Beth found herself staring at the older woman and knew it was she that she should be identifying with, not the young bride.

Turning away quickly, Beth hailed a passing cab and jumped in.

Huddled in the corner of the car, she felt numb. Could she really start life all over again? She was nearing forty and was thinking of getting remarried, and having a baby. She put her hand over her eyes, trying to erase the wedding scene she had just witnessed. It would not go away. She had been so sure of her decision just minutes before. How could a chance sight of a young bride throw her into such confusion?

The children were asleep when Beth arrived home. Adam was not yet in. She felt calm and composed. She had spent the last few hours at her parents' apartment and had worked it all out in her mind. She would tell Adam the truth, quietly and rationally, and he would understand. It even occurred to her that he might be relieved. He was probably as bored as she was but was too much of a gentleman to admit it. He too had had different aspirations when they married. In a way, she might be doing him a favor by releasing him to pursue another course instead of living out a life of quiet desperation.

She thought of having a drink but decided against it. She had purposely not had any all day, wanting to be sober and clear headed when she spoke to Adam.

Beth undressed, took a bath, made some coffee and tried to occupy herself with various little chores around the house. At 1 A.M. she became restless. Fear crept into her mind. Adam was out most evenings in recent weeks, but he had never come home after midnight. She thought of calling Sam Ryan, but decided against it. She was about to take a drink, in spite of her earlier resolution, when Adam walked in. She saw that he was flushed as he came toward her, his arms outstretched.

"Don't you dare touch me," Beth said furiously. "Where have you been?"

He was startled by the rebuff but regained his composure quickly. "Beth, I must talk to you," he said, containing his excitement with difficulty.

She looked at him suspiciously.

"I've decided to run for Congress. The United States Congress."

Beth gasped audibly.

Adam didn't seem to notice her reaction as he rushed on. "I feel it's important. I've been thinking about it for a long time, and now it seems to me that this is the right time. The assassination sort of brought it into focus."

"You've been thinking about it for a long time?" Beth could not believe what he was saying. "And you never mentioned it to me?"

"It's a very personal decision."

"Personal decision!" Beth exploded. "You're about to change the whole structure of this family, plunge us into a completely new existence, and you call it a personal decision?"

"Please don't make a scene," Adam said quietly, but his face grew white.

"Don't you order me around," Beth screamed. "I think it was your duty to tell me what you were planning!"

"I thought you'd be pleased," Adam said helplessly. "I thought it was what you always wanted."

"That was fifteen years ago." Beth tried to lower her voice.

"I wasn't ready then. The timing was wrong. I couldn't have done it as I know I can now."

"Well, now I'm not ready." She caught her breath before rushing on. "I want a divorce." The words tumbled out uncontrollably.

"You what?"

"I want a divorce. I'm going to marry someone else."

"Who?"

"Dan Bradbury."

Adam began to laugh. "You're being funny, aren't you?"

"It's hardly a joking matter."

"I've met him only once, but I know a great deal about him. He's all wrong for you."

"I'm going to marry him." Her voice grew shrill again.

"You mean you are going to leave this house, desert the children, destroy everything to satisfy some romantic fantasy?" Adam asked, almost politely.

"It's not a fantasy," she cried out desperately. All the thoughts, the rationales she had composed during the evening were forgotten. She had had it all figured out. Adam was misunderstanding what she was saying. "Adam, I'm not happy. There are things I want, things I need."

"Are you aware of how destructive you're being?"

"What's so constructive about living an unhappy life, growing resentful and bitter? Staying around would be a hell of a lot more destructive to you and the children."

"Beth, you're behaving like a spoiled, self-indulgent brat, who's never grown up." He stopped and eyed her for a minute. "Have you been drinking?"

"I haven't had a drink all day." She felt her mouth go dry. "But wouldn't you like it if I had. That would make it better. The drunken wife who doesn't know what she's talking about." She swallowed hard. "I don't need a drink to make it through the day since I met Dan."

"Are you implying that I'm to blame for your drinking?"

"What do you think?"

"You were hardly a teetotaler when we met," he said drily.

"You're revolting," Beth hissed.

"Calling me names isn't going to solve anything." Adam was suddenly completely in control.

The silence that followed his last statement frightened her, and the need to hurt him, break his smug self-righteousness was overwhelming.

"Does my father know about your plans?" she asked as a new thought crossed her mind. "Is that why it's so important we go up to Greenwich for Thanksgiving?"

"He knows I'm thinking of it."

"And you couldn't wait until the weekend because it's more important to shore up the Republican Party than consider Jimmy Jay's feelings, is that it?"

The question seemed to shake him up. "That's the most twisted thought I've ever heard." He became angry.

"No, it's not." Beth relished his change of mood. "When do you start taking advantage of Jimmy Jay as a political pawn in your campaign, or are you going to hide him from the conservatives who might vote for you?"

"Jimmy Jay is a fact of our lives. His color seems to bother you more than it does me."

"How dare you!" Beth stood up and faced him. "If it were up to me I would have informed my father that Jimmy Jay *and* Hannah were coming with us for Thanksgiving dinner, or we would not be coming."

"I'm more tactful than you are."

"You're lying."

"No, I'm practical." Adam's calm manner returned, and it was maddening. "I am completely aware that Jimmy Jay is colored and there is no changing it, just as there is no way for me to change the color of my eyes. I shall neither hide him nor expose him. If there is someone sick enough who will not vote for me because my nephew is a Negro, I don't want that vote. But I believe there are more people who will clearly see my indifference to the color of people, and they will vote in my favor."

"So you are planning on using him to get elected."

"Just as much as I will 'use'—and I say the word advisedly—the rest of my family to help me." He was very pale, but his voice was firm. "I'm in this race to win, Beth."

"Well, I won't be around."

They stood glaring at each other for a long moment.

"If you think I'm going to plead with you, Beth, you're wrong." Adam broke the silence. "But I'm telling you right now, I'm not going to give you a divorce." He turned quickly and walked out of the room.

"I'll get it somehow," she cried, running after him. "You won't be able to stop me."

He turned to look at her. "You're hysterical and you don't know what you're saying."

"I do, I do, I do," she screamed uncontrollably.

The door slammed loudly and he was gone.

"I hope I never see you again as long as I live," she wailed loudly at the closed door.

"You chased my daddy away."

Beth swung around and saw Sarah standing in her nightgown, her hair disheveled, tears streaming down her face.

Getting hold of herself quickly, Beth walked over to the sleepy child. "It's all right, darling," she said softly, getting down to her knees. "It's nothing serious." She tried to hug the child.

"I want Daddy," Sarah whispered, pushing Beth away from her.

"Daddy will come back, honey, don't worry."

"I hate you." Sarah's voice shook, and she started hitting Beth with clenched fists.

Beth tried to grab the child's arms. "Stop it," she said firmly, without raising her voice. "It will be all right."

Sarah struggled for a minute and suddenly she threw herself into Beth's arms. "You won't leave me too, will you, Mommy?"

Cuddling Sarah in her arms, Beth knew she had to stay. Tears trickled down her cheeks as she stroked her daughter's hair. "I won't leave you, pet, I promise." Dan and her life with him were moving farther and farther away. Her dreams were clouding over. She continued holding Sarah and felt the dampness of her tears falling on her hands.

Drew Van Ess collapsed shortly after they finished their Thanksgiving dinner. They were all sitting in the library. The fire was lit, the children were playing on the floor, Mary was watching television and Adam was in the middle of a conversation with him. Beth was just walking into the room with a tray when she saw her father keel over.

Mary began to scream. Beth put the tray down quickly and shouted for Martha to come and get the girls. That they had seen too much death was her first thought. They were too young to be involved in it to such an extent. Adam was on the phone calling the doctor. In spite of the commotion around, Beth wondered how Adam knew whom to call and what to say. She tried to calm her mother, and saw Martha lead the children out of the room, but her ear was tuned into Adam's conversation. It occurred to her that he knew how seriously ill her father was and suddenly understood his adamance about spending the day in Greenwich. Adam knew and never told her.

The doctor pronounced Drew dead at 10:00 P.M.

Mary, who had been given a sedative shortly after Drew collapsed, went into another hysterical fit, then fell into a fretful sleep. Beth sat down in what used to be her father's chair. It was then that the full impact of his death struck her. The house was dead. Everyone was dead. She was dead. Allen was dead. She closed her eyes and thought of her brother. What would he have been like, had he lived? What would she have been like if Allen had not died? Would she have married Adam? Probably not, she decided. It would have been someone like Dan. Dan! The mere thought of him and the idea that she would probably not see him again, pained her more than what was taking place around her.

Beth sat in the library watching the fire die and a chill came into the room. She looked over at her mother and was surprised to see her awake, staring into space.

"Are you all right, Mother?"

"I should have let him go when he wanted to, years ago," Mary said listlessly. "Had I let him go then, he would not have been able to leave me now that I'm old and have no one to care for me. He was a lecherous old man from the day I married him."

Beth was horrified at what her mother was saying, but dared not move.

Mary continued, but her tone changed. "I did love him, though. He was kind." She stopped and Beth hoped she would doze off. She knew she was listening to the ramblings of an old, distraught woman and, as Drew's daughter, she did not want to be there. Her mother began to speak again, and Beth got up and took a drink. She would shut out what Mary was saying. She had to. The rambling went on, and the love, hate, passion, disgust, adoration, deification and slander overlapped, so that it was hard to tell what Mary felt about her husband. She was totally unaware of Beth sitting in the room.

Beth was half dozing, still listening to her mother's monotonous voice when Adam came in. Dawn was breaking and the eerie light coming through the large Gothic windows was frightening.

Mary sat up when she saw Adam. "I don't want that Jew in my house."

Beth was about to react, but Adam restrained her. "I'll go get Martha," he said, and walked out.

Drew was buried Monday following Thanksgiving in the church he loved, in Southampton. It had been opened especially for the funeral and everyone who ever knew Drew was there. Mary conducted herself with the greatest decorum and ran the show as though it were a major motion picture production. She was dressed in black, her hat and veil were correct, her manner perfect. Beth looked at the massive attendance and was moved. She caught a glimpse of Sam Ryan and was surprised to see him. The only person absent, at Mary's request, was Adam.

Drew Van Ess's will was cynical, cruel and enlightening.

He left the apartment on Park Avenue to Beth and Adam. He left Beth a sizable sum of money. Trust funds were set up for his two granddaughters, the principle of which was to be given to them when they were twenty-five. Various sums were left to Martha, Joseph and Drew's secretary, who had served him for many years. Money was left to his Republican club. The rest of his fortune, which was a sizable one, was left to his beloved wife, Mary. It was to be placed into an irrevocable trust, the income to be given to her until her death, at which time it would be given to his granddaughters. The trust was to be administered by his loyal and devoted son-in-law, and friend, Adam J. Stillman. In return for the work involved in administering the inheritance, Adam was to receive $100,000, which he hoped would enable Adam to resume his political work, which he had so long neglected.

Part II

TODAY

1

"Super," Tony Abbot called out and the assitant cameraman shut off a fan and the glaring flood lights.

Lauri Eddington stooped slightly and relaxed her body in relief from the heat. Her hair, which minutes before had been wind-blown for the picture she was doing, now settled wispily over her face.

"That was great, Lauri," Tony said as he came toward her and lifted her face to his with one hand while the other smoothed away the hair, exposing the perfection of features which had made her the top model in the United States.

"Thanks, Tony," Lauri said as she moved toward the tall straw peacock chair which stood in the corner of the huge room and threw herself into it. "But I'm completely pooped, dead, beat and thirsty."

"I'll get you some coffee," Joey, Tony's assistant, called out, and Lauri smiled her thanks, shook her head and closed her eyes.

Tony went about putting things in order, rolling up the white canvas screen which was used as a backdrop for the perfume ad he had just photographed, pushing the fan to a far corner of the room, fluffing up the numerous pillows on which Lauri had sat while being photographed, and rearranging the long-stemmed red roses on the coffee table. Finished, he turned off some more lights, leaving an air of mystery in the Central Park South studio. Only one table lamp still glowed in the far corner of the room, the rest of the light coming from the double, ceiling-high windows that faced the park. It was early evening and Tony stared down at the miniscule people walking in the twilight and marveled at the magnificent sight of the bare, stark-looking trees which had a few dry leaves still clinging to their branches. The picture, although desolate, was startling and beautiful. For a brief moment, he felt breathless at the sight; then, sighing contentedly, he turned toward Lauri and stared at her.

He had photographed most of the beautiful women in the United States and abroad, but somehow no one compared with Lauri Eddington. In fact, some were probably more beautiful, more perfect when taken feature for feature, but none of them had the grace, the elegance, the special quality that Lauri had. It was her coloring, he decided. Being half Italian, she had her mother's olive-toned skin, amazing amber-colored eyes, set wide apart and slanted upward, framed by incredibly long, dark lashes. She also had her father's Anglican square chin and high cheekbones. Her hair was a dark auburn and hung straight down to her shoulders, accentuating her long, graceful neck. It was her mouth, however, that was most extraordinary. It was almost too full, but its shape was soft and frighteningly expressive. Tony was so captivated by her beauty that it took him a minute to realize she had fallen asleep while he had been cleaning up. The lips quivered slightly and he suddenly knew she was not only tired, but hurting. She had changed, he thought sadly. Although still lively and amusing, filled with a warm spirit, there was a shadow of sadness about her in recent months and now, in this unguarded moment, it had surfaced.

Walking over to her, he pushed her hair back from the high forehead and she opened her eyes and looked at him gratefully.

"And I don't particularly like women," he said, as he smiled down at her. The pain in her eyes hurt him. "George is jealous of you, even without having met you," he said lightly, trying to make a mockery of his statement.

Lauri pressed his hand and smiled affectionately at him. "I love you, too, Tony, and if I were photographing you, I'd probably do for you what you've done for me." She paused and a serious look came into her eyes. "Why, you've made me one of the top models in the country and don't think for a minute that I don't know it and appreciate it. No one has ever been able to get me to look like you do. It's unbelievable."

"I've got an awful lot to work with, you silly girl." Embarrassed, he turned away and picked up a pack of cigarettes. "How about having dinner with George and me? He's a great cook, you know, and he's simply dying to meet you." His tone changed and he became uncharacteristically effeminate.

Lauri lowered her eyes. Tony was behaving strangely. He had never before pressed his homosexuality as he was doing at that moment. And who was George, she wondered.

"I'd love it," she said slowly, "but Sam Ryan is taking me to the Roosevelt Hotel where the results of the election will be announced."

"Roosevelt!" Tony said with mock horror. "Why would anyone go to that rat hole? No one goes there anymore, ever."

"Stop it, Tony." Lauri tried to keep her tone light. "You know damn well they use the Roosevelt for all sorts of political affairs. Adam Stillman has his headquarters there, and tonight we'll know if he's been reelected to Congress."

"Adam who?" Tony said facetiously.

"Adam *who?*" Lauri started and then realizing Tony was joking, she burst out laughing. "You really are too much."

"You bet I know who Adam is." Tony smiled. "Luv, I've learned enough about politics, civil rights, civil liberties, due process of law, and all that crap since you got involved in politics to last me a lifetime. Why, thanks to you, I might even vote for Adam J. Stillman, Liberal Republican Congressman from the silk stocking district, fighter for all fine causes, good looking, honest, upright and a yid to boot."

"Tony!" Lauri gasped. "I hate it when you use those expressions."

"Can I help it if he's a Jew?" he said with pretended innocence. "Besides, I love it when you get mad."

"Oh, you know what I mean," Lauri calmed down.

"I know what you mean, Lauri, but when you can finally call a spade a spade, then you're really free of bigotry. Adam Stillman is a kike, Sam Ryan is a mick, I'm a fag, and you're a dago. We're all ethnics and I love it. Combined, I no longer feel like a minority in the city. I almost feel sorry for the poor wasps."

Lauri smiled briefly. She had never seen Tony so frivolous or so outspoken. Something was troubling him and she could not imagine what. She stood up and started toward the dressing room which was at the far end of the room and quite invisible since the wooden door blended into the wood paneling of the room.

"Incidentally," Tony called after her, "have you ever met him?"

The phone rang at that moment and Lauri quickly closed the door behind her, relieved at not having to answer Tony's question.

Turning on the light in the room, she stood for a long moment and stared at herself in the full-length mirror. After all the time she had known Adam, she still got nervous when anyone associated her directly with him.

Walking over to the stall shower, she turned on the water. She was feeling ill and hoped a shower would refresh her. She had to be in full control of herself on this special evening.

She took great pains when applying her makeup, dabbing extra rouge on her cheeks and darkening the makeup around her eyes. She rarely used the stuff, but now she felt drawn and tense. Done with her face, she slipped into the Oscar de La Renta gown. She wore no undergarments, since the dress called for a smooth look. Turning, she looked at her figure in profile. Her breasts were firm, her stomach flat, her slim, tall, lithe figure beautifully outlined in the simple dress, but she was aware she had gained some weight. It did not show, but she felt it. With a sigh, she clipped on large gold looped earrings and carefully latched a heavy gold Tiffany love bracelet onto her wrist. Stepping into beige sandals, she stood back and looked at herself carefully. Weight gain or not, she looked well and was grateful for her appearance. Picking up her luscious red-fox coat, she reentered the studio.

"How do I look?" she asked.

"You've looked in the mirror, Lauri, and you know you look sensational." He seemed preoccupied and lit a cigarette and poured himself a drink. "Your coffee is on the table," he said, indicating the low coffee table which stood in front of a pillow-laden couch, "or would you rather have a drink?"

She did not want the coffee, and the thought of having a drink made her shudder. Slowly, she walked over to the sofa, aware that Tony was now observing her too closely.

"You've gained weight," he said, not taking his eyes off her.

"It's the dress," she answered quickly.

"Yeah, maybe," Tony said, although not convinced. "Which brings to mind the question of what's with the new style you've suddenly gone into. The dresses, the jewelry, the makeup. What gives?" He was used to seeing her in tight fitting dungarees, massive shirts tied around the waist carelessly with ribbons and belts, high heeled boots and no makeup.

"I'm trying on the grown-up look," she answered, and threw herself down on the couch. "Don't you like it?"

"What about that drink?" He ignored her question.

Lauri looked over at the mantel clock. "Sam won't be here for another half hour, so make it a light scotch."

Tony poured her drink and came over to sit beside her.

"How old is Sam?" he asked, handing her the glass.

"Gee, I don't really know," Lauri said as she smiled her thanks. "One never thinks of age with Sam."

"Well, I'd say he's well over sixty, and, frankly, if I were your father I'd be furious. For Christ's sake, he's more than twice your age."

"You never really got to know my father," Lauri answered haltingly, aware that Tony had used a colloquial expression rather than a specific reference to her father, but Larry Eddington's presence separated them and she treaded lightly in her reply. "He was an artist, and to him age was immaterial." A far away look came into her eyes. "As a matter of fact, Papa met Sam and they got on very well." She turned to Tony. "Besides, there's nothing between Sam and me. We're friends. We have the same interests, enjoy the same people, the same jokes, the same politics. I've known him for years, you know. My husband introduced him to me when we were first married, and we spent many evenings together."

"That's probably why he's your ex-husband," Tony said sagely. "I'll tell you one thing for sure, if I had a wife who looked like you—heaven forbid—and someone as suave and rich as Sam Ryan was always hanging around, I'd get suspicious."

Lauri smiled. "If it were up to Brad, I'd have gone to bed with Sam if he thought it would help him in his career."

"That's disgusting," Tony said angrily. "I don't believe it."

Lauri stared at him and was aware that it was the first time she had downgraded Brad to anyone.

"Thank God I'm gay," Tony said, with conviction. Then, "So you're not sleeping with Sam?"

"No, I'm not," Lauri said and stood up. Tony was one of her closest friends, and in the past she would have confided in him, but now the conversation had grown too intimate and she did not want to continue. "I'd better get my things together," she said, and hurried toward the dressing room.

"So if it's not Sam, who is it?" Tony called out after her, surprised at her secretiveness. It was unlike her.

He leaned back, trying to figure out the change that had taken place in her. He had known her since she was a sophomore at the High School of Performing Arts and he was her dance instructor. She was a sweet, warm girl who was no beauty at the time. Her eyes were enormous in proportion to the thin face, the dark hair stringy, her body undeveloped. Yet there was a quality in her that attracted him from the day they met. She was studying to be an actress and he could not understand why she was trying for the stage; it held no special interest for her.

"My father wants me to be an actress," she said simply.

"My mother wants me to be a dancer," Tony remembered answering.

As their friendship developed, Tony discovered her most captivating trait. She was like a chameleon. She had the ability to take on the moods and personalities of all who touched her life. She lived with her father, and she made a greater effort than any other student trying to please him. When Tony confessed to her that he wanted to be a photographer rather than a dancer, she promptly became interested in photography and helped him compose a portfolio. Her devotion to him was boundless, and he was deeply grateful.

It was a difficult time in Tony's life. His father had died when he was an infant and his mother, an overbearing woman, devoted all of her time to her only son. Girls frightened him, boys attracted him. The thought that he was a homosexual terrified him. When his male dance instructor seduced him, his confusion and embarrassment were overwhelming. He had enjoyed the affair with the man but was still not willing to admit he was a homosexual. His attraction and friendship with Lauri relieved some of his fears, and just before his first solo dance recital he went to bed with her. He knew she was a virgin and that she was infatuated with him. He was fully aware that he was using her. With feelings of unbearable guilt, he canceled his appearance and left for London, where he accepted homosexuality and gave up the idea of becoming a dancer. His letter of explanation to Lauri was the only love letter he ever wrote. He did not ask or expect her to understand, much less forgive, but the deep love he felt for her was evident in every line.

He took up photography and devoted all his energies to it. He rose rapidly in the field and became one of the best-known fashion photographers on the Continent. His sexual preferences became progressively mixed, and although his companions were predominantly men, he did have affairs with women. The fears of his early youth were realized and dismissed. The idea that he would one day marry was not out of the question. He thought of Lauri often and, although she had never answered his letter, he was sure that one day they would meet and resume their friendship. When he returned to New York, years later, and she walked into his studio, he knew instantly that she had not changed and that further explanations about their aborted friendship were not necessary. It was as though he had never been away. He had been expecting her, having chosen her picture from a set of photographs sent to him by a modeling agency. The pictures he had seen were not very good, but he knew she had developed just as he had imagined she would. He was nervous that morning while waiting for her, and he was pleased. Continuity was sorely lacking in his life, but he had learned to live with it. Lauri brought back the only bright period in his unhappy youth.

She was a struggling model the day she came into his studio. She had her back to him when he walked in and he had a minute to observe her. She was taller than he remembered and quite thin, but the silhouette was extraordinarily graceful. Then she turned and he caught his breath. She was perfect. He saw her cock her head and bite her lip, then she rushed toward him and threw herself into his arms, and feelings he had never allowed himself to experience washed over him. After a brief moment, he pushed her away and searched her face.

"You're as beautiful as I knew you would be," he said, touching her face.

"Am I really?" she asked, as large tears of happiness started streaming down her cheeks.

He lowered his eyes. He knew she meant it. This lovely creature was totally unaware of what she looked like or who she was. He could see the insecurity, the lack of identity, the fear.

"Yes, you are," he said, trying to hide the pain he was feeling for her.

The touching humility, the loyalty, the involvement with friends were all still there.

They spoke for hours that day and although she talked a great deal about her life, detailing everything since he had last seen her, he sensed the obvious gaps in her story. What came across clearly was that she was struggling both emotionally and financially. She was alone and frightened. He did not pry but was surprised. Somehow it made no sense that Larry Eddington would not be on hand to help her. She did not elaborate about her father, except to mention that he was living in Palm Beach, and Tony gathered their relationship was strained.

Three years had gone by since then. They were years of grueling hard work. Beautiful as she was, instinctive and willing, she had not been prepared for life and did not understand the fundamental requirements for survival or the need for discipline. Larry, with all his love and devotion, had crippled her. Tony fought with her, pleaded with her, threatened and bribed, but finally he succeeded in teaching her the basics that enabled her to become a top professional model.

He started off by making her work as a fashion model in the garment district.

"You've got to learn everything from scratch. Walking is an art, movement is dance. There must be a reason for every action, and you must know what that reason is."

"I hate Seventh Avenue," she wailed. "I did it for a while, and I can't take it."

"You'll take it and like it," Tony thundered back. "Then you'll start walking down runways for various designers, and what you wear and how you wear it will become outstanding. You'll be seen by the people who count, the editors, the other designers. I want the people who look at you to know they need Lauri Eddington as much as you need them."

As her career took shape her social life became more active. Tony was pleased. She was young and beautiful, but she needed the reassurance about herself to enable her to grow and realize her fuller potential. He watched her form various liaisons with men, involve herself totally every time, and when they were over, she would come back to him with a fuller awareness as to who she was. When Lauri suddenly became interested in the New York political scene, Tony took it for granted that Sam Ryan was her newest lover. But as the weeks and months went by and Lauri never mentioned Sam, except in passing, Tony became concerned. He could see her sliding back emotionally, and he blamed Sam for it. He was too old for her, too sophisticated, too demanding. Lauri was in over her head, and Tony was convinced she needed help. She needed his help. She depended on him.

Tony lit a cigarette, trying to avoid a thought he had been suppressing for a long time. Yes, Lauri did need him and depended on him, but somehow, with the passage of time, he had grown to need her and depend on her, as well. Lauri had become indispensable to him. It seemed unfair. He had worked hard to become emotionally independent, be free of the need for people or things. He had succeeded in uncluttering his life, and although he loved Lauri, he knew he could never make a serious commitment to her. He was not a monogomous person. Anyone living with him would suffer. For Lauri it would be a disaster.

Nervously, Tony got up and poured himself a drink. Lauri needed someone who would love her, marry her, give her a home and security. She had come a long way from the insecure girl who walked into his studio years back. But in spite of her success as a model and her potential for even greater achievements, she still needed a frame, a base. She needed someone who would serve as a buffer against the daily realities of living. He could not give it to her. He was sure Sam could not either.

Suddenly Tony remembered Lauri saying she was not involved with Sam. He was sure she was not lying. He looked toward the dressing room, puzzled. If it was not Sam, who was it? The idea struck him like a thunderbolt. It was Adam Stillman! The thought distressed him even more. Lauri was not one to be embarrassed by or hide a relationship. Certainly not from him. And if she did not confide in him, the affair was serious and was probably an unhappy one. Somehow, Adam Stillman was hurting Lauri, and no one had a right to hurt her. He would not allow it.

At that moment the downstairs buzzer sounded and Tony knew it was Sam. He had hoped to have a chance to talk to Lauri before she left. Now it was too late.

2

Lauriana Eddington was born on New Year's Eve, one minute after the year 1950 was ushered in, at the elegant Doctor's Hospital on York Avenue in New York City. Although far away from her parents' home on Bank Street in Greenwich Village and certainly above Larry Eddington's means, the hospital was the only one he considered.

"My child will come into the world in style," he stated when his wife protested, "and will get used to it from the start."

Larry was a minor painter who worked as a commercial artist and taught drawing at the New School for Social Research. These menial jobs were, as far as he was concerned, a passing phase until such time as fame and fortune sought him out.

A loose-limbed, six-foot-tall man, Lauri's father looked more like an athlete than an artist. His Scottish and Norwegian ancestry was easily discernible. He had blond hair and blue eyes, a square chin with a deep cleft, and full, sensuous lips. He smiled easily and his laugh was spontaneous and contagious. Aware of fashion, he was meticulous about the way he dressed and spent a great deal of time achieving a casual look. A dreamer with a romantic soul and a tendency toward irresponsibility, he loved colors. Moods were described in color, people and places had their hues. Long before men's fashions gave license for colorful shirts and scarves, Larry wore them. Being highly opinionated, he coped well with his own life-style. For the people involved with him it was more difficult. His mercurial personality made a mockery of daily living since it hid a moral standard verging on the puritanical and an insatiable desire for acceptancy by society.

Everyone who knew Larry was shocked at his choice of a wife. A Neopolitan girl who came from the ravages and poverty of post-war Italy, Anna was a most unlikely wife for Laurence Eddington from Londonderry, Vermont. She stirred something in Larry that excited him from the minute he saw her. She was living in a cold-water flat in lower Manhattan when she began posing for his class at the New School, and in spite of her aggressive, almost arrogant manner, Larry could sense her vulnerability and fear. Within days after meeting her, he invited her to move in with him. They were married one month later.

Lauri's life was a happy one until she was four. Her father and mother doted on her. Their apartment, on the top floor of a brownstone on Bank Street, was spacious. The living room had a huge wood-burning fireplace and a slanting skylight that covered half the room. The master bedroom was large and comfortable. A small room in the back was used for storage until Lauri's birth, at which time it was converted into a nursery. Lauri could not recall when the fights between her parents started. She was very young and she could hear them arguing. One fight grew louder and louder, and Lauri, lying in her bed, trembled with fear. It was only when she heard Robbie, her parents' best friend, interfere and subdue the voices, that she was able to fall asleep.

Then, one day, Anna was gone. Lauri remembered being picked up by Larry from kindergarten, and when they arrived at the apartment Anna was not there. Instead, there was a letter which he tore open and read with great haste. He made no sound, but Lauri saw his expression change and she watched the tears begin to stream down his face. She walked over to him and stood close. With an anguished cry, he picked her up and held her close.

"We don't need her, do we, princess?" he whispered hoarsely.

"Where's Mommy?" Lauri asked, frightened now that her father had spoken.

"Mommy had to leave for a while," he said, more in control. "But Papa is here to take care of you. Just remember that. Papa is here."

The mood of sadness prevailed for a while. Larry seemed unable to adjust to life without Anna. It was in that period that Robbie came often and spent the evenings with them. During the day, Roza Marchiano, the superintendent's wife, who had been Anna's best friend, came in to help. Still, when Roza would be waiting for her at the end of the school day, Lauri would be disappointed that Anna was not the one to take her home. She missed her mother dreadfully and could not understand why she had left her. Instinctively, she knew she could not talk to Larry about it. Instead, she talked to Robbie.

He looked uncomfortable as he told her Anna had gone back to Italy to visit her family.

"But aren't I her family too?" Lauri asked innocently.

"Of course you are," Robbie answered in confusion. Her logic threw him. "But you have your papa and she missed hers," he said lamely.

"Will she ever come back?" Lauri persisted.

"I'm sure she will, baby. I know she loves you and misses you, and I'm sure she won't stay away too long." He said it with an air of assurance, but his ambivalence did not escape her.

Painfully, she began to push thoughts of Anna into the dark recesses of her mind.

Except for a large framed portrait, which Larry had painted and which hung over the fireplace, she did not even remember what her mother looked like, and Larry became her whole world. It was a wonderful world. Fantasy, her father's greatest ally, finally took hold and, when he recovered from the shock of being deserted, he pursued his quest to create a princess of his child. His adoration of her as an infant grew to worship, and he spent every waking hour grooming her for happiness and success. What that success entailed he could not define, but it was to be in the realm of the arts and it would bring her fame and fortune.

Inadvertently, Lauri helped perpetuate these fantasies. Although not beautiful in the conventional sense, she was quite extraordinary looking. Her large eyes were far too big and serious for the little face, framed by long auburn hair. Her mouth was too full, her forehead too high, her cheekbones too pronounced. She was rail thin, and when first meeting her the over-all impression was of a sad, wispy, fragile waif. Her looks, however, were deceiving. She was neither sad nor fragile. She was a bright, uninhibited child, filled with love and compassion. Her humor and easy laughter were in contradiction to the dramatic appearance, and it was that which convinced Larry that she was destined for a career on the stage.

He tried not to pressure her with his ambitions. Until she entered first grade, Lauri had a normal life, surrounded by people who loved her and cared for her every need. When she entered elementary school, Larry began to mold her. Lauri was registered at the Little Red School House and began a rigorous schedule. School, dancing classes, drawing lessons at the Museum of Modern Art, rehearsing for school plays, excursions to the country and attending children's theaters took up all of her time. Larry did not neglect her social life either. He sought out parents of children he felt were worthy of Lauri and gave amusing, fun-filled parties, to which he sent individually painted invitations, and encouraged the mothers to stay and enjoy the festivities.

Having Robbie around helped. He was a perfect balance to Larry's demanding schedule.

A Puerto Rican in his mid-thirties, Roberto Galandez had come to the United States when he was sixteen years old. He was olive-skinned, with dark hair and dancing black eyes. A fairly successful dress designer, he had been part of Lauri's life from the time she was an infant. He had met Larry through Anna, who did some modeling for him before she married, when he first opened his Seventh Avenue dress designing studio. Uneducated and almost crude in manner, he designed instinctively and had an incredible eye for the fashion trends. Being accepted by the Eddingtons was a turning point in his life. Larry brought him to the attention of some small boutiques in the Village and as a result was partially responsible for Robbie's success. He loved Lauri as though she were his own and, in his primitive way, helped relieve her of the pressures imposed by Larry.

The jeans and overalls which Robbie brought her were the perfect contrast to the lacy dresses and organdy pinafores. The doll collection, which was magnificently displayed on her shelf, was made enjoyable when Robbie began to teach her how to make up little dresses for them; the elaborate paint set Larry bought for her sixth birthday was countered by crayons and chalk and colorful paper on which he encouraged her to design outfits for her dolls. While Larry concentrated on the intellectual stimulation, Robbie supplied the tickets for the circus and spent time with her at Coney Island riding the cyclone and walking along the boardwalk eating sugared candy. Occasionally, Larry went with them, but his distaste for the teeming multitudes eventually won out and Robbie spent time alone with the child. Larry accepted Lauri's need for what Robbie offered her, knowing that in the end he alone would prevail. He was there when she woke, he was there when she went to bed, he nursed her when she was ill and he helped her through all the hurdles encountered when she became aware of her peers and started reaching out for friends. Just as he was there the day he held her close and told her Anna had died in a car accident on the Amalfi Drive in Italy.

It was a hot Sunday in August when Lauri awoke to find her father sitting in a lounging chair on the little terrace outside the living room. Taking her juice from the kitchen, she walked out, climbed into his lap, and rested her head against his shoulder. Looking up at the clear blue sky, she heard the words but their meaning escaped her. The sadness in her father's voice made her want to cry.

"Does it mean it will be a longer time before Mama comes home?" she asked, not daring to look at him.

"It means your mama is never coming home," he answered wearily.

Never. The word made no sense. Never had to have an end, she reasoned childishly. It simply meant a longer time before she could see her mother. She stared vacantly at the sky and saw a little white cloud drifting by. It looked like a bird in flight. She followed it with her eyes until it disappeared behind some buildings. Still she held on to its image. Closing her eyes, she visualized its flight toward the sea. Never would be over, she decided, when her little cloud reached the horizon. She tried to prolong its journey. Never was a long time, she understood that. Slowly she brought the cloud to the water's edge and held it briefly before it sank out of sight. The cloud had gone down, but like the sun, it would rise again, Lauri thought with relief. She opened her eyes. A white cloud was drifting by. It was moving more quickly and Lauri tried to keep up with it. As soon as it hit the horizon again, she thought more frantically, never would be over . . . Her mind began to spin as the cloud went down into the water, rose again, circled by her house and went toward the horizon yet again . . . Never would never end . . .

Lauri was eight years old and she knew she would never see her mother again. She tried to remember what her mother looked like, but the image was blurred.

"Papa, may I go visit Robbie?" she asked.

Larry was taken aback. He had been concerned with what her reaction would be and was stunned at how little it mattered.

"I'd like you to stay with me for a little while," he answered, pressing her closer to him. "Papa needs you and wants you near him."

Lauri nestled closer to him. Her father needed her! She mulled over the thought. It was a strange revelation and she liked it.

When Lauri graduated from elementary school, Larry took it for granted she would enter the High School of Performing Arts and take up acting. She was fourteen and had grown into a shy, gangly adolescent who was suddenly too tall, still too thin and quite awkward. She was not at all sure she wanted to be an actress. She would have preferred the Parson's School of Design. Larry was very upset. Not wanting to disappoint him, she auditioned for the school board—which was torturous—was accepted, and went along with Larry's wishes rather than her own.

Lauri's freshman year was grim. She did not like her schoolmates, finding them pushy, phony and aggressive. She had no idea how to compete with them, and slowly the gay little girl withdrew into herself. It was during that period that she suddenly missed her mother and wondered why she had deserted her. The thought that she had done something to cause Anna's departure began to prey on her mind. It also caused her to have great feelings of guilt toward Larry. She was fully aware of how hard he worked at giving her a full and complete life, and she felt disloyal. She tried to hide her misery, but in spite of her efforts, she became morose and brooding.

Larry watched Lauri's growing unhappiness but had no idea how to reach her or make her pain disappear. He redoubled his efforts at entertaining her. They did not miss a Broadway show, a ballet or a concert. He went out of his way to discover elegant little restaurants that he hoped she would enjoy, gave small dinner parties with entertaining guests, and personally designed a more grown-up wardrobe for her which Robbie dutifully had executed by his dressmakers. He also started taking her to the various parties given by New York's social elite.

For the most part, Lauri enjoyed and was grateful for the extra attention. Going to the homes of the wealthy, however, bothered her. She felt out of place and was convinced their presence was forced rather than spontaneous. She also noted that Robbie was never invited to join them on these occasions. It did not seem to bother him, but it upset Lauri. When she asked Larry about it, he became uncomfortable.

"He comes from a different world," he said seriously. "He'd be bored."

"It's because he's Puerto Rican and polishes his fingernails," Lauri said more to herself than to her father.

"That's ridiculous," Larry exploded.

"No, I don't think it's ridiculous at all." Lauri looked directly at him. "Your hosts are pure white, rich and social. Robbie is poor, Hispanic and uneducated." She was tempted to point out that they too were fringe guests, but she knew it would be pointless.

"Don't be so quick to knock appearances." Larry regained some of his composure. "Being seen in the right places with the right people has never done anybody any harm."

Appearances, social standing, trying to be part of a world that did not want you, Lauri thought bitterly. It was all wrong, of that she was sure. Why it was wrong eluded her.

It all changed when Lauri entered her sophomore year and met Tony Abbot, the dance instructor. Dark and strikingly handsome, Lauri was attracted to him. It was the first time she felt a physical need to touch someone of the opposite sex, other than her father. Physical attractions, sexual relations were fathomless mysteries. Dance classes, until she met Tony, were a nightmare. He seemed to sense her discomfort and went out of his way to stand beside her during class, helping her with the difficult steps, and giving her a feeling of security. When he offered to help her after school, she accepted.

It was a turning point in her life. They would meet after the school day was over and he would work with her. The hours spent with him at the studio were the highlight of her existence. Often when she arrived there, she would watch him practice his step and dance routines. Their relationship was of a dance instructor and pupil. Then one day Lauri arrived early and found him engrossed in an impromptu dance. She stood aside and watched. He was magnificently built. Dressed in black tights and a fitted white shirt, every muscle was emphasized and seemed to vibrate. Her eyes swept over his body, taking in the muscular thighs, the flat stomach, the thin but powerful rib cage, the controlled movements of his arms, and the beauty of his hands. It was his face, however, that made her catch her breath. It was wet with perspiration; his dark hair falling over his forehead almost covering his eyes, his mouth was slightly open and he was breathing heavily. Suddenly he stopped dancing and threw his arms up over his head, his eyes opened wide and were staring at the ceiling. The look of desperation and pain emanating from the statuelike figure frightened her. She felt as though she was seeing the depths of human despair. It was then he saw her. The look disappeared and a warm smile came to his face.

It was the beginning of a deep friendship. From that day, her schooling took on a new meaning, and within a short time she began to rebel against her father's domination. It wasn't anything Tony did or said; it was simply having someone who listened to her and accepted her as she was, without criticism or recriminations.

The change in Lauri was abrupt and obvious. It started with her refusal to wear the clothes Larry thought appropriate. Instead, she emulated the manners and dress of her schoolmates. She became sloppy and careless about her appearance, behavior and speech. Larry hated obscenities, and Lauri found herself purposely injecting words which offended him whenever possible. His disapproval no longer frightened her. As a child she accepted her father's opinion about everything without question. Now she disregarded him completely. She became part of the school scene. The Eddington household was turned into an on-going party, with everyone coming over at will. The cultured times which she and Larry had shared were replaced by a stream of youngsters who were too loud, played their records endlessly, stayed too long and threw beer and soda cans all over the floor. It was open house to everyone but Tony. He was her private and special friend and she did not want to share him with anyone.

Their friendship was exposed the day she went to the ballet with him —without telling Larry—and did not come home until 10:30 that night. She had tried calling her father, but could not reach him.

When she walked into the apartment, Larry was settled in the wing chair in the living room, pretending to be absorbed in a magazine.

"Hi, Papa." She walked over and kissed him on the forehead. "Sorry I'm late."

"Where've you been?" he asked nonchalantly.

"I went to the ballet with a friend, Tony Abbot," she said, deciding at that moment to drop the charade.

Larry raised his brows in surprise. "Who's he?"

"A dance teacher at school." She dropped her books and went into the kitchen.

"You've never mentioned him before." Larry was standing in the doorway.

"Didn't I?" Lauri simulated surprise.

"You know you didn't." Larry tried to sound patient.

"Well, I'm mentioning him now," Lauri said, with irritation. "He's a wonderful, good looking and talented friend. He's a great dancer, and if he decides to take up ballet seriously, Ballanchine will grab him."

"Has he been accepted?" Larry asked with disdain.

"He would be if he wanted it."

Larry placed her food on the table and sat watching her in silence. Lauri was upset. Her father never really liked any of her friends. He always acted gracious and charming, but somehow he would find fault with them when they were out of earshot. Now he was tearing Tony down without having met him. "Papa, I think it would be nice if I introduced you to Tony. He's awfully nice and very bright. I know you'll like him."

"Why not invite him to dinner," Larry said carefully. "You know I'm always pleased to meet your friends."

To Lauri's great surprise, Larry liked Tony, or appeared to. They had a great deal in common, talking about art, theater, painting and dance. When Tony left, Lauri dared not ponder her good fortune.

Relieved of the deception, Lauri began to see more and more of Tony. When she discovered his interest in photography, she immediately took it up as an avocation. He was doing free-lance work, and she would wander the streets with him scouting locations for pictures he wanted to take. He taught her how to develop film and she became quite adept in the darkroom. She carried equipment for him when he had an assignment or needed pictures for his portfolio. When his time was taken up preparing for a solo performance at the YMHA, she relieved him of the burden of worrying about arranging his schedule so that it would not interfere with his dance rehearsals. He reciprocated fully. Her schoolwork improved with his help. He listened to her talk about her inner turmoil and tried to guide her toward independence from Larry without promoting outright rebellion. He gave her confidence where friends were concerned. Her inability to form relationships with her peer group was deep-seated.

As the date of the dance recital grew closer, Tony became more agitated. He broke several appointments with her and Lauri became concerned. A week before the performance, Tony did not show up for his class. She rushed to his house.

Tony opened the door for her and her heart sank. He was pale and disheveled, and the rings around his eyes indicated that he had not slept.

"Are you sick?" she asked, putting her hand out to touch his forehead.

"No," he snapped and walked into the apartment, leaving the front door ajar.

She followed him into the living room. "May I make you a cup of tea, or something?" she asked tentatively. She was unaccountably nervous at being alone with him, although they had spent many afternoons in the apartment while his mother was out.

"I don't want to be a dancer. I want to photograph beautiful people, beautiful things," he said angrily.

"You can do both."

"Never. I want to be the best in one field, not second best in two."

She came to sit beside him. "Calm down, Tony," she said. "First, do the recital and then decide." She felt calmer as she continued reassuringly. "Why, you're the most talented and beautiful man I've ever seen, and it's just a matter of finishing what you started. You've committed yourself to the 'Y,' and I think you have to go through with it. Then you can make up your mind."

He put his arm around her thin shoulder and a small smile appeared on his face. "You sound so grown up, Lauri."

"I am grown up, except that no one is willing to admit it," she answered defiantly.

He lifted her face to his and kissed her gently on the lips. It was the first time any boy had ever kissed her, and it excited her. When he moved his face away, she put her hand to his cheek and caressed it.

"Would you do it again?" she whispered. "It was so nice."

He kissed her more passionately and she responded, turning her body toward him.

Lauri could not remember undressing, but suddenly her dungarees were lying beside the couch, her sweater was off, and Tony was spreading her legs apart and pushing himself gently into her. She dared not move.

"Are you all right?" he asked in a strained voice.

"I want you." She found it difficult to talk.

Gentle as he was in his lovemaking, a cry escaped her and she saw him wince.

"It's all right," she said after a minute, and slowly began to move her body rhythmically, accepting him deeper and deeper, the lips of her vagina contracting around his genitals.

He lay on top of her long after the warm semen seeped down between her thighs, his body relaxing and his breathing returning to normal.

Lauri was sure he was asleep. Carefully she wrapped her arms around his shoulders and pressed him to her.

"Thank you, Lauri," she heard him whisper in her ear. "Thank you for everything you've done, for everything you've said. Thank you for being."

She put her hands to his face and lifted it so she could look at him. His eyes were dark and somber. "Thank *you*, Tony," she said seriously. "Now I'm really grown up."

They did not meet for the next few days. Tony was busy rehearsing and Lauri was preparing for his debut. She designed a special dress which Robbie had made up by one of his dressmakers. Larry helped her with the accessories and she went to Vidal Sassoon to have her hair done. Thoughts of her affair with Tony sent shivers of happiness through her and she could not wait to see him after the performance. She was his date and they were going out to celebrate.

Tony was to pick her up at 7:00 in the evening. She was fully dressed by 6:00 and sat on the balcony waiting for him. Larry was painting in the living room and she noticed he was agitated.

The hour slipped by and Tony did not show up. At 8:00, she called his home. The performance was scheduled for 8:30. There was no answer. At 9:00, Larry called up the YMHA. The performance of Tony Abbot was canceled. No explanation was given.

Lauri undressed slowly and got into bed. The hurt and disappointment were too great even for tears. Larry came into her room and sat on the edge of the bed. He wished she would cry.

"I'm just ugly, I guess," she said finally. "I'm just nothing, and he couldn't stand to have me around anymore."

"That's ridiculous," Larry said angrily. "You're beautiful, princess, and don't you forget it."

"There's something wrong with me, Papa," she persisted. "I have no real friends because I do and say things that are . . ." The tears began to flow and the words choked in her throat. "Oh, Papa, what's wrong with me, what's wrong with me, what's wrong with me?"

Larry sat by helplessly listening to her question being repeated over and over. Finally, unable to let her think she was responsible for what had happened, he said very quietly, "Princess, there's nothing wrong with you. You're beautiful, you're young, you're kind and gentle. It's Tony who has the problem."

"What do you mean? What problem?" Lauri asked sitting up.

He cupped her chin in his hand. "You see, my little love," his voice was very low, "Tony is a homosexual."

She stared at him in disbelief. She wanted to laugh but did not dare. She had gone to bed with Tony and, although he was the only man she had ever slept with, she was sure he had made love to her. The memory of the afternoon with him was vivid in her mind. Tony was a man.

"Papa, you're wrong." She wiped her eyes and got out of bed. She could not stand looking at Larry. "I know you're wrong," she said more defiantly.

"No, I'm not," Larry said with assurance. Suddenly the truth dawned on him. "You've been to bed with him!" It was not a question, it was a statement.

Lauri ran out of the room. Larry followed quickly behind. "You have, haven't you?" he screamed, totally out of control.

She turned and looked at him blankly. Without warning, he picked up his hand and struck her across the face. "You have, haven't you?" He hit her again. "You little tramp. You little ungrateful whore. You're just like your mother."

As soon as the words were out of his mouth he turned and rushed into his bedroom.

Lauri watched him go. In the years since Anna left, her name was rarely mentioned, and when it was it was usually in the most flattering and pleasant way. But more devastating was the accusation about Tony. Larry had said it with great authority, and although he usually spoke in that manner, it was different this time. He seemed to know. She closed her eyes trying to suppress a thought which was surfacing and which she was not willing or ready to accept. She shook her head, hoping the motion would push it away. Walking into her bedroom, she threw herself on her bed, sobbing.

Lauri did not know what woke her, but suddenly she sat up and realized she had fallen asleep. She looked over at the clock. It was past 2:00 A.M. Her mouth was dry and she wanted a drink of water. She was walking toward the kitchen when she heard sounds from the living room. She peeked in and saw her father sitting in an armchair, his head in his hands. Robbie was standing beside him, his hands on Larry's shoulder. It was a completely innocent sight, yet there was an intimacy between the two men that was totally revealing, and the truth which she had ignored in the past was unveiled. Robbie and Larry were lovers! A grotesque picture fell into place. Her whole life up to that moment took shape. Incidents through the years of growing up, hints by people which she had ignored, tiny insignificant gestures which she had accepted as natural between Robbie and Larry, her mother's sudden departure. Often she had wondered why her father had no girlfriend. She had always dismissed it, knowing he had many women friends. None ever slept over, but it was obvious that he would not expose his daughter to a mistress. Certainly no man had ever slept over. Evenings when Robbie stayed for dinner would often end with Larry leaving with him and returning in the early hours of the morning, but it had never dawned on her to sus-pect their relationship. They were, as far as she was concerned, two at-tractive men who were going out on the town. All these thoughts flashed through her mind in quick succession, but the most dominant was the duplicity in Larry's attitude toward Robbie. Robbie was good enough to have as a lover, but not good enough to take to the elegant social parties he went to. Lauri felt sick. The taste of spittle rose in her throat and she began to gag.

Both men looked up and Robbie ran to her.

"You okay, princess?" he asked with concern.

"I'll be all right." She smiled wanly and looked at her father. He was ashen. She walked over to him and forced herself to touch his arm.

Their eyes met and held for a long minute. She refused to be stared down, and it was at that moment that Larry knew she had guessed his relationship with Robbie. He lowered his eyes in confusion.

3

On the surface nothing changed in Lauri's life. She continued with her schooling but stopped inviting friends over, convinced her discovery about Larry was common knowledge and she was deeply embarrassed. She brooded over Tony and wondered where he was. She was not angry at him, assuming he had reasons for his actions. When a letter from him arrived, postmarked London, England, she was pleased, but it did little to relieve her unhappiness. Although the letter was filled with love and overflowing with sincere sorrow at having caused her pain, there was no explanation for what he had done. Somehow it gave credence to what Larry had said, and her feelings of separatedness, of being different, became more acute. Her affair with Tony and the revelation about her father, had stripped her of innocence. Having misjudged the sexuality of the two men in her life, her insecurities were greater than ever. She was no longer a little girl, but she was completely unable to face womanhood.

Moving away from Larry was the solution, but she knew she was too young to go it alone. She also had nowhere to go.

Summer vacation arrived and Lauri was determined to spend it away from New York. When an advertisement in the *Village Voice* for a mother's helper on Fire Island caught her attention, she applied for the job without telling Larry. Once accepted, she informed him of it as a *fait accompli*.

The idea that Lauri was going to spend two months away with people he did not know was an horrendous blow to Larry. He had walked around Lauri like a shadow since the night of the scene about Tony Abbot, trying to maintain the air of a hurt father who was displeased with his daughter's behavior. His facility at sidestepping painful realities obscured the truth of what had actually taken place between Lauri and himself. As far as he was concerned Tony Abbot had taken advantage of his precious little girl, and time would wipe out the memory of that dreadful evening. Being informed that Lauri wanted to be away from him was therefore staggering.

"Who are the people?" Larry asked, controlling his dismay. Lauri had never been away from home. On occasion he permitted a friend to sleep over in their home. She was never allowed to sleep out.

"A Mrs. Joyce Green," Lauri answered.

"Is there a Mr. Green?" he asked.

"I don't really know."

"Where does she live on Fire Island?"

"I don't know."

"I won't let you go unless I can speak to the woman," Larry said adamantly. "Where does she live in New York?"

"West End Avenue and Ninety-third Street."

"It's not the best neighborhood," Larry said almost to himself. "Does she have other help?"

"Papa, I didn't interview her. She interviewed me," Lauri said patiently. "She's pleasant, friendly and her five-year-old son is adorable. She wants me to go with her, and I'm going."

"Not before I meet her," Larry thundered.

Joyce Green understood Larry's reservations and invited him up for a drink. Lauri went along, concerned with the impression Larry would make.

The meeting went well. A large woman in her mid-thirties, Joyce had been a former Seventh Avenue model who married her boss and divorced him shortly after her baby was born. She was properly impressed with the elegant Mr. Eddington, listened with attention to his various comments and opinions and appeared genuinely interested in his requirements for his daughter's safety and comfort. During the hour-long visit, she looked over at Lauri several times, with genuine affection. She had liked Lauri from the minute she came in for the first interview. There was a sensitivity about her, a desire to please mingled with a pride that were touching. Joyce had made up her mind about Lauri before meeting Larry. Now she was convinced she had made the right choice. Faggot or no faggot, he brought up his daughter with love and concern and it had borne its rewards.

"Isn't she nice?" Lauri asked when they left, feeling relieved.

"Hardly my cup of tea," Larry answered cryptically. "Much too aggressive and rather vulgar. She's also a slob. Her house is a mess, and she's let herself go in a most revolting way. I can just imagine what the place is like on the Island. You'll hate it, Lauri, I know it."

As always, every word was spoken with authority.

"At least they don't live in Cherry Grove," Larry continued. "It's a part of the Island I abhor, and I want you to promise me that you'll avoid it at all costs."

Lauri lowered her head. She knew Cherry Grove was overrun with homosexuals and wondered about Larry's disdain for the area.

"Were you ever there?" she asked curiously.

"Once," Larry answered without hesitation, "and I hated it. It's sick, completely sick and littered with degenerates."

Larry watched her pack and was critical of everything she took. Lauri ignored his comments. It was a repetition of her whole existence with him. She could do nothing right if he was not in charge.

"You're not equipped to handle the job, you know," he said, the night before she left.

"What equipment would I need to go to the beach with a little boy and baby-sit for him at night?"

"You don't know how to swim, for starters. You'll be alone a great deal of the time. That Green lady looks like a real social butterfly. Probably plays poker till all hours and drinks beer."

"Papa, stop frightening me. I don't think it's fair. I told Mrs. Green I don't know how to swim, but she felt I could learn. And I won't mind being alone." She had trepidations about the trip, but knew instinctively it was important to begin to separate from Larry.

Sitting in the back of Mrs. Green's car, Lauri listened to the light banter between Joyce and little Billy, and her heart broke with envy. The child was loving and affectionate and his mother lavished him with praise and unabashed adoration. Lauri knew Larry loved her, but he exhibited his love in such a tangled and warped way. As always, at moments of emotional stress, she missed Anna.

Most of Larry's statements about Joyce turned out to be accurate. The house, although large, was a shambles of disorder. Joyce had no interest in housekeeping. It was just as well. Other than making beds, Lauri had never been required to do anything in her own home and would not have known how to go about it. The atmosphere however was warm, friendly and undemanding.

Lauri was treated like a member of the family and fell into the job of caring for Billy with ease. Still she was very unhappy. The first time she put on her tank-shaped bathing suit which Larry deemed appropriate and chic and looked at her thin, underdeveloped body, she quickly covered herself with a large, old shirt she had taken from Larry. Claiming to be allergic to the sun, she spent her first few days at the beach under a beach umbrella, feeling displaced. There were many young girls around, all approximately her age, but they appeared mature, self-assured and seemed to be having a wonderful time. No one paid attention to her and she had no idea how to approach them. It was therefore a pleasant surprise when one of them came over to her about a week after they arrived and introduced herself.

"I'm Sissy Smith, and you're Lauri, aren't you?" she said pleasantly. "We're having a party on the beach tonight. Would you like to come?"

"I'd love to," Lauri accepted cautiously. "How did you know my name?"

"Joyce told me," Sissy answered. "Will you come?"

"I'll have to ask Mrs. Green."

"She'll say it's all right. They're having their poker night at her house."

It turned out to be a pot-smoking beach party and Lauri had her first taste of the drug. It had little effect on her, but she enjoyed the evening. Everyone was ebullient, and although she felt somewhat of an outsider, she did not mind it. She was with a group of kids, on her own, without having to account to Larry.

Lauri became part of the gang. She turned out to be the youngest of the group and was treated like a mascot. Accentuating her youth, she exaggerated her naïveté and became the party clown. It enhanced her popularity and helped her avoid any serious relationships with the opposite sex. She would watch with hidden curiosity the various couples necking, envied them secretly, but the comaraderie shown toward her by everyone offset the fact that no one boy showed special interest in her.

"I'm happier than I've ever been," she said to Mrs. Green one morning while they were having breakfast.

"You're a changed young lady from the one I met in New York, I'll tell you that." Joyce smiled warmly at her. "What's your life like with your father?" she asked suddenly.

"He's great," Lauri answered quickly. "Papa is the greatest on all levels."

"Where's your mother?"

"She died when I was eight." Lauri purposely did not mention Anna's departure.

"What was she like?"

"She was wonderful. Kind and sweet. She loved my father more than anything in the world. It was terrible when she died." Lauri spoke quickly and could not understand why she was lying, but it came automatically.

"Was she beautiful?"

"Unbelievably beautiful."

"I could see that. You've got a great deal of your father about you, but there's more to your appearance and that must come from her."

Lauri blushed. Her father was always telling her she was beautiful, but no stranger had ever said it.

"Does your father have a girlfriend?" Joyce continued the questioning. She was almost positive Larry Eddington was a fag, but she was curious about him. He did have a daughter, and it was possible she was wrong.

"Oh, yes," Lauri said with exaggerated assurance. "Her name is Darlene Clark. She's a dancer, and they're going to get married as soon as she gets her divorce." The fantasy took form without effort.

"Damn it." Joyce smiled. "I have several girlfriends I could have introduced him to."

Lauri, although embarrassed about the lies, was relieved by the conversation. Joyce had not guessed that Larry was a homosexual, she decided. Although not consciously aware of it, she had been worried about it. The brief exchange wiped away the last barrier of inhibition. No one would know about Larry. Whatever stigma she carried could temporarily be put to rest. Her summer loomed more glorious than ever.

Sissy's boyfriend, Mike, started teaching her to swim. She stopped being self-conscious about her appearance. She was thin, but she carried herself with grace and felt quite chic. She tanned well, her hair grew long and wild, and she reveled in her new-found freedom.

She'd been on the Island for four weeks when Larry called to say he was coming to visit. It was a Wednesday and Joyce immediately invited him for the weekend. It threw Lauri into a state of misery.

That night, sitting on the deck of Sissy's house smoking pot, Lauri watched the reflection of the full moon on the calm waters of the Sound. She had to stop Larry from coming. Somehow she was not going to allow him to put an end to her first happy, independent experience.

"Cool it, Lauri," Mike said at one point. "You're going to get awfully sick from all that stuff."

"I'll be all right." She found it difficult to talk and she felt drowsy. "I'll be fine. And if worse comes to worse, you and Sissy can drop me on Joyce's deck before dawn. She'll never know the difference." She dozed off, almost forgetting why she was so unhappy.

It was very dark when Lauri opened her eyes. The moon had disappeared and for a moment she felt frightened. It took her several minutes to remember where she was. A dim light was shining through the picture window of Sissy's house and Lauri heard whispers from within. She strained her eyes and a vague silhouette of Sissy lying on the low sofa emerged. Her head was thrown back, her hair falling over the side of the couch. Lauri was captivated by her beauty. Suddenly she realized Sissy was not alone. As her eyes adjusted to the contrast of the darkness around and the light from within, she made out Mike's features. They were both naked and Mike was lying on top of Sissy, crushing her body deeper into the sofa. There was a dreamlike quality to the scene and it all seemed to be happening in slow motion. Lauri watched Mike roll off the couch and place his head between Sissy's legs. Sissy began to laugh quietly, arching her back. Her firm, full breasts, with nipples pointed, were in full view. Lauri's mouth went dry. She wanted to avert her eyes but could not. She felt paralyzed. Mike stood up, and his body was clearly outlined in the dim light. Lauri barely noticed him. Her eyes were glued to Sissy's nakedness. She was completely mesmerized by the girl's body. She saw Mike lower himself toward Sissy, taking one breast in his mouth and begin to suck it as his hand massaged the other. His face disappeared into the soft flesh. With a frightening clarity Lauri knew she wanted to run into the room and push him away. She wanted Sissy's breast in her mouth, wanted to feel the softness of the flesh next to her face. Unconsciously, she raised her hand and felt her undeveloped chest. Her vagina began to throb with desire, and she knew the desire was for Sissy.

A dry sob escaped her. She *was* abnormal! Like Larry, she was not a complete woman just as he was not a complete man. She was a lesbian and that explained why no boys were interested in her, and why she avoided them.

Lauri did not remember getting up and leaving the deck of Sissy's house, but she found herself running along the beach, tears streaming down her face, bitter saliva choking her throat.

"What's the matter, Lauri?" Joyce was looking at her and Lauri realized she was in front of the Green's house and she was on her knees, throwing up.

"I'm sick," she mumbled.

Joyce led her into the house and helped her undress. Gently she lifted Lauri onto the bed and went out of the room. Lauri closed her eyes and was about to doze off, when she felt Joyce wiping her face with a damp cloth. Blindly she grabbed the woman's hand and kissed it.

"Please don't leave me," she pleaded, never opening her eyes.

"I won't baby," Joyce said tenderly. Then, lying down beside Lauri, she pulled her into her arms.

"You've got such a lovely body," Joyce whispered emotionally, and Lauri felt Joyce's fingers run down her shoulders toward her lower back. It felt good. The fingers moved over her small breasts, pausing briefly over the hardened nipples, then moved down her stomach, until they reached her pubic hair.

The memory of the overwhelming physical desire for Sissy returned and Lauri lay very still. Joyce's hand was resting between her thighs and Lauri had a strong urge to press her thighs together, forcing the hand to remain locked between them. She also had an uncontrollable desire to push her fingers into Joyce's warm, damp vagina. Terrified by her thoughts, Lauri found herself clawing at the sheets.

Joyce's hand moved down her legs. "Poor baby," the older woman whispered. "Your feet are frozen."

Lauri's heart was pounding and her eyes flickered open. Joyce was naked, her back was to Lauri and her full breasts were resting on Lauri's stomach, and she was kissing her lower body.

Losing control, Lauri lifted her hand and touched Joyce's soft curved back. The texture of the skin was intoxicating. The woman reacted to the touch. With a swift motion, she pushed Lauri's legs apart, placed her face between them and Lauri felt the woman's tongue begin to toy with her clitoris.

In spite of herself, Lauri's body began to gyrate and her hands grabbed Joyce's head, pushing it closer to her.

The sun was streaming through the louvered shades when Lauri woke up. The house was quiet and she knew it was very early in the morning. She was alone. The scene with Joyce the night before came immediately. She got up quickly and dressed. With equal speed, she packed her suitcase. She could never face Joyce again. She could not bear to see any of her friends now that she knew the truth about herself. She certainly could not stay on Fire Island. Larry had told her she would not keep the job, and he was right. He was always right, and now she wanted to be with him and Robbie. With them she was safe.

Tiptoeing into the kitchen, she prepared Billy's breakfast, put coffee on for Joyce and started composing a note.

"Feeling better?" Joyce was standing in the doorway.

"I've got to leave for New York," Lauri said nervously. She could not look at Joyce.

"Why, honey?"

"I'm still feeling sick, and I've had this sort of thing before. When it happens I've got to see a doctor. Our doctor." She said it sincerely and was fascinated at how easily she had learned to lie. "I told you I was allergic to the sun, but I thought I'd outgrown it. I obviously haven't."

"Will you come back?"

"If the doctor lets me."

"Let's wait for Billy to get up and we'll walk you to the ferry." Joyce poured herself some coffee and sat down opposite Lauri.

"Lauri, I loved having you here and I hope you can come back."

"Thank you, Joyce." Lauri lowered her eyes in confusion. "I'll call you as soon as I know, and I'm sorry to leave you in the lurch."

"You were a joy to have around and it's a shame you're leaving."

At the ferry, Billy cried and Joyce hugged Lauri affectionately. The contact upset Lauri. She hated the feel of Joyce's fleshy body.

4

Larry was delighted to have his daughter back, although he was shocked by her appearance when she arrived home. Her hair was unkempt, her skin was peeling, her nails were long and dirty. It was, however, the vacant look in her eyes which disturbed him most. She seemed lost and frightened, and he held back the temptation to point out that he was against the trip in the first place. Fire Island was never mentioned, and he assumed the atmosphere in the Green's house was simply not up to her standards and that she missed her home. Within a short time he had her back to looking like herself, but he could never reach her beyond the simple exchange of mundane subjects. He kept hoping that when she returned to school her mood would change. He hid his concern, tried to be patient, but he resented her remote behavior. He could not even bring out her anger.

Lauri returned to school; still the distant mood prevailed. She rarely went out, and if she had friends they were never brought to the house. At the end of her junior year, she dropped out of Performing Arts. She did not ask Larry's permission; she simply announced that she was not going back. He accepted her decision quietly. His suggestion that she enroll in one of the better private schools on the Upper East Side was turned down. She did agree to enter a public high school in the Village. Her adamance baffled Larry. Since returning from her summer on Fire Island, she had acquiesced to most of his requests.

Lauri's decision to leave Performing Arts was simple. She wanted to remove herself from any relationships that involved Larry. She wanted a new set of friends who did not know him. Fire Island and what had occurred there haunted her, and she was looking for an atmosphere which was more relaxed, less competitive, a place where she could lose herself in anonymity.

The new surrounding suited her to perfection. Scholastic achievements were easy for her since none of the students were interested in their studies. Everyone there was simply biding time. It was a halfway house between childhood and maturity. Within a relatively short time, Lauri found a group of youngsters who were delighted to have her as part of their crowd. They did not care who she was or where she came from, and she felt safe with them. She had no problems with Larry. The art of manipulation, learned during the summer, served her well. She had lied glibly to Joyce and now she lied to Larry. Often she wondered if he believed all her stories about her schoolwork and her new friends, but in his concern for her, he gave her free rein and she did not abuse it. His requirements of her were minimal and she made sure not to overstep the boundaries. She was always home by midnight, she kept her grades at a certain level and she ate Sunday dinner with Robbie and Larry at some elegant restaurant, at which time she was expected to dress properly.

The need to move away from Larry grew greater as her graduation from high school came closer, but so did her apprehension. In spite of the bravado of her schoolmates, they were lonely and frightened at the thought of facing life on their own. All things considered, Larry was there when she came home at night.

It was after Lauri graduated from high school that she met Bradford DeHaven. It was New Year's Eve and Larry invited her to accompany him to Mrs. Vincent Mortimer's annual party.

It was a society-studded affair which Lauri had attended since she was quite young and which she had always hated.

"Can't we just go out to dinner with Robbie?" she asked wearily.

"Lauri, I ask so few things of you these days." Larry tried to keep the plea out of his voice.

They rarely talked anymore, and suddenly Lauri felt sorry for him. For the first time she noticed his hurt, and it occurred to her she was punishing him for being a homosexual, and it made no sense. He had been a good and sincere father and asked so little in return for his efforts. Going to a New Year's Eve party was little enough to ask.

Lauri made a supreme effort to please him that evening.

She permitted him to design the dress she was to wear, had her hair done as he liked it, and accepted a magnificent ruby necklace which had belonged to Anna. While the preparations for the forthcoming event were taking place, a serenity settled over the household and Lauri found herself strangely relaxed. Although Larry did not approve of makeup, he had asked her to accentuate her eyes and put lip gloss on her mouth. Looking at herself in the full length mirror she had to admit that everything he had suggested achieved a perfection which was almost embarrassing. Nothing within matched the vision she presented. It was all a lie.

The anger which had been set aside was perking inside her while she stood in front of the lit fireplace waiting for Larry to finish dressing. She was deeply absorbed in watching the dancing flames, trying to understand her sudden rekindled discontent when she heard Larry walk in, and she looked around.

"God, you look like your mother," he said, and the pride of possession in his voice did not escape her. She looked up at Anna's portrait and, for the first time, she felt she understood why her mother had left. It was not only Larry's homosexuality; it was not the extravagances or impractical and unrealistic life-style which Larry insisted on. It was that overpowering possessiveness he had toward the people who were close to him; the need to mold, the need to control. He had drawn the rope around Anna too tightly and she had had to escape. Now he was doing it to her. In a strange way, she was not angry at him. Instead, feelings of resentment toward her mother choked her. It seemed unfair to have left a little helpless child to be brought up by Larry.

"Why didn't she want me?" Lauri asked, still looking at the portrait.

"She did," Larry answered, and she heard him pour himself a drink. He rarely drank, and Lauri knew he was nervous. She wanted to drop the subject but felt compelled to continue.

"She never showed it." She turned her head and watched him.

"She fought for you in every way. She even went to court, but I wouldn't give you up, and no judge would allow an American child to be taken out of the country, which is what she intended to do." He spoke very quietly.

"You never told me."

"I didn't think it was important."

"Good God, Papa, every child wants to know he's wanted by his mother." Lauri lost her temper.

"I had no idea you missed her, or even thought of her," Larry said, and the look of pain on his face was unbearable to watch. "I really thought I made up for her not being here."

Lauri lowered her eyes. They finished their drinks in silence.

"I think we should be going," Larry said.

Larry had rented a limousine for the evening, and in spite of herself, Lauri felt like a princess in a fairy tale as the driver opened the car door for her and she and Larry walked into the elegant town house. Standing in the large gallery, milling with people, she felt the admiring glances that were being thrown in their direction. The butler helped her with her coat and she looked over at Larry. His blond hair was quite long and his square-chinned face was handsomer than she had ever seen it. Self-consciously she kissed him on the cheek. She knew she had hurt him with her questions about Anna and regretted it. He smiled his gratitude.

Within minutes after entering the large living room, she was besieged by several men whom she had known from past parties. Most were older and were pathetic in her eyes as they attempted to flirt with her. A butler came over and poured her a glass of champagne. She did not enjoy alcohol, but she felt restless and decided to get drunk. She was actually enjoying herself when she became conscious of a young man standing a few feet away from her, staring in her direction. When he caught her attention, he came over.

"I'm Bradford DeHaven the Third," he said with a smile. He was tall, had dark hair and was extremely handsome. His teeth were very white and even, his eyes, a pale blue, were rimmed with dark lashes. He was exquisitely elegant and exuded a masculinity and self-assurance that excited and frightened her.

"I'm Lauriana Eddington the First," she answered, smiling uncertainly.

Just then the lights were lowered and the clock struck the midnight hour. She was surprised that the time had gone by so quickly, but her thoughts were interrupted when Brad leaned over and kissed her on the mouth. She was taken aback and was trying to regain her equilibrium when she saw her father standing next to her.

"Happy New Year, Papa." She kissed him quickly, and he put his arm around her shoulder and held her close. She nestled up to him and, feeling more secure, she looked over at Brad, who was obviously waiting to be introduced. "Bradford DeHaven the Third," she said politely, "this is my father, Laurence Eddington."

"Are you related to the DeHavens from Virginia?" Larry asked conversationally.

"Afraid so, sir." The young man shook Larry's hand respectfully. "Do you know my mother?"

"No, I don't," Larry answered, obviously impressed, "but I know a great deal about your family. I used to ski with James DeHaven years ago in Vermont."

Lauri bit her lip with annoyance. The pretentious name-dropping was a need Larry had, and it bothered her.

"He was my uncle," Brad said solemnly. "He died, you know."

"Yes, I'd heard about it," Larry answered in a somber tone, and Lauri could tell he felt comfortable with Bradford DeHaven. "What did he die of?"

"Drank himself to death," Brad answered almost flippantly, and there was a note of malice in the way he said it.

"Yes, he overdid it even when I knew him." Larry seemed not to have noticed Brad's tone as he plunged into an elaborate, irrelevant reminiscence about the past. She wanted to move away. She had watched her father push himself into similar conversations with the "upper crust" of society, pretending to be one of them, always ignoring the fact that he was not. Larry, however, was holding on to her shoulder and she could not escape.

"May I take your daughter out for a late supper?" Brad asked Larry, when the latter had finished his story.

Larry looked over at Lauri, and she could tell he wanted her to go.

"I think you'd better ask her." Larry smiled happily.

Lauri was tempted to refuse, but her father was pleased and proud, so she accepted.

She sobered up the minute they stepped into the cold, brisk, night air. She felt an instinctive need to be on guard, but could not explain why.

They went to several parties and she began to feel more comfortable. Everyone she met seemed to like her, and whatever trepidations she had about being with Brad evaporated. He behaved impeccably. He was warm, considerate and affectionate. As the evening was drawing to a close, Lauri had put aside her apprehensions and mentally prepared herself for the moment he would ask her to go to bed with him. Still when he gave the driver a Sutton Place address, she felt deflated.

"I want to pick up my car," he explained as he sat back and took her hand in his. She felt her stomach muscles contract.

They got out of the taxi in front of an apartment house on Sutton Place and Lauri headed toward the main entrance.

"The garage is this way," Brad said, guiding her toward the corner where the garage ramp was located. She felt foolish.

"I'm going to marry you, Lauri," Brad said. "You're not just a one night roll in the hay in my life." He pulled her toward him. "I had to pick up the car since I'm driving down to Virginia to see my mother when I leave you. It's a family ritual which means a great deal to her."

She snuggled up to him and rested her head on his shoulder. It felt like the happiest moment of her life.

It was 5:00 A.M. when they reached her house and Brad insisted on escorting her up.

Larry was home, having just arrived a few minutes before, and was still in his evening clothes. Robbie was there too, and they were having some champagne. Lauri watched to see Brad's reaction to Larry and Robbie. There was none. He behaved like the proper young man, making an obvious effort to impress them. Larry offered them champagne and they drank a toast for the New Year.

Curled up in the big armchair, Lauri felt content for the first time in many months. She was exhausted and she closed her eyes. Larry, Brad and Robbie were chatting amicably and their voices were soothing. Vaguely she heard Brad tell her father about his schooling; Collegiate,

Choate, Yale. Horse racing was his passion, and he trained his mother's horses on their farm in Virginia. He worked in a stock brokerage house on Wall Street. She fell asleep, unaware when Brad left.

She woke up on New Year's Day at two in the afternoon. She could smell the fresh coffee and the fried bacon, and she stretched happily. She could hear Larry whistling happily while preparing for their usual New Year's Day open house. Life was wonderful. She was going to marry Bradford DeHaven the Third, would become a person in her own right, would make a lovely home for her husband, have children and live happily ever after. Getting married would enable her to leave Larry gracefully.

Brad called late that evening from Virginia. She was genuinely pleased to hear from him. He would be back in New York the next day and wanted to take her to dinner.

Brad was Lauri's first boyfriend, and her dates with him were the first formal ones she had ever had. He insisted on picking her up at her home and was shocked when she appeared, on their first date, in dungarees and sneakers. Quickly she reorganized her thinking and found herself dressing, again, as her father would have expected her to. Whatever irritation she felt about it was erased when she saw the pride which Brad exuded when she appeared with him in public. The phrase, "this is my girl," sent a thrill through her. She belonged to someone! Whenever he picked her up, Brad would have a drink with Larry and, although Larry said little, he seemed pleased at what was happening. They still did not communicate, but Lauri sensed his relief when she arrived home at a reasonable hour, satisfied she had been seen to the door.

Brad spent money lavishly. They dined in elegant restaurants, went to the theater and the races. His passion for horses was all-consuming. He spoke of their future together, constantly. They would live in New York for a while, but eventually they would have a house in the country with stables in which Brad would breed the finest yearlings who would win races at the great tracks around the country. He was a magnificent horseman, and watching him ride at the country homes of his friends, Lauri's physical desire for him was overwhelming. On occasion, they would double date with people he worked with. She found these evenings trying. Brad was highly opinionated and argumentative. Lauri would look at the faces of their companions and try to decide what their reactions were to Brad's almost irrational rage. She could never quite figure out what they thought. Somehow the evenings would end on a pleasant note and Lauri would promptly put her doubts to rest. What was most important was Brad's love and desire for her. His respect and concern were almost touching. She was in love with Brad. He was in love with her, and they were going to get married. That was all that mattered.

Her main concern was that she had little to offer him other than a pretty appearance, and that he would grow tired of her. She was brooding over her deficiencies as a woman and a person, when Brad informed her that they were invited by Sam Ryan, his boss, for a Sunday brunch at his home in Croton, New York.

Her self-confidence was at low ebb the morning they drove up. She knew Sam Ryan was important. When mentioning the forthcoming trip to Larry, he was visibly impressed.

"You're in for a treat, princess," Larry said, and he could not hide his feelings. "His home is a showplace."

"He's Brad's boss and apparently he wants Brad to see his new colt."

"Lauri, Sam Ryan is one of the most powerful men in the political world, a fine art collector and a serious sportsman. His stables are famous."

Larry hovered over her while she dressed and made her redo her hair several times. Just before she left the house, he insisted she choose a different belt which he thought more suitable for the outfit she was wearing. It had been a long time since Lauri had given in to her father's fetish over appearances, and she was fully conscious of her own nervousness when she followed his advice without argument.

Sam Ryan was delightful, and Lauri found herself relaxed and happy from the minute they met. They spent the time before the midafternoon meal in an enormous library in front of a big wood-burning fireplace. Sam went out of his way to show his appreciation of Lauri. At one point, when Brad went out to the stables to look at the horses, Sam stayed behind to chat.

It turned out he had met her father and had seen his paintings at a one-man show a couple of years back.

"Fine painter," he said seriously, and Lauri could not help but smile.

"You didn't like his work, Mr. Ryan," she said, and he looked up. Seeing her expression, he returned the smile.

"How did you know?"

"I take you for the sort of person who would buy a painting of a struggling young artist if you remotely liked his work."

"But I *did* like your father," he said, with genuine appreciation for her perception and honesty.

"He's a wonderful man," Lauri agreed enthusiastically. "And now that he's taken to painting portraits, I think he's going to make it." She stopped and thought for a minute. "As a matter of fact, it occurs to me that the reason it has never been right before was because my father is too inhibited to do anything but straight portraits. He has feelings for people, but not for the abstract." She was pleased with the revelation and was aware that she had spoken intimately to a man she barely knew.

"Thank you," Sam said with warmth. "That was a great compliment you just paid me."

She felt herself blush. To her relief, Brad returned and the conversation turned to horses.

On the way back to the city, Brad was euphoric. "He adored you. He thought you were the living end," he said enthusiastically. "Do you know how important that is? Do you know what this can mean?"

"What can it mean?" Lauri asked rhetorically.

"Oh, stop being childish. It's important when the big man likes the wife of his executive. He sees me now as a man of quality, and it gives me an edge, a dimension that others don't have. I'm no longer just the son of Mrs. Cynthia DeHaven."

Lauri was pleased for Brad, but she was even more pleased with herself. Sam Ryan knew her father, identified her as a person who came from somewhere, had a background, had a base. She was not *just* Brad's girl. Shades of her old respect and appreciation of Larry returned.

It was therefore a great surprise when Brad asked her to meet his mother, but became visibly agitated when she suggested Larry join them.

"Another time." Brad laughed uncertainly, and a nervous rigidity crept into his manner. "For now, I'd rather she meet you alone."

"Why?" Lauri asked, suspecting for the first time Brad's awareness of Larry's homosexuality. She had learned to live with it and rarely thought of it anymore. The idea that Brad knew and was ashamed of Larry was distressing.

"I just know my mother," Brad said with determination.

She relented in spite of herself. She had never mentioned Brad's proposal to Larry, and now she was pleased at the omission.

The meeting was at 11:00 o'clock in the morning at the apartment on Sutton Place, which Lauri had never seen in all the time she had been dating Brad.

Cynthia DeHaven was, according to Brad, a genteel Irish Catholic from Dublin, Ireland, who was wooed for a long time by Bradford DeHaven II before she consented to leave her home and come to America. They were married in the Catholic Church where Brad's father promised to rear the children in her faith.

"That sonofabitch reneged on his promise," Brad said angrily. "And shortly after I was born he left my mother for some cheap little tramp and got a divorce."

"Are you Catholic?" Lauri asked, amazed. She was Episcopalian, but except for Easter and Christmas, religion was not a prime concern in her life.

"Of course," Brad said. "As a matter of fact, that's one of the reasons I want you to meet my mother."

She was about to say she'd convert, if it would help, but something stopped her from making the commitment.

"You see, Lauri, my mother is against divorce. Her family did not recognize her divorce, and she was never able to face them after my father divorced her." He was very somber. "That's why she lives a solitary life in Virginia, raising horses and having little social contacts. I'm her whole life." He looked genuinely miserable.

Riding up in a taxi to the DeHaven apartment, Lauri tried to imagine what Mrs. DeHaven looked like. A demure, gray-haired lady, with a sad face came to mind.

Nothing could have been farther from that image. Cynthia DeHaven was a monster. A bleached blond with a tight permanent, she had pinched features and icy-blue eyes. She greeted Lauri as if she were a maid being interviewed for a position.

"I'll go and see about coffee," Brad said after the brief introductions, and left them alone.

"Bradford tells me you want to marry him."

"He asked me to marry him."

"You understand that I don't approve."

Lauri remained silent.

"Bradford is totally dependent on me for money," Cynthia DeHaven continued, "and if he marries you I will cut him off without a penny."

"Since I'm not marrying Brad for his money, Mrs. DeHaven, I'm afraid it won't make any difference to me." Lauri spoke slowly. "Besides, Brad works, and from what I've seen, Mr. Ryan seems quite impressed with him."

"Sam Ryan took Bradford on only because I am a major stockholder in his company," Cynthia said, with disdain.

"I don't know why you're doing this, Mrs. DeHaven," Lauri's voice matched Cynthia's tone. "You are implying that without you Brad does not exist. It's cruel and I can't accept it. He's bright, well liked, hard working and if I were his mother I'd be proud of him. You must have your reasons, but I'm really not interested in what they are."

Cynthia was about to reply when Brad walked in.

"Isn't she great?" he asked, putting a tray down. He poured a coffee for Lauri and two vodkas with orange juice for his mother and himself. Lauri was shocked to see Mrs. DeHaven down the drink and hold her glass out for a refill.

"Bradford," Mrs. DeHaven, ignoring his question, took the second drink, held it in her hand and looked directly at her son. "I've told you my feelings about your intentions. I grant you she said all the right things. It won't, however, make me change my mind." She took a sip of her drink. "At twenty-one I hardly think you'll be able to make it without my help."

Brad looked from his mother to Lauri. His embarrassment was evident.

There was a heavy silence as Brad finished the contents of his glass and headed toward the tray holding the liquor. Lauri was disturbed by the conversation, but she was more upset by the thought of anyone drinking vodka that early in the morning.

"I'd like to leave now, Brad," Lauri said, and stood up. Brad put down his glass and threw a look at his mother, who was preoccupied with lighting a cigarette.

When they walked out of the room, Cynthia DeHaven did not bother to look up.

Walking slowly up the stairs to her home, Lauri tried to understand the contrast between what Brad had told her about his mother and what the woman really was. In a strange way she was touched. Brad's love for his mother had colored his impressions, just as she probably saw Larry differently than others.

Larry was standing in front of his easel when Lauri arrived home. She noticed he was tense, and she walked over and looked at the painting he was working on. She knew he disliked painting portraits and had fought against doing them, feeling it was a compromise. She attributed his state of agitation to that.

"I don't think you should go on seeing the DeHaven boy," Larry said suddenly.

"Why not?" Lauri turned in surprise. "I thought you liked him."

"Well, you were wrong." Larry went back to his work.

"Wait a minute." Lauri felt her temper rise. "I've been seeing Brad since we met on New Year's Eve. I haven't dated anyone but him, and you seemed pleased."

"I was pleased. Pleased that you weren't running around with God knows who, were dressing properly, were behaving like your old self. But I didn't think you'd be foolish enough to get involved so deeply with someone like him." He stopped when he saw the look of defiance come to her face and knew he was pushing too hard and if he continued she might do something foolish to spite him. He put his drink down carefully and started out of the room.

"You're not going to tell me he's a fag, too?" Lauri yelled after him, and realized the minute she said the words that they would be misunderstood.

Larry turned slowly in the doorway and looked at her. "No," he said very quietly, "he's much worse." And then, turning around, he walked into his bedroom and slammed the door behind him.

Lauri felt confused. Although she had not yet decided to marry Brad, she was sure her father was wrong about him. Brad was a gentle, considerate and decent man. He was well brought up, had a good education and seemed to have proper values. If Mrs. DeHaven did cut Brad off from his inheritance, Lauri was sure they could manage. She had met the people Brad worked with and he got along with them. She had met Sam Ryan, and she was sure that no employee who was hired because of his mother's connections would have been accorded such an honor if he were not deserving in his own right. But more important, she was convinced she was in love with Brad. He was a gentleman and he treated her with love and respect.

Larry was gone when Lauri woke up the next morning. The note he left said he had gotten a commission to do a portrait of a woman in Palm Beach. It did not indicate when he would be back. It was not an unusual occurrence. Larry was getting more and more such commissions. The fact that he left without telling her about it in advance was the shock.

When Brad called she said she wanted to get married as soon as possible.

Lauri and Brad were married that evening by a justice of the peace in Connecticut. She had no wish to call her father, but she did call Robbie. He sounded sad as he wished her good luck. The conversation depressed her, and doubts about her impulsive act mounted.

The weekend spent at an inn in Ridgefield, Connecticut, was an unhappy one. They were shy of each other sexually, had little to talk about and Lauri suspected Brad was as nervous and uncomfortable as she was. The tension eased when they finally headed back to New York. She was resting in the crook of Brad's arm when the car came to a stop in front of a highrise building on Fifty-fourth Street off First Avenue.

"We're home." Brad tried to sound cheerful.

Lauri looked around bewildered.

"Lauri, I never told you I lived on Sutton Place," he said, as though reading her thoughts. He sounded both indignant and defensive.

She tried to laugh. "I know you didn't, I simply assumed . . ." She felt contrite. "It was a stupid assumption and I'm sorry." Then, sighing with relief, she put her hand on his arm. "As a matter of fact, I don't think I would have felt comfortable in that huge house."

Putting his hand in his pocket, Brad pulled out a small blue Tiffany pouch and handed it to her. "It's a wedding present." He smiled for the first time.

Lauri pulled it open and found a small gold key wrapped in tissue paper.

"Your key to your new home," Brad said shyly.

Lauri stared at it. The key to her new home! Brad was her husband. She was Mrs. Bradford DeHaven III. But home was on Bank Street and she was Lauri Eddington. She closed her fingers over the key and leaned over to kiss Brad on the cheek. She was being childish and knew she had to stop it.

Brad drove off to park the car, and Lauri went up to the apartment.

It turned out to be quite pleasant, although it was evident from the dust and meager furnishings that Brad rarely used it. Lauri walked around and was convinced everything in it was taken from Mrs. DeHaven's attic. The furniture at Sutton Place was hideous; the discards were worse. She wandered into the bedroom. The bed was unmade and a shudder went through her. Haltingly, she started opening various closet doors. Brad's extensive wardrobe was hanging neatly in the large walk-in closet, grouped in unbelievable order. The jackets, the slacks, the suits, the evening clothes. In a second closet, she found his sweaters neatly folded on the shelves. Here they were stacked by color. His shirts were all wrapped in cellophane, his ties were neatly hung on a tie rack, his scarves folded on separate shelves. The shoes and riding boots were in a third closet. All were gleaming from constant polishing and care. In contrast, the linen closet was almost bare. Taking a couple of sheets and pillowcases out, Lauri had to control the tears. She could never be the wife Brad expected. She had nothing to offer him. She missed Larry desperately.

Lauri was making up the bed when Brad walked in.

"Is that all the luggage you brought with you?" he asked, putting down her two suitcases.

"I left most of my clothes at home." She blushed. "I mean, at my father's."

"Would you like me to go pick them up?" he asked obligingly.

She realized she had not told Brad of Larry's feelings about him. "I don't really have anything I want there." She hid her embarrassment. "You know, everything was sort of old." She paused. "I thought I'd buy new stuff."

"Oh." Brad looked away.

"It's just as well, though." Lauri tried to sound light, although his reaction puzzled her. "Your clothes take up most of the room in the closets, and there wouldn't have been any place for mine."

"Come on, Lauri, we'd find room for anything you need." He sounded hurt.

"I'm exhausted, Brad," Lauri whispered, not knowing what else to say.

"Sure you are, honey." He started toward the living room. "I'll go out and buy food. You rest as long as you like and we'll eat later."

He looked as though he could not wait to escape.

For the first few months of marriage Lauri felt as though she were on a roller coaster. They rarely spent an evening at home, and she had the uncomfortable feeling that Brad was afraid to spend time alone with her. No sooner would he come in from work, then he would be ready to meet people for a drink or go out to dinner. If the people they spent time with were never around for very long, Lauri had little time to ponder the changing faces. She never got to know any of them well, but everyone seemed to like them and it made Brad happy. His pride in her was flattering and her confidence rose.

In many ways, her life with Brad was not different from what it was with Larry. Brad took care of every detail of their daily existence. All he expected of her was to look well, be friendly and be liked by his friends. He enjoyed shopping with her and insisted on her buying designer clothes and expensive accessories. He brought her several pieces of jewelry, which were ostentatious and not quite to her liking, but he had a way of giving them to her which was touching and she did not want to hurt his feelings. But unlike Larry, he had no interest in their home. Her suggestions concerning furnishing the apartment were ignored, although on occasion he would show up with outrageous accessories which baffled her. A Tiffany chandelier which was too large for the simple round table in the tiny dining area, a set of twelve cut-crystal glasses, totally inappropriate for their simple ceramic dishes; heavy silver cutlery, almost laughable for their style of living. Her feeble protests were answered by near tantrums and Lauri was quickly intimidated.

Still, she was not unhappy. She began to enjoy their physical relationship, and her concern about her sexuality diminished. She also felt less restricted. She was a married woman and the status was appealing.

It all changed the night Lauri discovered Brad had never been to Yale. Someone mentioned it and Lauri pretended not to hear it, but as the evening progressed, she noticed Brad began to drink heavily, becoming abrasive and argumentative. His usual glib manner when in public, his easy-going manner disappeared, and Lauri could not wait for the evening to end.

After that evening Lauri began to take greater notice of who her husband was. Deficiencies in him that she had glossed over since they were married took on new proportion. His erratic behavior, warm and loving one day, verbally abusive the next, the mood changes from euphoria to depression, the tantrums followed by abject apologies, became jarring realities. It was his lying, however, that Lauri found most difficult to cope with. He was so adept at it that it took quite a while before she realized he lied out of habit. His seeming wealth turned out to be a myth. Once his mother withdrew his allowance, he was totally dependent on a rather small income from his job. Lauri's designer clothes were bought on his mother's charge accounts, until the older woman put a stop to it. He was driving Cynthia's car without permission, and he was seriously in debt. It all came to light when Cynthia called and made a scene about the car. At first Lauri refused to accept what Cynthia said, convinced the older woman was being vengeful, but when the debt collectors began to threaten, she knew she had to confront Brad with the facts.

Scared as she was of Brad's rages, Lauri finally told him what she knew. To her surprise, he took it quietly. His only explanation was that he loved her and wanted to give her everything.

Faced with the reality of her life, Lauri knew the over-all picture was not a pretty one, but she found it difficult to believe that there was something drastically wrong with her marriage. She refused to admit to herself that Larry had been right. But more than anything, she was unwilling to give up her first taste of freedom.

The role reversal occurred within a short time. As Lauri became more assertive, Brad accepted her decisions with little argument. She got a job as a receptionist at an art gallery on Madison Avenue, and although Brad was upset at first, he was mollified when she took over some of the household expenses. They went out rarely, and Lauri put most of her energies into making their home cozy and warm. Brad began to travel and his earnings rose. They even discussed having a child.

Lauri did extremely well at the gallery. Her instinctive sense for color and design were appreciated by the people she worked with, and shortly after going to work the owner of the gallery began to consult her about various artists' works. She started to draw and sketch designs in her spare time. It was extremely gratifying and thoughts of a designing career took root.

A harmony descended over their home. Lauri enjoyed her work and Brad, although away a great deal, seemed happy with what he was doing. Occasionally they were invited to Sam Ryan's home in Croton, which convinced her that Brad was doing well. Her state of contentment was only marred by Larry's silence. She had seen him passing by the gallery, and although she was sure he saw her, he never acknowledged her presence, and it caused her great unhappiness. She thought of calling him, but kept putting it off, looking for a special occasion that would justify the resumption of their relationship.

The opportunity came on a Saturday at the beginning of December when Sam called to invite Brad and her up for Sunday brunch. Lauri was surprised, since Brad was away.

"Well, you come alone," Sam assured her graciously. "I'll send a car around ten tomorrow morning."

She was about to refuse when he continued.

"As a matter of fact, why don't you bring your father. I really did enjoy meeting him, and I would like to get to know him better."

"I'll ask him," she promised and could not wait to hang up. In her excitement she forgot that Sam seemed unaware that Brad was away. Being given an opportunity to call Larry crowded out all other thoughts. Finally, she had something to offer him—an invitation to a magnificent country estate, owned by a powerful, rich and known personality.

"Papa," Lauri said breathlessly when she heard his voice.

"Princess," he said, and she knew he was as choked up with emotion as she was.

"I love you, Papa."

"Nowhere near as much as I love you," he answered.

Lauri basked in the warmth that was transmitted over the phone.

"I'm invited to Sam Ryan's house for the day, and he specifically asked me to have you come up too."

"Sam Ryan, the stockbroker?" Larry could hardly contain his excitement. "I met him, you know," he continued quickly, trying to hide his pleasure.

"I know." Lauri smiled to herself. He would never change. "He told me," she said out loud, "and he liked you and wants to see you again."

"When?" Larry took on his old familiar blase manner.

"Tomorrow at ten in the morning." She paused, allowing him time to accept with dignity.

"I'm sure I can make it, princess."

The game was being played, as it had in the past, but she did not mind.

It was a cold brisk day and Lauri, knowing how important it was to Larry, went out of her way to dress so as to please him. She chose a camel-colored woolen mini tunic, kid boots in a darker shade and matching bag. A bright orange scarf tied around her dark hair was the perfect accent color for the simple outfit. Going down to meet him, she felt elegant and grown up.

Larry was waiting for her on the corner. For a brief moment she was not sure it was he. His hair had grown quite long and he had a beard. He was leaning casually against a lamppost, smoking a cigarette. The gray flannel slacks were tight fitting as was the white turtleneck shirt. The fur-lined jacket was open and the numerous gold chains and medallions were clearly visible. She was taken aback and was trying to regain her composure when he turned and saw her. She started to run toward him, but stopped when she saw the look of shock on his face.

"Baby," he said hoarsely, "are you all right?"

"Of course I'm all right." The reprimand, the old reproach destroyed her confidence. "Why do you ask?"

"You've lost so much weight."

She laughed uncertainly. She knew she was thinner than she had ever been, but she was convinced she was extremely chic. "I thought you'd be pleased," she said feebly. "You always told me you hated overweight women."

"I'm not, however, enchanted with skeletons," he said soberly. Then he smiled and took her in his arms. The unhappy exchange was quickly forgotten. She was his daughter and his concern was touching.

Larry and Sam took to each other immediately. There were several guests who were involved in the art world, and Lauri enjoyed watching her father captivate them. If only Brad were around, she thought, the day would have been complete.

"Where is Brad, anyway?" Sam asked at one point.

"Why, he's away on business for the company," she answered, but the question stunned her.

"We're not traveling salesmen." Sam laughed pleasantly. "Although come to think of it, he's probably at his mother's now that she's asked him to be in charge of her portfolio again."

Lauri bit her lip, trying to hide her shock. Brad had never stopped lying to her, and she had been living in a fool's paradise.

The rest of the day was a blur in Lauri's mind, and she was relieved when she finally dropped Larry at his apartment and she could escape to hers.

Her first thought was to call Mrs. DeHaven's house, but she rejected the idea. There was nothing she could say over the phone, even if Brad did come on the wire. Packing and walking out was the other possibility, but she had nowhere to go. She spent a sleepless night trying to figure out what she should do. Her marriage was over, of that she was sure. The question was how she would manage without going to Larry for assistance. She had a job and could probably look for something more lucrative, but she needed cash to tide her over. It occurred to her to sell the jewelry Brad had given her, but she did not want to take anything from him. Pawning them, with the idea of getting them back eventually, made sense. Quickly she sifted through the jewelry and picked up a large diamond and sapphire brooch set in heavy 18 karat gold. Ugly as it was, it looked expensive, sitting in a Cartier box.

Brad called while Lauri was dressing to go to work. She was exhausted and her nerves were raw.

"Have a nice trip?" she said in a strained voice.

"Great. Big deal in the offing," he answered happily.

"Brad, don't you ever tell the truth?" Lauri exploded.

"What are you talking about?"

"Stop it." Lauri lost control. "Were you at your mother's?"

"I was away on company business," he insisted, but he sounded nervous.

"You were at your mother's," she persisted.

"What makes you think so?" he said cautiously.

"Sam made me think so. Larry and I spent the day in Croton . . ."

"Larry!" Brad screamed into the phone. "Are you telling me you took your father up to Sam's?"

"Why yes, Sam invited him." Lauri became defensive.

"I don't believe you. I don't believe for one minute that Sam Ryan would have anything to do with that fag . . ."

Lauri slammed the phone down. She was shaking. Beads of perspiration started forming on her forehead and her head began to throb. Sitting down on the bed, she felt faint. Brad's infantile behavior, his lying, his relationship with his mother were nothing compared with what he said about Larry. The words sounded like an accusation and kept echoing in her mind. She knew she would never forgive him for that.

Dragging a suitcase out of the closet, Lauri began throwing things into it. She was determined to be out of the apartment before Brad got home. The marriage, as far as she was concerned, was over.

"Where the hell do you think you're going?" Brad was standing in the doorway.

Lauri looked up and something about his manner frightened her.

"I'm leaving you, Brad." She tried to sound calm.

"Why?"

"We've reached a crossroad in our lives. We need a rest from each other."

"Bullshit," Brad said, and his voice was ominously quiet. "It's what I said about your father, isn't it?" His tone did not change. "I can't help it if he's . . ."

"Don't say it again," Lauri's voice rose.

"Damn it," Brad disregarded her interruption. "I've known all along he was queer. Everyone does. It hasn't affected you, and it didn't really matter to me. I married you, didn't I?"

"Thanks a lot," Lauri hissed and turned back to her packing. "Why did you marry me, anyway?" she asked curiously.

"Because Sam liked you, if you must know."

"That's revolting."

"Have you been to bed with him, yet?" Brad asked maliciously.

"You are sickening." Lauri snapped her suitcase shut and started toward the door.

"I won't let you go." Brad's voice was tight.

"Stop being a masterful husband. It doesn't suit you." Lauri tried to hide her rising fear as she passed him. Brad grabbed her arm. "Please let me pass." She tried to pull away.

"You're not leaving me, Lauri." He pulled her toward him.

"Brad, please let me go," she repeated.

The first blow struck her face and were he not holding on to her arm she would have fallen. Lauri felt a trickle of blood start down her lip. Struggling frantically, she was about to free herself from his grasp when he lifted her physically and threw her on the bed. She felt him rip her dress and in seconds he was on top of her, his legs straddling her body. Pressing his hand over her face, he unzipped his pants. She stopped struggling. She was going to be raped by her husband, and as dreadful as it was, she knew it would be over in a few minutes. She closed her eyes and tried not to move. She felt him push her legs apart, pressing himself into her when simultaneously he started pummeling her face and body with his fists.

When Lauri awoke she saw someone standing beside the bed. For a minute she thought it was Brad, and she tried to get up and escape.

"I wouldn't do that if I were you," the man said gently. "I'm Dr. Stan Blyden and I live in the building."

"How did you get here?"

"The doorman called me. He saw your husband run out of the building hours ago and it made him nervous. He tried reaching you on the house phone and when you didn't answer he called me."

Lauri began to cry.

"You're a bit of a mess," Stan said, taking her wrist in his hand. "But we'll have you back in shape in a very short time."

"Have I been unconscious for a long time?"

"On and off during the day." Stan sat down on the edge of the bed.

"And you've been here all that time?" Lauri asked controlling her tears.

"My girlfriend Peppy took over while I was working." He smiled reassuringly. "As a matter of fact, she was the one who said it would be wrong to send you to the hospital. She's an actress and is very publicity conscious."

"Thank God for Peppy." Lauri tried to sit up but found it impossible.

"Just relax," Stan said soothingly. "You're still quite weak." He wiped her brow with a towel. Then, looking directly at her his manner changed and his voice became officious. "I don't know the man you are married to, but if you'd like to press charges, I'll be happy to testify on your behalf."

"Good God, no."

"Okay—just relax," Stan said soothingly.

"What about my job?" she suddenly remembered.

"I think you should call them and ask for a week off."

During the week of recuperation, Lauri tried to take stock of her life. She was strangely relieved at being separated from Brad. Their life together had been a great strain, although it pained her to admit it. She had little to show for it, except that she was no longer Larry's little girl. In spite of everything, she had come into her own.

On the morning before going back to work, Lauri went down to a pawn shop on Eighth Avenue. The man sitting behind the barred cage looked up at her suspiciously. Haltingly, Lauri took out the brooch and handed it to him. He took out his small magnifying glass and peered through it.

"Is it yours?" he asked, and Lauri felt she was being accused of a crime.

"Of course it's mine." She tried to hide her nervousness.

"I'll give you a couple of grand for it. Take it or leave it."

Lauri gulped. Two thousand dollars seemed unbelievable. If a pawnbroker was willing to give her that much, the brooch was obviously worth much more.

"Well?" the pawnbroker asked. "Do you want it?"

"Yes," she said with assurance.

"Name?"

"It's Lauri." She paused. She did not want to give her married name. "Lauri Eddington," she said firmly.

"Address."

She gave Larry's home address.

The man handed her the ticket and a pile of one-hundred-dollar bills. She ran out of the shop. The experience was embarrassing, but she had two thousand dollars and she was about to start a new life.

5

The gallery closed at 5:30 P.M. and Lauri, finished with her day's work, was locking the front door of the shop when she heard someone call her name.

"Mrs. DeHaven?" A heavy-set man with short cropped hair was standing at her side. She looked at him. He was not alone. Another man was with him. She knew neither.

"Yes," she answered, but a feeling of great discomfort overtook her.

"I'm Detective Grant, and this is my partner, Mr. Jarvis. We're with the nineteenth precinct," the man said.

Lauri nodded.

"Could we ask you a couple of questions?"

She nodded again.

"Well, it seems you pawned a brooch recently," Mr. Grant said. He too seemed uncomfortable. "It was a large diamond and sapphire piece in a gold setting."

"Yes, I did."

"May I ask where you got it?"

"I don't know that it's any of your business," she answered firmly, although feelings of panic were rising within.

"Mrs. DeHaven, please try to understand, we're simply doing our duty."

"What is your duty?" she said indignantly. "I had a brooch and I decided to pawn it."

"Was it your brooch?"

"Of course it was."

"Why did you pawn it under the name of Eddington?"

"That is my maiden name." She tried to sound rational and calm. "I do quite a few things under my maiden name. I work at the gallery under the name of Eddington."

"Did you buy the brooch?"

"No, it was given to me."

"By whom?"

"I don't think that's any of your business either." As she spoke the picture began to take shape. The brooch was not Brad's to give. The next thought was more difficult to come by; Brad had taken the brooch from someone.

"Mrs. DeHaven, please try to cooperate with us. We're not enjoying this any more than you are. Could you tell us who gave it to you?"

"Who wants to know?" she asked, suddenly fully in control of herself.

"The person from whom it was taken."

"And who's that?"

"We're not at liberty, at this point, to tell you. For now, we're simply trying to establish possession and how it came into your hands."

"Supposing I refuse to tell you?"

"We'll have to ask you to come to the precinct with us."

"And if I refuse?"

"We'll have to arrest you as a material witness."

"What does that mean?"

"Well, you're innocent of theft until proven otherwise, but since you will not cooperate with us, we must take you in as an accomplice on a charge of harboring information that would lead us to whoever is responsible for the theft." He paused. "The brooch is worth a great deal of money and the charge is grand larceny."

She looked around and saw a police car standing at the curb. She had not noticed it before. Looking back at the gallery, she was relieved that everyone was gone.

The drive to the police station was a nightmare. Lauri slid down in the seat hoping she could become invisible. The sight of curious pedestrians on the street watching her entering the police car made her shudder.

The station house was brightly lit and she felt ill. She also felt conspicuous in the drably painted room where policemen were walking around handcuffed to swarthy looking men and disheveled women. Someone was screaming obscenities, another was lying on the floor refusing to move and was being dragged by his ankles toward a separate room. The commotion made Lauri's terror grow.

Mr. Grant walked over to a uniformed man and whispered in his ear, and she watched them nod at each other in agreement. Then he came over to her.

"Mrs. DeHaven, before we go any further, I must again ask you to tell us who gave you the brooch, and do you have any other stolen goods in your possession."

"I don't have stolen goods of any sort," she replied, trying to sound indignant, but she did not sound convincing even to herself. Stolen goods! The Tiffany chandelier, the crystal goblets, the sterling silver cutlery, Brad's car . . .

"You may call your lawyer, if you wish," he said almost gently. "I think you should."

"I don't have a lawyer," she answered feebly. "I don't need a lawyer. I haven't done anything wrong. I'm not a thief." She felt the tears begin to choke her.

"You should call someone. Your husband, a relative, your boss?" Mr. Grant said kindly.

"I don't understand what you're talking about. I didn't steal anything. I got the brooch as a gift." She was completely terrified.

"I believe you," he said, "so if you'd just tell us who gave you the brooch, we'd check it out and go from there."

The uniformed policeman came over. "I think we can book her," he said firmly. "Get her fingerprinted," he ordered.

"Fingerprinted?" she screamed with horror. But even as she was protesting, another policeman walked over and, taking her firmly by the arm, led her into another room. Her hand was placed onto an inkpad and then each finger was pressed onto a blotter. She watched the action as though it were a bad dream. A piece of cloth was shoved at her. "You can wipe your hands now, miss."

Paralyzed with fear, she was led back into the main room and the uniformed policeman started asking her questions. Her mind was a blank. She could not follow what he was saying.

"I think you should call someone," Mr. Grant was standing beside her. "Just give me the number and I'll dial it."

Larry. She would call Larry. How she would explain where she was and what was happening was not clear to her, but there was no one else she could call.

The phone rang several times and she was about to hang up when Larry's breathless voice, sounding as though he was running, came on the line.

"Papa," she said as calmly as she could, but a sob of despair escaped her. "Oh, Papa, please come quickly." She could not go on. Mr. Grant took the phone from her, explained where she was and hung up.

She sat on a hard bench, dazed, waiting. Brad had stolen the brooch. She knew it. But from whom? The answer came immediately. He had taken it from his mother. She closed her eyes. The nightmare was too ghastly to digest.

Larry arrived with Robbie, and after kissing her and reassuring her that everything would work out, they proceeded to work out the details which enabled her to leave with them.

They drove down to the Bank Street apartment. Lauri lay down on the living-room sofa, feeling numb. She wanted to sleep, to escape from the realities she knew she would have to face at one point, but for now she wanted to be away from everything.

"I think we'd better get a lawyer," Robbie said.

"It's a hell of a situation." Larry sounded uncharacteristically unsure of himself. "I wonder if we shouldn't think about it more carefully."

"There's nothing to think about. And we'd better act fast," Robbie persisted. "What about that Ryan guy?"

"I don't know," Larry hedged. "Lauri?" He came over to the sofa. "Lauri, Robbie thinks we should call someone like Sam Ryan. What do you think?"

Larry's indecisiveness upset her. She opened her eyes and saw him standing over her, his brows knit, his hand running nervously through his hair.

"Why do we have to call anyone?" she asked, feeling uncomfortable.

"I have a feeling Mrs. DeHaven is going to press charges against you."

"What has she got to do with it?" Lauri asked carefully.

"It was her brooch," Larry answered, the halting manner in his voice was more disturbing than what he was saying.

She did not answer. The room was very quiet.

"Lauri," Larry finally spoke, his voice muffled. "Lauri, have you got a key to Mrs. DeHaven's apartment?"

She sat up slowly and looked from Larry to Robbie and back to Larry.

"Papa, I was there once in my life. It was the day I met her." She stopped as the full implication of his question hit her. "Papa, you don't think . . ."

"I don't know," he said quietly. "It's been a long time since you've lived with me. I knew you then . . ." He paused uncomfortably. "People change."

At that moment, Robbie lunged at Larry and hit him across the face with the back of his hand and Lauri began to scream hysterically. She tried to stand up. She wanted to run. Her legs buckled and she felt Robbie catch her and carry her into her room. She sank into a deep sleep.

"Lauri," she heard Robbie's voice and woke up immediately. "Lauri, Sam Ryan is here, and I want you to come into the living room and talk to him."

Robbie was looking down at her.

"It's going to be all right, baby. We just want you in there when he calls Mrs. DeHaven."

Sam walked over to her when she entered the room and hugged her. Larry was standing beside the fireplace, his back to them.

"I'm sorry, Lauri, for the mess," Sam said gently. "Now, if you'll just sit down and give me some of the facts, we'll clear this whole thing up tonight."

She looked around uncertainly.

"Who gave you the brooch?" Sam asked.

"Sam, does it matter?" she asked. "I can honestly tell you I didn't steal it."

"I know that," he said impatiently. "Who gave it to you?" he repeated the question.

"Brad gave it to me," she whispered.

"Did he give you a Tiffany chandelier as well? Silverware? Crystal goblets?"

She nodded, feeling dumb.

"Okay," Sam said, and he looked tired. "Let's get that witch on the phone and tell her the facts."

He dialed Cynthia DeHaven's number. Lauri looked over at the clock on the mantel. It was 3:00 A.M. She was about to suggest that they might be waking her, but stopped herself. It was a stupid thought.

"Cynthia? It's Sam Ryan."

The high-pitched anger of the woman could be heard.

"Shut up and listen," Sam ordered. "That little creep you raised stole your stuff, and his wife is being accused of the crime."

He listened, and except for the barrage of hysteria over the wire her words to everyone in the room were unintelligible. Sam held the phone close to his ear as he let her rant for a minute.

"Okay. Now let's get back to the facts. I'm telling you he stole your jewels, your chandelier and the rest of that crap you had in your apartment, and I'll prove it." He sounded menacing. Cynthia was screaming again. A sinister grimace spread over Sam's taut face. "Don't you worry, I'll prove it. I'll also prove he's an embezzler. And I'll see to it that it gets coverage in every newspaper in the country. I'll humiliate you and him to the point where you'll be run out of the country. So, I suggest you drop the charges first thing in the morning. My lawyer will phone you and tell you exactly what it is you are to say." He paused and there was no sound from the other end. "Or I'll press charges of my own."

Cynthia said something, but now her voice could no longer be heard.

"And, Cynthia, I don't want to see him around the office ever again, and, for whatever it's worth, I refuse to go on handling your stock holdings." He slammed the phone down.

"Did Brad embezzle money?" Lauri asked in awe.

Sam's face twisted into a strange, almost ugly smile. "Cynthia doesn't know if he did or didn't, but she does know her offspring, and if ever there was a rotten egg, he's it."

"What happens now?" Larry asked after a long silence which had fallen over the room.

"Well, I think it would be a good idea if Lauri came up to Croton with me. Cynthia is scared right now, but she's going to wake up in the morning and go at Lauri with everything she's got. She'll figure out she's here, and she'll stop at nothing." He smiled wryly. "You innocent people couldn't begin to know how to fight her. I do. We come from the same gutter."

Lauri kissed Robbie, but left without saying good-bye to Larry.

Lauri was quite ill for the first couple of weeks of her stay in Croton, and was under a doctor's care. Sam was away most of the time and she had the house to herself, except for the housekeeper, who doted on her. When he did come in for the weekend, they would avoid talking about what was happening with Cynthia, Brad or the events surrounding the theft.

It was six weeks later when Robbie called to tell her that Larry was moving to Palm Beach. He asked her to come in and say good-bye.

"You mean he's moving there permanently?" Lauri asked, fear creeping into her voice. Angry as she was with her father, not having him close by was frightening.

"Afraid so, princess." Robbie sounded sad.

Driving in to New York, she rehearsed her meeting with her father. She wondered if it would do any good to thrash it out, to see if it was possible she had misunderstood what he meant. She had been upset and he was, too.

She rushed up the stairs to the apartment and found Larry standing in the living room. Packed suitcases stood by the door. He looked ill. His tall frame seemed slightly stooped, his face was wrinkled with sorrow. They looked at each other for a long moment, while he searched her face for some indication that she had forgiven him. The spark of arrogance, the self-assurance were all gone.

"How did it happen?" he finally asked, breaking the silence.

"Papa, you've never really understood who I was or what I wanted." She tried to speak gently.

"I thought I was doing the best for you. I tried to be understanding, to protect you."

"Did you?"

"Lauri, it all began with that young man. I knew it and I had to tell you."

"Who, Brad?" The conversation made no sense.

"No, Tony Abbot," Larry said adamantly. "I know I shouldn't have said it the way I did. I certainly should not have hit you, but I loved you so much and I didn't want him to hurt you."

"Tony?" She was staggered. "What has Tony got to do with it?"

Larry looked puzzled and, in a flash it dawned on her that he had no idea where her anger lay, what he had actually done to her life from the time she was a child. He had picked one incident he could justify and still maintain his position as a father.

"Oh, Papa," she cried out in despair. "It wasn't Tony that made our life go sour. It wasn't your hitting me, or telling me about him that made the house of cards you built fall apart. It was the deception, the lie we lived together."

"I never lied to you."

"I'm sure you never actually told me a lie. It was much worse. You lived a lie. You never trusted yourself, and you never trusted me." She caught her breath trying to figure out how she could actually say what she wanted to. "Papa, the idea that you could even doubt for a second that I would take something that did not belong to me . . ." She could not bring herself to say it all.

Larry's expression of confusion deepened, and Lauri knew he was not able to understand what she was saying. It was useless. His pretense was his shield, and like a false heartbeat, he could never correct it. She turned away and walked out to the little terrace. She heard the front door slam, and in a few minutes she saw him walk out of the building, hail a cab and get in.

She stood for a long time looking down at the empty street; then, turning around, she walked back into the living room. She was all alone for the first time in her life.

6

Lauri was unable to pull herself out of the deep depression that had settled over her after Larry left. The months rushed by and she was aware of the passage of time by the changing seasons. The brief independence she had begun to feel in the last few months of her marriage to Brad disappeared. She drifted from day to day, week to week. Occasionally she got modeling jobs on Seventh Avenue through Robbie, although she refused to work for him directly. Otherwise, her life was taken up with companions who were as lonely as she. She met them at parties or singles bars. Her pattern became that of many young women in the late sixties. She got involved briefly in the anti-war movement and the soft-drug scene. Pot smoking was an antidote to reality, and drinking, which she never enjoyed was her way of accentuating her self-loathing.

It was Robbie who finally persuaded her to consider a career as a photographer's model. He introduced Lauri to an aspiring photographer who was trying to get a soap ad campaign. He was a pleasant young man, and with his help and encouragement, feeling she was doing it for him, she was able to throw herself into the work. He did not get the commission, but Lauri had some pictures. The relationship ended when the young man left for California and Lauri returned to her solitary existence.

Lauri was at the lowest point of her depression when she was awakened one morning by a call from June Smythe. June had one of the most successful modeling agencies in the city and was a friend of Robbie's. She had refused to sign up Lauri, but promised Robbie she would try to find her work if a job presented itself. In the two months Lauri had known her, June had sent her out on three jobs. She had gotten none of them.

Lauri had a dreadful hangover from the night before, and in spite of having lived alone for a long time, her first thought when she heard the phone ring, was that Larry might answer it. The ringing would not stop, and finally she reached out and picked up the receiver.

"Lauri, it's June Smythe," the woman said officiously.

Lauri was awake within seconds. Her eyes wandered to the nightstand clock. It was 8:45 A.M. "Hi June," she said, trying to sound fully alert. June Smythe rarely called her models, personally.

"Get a pencil and write this down," June ordered. "You've got an interview at twelve noon. It's at 220 Central Park South, on the twelfth floor." The voice was commanding. "Bring your pictures and, honey, be on time." The phone went dead before Lauri could ask the name of the photographer or if she had to bring any special clothing. She dared not call back.

Broke as she was, she took a taxi up to Central Park South. She could hear a clock chiming the midday hour as she hurried into the building.

Austere oak-paneled doors greeted her as she stepped out of the elevator. There was no sign on it to indicate she had arrived at the correct destination. She turned around to ask the elevator man who the apartment belonged to, but he had already gone. Filled with trepidation, she rang the bell. Deep chimes echoed through the apartment.

A young man, dressed in jeans and a tight ribbed turtlenecked sweater, answered the door. "Miss Eddington?" he asked pleasantly. "Please come in."

He allowed her to precede him into an enormous room with double-height windows through which one could see nothing but clear blue skies. Loud rock music came from every corner of the room, giving the place an atmosphere of joy.

"I'm Joey," he said, "and if you'll be kind enough to wait a few minutes, we'll be right with you."

Left alone, Lauri looked around.

The room was sparsely furnished, but every piece was in proportion to its size. A long, comfortable couch faced a fireplace. A huge coffee table stood in front of it, laden down with books and magazines. Two smaller settees stood on each side of the table. All three pieces were covered with pillows in a melange of colorful fabrics. The rest of the space was devoted to camera equipment and other paraphernalia needed for photographing. A stairway hugged one wall of the room, indicating a second floor was part of the apartment. In spite of the starkness of the decor, a feeling of warmth and well being descended on her.

"Lauri?" She heard her name and turned around slowly. She recognized the voice, but was too stunned to react.

Standing a few feet away was Tony Abbot. She bit her lip for fear of bursting out crying. Then, with unrestrained joy, she ran to him and threw herself into his arms. After a brief moment, she pulled back and continued to stare at him as the tears of happiness streamed down her cheeks.

They never got any work done that day. Tony took her up to his living quarters. There were four rooms on the upper level, each decorated with simplicity and good taste. The room, however, that was most startling and indicative of who Tony Abbot had become, was his bedroom. It was a large room containing a king-size bed, tautly made up with crisp white sheets and a blanket resting on the foot of it, a small nightstand and a floor lamp for reading. The walls were lacquered navy blue; the deep mahogany floors were bare. The large windows did not have blinds or shades, and as in the living room, the sky was the sight that greeted the eye.

They settled themselves in the library, which was lined with books and was done in varying shades of gray flannel and soft camel-colored suede. Tony turned on the record player and, in contrast to the rock music that greeted her when she walked in, a magnificent recording of Joan Sutherland filled the room. Tony picked up the phone and asked Joey to bring up some tea. As they waited, Lauri settled herself into one of the armchairs, never taking her eyes off him. He was as handsome as ever, and she tried to detect a sign of his homosexuality in manner or gesture. There was none. Then, remembering the young man who opened the door, she wondered if he was Tony's lover. She regretted the thought.

Just then Joey walked in with a tray and two cups and a teapot. He poured the tea and handed it to Lauri.

"Do you take milk, sugar?" he asked respectfully.

Lauri shook her head.

"Will that be all, Mr. Abbot?" Joey asked.

"Yes, Joey, you can go now," Tony said absently. "As a matter of fact, you can take the rest of the day off. Just call June Smythe and tell her Miss Eddington is perfect for the job and I will be using her." He smiled pleasantly and the young man left.

That was not a conversation between lovers, Lauri thought, and was both relieved and embarrassed by her feelings.

They talked late into the evening. Tony told her about his life in England in great detail, trying to bridge the gap of years. He seemed to include her, make her feel that she was still a part of his life. Lauri, in turn, delved into the past five years of her life, but found herself editing some of the horrors that had taken place. She mentioned Brad and her marriage which ended in divorce. Still, she did impart her feelings freely.

It was seven o'clock in the evening and it was growing dark.

"Now, my sweet," Tony said firmly, "I shall take you to dinner, and then we'll come back here and we'll go to work."

"What is the job?" Lauri asked, remembering why she was there. "Do you want to see my pictures?" She tried to sound professional.

"Lauri," Tony said seriously, "those pictures couldn't get you a job posing for a peep-show ad for a girlie house." He was not smiling. "You can be one of the top models in this city, but it will mean work, hard work." He paused. "And I'm going to make you do it."

"But I thought you said I had the job?" she said, trying to sound as impersonal as he now sounded.

"You do. It's a portrait shot of a girl holding a glass of wine. You can do that without any problems, with my photographing it. But that's not what I'm talking about. I'm going to make you start using your body, your face, your mouth, your eyes, your hands, your guts and your brains." He did not look like her friend when he spoke. "By the time I'm through teaching you to work in front of a camera, you will have discovered every fucking part of who and what you are, where you live and why you're doing it."

Lauri was frightened. "Tony, I don't think I . . ."

"Shut up, Lauri," he said, but his tone softened as he became aware of her again. "You have it at your fingertips, and I'm just going to help you make it come to the fore." He put his hands out and helped her up. "Now for dinner." Putting his arm protectively around her shoulder, he led her out of the apartment.

It took nearly two years of grueling work for Lauri to come up to Tony's standards of what a model could and should achieve in a sitting. She stopped seeing the people she had been involved with and concentrated on what Tony wanted. She worked all day, and would be too exhausted to go out at night. He was a tyrant when it came to work. At times he reminded her of her father and of Brad, but she knew there was a difference. Tony was doing it for her, whereas, Larry and Brad were feeding their own egos. Tony was helping her acquire an identity and a goal. Her perceptions, whether in people, clothes, art, literature or music, were suddenly respected. A disagreement did not end in dismissal, but in discussion. Tony listened to her, considered her opinions, respected her views. She began to emerge as a person.

Tyrannical as he was when it came to his work, the minute the camera was put away he became her friend. She knew little about his personal life, but spending as much time with him as she did, she was more puzzled than ever about who he really was. There was a maturity about him that far exceeded his age. He was one of the most prominent fashion photographers around, but it did not affect him. She knew he had lovers, both men and women, and on occasion she was introduced to them. None, however, played a serious role in his life. Tony, as far as she could tell, lived a totally independent emotional life. He read a great deal, loved the opera as much as he did popular music, was serious and introverted. Able to be vivacious when people were around, he would close up when alone and the thoughtful solitary man emerged.

When Lauri first started working with him she had secretly hoped they would become lovers, but warm as he was, he made it clear he was her friend, no more. Often, she would sit and stare at him engrossed in his work and would wonder why she was not attractive to him as a woman. Many men wanted her. It was the only subject she could never discuss with him.

Being Tony Abbot's top model boosted her career and she was in great demand. She did a television commercial, which was being considered for an award, and she was becoming a minor celebrity. Her pictures were everywhere and people she had not seen in all the time since she left Brad began calling. Even her father's friends, who had always treated them like poor relations, were now inviting her to their homes as an equal. On those occasions she missed Larry and wished she could bring herself to call him and offer to share her success with him. She kept putting it off. The time had not yet come, and she knew it.

Lauri could feel the change in herself. The frantic need for people, movement and noise was gone. She worked hard, took each assignment seriously and concentrated on what she was doing. Her mind was receptive, her inner need for creativity was flowering. When Robbie asked her to create a line of Lauri Eddington sportswear, she threw herself into the job with enthusiasm.

Robbie was thrilled with her work and accepted all her sketches. When she saw the first outfit finished she finally felt secure enough to call Larry and try to reestablish her relationship with him.

The conversation with him was reminiscent of her call to him after she married Brad. Now, however, the gift she was bringing was her own personality rather than Sam Ryan's. Larry was overcome with emotion and invited her down to Palm Beach for the weekend.

Lauri's sense of security began to falter even as she was packing for the trip. She was anxious about her wardrobe, her appearance, her new-found independence. She modeled the clothes she was planning on taking for Tony and ended up with two laden suitcases for the brief stay. She traveled in an outfit she had designed, which headed the Lauri Eddington collection. The tight-fitting magenta pants, combined with a purple man-tailored shirt and a fuschia sash, were striking, and Lauri knew she attracted attention as she stepped off the plane in Palm Beach. With admiring glances being thrown in her direction, she felt fortified.

Larry was waiting for her, and she ran toward him, breathlessly. He gathered her in his arms and they clung to each other for a long time.

"How do I look, Papa?" was her first question as she moved away from him.

The imperceptible pause before he answered shattered all vestige of self-confidence. "That's some color combination." He tried to smile.

"You don't like it." She was angry at herself for asking his opinion. She was furious for caring.

"I do, princess," Larry insisted. "It's just that I'm not partial to those colors." He put his arm protectively around her shoulder. "But that's my problem, sweetheart."

The sense of self, the feelings of achievement, of being her own person were gone. She was Larry's little girl, unhappy about not getting her father's approval.

Sitting in the open convertible car, Lauri glanced over at him. If Larry was aware of what he had done, there was no evidence of it. He chatted amicably, telling her anecdotes, outlining the plans for her stay. In no way did he indicate an awareness of the passage of time since he had last seen her, or the circumstances under which they had parted.

By the time they reached his house, Lauri was completely miserable. She knew she would not show him any of her designs or tell him about what had actually happened to her in the intervening years.

Larry had finally made it as a personality, and Lauri was pleased for him, but she could not wait to get away. Larry was the same overconfident authority about everything and everybody. He had re-created a social group of friends who admired and respected him, listened to him and enjoyed his company and Lauri found herself bowing to his commanding manner.

"Why do I do it to myself?" she asked Tony, the first night she was back in New York.

"We all have needs," Tony answered soberly, "and until the needs change, we go on feeding them."

"I don't have a need to be made to feel tasteless and stupid," she protested.

"No, you have the need to be Larry's little girl, and he has the need to have Lauri as an obedient daughter."

"When does it change?"

"When you accept it for what it is." Tony smiled and a faraway look came into his face. "Someday it will happen," he said with assurance. "Give yourself time."

Lauri won the television commercial award, which was gratifying, and she threw herself more seriously into designing. She loved designing, and although her clothes were accepted by the younger set of fashion-conscious working girls, she could not make it into the "big league." It did not daunt her enthusiasm. She was convinced that one day when she had more time, she would turn her attention exclusively to designing and would make it.

She was busy from early morning until late at night. She was closer to Tony than ever and she even cultivated a taste for the opera, and they became an "item" in the gossip columns. Everything was falling into place for her. Still, the loneliness of the soul persisted. She had several affairs, which she hoped would develop into serious relationships. They did not. She kept looking for someone who could fill a void that had been in her since she was very young and which was now more acute since her life had taken shape.

7

Lauri was at the height of her success when she met Adam Stillman. It was just before Christmas when she got a call from the Van Ess-Stillman law firm asking her to come in. Her suit against the DeHavens had been settled. Hard as she fought against suing Cynthia, Sam insisted, saying that in defeat Cynthia was a raging tigress, and unless a counter-suit for damages was established, Lauri would come off badly.

The young lawyer was extremely pleasant as he waited with her at the elevator after she'd signed the papers. It was late afternoon on a cold December day and she was wrapped in a huge parka, her head covered with a knitted cap and a matching scarf was flung around her neck. Her dungarees were tucked into the leather boots and she wore no makeup. Just as the elevator door was closing behind her, someone forced it open and Lauri found herself staring at a man who was vaguely familiar.

He pressed the button for the ground floor and they stood awkwardly next to each other, with Lauri trying to recall where she had met him. He looked over at her and smiled self-consciously.

"We've met, haven't we?" she asked.

"We might have." His voice was deep and he seemed preoccupied. "I'm Adam Stillman."

"Oh, my God, of course." Lauri became flustered. "You're the Congressman." She smiled and felt herself blush. "Please forgive me for not recognizing you, but the truth is we have met."

"When?"

"I was sixteen years old and you came down to my high school and I gave you an award." She paused, recalling the day vividly. "You even leaned over and kissed my cheek after I finished my speech."

"That would account for my not recognizing you." He smiled more comfortably. "I couldn't have forgotten someone as beautiful as you had we met more recently." He said it gracefully, but Lauri knew the words were forced.

"Which reminds me, I must thank you, or rather your office, for taking up a lawsuit for me and winning it."

"I'm sorry, but I'm not really involved in the legal work anymore."
He frowned.

"I'm Lauri Eddington," she said. "Sam Ryan called you almost three
years ago when I was unjustly accused of a theft."

"Of course, I remember." He seemed relieved. "It was an ugly, terrible thing that happened to you. I'm glad it was resolved."

The elevator door opened. "May I buy you a victory drink?" he asked
politely, and seemed confused by his suggestion.

"I'd love it."

"Do you have a preference?" he asked, and Lauri got the feeling he
was surprised at what he was saying.

"How about the Regency Bar?" she said. "It's only a couple of blocks
from here."

He smiled. "I know where it is. I live in the city."

She returned the smile. He appeared unsure of himself, and Lauri
found it attractive.

When the waiter came for their order, they were embarrassed since
neither wanted an alcoholic beverage.

"I'll have a glass of white wine," Lauri said, making the concession.

"Make that two." Adam turned to her and for the first time seemed at
ease in her presence.

It was past eight o'clock when they left the bar. Lauri was completely captivated. "I don't know when I've enjoyed myself more," she
said genuinely.

"May I call you?" Adam asked.

"I wish you would." She dug into her large bag and took out a pad
and pencil and jotted her home number down. "I really hope to see you
again."

On her way home, Lauri wondered if Adam would call. He had told
her a great deal about his work, his life, his travels. He was married, but
his wife was in Greenwich, Connecticut, visiting her ailing mother for
the holidays. He had two daughters and a nephew. It almost sounded as
though he had three children. Several times he mentioned the nephew as
his son, but each time he corrected himself. He had also spoken with
great passion about his recent trip to the Middle East, and Lauri could
not help but feel his deep sadness when he mentioned his visit to Israel.
Lauri knew about the recent war there, and made a mental note to ask
Tony for more details about it.

Adam called Lauri early Saturday morning. In the three days since
they met, she had not stopped thinking about him. She made a point of
finding out more about Adam Stillman, Congressman from New York,
and discovered that he was very much married, was a dedicated public

official, a sincere, thinking man and not someone who would play around while his wife was away.

"How about brunch at my place?" Lauri said and was touched by the note of relief in his voice at her suggestion.

"That would be lovely. But are you sure it won't be any trouble?"

"I'm not the greatest cook, but I'll get something together. Besides, I love listening to you, and it would make no difference if we were sitting in a restaurant or at my place. I'll get a good fire going and we can relax."

He was there on the dot of noon on Sunday and the hours flew by just as they had when they were at the Regency. Lauri was unusually attracted to him and was amused and amazed at being self-conscious by her feelings. She covered her nervousness by talking a great deal.

"You're a total revelation to me," Adam said at one point. "Your generation is being cruelly maligned if you are in any way representative."

Lauri was flattered. "I'm less than most of them," she said in her forthright manner. "I know less than most people my age."

"You're being modest."

"No, I'm not. Things happened in my life that made me stop my education, and I feel it especially when I'm talking to someone like you."

"Formal education could not give you the instincts you have," Adam said seriously. "Those don't come out of textbooks, they come from living, feeling, seeing and having basic compassion for your fellow man. You have it."

When Adam left, he kissed her on the cheek and promised to call when he was next in New York. He did not tell her where he was going, but she assumed he was spending time with his wife in Greenwich.

On Christmas Eve, Lauri spent the evening with Tony, as she had been doing for the past few years. It had become a ritual since they were both alone and considered each other family. They decorated the tree together, and when the clock struck midnight, they opened their gifts and drank champagne. Lauri usually spent the night, and they would go to the Plaza for breakfast on Christmas morning. This evening, Lauri felt restless and wondered how she could leave gracefully. They opened their gifts and drank their champagne, and then Tony asked if she would forgive him if he went out for the evening. She knew he was lying—was giving her an out. She reached out her hand to him and he took it and held it for a long time.

"You're my love, Lauriana."

"And you're mine." She smiled and kissed him warmly.

The phone was ringing when Lauri entered her apartment.

"Merry Christmas," Adam said.

"Where are you?"

"In a little bar around the corner from where you live."

"Would you like to come up?"

Lauri could not remember ever being so completely happy and feeling so desired as when Adam made love to her. He was a good lover, gave of himself as no man she had ever slept with. Past relationships faded into oblivion. All she knew was that she wanted to please him, satisfy him, show him her gratitude.

"You're like a little girl." Adam was lying beside her, holding her close.

"Did I make you happy?"

He looked down at her and kissed her brow. "Yes, Lauri, you've made me very, very happy." He was silent for a long time. She snuggled up to him. "You're very shy for a successful, liberated young lady, aren't you?" he said finally. He sounded surprised.

Lauri thought about it briefly. "Yes, I guess I am."

"Do you have a boyfriend?"

She laughed. "Hardly, Adam. I can only handle one affair at a time."

He looked disturbed and leaned over to get a cigarette.

"Adam, you said when we first met that my generation is being maligned. Well, all the stories about the liberated ladies of the sixties and seventies are mostly stories. Yes, I've had lovers. I enjoy sleeping with men. But I choose the men I sleep with and I choose them carefully. Most women do."

Lauri thought she had been in love several times since leaving Brad, but her love for Adam seemed to be the culmination of every dream she ever had. He fulfilled her completely. Within weeks after meeting him, she could not stand to be without him. The days when he was in Washington, she would suffer miserably. Often she would take a plane in the late evening and meet him there. The weekends were the most difficult. He spent them with his wife, whom Lauri remembered from the day when she gave him the award at her school. That day when he leaned over and kissed her, she caught sight of his wife, who was standing in the wings. The features of the woman were blurred in her mind, but she recalled a vision with light red hair, which looked like a bright halo, dressed in a flaming red dress and a mink coat thrown over her shoulders. At the time, Lauri remembered thinking she was the most beautiful creature she had ever seen.

Adam never again discussed his family with her, but he did talk a great deal about his work in Washington. Her ignorance in matters of the political world upset her. It did not bother him. He became her lover, her teacher, her father. Except for Tony, Robbie and her work, her life revolved around him. Since leaving Brad, Lauri smoked pot as a matter of course. It enhanced her enjoyment of her sexual experiences and it helped her fall asleep on the nights when sleep seemed impossible. With Adam, she discovered a sexual relationship that was thrilling without the stimulation of the drug. He was gentle, caring and in contrast to her other lovers, he seemed to draw his physical pleasure from her. He was older than any other man she had ever slept with and lying in his arms after their lovemaking, she would feel protected, cared for and completely loved.

His being married did not bother her. She was disinterested in marriage, and she was sure he had no thought or desire to leave his wife. Her future, however, as an independent person began to preoccupy her. She was twenty-five and was fully aware that she could go on modeling for several more years, but she refused to let her future hinge on those tenuous years. She was making headway with her "Lauri Eddington" label, but it was still not lucrative enough to support her. She needed national exposure to bring it to the attention of the public, and although she was earning good money as a model it was hardly likely she could do it on her own.

When Lauri was offered the job of being the Aden Girl, a highly coveted plum in the modeling world, she accepted with alacrity. It meant greater financial security, but it also represented other possibilities.

"It's a beginning of an end to your modeling career," Tony said when she told him about it. "You become identified with their product and it's hard to break it."

"I'm getting a five-year deal," Lauri answered. "And I don't intend to just be their model. I'm going to work out a tie-in of my designs with the Aden Girl people."

"What are you talking about?"

"I'm going to persuade them to allow me to wear my collection when I do their campaign."

"Can you swing it?" Tony smiled with appreciation.

"With your help I can. I've sold the idea to Kim Sloan, the account executive. What I need now is a set of pictures, with me wearing my designs, identical to the pictures they want with their wardrobe." She paused, letting the thought sink in. "It will mean double work for you and for me, but it's worth it. Kim promised to help, and she's great. Bright as a whip, inventive and adores my clothes."

"That's quite a plan," Tony said somberly.

"I've got the sketches for the spring and summer lines right here," she started sifting through her briefcase and pulled out a batch of drawings and swatches of materials. "Robbie is gung ho on the whole thing." She was breathless with excitement. "It's the break I've been looking for. There's no way I can get the Lauri Eddington line displayed nationally on my own. This can put us into the big league."

The work load was enormous, but Lauri thrived on it. She felt more alive than ever. Robbie helped in the execution of the designs; Tony photographed each set of pictures in duplicate; Adam was her cushion of emotional security.

When Adam started campaigning for his seventh congressional term, Lauri knew she could not work on the campaign, since his wife was involved, but she did start seeing Sam Ryan again. He was backing Adam and through him she felt close to Adam and felt she was involved in his life.

The morning of the election, Lauri voted early, then spent the day posing. Now, standing in the dressing room, she was putting her things into a Gucci tote bag when she heard the doorman of Tony's building buzzing from the lobby. Sam was early and Lauri was pleased. The conversation with Tony was getting too intimate and she was afraid she would break down and tell him about Adam. She threw a last look at herself in the mirror. She had to look her best, and she had to be poised and calm. The evening was bound to be difficult.

After knowing Adam for a year, she was going to meet Beth Stillman for the first time, and the prospect was frightening.

8

Jeb, Sam Ryan's driver, held the door open for Lauri as she stepped into the black Rolls-Royce and leaned over to kiss Sam's cheek.

"You look like you're ready for a victory party, Lauri," Sam said as he took her hand in his.

"He's going to win, isn't he, Sam?" Lauri asked as she looked at the older man sitting comfortably in the opposite corner of the car.

Sam Ryan was a large, heavy-set man, yet his features were amazingly refined. His white hair was thinning, his eyes were blue and almost cold behind the rimless glasses, his nose long and aquiline, his lips thin and serious. He was in his mid-sixties but looked younger, being an athlete who spent many hours on the golf course, playing tennis, swimming or riding his horses which he kept on his country estate in Croton, New York. He had come to the United States from Ireland when he was barely two years old and had grown up in New York. He had made it the hard way, working as a messenger boy on Wall Street after school hours, slowly rising in the firm that employed him. When he graduated from CCNY Law School, which he did by attending night school, he continued his ascent until he was able to buy his own seat on the Stock Exchange and had earned the enormous fortune that made him one of the richest men in the country and one of the most powerful leaders in the political arena both in New York and Washington. An advisor to Presidents was the way the press referred to him. Being blessed by Sam, a non-party-affiliated elder statesman, was a coup for any aspiring politician. Adam Stillman was Sam's man, and as Lauri nestled down into the plush comfort of the huge car her confidence was justified.

"He deserves to win," Sam said quietly. "But the voting public is fickle, you know that, Lauri, and although, to date, Adam has made no visible mistakes, there's always a possibility that the unknown will rear its ugly head."

Lauri felt herself grow cold as she threw a sidelong glance at the older man. Was he warning her? Did he know? Did he suspect?

"But at this late stage," Lauri found her voice, "if there was something in Stillman's background that could ruffle the nest, wouldn't it have come up by now?" She knew she was talking too quickly, and she caught her breath before continuing. "After all the times he's run for Congress, surely the opposition would have dug up any dirt if there was any."

"True," Sam said quietly. "But somehow this Congressional race is different." He was silent for a moment. "You see, Lauri, Adam is not going to serve out the congressional term. He's planning on running for mayor." He looked over at her, letting his words sink in. "Assuming he wins tonight," he went on, "which I sincerely hope he does and frankly believe he will, he's going to have a hard and long fight to get the nomination next year for the mayoralty against a pretty strong incumbent."

Lauri retreated farther into her seat. Mayor of New York. Adam Stillman, Mayor of New York. The thought was staggering and gave vent to her greatest fears. As long as Adam was in Washington, coming into town only on weekends or late at night, they were able to keep their affair out of the peering eyes of the public. But being the mayor would mean he would be living in New York, living with his wife.

"You're really a beautiful young woman," she heard Sam say, and she looked over at him. "As a matter of fact, you will probably grow more beautiful as you grow older, which will be a disaster." He reached over and touched her cheek. "I'm glad I won't be around for that."

"You're sweet, Sam," Lauri said, pleased with the change of mood and subject. She threw her head back and stared at the darkening sky through the rear window.

She had not seen Adam since Friday, when he had to go with his wife to visit her mother in Greenwich. She was in her apartment when he called. It was noon and she was expecting to meet him for lunch.

"Sorry about not being able to make it, hon," he said, "but Beth insists I go with her. She feels I might persuade her mother to do some last-minute politicking for me among her rich New York ladies."

"That's ridiculous," Lauri answered seriously. "Her father was a registered conservative Republican, and you know better than I that they didn't endorse you this time around. Good God, they have their own candidate to think about."

"What you don't understand, honey, is that Beth has been determined, ever since she was a little girl, to break her father's heart and her mother's back. She succeeded in the first effort when she married me. She's never stopped going after her mother." He sounded gay, and Lauri realized she resented his good mood.

Lauri did not answer. Ever since she got involved with Adam she avoided talking about Beth. Instinctively, Adam felt her reticence, but he was now high with the smell of victory and was being insensitive to her feelings. She did not blame him, yet the pain she felt was indifferent to logic.

"You there, Lauri?" Adam asked as the silence grew longer. "Are you all right?" he asked more anxiously, when she did not answer.

"Yes, Adam," Lauri said, and tried to make her voice light. "Of course I'm all right, silly." She cleared her throat. "You'd better hurry, though, or you'll be late."

"What are your plans for the weekend?"

"Nothing much. I might go to Tony's and spend some time with him. And Sam invited me to go up to the country."

"Will you go?"

"Would you like me to?" she asked, resenting the question. For a minute Adam sounded like Brad.

"Stop it, Lauri," Adam said coldly, "and cut out these stupid insinuations. I don't give a hoot in hell if you ever see Sam or ever talk to him again." He paused, controlling his anger. "You know my feelings. You know damn well where you stand with me, so why torture yourself?"

"I'm sorry, Adam," Lauri answered immediately. She was being oversensitive and was reading things into the innocent query. "I'm just upset that I won't be seeing you this weekend, that's all." She paused briefly. "Actually, I'll be fine, and you go on and have a good time, and don't forget to charm the pants off the old bags. As a matter of fact, once they meet you I'll bet quite a few of them will abandon their candidate and vote for you." Before she hung up she clutched the phone and whispered, "I do love you so, Adam."

Adam did not call during the weekend, although she had purposely not gone to Sam's. She stayed in town and spent some time with Tony. She spent all day Sunday in bed, feeling weepy and depressed. Several friends called to invite her out, but it was Tony who called almost every hour to find out how she was.

"You looked like hell yesterday," he said the first time he called. "Shouldn't you see a doctor?"

"I'll be fine, Tony. I'm just tired," she said reassuringly.

"It's the Tuesday sitting I'm worried about," he said, trying to sound nonchalant. "We've still got quite a few pictures to shoot."

"Sure, baby," she laughed. "I know you're not worried about me. It's simply your career, right?"

"Okay, so I worry about you. I always worry about you. Can I help it if I'm queer?"

"In more ways than one, my love. But so am I, and I'll be smashing on Tuesday. I promise, for the sake of your career."

She hung up feeling better. Her friendship with Tony was the most solid relationship in her life, and she cherished it as she knew he did.

Monday, Lauri felt better and went out to buy a new outfit for the victory party. She bought a long body-hugging taupe silk dress with shoelace-thin straps, and a matching stole. High heeled shoes were dyed to the exact shade of the dress. She had a small gold clutch bag her father had given her years back, and her full-length red-fox cape was to complete the outfit. She rushed home from her shopping spree hoping to have a message from her service that Adam had called. There was none. She had been thrilled with her purchases, but as she started unpacking them, she felt foolish. Everything she had bought was so unlike her usual style of dressing. As she tried it all on, the tears would not stop flowing.

Now, late Tuesday, sitting next to Sam in his car, she was feeling a sense of uncontrollable impatience at the thought of seeing Adam.

"We'll stop at Le Mistrel for a bite before going to the Roosevelt," Sam said and brought Lauri back to the present. "Is that okay?"

She nodded as the car came to a halt outside the East Side restaurant. "I thought it would be wise. We won't really get a chance to eat again until quite late, and that's provided Adam wins," Sam was saying as she stepped out of the car. "And if he wins, I promised to take Beth and Adam for a nightcap at El Morocco." He took her arm and guided her into the restaurant. "I think it would be nice for you to meet them, considering you're such an avid supporter."

"Sam," Lauri said suspiciously, "you must be getting senile. You told me of this plan a week ago, in almost the exact words."

"Did I now?" Sam answered. "I forgot." He smiled a strange little smile. "It's always amazing to me that you've never met the Stillmans."

"Sam, I'm just a voter, remember?" Lauri said lightly, as the maître d' led them toward their table. "And I did meet Adam Stillman once," she continued trying to be as nonchalant as possible.

"Oh, you did?" Sam said as he looked carefully at the menu which the waiter handed him.

"Yes, I even have a picture of him and me as he leaned over and kissed my cheek. I was sixteen and giving him an award from Performing Arts. Thank God, it wasn't in color. I was blushing like mad."

"You never told me that," Sam said soberly.

"Why should I? It was years ago," she said pleasantly. Again she wondered if Sam knew of her relationship with Adam.

She concentrated on the menu, and the thought of eating made her ill.

"What will you have, madam?" the waiter was standing beside her table, pen and pad in hand.

"I'll start with some clear broth," she said feebly. "Then I'll decide on what else I want." When she saw Sam raise his brows in wonder, she decided to ignore the look. Sam proceeded to order a huge meal for himself, choosing the wine carefully. Finished with his order he turned to her, "Sure that's all you'll have?"

"I've put on weight," Lauri said lightly. "Even Tony noticed."

"He's a nice boy," Sam said sipping the wine which was delivered to the table. "You've known him for a long time, haven't you?"

"We were in high school together. He wanted to be a dancer, or so he thought, or rather so his mother wanted him to think." She smiled, "Just as I thought I wanted to be an actress, or so my father thought." Mentioning her father made her grow serious for a brief moment. "Anyway, Tony left suddenly and went to England. I don't think I've ever missed anyone as much as I missed him. He was truly my best and only friend."

"We should have asked him to join us this evening," Sam said suddenly. "I've only met him a couple of times, but I like him. He's not the run of the mill . . ." He stopped, not knowing how to finish the sentence.

"He's not," Lauri said emphatically. "And he wouldn't have come. He suspects that there is a mad love affair going on between you and me, and he disapproves totally."

"And right he is," Sam agreed. "I'm old enough to be your grandfather."

They both smiled.

The meal was eaten in uncomfortable silence, and try as Lauri did, she could think of nothing to say. Sam seemed equally uncomfortable.

When they stepped back into the limousine, Lauri had to suppress the impulse to ask to be driven home rather than join Sam at the Roosevelt. It was, however, out of the question. She had to go.

"Are the results in?" Sam asked Jeb as they settled into the car seats.

"He's won big." Jeb smiled into the rearview mirror. "Both opponents conceded."

Sam looked at his watch. "That was quick," he said with appreciation. "You'd better step on it," he instructed and looked over at Lauri. "I knew he could do it." He sounded relieved.

Adam rose from his seat the minute Lauri and Sam walked into the ballroom. He flashed a triumphant smile in their direction and Lauri nearly tripped, unable to take her eyes off him.

Once seated, Lauri tried to relax and with great effort tore her eyes away from Adam and shifted her gaze to the tables flanking the speaker's podium. She caught sight of Beth Stillman almost immediately. She was a regal-looking woman, beautifully groomed and poised. She was looking at Adam with interest and appreciation. Still, as Lauri explored the woman's face, she felt inexplicably sad. The memory of the candidate's wife standing in the wings of the school auditorium, years back, flashed through her mind. The resemblance was inescapable, but the woman sitting on the dais looked strained, uncomfortable and faded. The excitement that emanated from that long-ago image was nowhere in sight. Lauri felt sorry for her.

"Sam," she whispered, "I don't feel well."

He leaned toward her and touched her brow.

"You're quite warm," he said with concern.

"I don't think I'll join you later." She found it difficult to talk. She felt like crying and could not understand why.

"Can you last through Stillman's speech?" Sam asked. "And since you're already here, I'd really like you to meet him."

"Of course," Lauri said in a resigned voice. She would have to meet Beth Stillman. It was unavoidable and quite distasteful. Settling back, she tried to follow what Adam was saying, but found herself puzzled by her reaction to Beth. In all the time that she had been seeing Adam, she had never thought of herself usurping his wife's position in his life. She had no qualms about having an affair with a married man, since their relationship did not seem to infringe on his marriage or his home life. Marriage to Adam was the farthest thing from her mind, and she was sure he had never given it any thought either. They were two mature people who were in love, who fulfilled a need in each other, independently from anyone around.

". . . and last, but not least, my appreciation to my wife, Beth, without whom I believe I could not have won as handily as I did. She's a pro in more ways than one, and I would be remiss if I did not mention her."

Lauri shifted uncomfortably in her seat. That was not in the speech Adam had read to her the week before—"appreciation to my wife . . ."

The thunderous applause of approval when Adam finished his speech reverberated through the room, and Lauri was overwhelmed by her feelings of pride in Adam which were not mingled with inexplicable guilt.

"He's a winner," Sam said in appreciation. "If only he weren't Jewish, he could have gone all the way."

"Isn't there ever going to be a Jewish President?" Lauri asked curiously.

"Maybe in your lifetime, Lauri," Sam smiled sadly. "I doubt I'll see the day."

Lauri was about to reply when she saw Sam rise. She looked around. Adam and Beth were approaching.

Beth extended her hand in greeting, and Lauri felt herself blush. She nodded briefly and quickly looked over at Adam, hoping to hide her confusion.

"Lauri isn't feeling well," Sam said as they all started toward the exit.

Lauri could not follow the exchange that was taking place, since Adam was walking close to her and she was conscious of his presence.

Beth said something, and Lauri heard the mockery in the voice.

Standing on the sidewalk, waiting for Sam's limousine, Lauri felt Beth's eyes boring into her. She looked over at the older woman and their eyes met. She knows, Lauri thought, and the feelings of sadness she had felt for Beth when she first saw her on the dais returned more forcefully. The poor woman knows about the relationship with Adam and is frightened. She wanted to reach out and take Beth's hand and reassure her that she did not want to take Adam away, assure her that she was safe. In spite of the cold she felt drenched with perspiration and her head began to spin.

"You all right, Lauri?"

She opened her eyes and found herself in Sam's car, leaning against him. Beth and Adam were sitting on the limousine's jump seats. Adam was very pale. Beth was somber.

"I feel like such a fool," Lauri whispered. "I've never fainted before."

"Nonsense," Sam said gently. "You work too hard. I must speak to Tony about that."

The car came to a stop in front of Lauri's building.

"Sure you won't let me get my doctor to come over?" Sam asked, helping her out.

"I'll be fine, Sam." She smiled at Adam and Beth. "Please forgive me for spoiling your evening."

"I'll call you in the morning," Sam said, and he watched while she unlocked the front door of her building.

Reaching her landing, she saw a manila envelope propped up against her front door. It was from Stan Blyden. Entering the apartment, Lauri threw her coat on a chair and opened the envelope. It contained a small package and a letter. She read it slowly.

"The results of the test are positive. Come in soon for a thorough examination." The words were neatly typed. The handwritten message beneath made her smile. "Congratulations, Lauri, if congratulations are in order. In any event, as your friend and doctor, I suggest you come in and talk to me as soon as possible." It was signed "Stan."

Removing the brown wrapping from the package she realized it contained a bottle of calcium pills. Sweet Stan. He had tried reaching her for the last couple of days, but she had avoided him. She did not really need his confirmation about the pregnancy. She had known it all along and had purposely put off taking the test. Now she was about six weeks pregnant and knew she had procrastinated hoping for some miracle that would make the decision about having the child easier. Instead, she was more confused than ever. How could she predict the chance meeting

with Beth Stillman and her feelings about the woman? How could she
have known about Adam's plans following his successful bid for his congressional seat? But most important, how could she have anticipated her
own ambivalence concerning the unborn child once it became a reality.
She was going to have Adam's baby, and it was something she thought
she wanted until a few hours ago. Now she was frightened.

Pills in hand she walked into her bedroom. She was completely
drained, but the overwhelming exhaustion was gone. She had to think
carefully about her future. She undressed slowly, throwing her clothes
down carelessly. Her future was no longer hers alone. If she were to
have the baby it would be "their future"—hers and a child's future. A
sense of excitement accompanied the thought. She stared down at her
naked body. Except for a slight thickening of the waist, it had not
changed. Her stomach was still flat. Her breasts were a bit fuller, but
never having been voluptuous, it was hardly noticeable. She could continue modeling for quite a while. She could certainly do head shots
throughout the pregnancy. Being pregnant would not preclude doing her
designing. It certainly would not interfere with her work as the Aden
Girl. She stopped as the thought struck her. Or would it? Broadminded,
liberated executives might not want an unmarried mother as their spokes-
person. Would she fight them if they turned her down, she wondered.
Would Tony stand by her? How would Tony react? The certainty of his
backing was suddenly in doubt. Impulsively she picked up the small
princess phone and started dialing his number, when the downstairs buzzer rang. She knew it was Adam. Replacing the receiver she slipped into
a robe and waited. He had a key and when she heard his footsteps
scrambling up the stairs, she walked into the living room to meet him.

"What the hell was that all about?" Adam said as he paced up and
down Lauri's living room.

Lauri sitting in a rocking chair, dressed in a long, royal blue silk
robe, her legs tucked under her, looked at him and let him vent his rage.

"Well, for Christ's sake, will you tell me what's going on?"

"There's nothing going on, Adam," Lauri said quietly. "I simply ate
something that disagreed with me and it made me ill. It was hot at the
Roosevelt. I'd worked a long day under scorching lights and I passed
out." She shrugged her shoulders. "I thought it very dramatic, if you
must know."

"I can assure you Beth didn't think it dramatic, and Sam went crazy
when you refused to see his doctor."

"I didn't do it on purpose, Adam, although I must say the prospect of
spending the evening with your wife was not exactly helpful to my state
of nausea." She stood up and, walking over to Adam, she put her arms

around his neck and pressed her lips to his. "Congratulations, my darling, on winning the election." She moved her head back, but her body pressed close to his and she looked intently at him. "I'm so proud of you."

Adam pushed her away gently and started pacing again. Lauri turned toward the door that led to the kitchen. "Want some juice or something?" she asked in a hostesslike manner.

"Thanks," he said absently and walked nervously over to the window. It was past 1:00 A.M. and the street lights were dimmed by the misty fog that had settled, giving the tree-lined street a strange yellow aura, accentuating the darkness around. Adam, standing in the light at the window, felt exposed. The impulse to move away, hide from possible prying eyes, embarrassed him. He was behaving like a frightened, unfaithful husband. The thought almost made him laugh. He *was* an unfaithful husband. He pressed his fingers to his eyes. He was being an irresponsible old fool, and he was angry at himself.

"Lauri," he said without turning around, "I won't be able to see you for a while. Several things have come up that I've got to work out as far as future plans are concerned. Political decisions I have to make, which I can only do if I'm alone. You understand, don't you?" There was no reply, and looking around he realized Lauri was not in the room. He walked over to the kitchen. She was leaning against the refrigerator, a glass of milk in her hand.

"Are you all right?" he asked, and could hardly keep the irritation out of his voice.

She smiled pleasantly. "I'm fine, Adam, and you needn't be so angry." She poured a glass of juice and handed it to him.

"I was saying, Lauri, I can't get away for the next few weeks. I want to stick close to home and come up with some important decisions."

"You mean the possibility of running for mayor?" she asked with seeming innocence.

"How did you know about it?" Adam stopped short.

"Sam mentioned it to me."

"It's only a possibility," he said quickly, hiding his anger and discomfort. Even Beth did not know about it. Sam had no right to speak of it to anyone. Sam was pushing him, and he did not like it. "You see, Lauri, I honestly think I can do more good for the city as mayor than I can as a Congressman. But it has to be my decision, and if I'm to make a run for it, I want to be sure I've covered all bases."

"Well, I think you're right, and I think you should reacquaint yourself with New York. In a way, you've been away from your home for many years," Lauri said, sipping her milk. "Where do you live, anyway?"

"On East Seventy-second Street. It's an apartment Beth inherited from her father. It's been in the family for a long time."

"And you've always had an apartment on Ninety-eighth Street." Lauri smiled pleasantly. "How cozy."

Adam winced. Lauri was the only person, other than Beth, who knew about the apartment.

"Adam," Lauri said more gently, seeing his expression, "I don't mean it that way. It's just that your life with your wife is so . . . so"—she paused, trying to find the word—"deceptive," she concluded. "It's almost like you're making fun of the voters. When there's that much dishonesty in your personal life, how can anyone trust you . . . if they knew."

"In its own way, our life is cleaner than most other politicians' lives," Adam said soberly. "Ours is a long-standing partnership. A give and take."

"She gives and you take," Lauri said quietly.

"Beth gets her share, Lauri," Adam said coldly. "And believe it or not, I've given her the life she wanted and probably couldn't have gotten without me. A position, a sense of power, a recognition."

Lauri turned away and started arranging a bouquet of flowers Adam sent her earlier in the day.

"I think you'd better go now," she said, quietly. "I'm tired."

"When will I see you?"

Lauri turned slowly, her eyes blazing with anger. "Look, Adam, a few minutes ago you said you wouldn't be able to see me for a while. I accept it; agree that it has to be that way. Now you start this shit about when will you see me. As long as you were in Washington and we had a semblance of a life together, it was fine. But if you think I'm going to start sneaking around for little pats on the ass from you when you can get away for an hour, forget it."

Adam was taken aback. Since meeting Lauri they had never once had a fight.

"What's wrong, Lauri," he asked, genuinely upset. "Something has happened, and I'm damned if I understand what it is."

"Nothing happened, Adam. I'm tired, I'm not feeling well and I don't think meeting Beth agreed with me. For some ungodly reason, I felt cheap this evening. She's a lady, Adam, and I'm infringing on her rights as your wife, as the wife of the Congressman from New York, as the lady who will probably be the mayor's wife." She paused briefly and turned away. "I don't like my position anymore."

"Next thing you'll be saying is it's either her or you," Adam said dryly.

"Not a chance!" Lauri's voice rose. "I've never made any demands on you and you know it." She spoke firmly, but the feeling of nausea welled up in her again and she started quickly out of the room, fearful of being sick. "I wish you'd go, Adam," she called out after her.

Adam watched her and his confusion mounted. What had started out as a happy, unencumbered affair had taken a serious turn. He had sensed it for a while and knew he had to put an end to it. When Lauri fainted on the street, his concern for her shook him. He felt responsible for her. He was preoccupied while Beth, Sam and he were having a drink at El Morocco. He could not wait for the evening to be over so he could go down to the Village and make sure Lauri was all right. But since walking in, the atmosphere was charged with uncertainty. Lauri was being irrational. Warm and loving one moment, biting and nasty the next. The thought that she was rejecting him stung.

He looked around for his coat. It was thrown over the desk chair. He started putting it on when he saw an open letter lying on the desk. He shifted his eyes away quickly, but not before the words registered.

"The results of the test are positive. Come in soon for a thorough examination."

Adam froze. He did not pick it up, but leaned over to read the letter more closely. The typed words implied nothing; it was the handwrittten postscript which revealed the truth.

Lauri was pregnant, and Adam knew she was carrying his child.

He felt trapped. The room seemed to be closing in on him. He looked over at the door which led to Lauri's bedroom and for a moment thought of rushing out of the apartment. It was an ugly thought, and he dismissed it immediately. Instead, he walked into her bedroom.

Lauri was sitting in the middle of the four-poster bed, dressed in a white old-fashioned silk nightgown, brushing her hair. She looked extremely young and helpless.

"Lauri," Adam said quietly, fearful of frightening her.

She looked up startled, then she smiled. "I thought you left."

"Lauri, I do love you. And I want to take care of you." He sat down next to her and took her in his arms. She nestled close and he lifted her face to his.

"I've decided to divorce Beth," he said, and was surprised by his statement, but did not regret it.

Lauri pulled away abruptly.

"You're going to do what?" Her eyes were wide with wonder.

"Lauri, I want to marry you. I want the baby to have a father and a mother. We'll have a good life together."

"How do you know about the baby?" Lauri disengaged herself from his embrace.

"The letter . . ." Adam said feebly.

"Well, I guess you had to find out sometime, and that's as good a way as any," Lauri answered, remembering Stan's note.

"Find out? Weren't you going to tell me about it?"

"Once I figured out what I'm going to do, I suppose I would have."

"What are you talking about?" Adam was getting angry. "It's my child and I had every right to know."

"Adam, I really am too tired to have a scene. I wish you would go." She was suddenly deathly pale.

"Lauri, I'm asking you to marry me. I'm going to divorce Beth and marry you."

"You want a divorce, Adam, you go right ahead and get one," Lauri spoke slowly and deliberately, "but don't put it on my back."

"I'm not putting it on you, or blaming you . . ." He stopped. He *was* thinking of a divorce because of her.

"Blaming me?" Lauri's voice rose. "Blaming me? How dare you, Adam, how dare you even say that word. I've never thought of marrying you. I've never indicated in any way, shape or form that it was what I wanted from you, and you know it."

"Lauri, I have a right to be a complete father to my child."

"Adam, that child is mine. I will have it or not, as I see fit. It's my decision and mine alone."

"What happened?" Adam was too bewildered to follow what was being said. "When did everything change?"

A small smile appeared on Lauri's lips. "Nothing changed, Adam. I adore you. I think you're the greatest. Right now, I'm just exhausted and I want to sleep."

He stood up. "I'll call you in the morning." Then leaning over her, he kissed her gently on the lips. "Just remember, I love you very much."

9

Lauri watched Adam leave and heard the front door close gently.

It was over, she thought as she lay back on her pillow. The affair that promised to be different from any other was ending. She knew it would, eventually, but the pain was overwhelming and she had no idea how to quell it. She also knew she was not yet ready to give it up. The feeling of emptiness was weighing on her, and it was reminiscent of the time she watched Larry leave for Palm Beach and she was left on her own for the first time in her life.

Pulling the huge handmade afghan over her, she nestled beneath its bulk. Unconsciously she ran her hand over the surface of the quilt and the familiar texture gave her a sense of long forgotten security. A memory of lying under this blanket, between her father and mother on a cold Sunday morning came to her. She was very small and they both hugged her and whispered intimately to each other. She could not remember what they said, but her mother laughed huskily and her father leaned over and kissed her. Lauri held on to the faded image of that day long ago. They had both wanted her. Lauri recalled Larry telling her that Anna had fought to get custody of her. Did she fight hard enough, Lauri wondered. Or was Larry's need to have his daughter so great that no one could extricate his child from him. And what was that need that made him so desperate as to separate a mother and her child? Exhibition of masculinity which he knew was not his? Probably. But there was another need. Fear of being alone. Having a child meant he would not be alone. He was afraid of loneliness, as everyone is. Poor Papa. Lauri wanted to cry. His fear of loneliness had blinded him to what was happening to the little girl who was brought into the world. Somehow, she could not fault him for that. For the first time in many years Lauri thought of Larry without a trace of resentment.

She drifted into a dreamless sleep.

The ringing of the phone woke her. Lauri sat up and glanced at the clock. It was 8:00 A.M. She picked up the receiver. It was Tony.

"Hi." He sounded strained. "Are you coming over?"

"I'll be there in twenty minutes," Lauri said and started to get out of bed. The feeling of nausea made her lie down again.

"You all right?" Tony asked.

"I thought I was," she said weakly, "but I guess I'm not." She took a deep breath, trying to swallow the vomit which started rising in her throat.

"Lauri, do you want me to come down?" Tony's voice was controlled but he was obviously upset.

"I think I'm in trouble," Lauri blurted out. She hadn't meant to say it. She did not really feel she was in trouble. It simply came out.

"That's obvious." Tony's voice grew tighter. "Want me to cancel the sitting?"

"No. I'll be there."

She got out of bed slowly and throwing on a pair of jeans, a wool sweater and a pair of boots, she walked into the bathroom. She looked haggard, the circles under her eyes were dark and ominous. She started to put some makeup on, hoping to hide the sickly pallor, but gave it up. The feelings of assurance with which she fell asleep, were gone.

Tony opened the door for her when she arrived at the studio.

"I'll just go and put some makeup on," she said, not looking directly at him.

"Cool it, Lauri. We can work later." He caught her arm and forced her to look at him. "You go sit down and I'll bring us some coffee."

She wrestled herself free and started toward the studio. "A coffee would kill me." She tried to smile. "Which might not be the worst thing in the world."

Tony followed close behind her. "Okay, let's have it. What's the matter?"

"I'm going to have a baby," Lauri said, and wondered again where the joyous feelings she had had late the night before had disappeared.

"You're what?" Tony gasped.

Lauri turned and stared at him. He was obviously shaken.

"You heard me," she said simply, and threw herself into an armchair.

"Do you want it?" he asked after a long silence in which he was trying to get control of himself.

"I thought I did. Now I don't know."

"Can you tell me who the father is?"

"Adam Stillman."

Tony was about to lash out, but controlled himself. When he felt he could speak without anger, he looked up. "I've always hated the liberal do-gooders. They do so much."

"Tony, he didn't rape me. I was a willing partner, and he certainly trusted me to avoid this scene."

"Why didn't you?"

"That's why I said I'm in trouble. I don't know."

"Does he know his good fortune?"

"Yes."

"Well, what does he have to say?"

"He wants to divorce his wife and marry me."

"Do you want to marry him?"

"No," Lauri said too emphatically.

"That's the most insane, ridiculous thing I've ever heard," Tony exploded. "You don't know what you want, yet you allow yourself to become pregnant, put yourself in the position of bringing a human being into this confused world to be brought up without a father. This so called liberated society we're living in is not that accepting, believe me." He stopped briefly. "Do you know how selfish and cruel you're being?"

Lauri listened intently. Tony's reaction was contrary to anything she expected. "For a civilized, enlightened human being, you're certainly saying all the wrong things," she said finally.

"Wrong things?" Tony laughed mirthlessly. "I've struggled with the feelings of being an outsider, being different, being unacceptable. You have too, and you know how painful it can be."

They stared at each other in silence. For no apparent reason Brad's statement about Larry's homosexuality came back to Lauri, and her embarrassment and shock were vividly recalled. She had buried those feelings deep inside; had learned to live with who Larry was and what it entailed for her as his daughter. Now Tony was saying it again. He was doing it tactfully, but saying it nevertheless.

"In a weird sort of way, you'll be repeating what your father did to you." Tony's voice became more gentle. "Lauri a child born to an unwed mother is acceptable today, but will it be acceptable tomorrow? And even if it is acceptable, you know damn well what the inner feelings are when you know you're somehow different than others. That feeling one has when the lights are off, late at night when no one is around." His voice broke and Lauri could hear his pain and unshed tears.

"Tony, why are you doing this?" Lauri cried out.

"And you think you'll be spared?" he continued ignoring her question. "Do you really believe the Aden people will go along with you and allow you to be their representative?" He stopped, as a new thought struck him. "Is that why you've been rushing through with the photographs?"

When she did not answer his manner changed.

"How pregnant are you anyway?"

"About six or seven weeks."

"What does it mean in terms of the appearance?"

"If we finish our presentation by December first and they accept it, then we're home free. I'll be back to myself for the fall collection next year." She paused. "If I decide to go through with the pregnancy."

"Lauri, forget it. If you decide to have the baby, they won't run those ads with you when they find out . . ." He got up and started pacing nervously. "Sure I'll go on using you as a model. Robbie and you will continue with your partnership, but we're the ones who are different in our own way. For a child you want the respectable, the norm, the average."

"I resent that," Lauri said angrily. "My child won't be stifled by stupid dull conventions."

"Bullshit!" Tony shot back. "Conventional and respectable are not necessarily synonymous with dull and stupid. What the hell do you think all those television commercials are anyway? Fathers and sons playing ball in the park, mothers preparing breakfast for their children, caring for their families in nice large, brightly lit kitchens. Television and movies depicting happy family life are the dream of every child and in a way every adult, everywhere in the world." He looked at her for a moment. "And what will you offer your child?"

"Love, care, understanding, compassion and decent values," Lauri said quietly.

"Lauri, you'll be mortgaging the next twenty years of your life, remember that."

"You make it sound like a real estate deal."

"No, it's much more complex. You can't sell a child at a profit or loss, you can't neglect it and you can't walk away from it as you would from a piece of property. The payments go on for a long time, and you can't suddenly decide to declare bankruptcy and go into a chapter eleven."

"I'm not going to have an abortion," Lauri said emphatically. "And you can go to hell with all your ideas of what is right and proper." She felt very calm and self-assured. "Because of who I am, because of what I grew up with, I'll be able to give my child a hell of a lot more than other mothers can. My life with my child may not make a script for a television soap, but I'll take my chances." She stood up. "I think we should get some work done."

"You're sure you won't agree to Stillman getting a divorce?"

"Never," Lauri said, and she felt she meant it. "I would no more be responsible for his leaving his wife or family because of an obligation he did not ask for." She smiled briefly. "I think Adam is one of the most wonderful people I've ever met. I think he's a fine man, a good Congressman who will go on to make an even greater career, and I don't want to be the one to ruin it for him." She stopped as a new thought struck her. "Besides, I don't need another father. Larry is a handful."

"Are you going to call Larry and tell him?" Tony asked curiously.

"About the baby?" Lauri nearly laughed out loud. "You've got to be kidding. I'll simply present him with the grandchild when it arrives."

"Lauri, are you sure you know what you're letting yourself in for?" Tony's voice softened.

"Tony, if I didn't before coming here this morning, I do now." She felt tired but determined. "You've frightened me enough for one morning."

Tony walked over to her and cupped her face in his hand. "I didn't mean to frighten you. I'm your friend, remember?"

She leaned her head against his shoulder. "Are you?"

She felt his arms encircle her shoulder and he held her close. "Well, for starters, I think you should come and live here for the next few weeks. No point in you running around when we have to finish the shooting of the ads."

She looked up at him. He was serious.

"After the sitting today, we'll go down to your place and bring back your stuff, and we'll play it by ear from there."

Lauri wanted to say something but the words would not come.

"I love you, Lauri." Tony smiled down at her. Then pushing her away, his expression changed abruptly. "Now to the realities. Get some makeup on and let's get to work."

He turned away quickly and started preparing the equipment for the photographing session.

10

It was just past midnight when Beth let herself into the apartment. The phone was ringing and she rushed to answer it.

"Mother?" It was Sarah. She sounded disappointed at hearing Beth's voice.

"How are you, sweetheart?" Beth asked, ignoring the tone. "And where are you?"

"I'm in Berkeley and I just saw the news on TV about Dad. I think that's great. And you looked sensational."

"Thank you, Sarah. It is a good face-lift, isn't it?"

"Mother! You didn't," Sarah shrieked in horror. "Why the hell did you do it?"

Because I want to look young, be loved, be wanted, desired, were the thoughts that rushed through Beth's mind. "I did it because I want to look as well as I can for as long as I can," she said out loud.

"You had character in your face." Sarah was still angry.

"I'll have character again, honey." Beth laughed quietly, although she was annoyed. "I can guarantee that. In any event, I wish you could have been with Dad this evening." She changed the subject and hoped her irritation was not too obvious.

"I'm sorry, too," the girl answered. "But . . ." she stopped.

"It's all right, honey." Beth covered the silence. "When will you be coming to New York?"

"That's why I'm calling. We'll be in over the holidays." She calmed down and sounded more pleasant than Beth remembered her being in a long time.

"A friend is coming with me, Mother." The aggressive tone was back. "His name is Philip Schmidt, and I want you and Dad to meet him."

"Who is Philip Schmidt?" Beth tried not to sound too enthusiastic, fearful of causing ripples in what was turning out to be a pleasant conversation.

"It's too complicated to go through over the phone," Sarah became defensive. "We'll be there when we get there."

"Why so indefinite?"

"We're traveling standby."

"Sarah, that's silly." She was holding back her anger. Sarah had a way of pushing her into rage. "All you had to do was call your father's office, and they would have arranged it all for you."

"Mother," the anger erupted, "I don't need that. I don't want help. I can attend to my plane flight on my own."

"Very well, Sarah," Beth said in resignation. Her conversations with her younger daughter reminded her of her own with her mother years back. She shuddered. "Will you call again before you arrive?" It suddenly occurred to her that Sarah had not called collect. "I'll tell Dad you called. And if you can let me know exactly when you're coming in, I can possibly drive out and pick you up."

"That won't be necessary. I'll phone when we get off the plane."

There was another pause, and Beth did not know how to end the conversation.

"Are you happy, Sarah?" she asked, and hoped she did not say the wrong thing. Communicating with Sarah was impossible.

"Very," Sarah answered. "Very, very happy." And she hung up.

Beth looked at herself in the hall mirror. Sarah's reaction to her face-lift was upsetting. She tried to remember what she thought when her mother had told her about her operation, years back. She was pregnant with Ali and wanted Mary to be concerned with her and her pregnancy. Why did her mother have a face-lift? The thought made her pause. She had hers done because she wanted to recapture her youthful appearance. She wanted to be noticed and appreciated as an attractive and desirable younger woman. She wanted some man to want her, to be wanted again, as Dan had wanted her. Married with children, she had never stopped looking. Were those her mother's thoughts as well? How could they have been? Mary was an elderly woman . . .

Picking up the morning papers which the elevator man had given her, Beth walked into the library, placed the papers on the desk and opened the door to the bar. A dim light flooded the room and Beth poured herself a drink. She had drunk quite a bit during the evening, but she was still not as drunk as she wanted to be. She downed the drink and poured herself another. As she did, she caught sight of herself in the antique mirrors lining the wall behind the glasses and bottles of the bar, and averted her eyes quickly. She hated looking at herself when she was drinking. The contrast in her appearance when she abstained from alcohol was most evident during the months of campaigning when she had not touched liquor. Her skin was clear, her eyes were bright, her whole expression was softer. Now her face appeared bloated, her eyes red and swollen, her mouth pinched. She reminded herself of her mother.

The thought of pouring the remains in the glass down the bar sink crossed her mind, but she could not bring herself to do it.

Instead, she turned toward the desk, switched on the lamp and glanced at the newspapers which she had placed there. Pictures of Adam and herself standing side by side after the election peered at her. Adam was attractive, self-assured, smiling directly into the camera, his arm carelessly draped around a middle-aged woman. She closed her eyes, trying to erase the thought. She was that middle-aged woman and there was no getting away from it. Mirrors could lie, people could lie, but photographs never did. In the black-and-white newspaper reprint, Adam was a handsome, appealing man, the picture of success. The woman at his side was someone who had passed her prime, for whom life was over.

Putting down her drink Beth removed one of a set of framed photographs hanging on the wall over the desk. It was taken after Adam's first congressional election. The Stillmans were huddled together, all smiling gaily into the camera. Ali was just entering her teens. She was tall and graceful, wearing a white dress bought especially for the occasion. Jimmy Jay looked particularly dark-skinned in contrast to his blond cousin. His expression was serious, almost defiant. Sarah, dressed in pants and a shirt, was clutching Adam's hand and looking adoringly up at her father. Hannah was sitting in front of everyone. She looked old, but there was a pride in her face. Adam, the triumphant candidate, had his arm around Beth's shoulder and she, too, was smiling. Bringing the picture closer to the light, Beth looked at the image of herself. She was a young, attractive woman, then, exuding self-confidence, ready to take on life.

With great effort she turned her eyes away and looked at the other photographs. They were identically framed and represented the other congressional races of Adam Stillman.

The second race was recorded much as the first one had been, except that Hannah was no longer in the photograph. The third race showed Adam, Beth, Ali and Sarah. Jimmy Jay had left them by then. Ali was missing from the fourth race. Sarah was gone too, by the fifth one. The sixth race showed Adam alone, Beth having been away with her mother who was ill.

The history of the Stillmans was fully recorded.

Ali changed from a fickle little girl to a young woman in love, ready to sacrifice everything to be a devoted companion to her art history professor, a man twice her age with two children. George Lothar, a gentle man, adored her and Beth watched Ali conforming to his demands of her, his needs of her. Although three years had gone by since Ali announced her decision to live with George, Beth was still upset by Adam's reaction to the affair. He refused to meet the man and spent endless days trying to convince Ali to forget him. To Beth he confided that he thought George was interested in Ali because of her inheritance. It was completely irrational and totally out of character for Adam to think in those terms, but he could not be dissuaded. It dampened the relationship between him and Ali, although Beth knew Ali and Adam spoke on occasion and met when Ali came to town. The mood between them, however, was strained.

Jimmy Jay left them when he was sixteen to go and march with Martin Luther King, Jr., over Adam's frantic protestations. Beth's accusation, when Adam first announced he was running for Congress, had proven prophetic. Adam, unconsciously, used Jimmy Jay as a peon in his political life. The boy was deeply hurt and rebelled by totally rejecting what Hannah had given him. As an up-and-coming rock star, Adam felt Jimmy was exploiting his Jewishness as a ploy to advance himself, deepening the friction between uncle and nephew. Neither was willing to understand and accept that they were taking and benefiting from what was legitimately theirs.

In recent years, Jimmy Jay had begun to bridge the gap, coming to understand and appreciate who he was. Adam was not as flexible. He clung to past points of reference and felt betrayed.

Beth never stopped talking to the boy and in recent years she saw the rage and mistrust abate. His basic instincts, nurtured by Hannah, were reappearing, and she was sure that he would one day reach out to Adam with love and would not be rejected.

And Sarah. She was the most crippled by what was happening around her. The loving, quiet, independent little girl grew defiant and filled with rage. Beth was so preoccupied with Ali and Jimmy Jay she was almost unaware that Sarah abandoned her intellectual pursuits and became involved in the drug scene and extremist political groups. She graduated from high school, hung around for a while and then went off to Berkeley. There was no stopping her.

A deep sigh escaped her. Somehow, they had all grown up. She had simply grown old. Everyone had let go, while she was still clinging.

"You're getting maudlin," Beth said out loud and smiled wryly. She looked at the desk clock. It was 1:00 A.M., and she wondered if she should wait up for Adam. She wanted to see him and talk to him, but could not remember why. With bottle and glass in hand she wandered aimlessly toward the front hall, gulping her drink down as she walked. The burning sensation of the alcohol made her shudder. She poured herself another and looked around. The foyer was lit by the sconces her mother had hung many years back. The marble floor was gleaming and the fresh-cut flowers were sitting in a large Venetian vase on the Empire console. The stairway leading up to the rooms Hannah and Jimmy Jay used, was covered in a lush beige carpet. Lydia had vacuumed it earlier in the week, and it would not have to be done again for quite a while. No one ever used that stairway anymore. Just as no one ever scuffed the marble foyer floor. Everything was in place, everything reeked of elegance. It was all exquisitely cultivated, nurtured, coddled and wasted.

A heart-rending scream started from Beth's throat. It wended its way through her vocal cords and she could feel the pain as the sound burst forth.

"Help me, please, someone help me." The voice was unfamiliar. Beth looked around bewildered. Someone needed help and she could not decide who it was. The sobbing that followed the plea brought her back to herself.

I'm going mad, she thought. Vaguely she heard the downstairs buzzer ringing. She stood very still hoping it would stop. It persisted and she knew she had to answer it.

"Are you all right, Mrs. Stillman?" the doorman asked.

"Why yes," she answered, and was surprised to hear herself speaking in her natural voice. "Why do you ask?"

"Someone heard a scream for help, and they thought it came from your apartment."

"I'm glad we still have concerned citizens in the city," she said pleasantly. "Thank you for calling anyway."

She hung up the receiver carefully and leaned her head against the wall. She was dizzy and she felt sick. With measured steps she walked through the living room and opened the french doors leading to the terrace. The fresh air felt good and turning around she scanned the vast room.

It too was rarely used and she had not been in it for quite a while. Reaching over she turned on a lamp. A pleasant light flooded in the room, giving it an aura of mystery. Its beauty was overwhelming. It had been decorated with so much care, so much thought. The down-filled sofas, flanking the unlit fireplace were inviting, the chairs, the tables, the bric-a-brac, were all in place. Once it had served the family, but as Adam's career took over, the room became the gathering place, the setting, the backdrop for his work, his career, his ambition. This living room was noted for being the epitome of what a man in public life should have in order to achieve his goals. With the years, the furnishings changed, the lighting, the color schemes, the seating arrangements. Everything was molded to show Adam Stillman off to the best advantage. Now the room was finally perfect, and it was no longer needed.

Deliberately, Beth walked over to the couch and sank into the softness of the seat, denting its perfection. With equal purpose she picked up the pillows, which were properly placed in the corner of the sofa, and flung them to the floor. Taking off her shoes, she threw them against a small fragile table. One of them caused an ashtray to slip to the floor, but the softness of the carpet cushioned its fall and it did not break. Beth smiled. Like her life, she could not destroy anything because everything around her was fortified by plush carpets. Angrily she got up and rushed into the front hall, picked up the brandy bottle and glass and returned to the living room. Resettling herself on the couch she poured herself another drink and stretched her stockinged feet on the large glass coffee table, purposely pushing a small elegant figurine out of place and tipping over a heavy crystal lighter. The messiness pleased her. Unsteadily she leaned forward and poured some brandy from her glass over the clear-glass table. The amber liquid spread slowly and trickled onto the rug. She shrugged her shoulders indifferently. The perfection of the room, which had captured her minutes before, now enraged her. She stood up and ran across it, disarranging it as she went. She wanted to recreate the room as it once was. The room where her children had romped, where voices were raised, where life existed.

Reaching the far end, she viewed her mild rampage. Her efforts were pale shadows of what an active family had once achieved. She stood very still as though waiting for something to happen. Suddenly, shadowy ghosts from the past began to dance before her eyes.

"Come to me," she pleaded. "I need you. I want you."

They flitted across the room slowly and disappeared.

It was all an illusion. Her whole life was an illusion. She closed her eyes as she sank into a state of utter desperation.

"Beth?" Adam's voice reached her and Beth struggled to come out of her stupor. He was standing in the doorway, smiling uncertainly.

"Hi." She cleared her throat and was conscious of the messiness around her. She stood up quickly and started putting the place in order. "Would you like a drink?" she asked nonchalantly, picking up the brandy bottle and turning to him.

"I think you're doing well enough for both of us," Adam answered, and regretted the statement. He had been watching her for several minutes before waking her. She looked so forlorn and lost. Changing his tone, he spoke more softly. "What's the matter, Beth?"

"I don't know," she whispered, not taking her eyes off him. There was something disquieting about him which Beth could not understand. For a brief second she had the impulse to walk over and touch him. Instead she lowered her eyes.

"Well, don't worry about it." Adam cleared his throat. "No harm done. You've worked hard in the last few months and you were probably all tensed up." He tried to smile. "As a matter of fact, I will have one. Let's toast our victory." He walked toward her and took the bottle out of her hand. Pouring his drink a small sigh escaped him. He was sorry he had wakened her. Discussing a divorce with Beth, who'd been drinking, was not wise.

"You've been a good sport, Beth, and I appreciate all you've done." He lifted his glass to her.

Beth watched him drink down his brandy and felt as though she were in a room with a stranger.

"I could have sworn you'd given up on alcohol," Adam said after a while. "I believe you haven't had a drink since we started working on this campaign. Am I right?"

Beth stared at her empty glass. The last time she had ordered a drink was the day Adam asked her to help him with the campaign.

"I didn't think you noticed," Beth said, and then remembered the newspaperman at the Roosevelt asking about Adam's running for mayor. "Adam," she said slowly, "why did you ask me to help you with this election?"

"You needed to get out, Beth. You'd become reclusive, and I felt you might get back to yourself if you were involved."

"How did you persuade Sam to allow it?" She kept the bitterness out of her voice. "By showing him the benefit of exhibiting the wife before a mayoralty race?"

"Jesus Christ!" Adam exploded. "Where the hell did that idea come from?"

"It seems yours plans for running are common gossip."

"I thought about it, but it was only a thought." He calmed down. "As a matter of fact, something has come up and I'm quite close to dropping the whole idea." What was Sam doing, Adam thought furiously. Why was he forcing a decision on him?

"Going to Washington tomorrow?" Beth decided to change the subject.

"No. I've got several meetings in the city and I've got to see Sam."

"Sarah is coming to town for Christmas," she said absently.

"Hey, that's great." Adam brightened.

"She's bringing a young man with her whom she wants us to meet."

"Who is he?" Adam asked.

"Philip Schmidt."

"Is he Jewish?" The question was out before he knew what he was saying.

"Is he *what?*" Beth gasped. "How the hell would I know. The fact that she knows his name . . ."

"Get off her back," Adam snapped nervously. "I'll never understand why you're always picking on her. She's a great kid."

Beth winced both at what Adam was saying and his obvious preference for their younger child. For a man who had worked with children, who had had a troubled younger sister, who was aware of so much of what was going on, he was completely oblivious to how badly Ali suffered from his neglect.

"Well, is he?"

"Adam, how would I know, and what difference would it make?"

"I don't know, except that I always assumed the girls would marry Jewish men."

"You've got to be kidding. For starters, you married me and I'm not Jewish. When I offered to convert, you poo-pooed it as totally unimportant. I personally wanted to give the girls a Jewish education, but you were disinterested."

"I didn't think I had to 'give' anything. I just took it for granted that they would know who they were." He stopped and was deep in thought. "It would have been different if they were boys," he said lamely.

"Oh, for crying out loud. You sound like an emir from Saudi Arabia." She paused to catch her breath. "Adam, are you hearing what you're saying? Took it for granted! What the hell does that mean? Eating a kosher meal your mother prepared on a Friday night when the children were small? Being vaguely aware that you fasted one day in the year and made jokes about it? I would have happily taken them to any synagogue you would have asked me to, but you never did. At least Ali went to church once in a while with my mother, which is more than Sarah ever did."

Adam raised his brows. "And what did that do for her? Living with a man twice her age, taking care of his two children, wasting her life away."

"Adam, stop it." Beth's voice became threatening. "In her own way Ali turned out to be quite a person. It would have been hard to predict that she, of all people, would be that devoted to someone, caring, concerned and anxious to please."

"What's going to happen to her when he throws her out?"

"Why would he want to do that?" Beth asked bewildered. "He's a responsible man. A serious professor in a good college, and he's in love with Ali."

"But he won't marry her."

"I don't think he can get a divorce. His wife is hopelessly paralyzed."

They stood staring at each other and Beth could not understand why they were fighting.

"As for whether Philip Schmidt is Jewish or not, I don't know and I'm too tired to begin to understand your sudden interest in religion. But that's beside the point. I think we should cancel our trip over the holidays and wait for her. Sarah wants you to meet him."

"I don't know," Adam said nervously. "I am exhausted and I could use a vacation." He had forgotten about their pending trip. "But if you think we shouldn't be away . . ." He shrugged his shoulders helplessly.

Beth watched him closely. After so many years, she wanted Adam, wanted him to take her in his arms, wanted him to make love to her. She was convinced that if she went over to touch him, he would move away.

"I think I'll turn in." She left the room feeling frustrated and foolish. Walking toward the bedroom the image of Lauri Eddington reappeared before her eyes. She was obviously responsible for Adam's strange behavior, and Beth knew there was nothing she could do about it.

As she started undressing, she felt restless. She had grown too dependent on Adam. The feelings were very reminiscent of her first year of marriage. It was different then. She was young and could afford to think of life on her own. Now it was too late.

"Damn it," she said out loud. The same thought had now crossed her mind several times during the evening and she was being a bore. Once she announced to Dan that she would not be leaving Adam, she had accepted being Adam's wife, Ali and Sarah's mother. This was a hell of a time to start regretting it. Still, she felt desperate. Everything was falling apart around her, and she did not know how to stop it.

Putting on a lacy pink negligee and matching peignoir, she glanced briefly in the full-length mirror of her dressing room. She was trying to be appealing and seductive, and it made her blush. She wanted her husband and wanted to be attractive to him as she had once been. Instinctively she knew it was hopeless. She raised her hand and stared at it. It was shaking, and she made a fist and dropped it into her lap. She was being a fool. Quickly she removed the peignoir and was taking off her nightgown when Adam walked into the room. Frightened by his sudden appearance, Beth got into bed and covered her nakedness.

"Beth," Adam started slowly, "I want to talk to you." He sat down in the small armchair that stood by the french doors.

"What about?"

"Beth, I'm leaving. I've decided to get a divorce." His voice was low and Beth was not sure she had heard him.

"Divorce?" she echoed the word.

"Yes, Beth." His eyes were lowered but his voice was firmer. "It's hard to explain, but I've met . . ."

"Don't say another word, Adam," Beth stopped him. "I don't want to hear it."

"But you have to, Beth. We're more than husband and wife. We're friends. You're my closest, most intimate friend, and if you'll let me explain, I know you'll understand."

She reached over and took a cigarette. Adam jumped up to light it. Leaning over her, the lamp light fell on his face. He was deathly pale.

"That girl, this evening. She's the one who's suddenly become the most important thing in my life. It doesn't take away from my feelings for you or the children . . ."

"Adam, you're a fool," Beth said sitting up, clutching the blanket around her. "You're an old fool. That girl is more than half your age. For someone who ranted and raved about his daughter living with an older man . . ."

"That's different," Adam interrupted.

"In what way?"

"Ali is a naïve, protected child. She doesn't know about life and men. Lauri is a mature young woman."

"Naïve, protected?" Beth said bitterly. "Oh, how old-fashioned can you be?" She inhaled deeply. "Have you any idea how long Ali's been on the pill? While you were being the big hero in Washington, fighting for an abortion law, I waited through two illegal abortions she went through. Ghastly, ugly affairs, with money-grubbing doctors treating girls as though they were whores." She caught her breath. "And I *know* about those two. God knows about the ones she did not tell me about." She waited for the words to sink in. "She may be naïve, but she sure as hell is not protected."

"You're lying, Beth." Adam stood up dazed. He wished he had not broached the subject that evening. He opened the french doors and a gust of cold wind swept through the room. "You're lying," he repeated with his back to her. "And if you're not, then you were one hell of a rotten mother."

"I was the best mother I knew how to be," Beth said, not letting the rage surface. "And I was here, which is more than you were. As for lying, why would I lie now? I lied all through the years about what was going on in your home, so you would not be troubled. So that you could make your career, so you could screw around." The anger could not be contained.

"Lauri is the only woman I've ever gone to bed with since we were married," Adam said, and turned around to face her. He wanted to walk away, but felt compelled to continue the conversation. "What about Sarah?" he asked and held his breath.

"What about her?" Beth became evasive.

"Since you've lied about Ali, what happened to Sarah while I wasn't looking?"

"I don't know," Beth said in a resigned voice. "She moved away from me a long time ago. I know she was heavily into drugs. We fought a great deal over that."

"Drugs? Sarah?" Adam was flabbergasted. "Little Sarah on drugs?"

"I don't think she's into hard drugs. When she was home, it was pot and maybe hash. What went on in Berkeley, I don't know." She felt she was betraying her children and was surprised at the thought. They were Adam's children as well, but protecting Adam from the serious household problems had become a habit. "That's why I thought it important that you be here when she brings her friend home. She obviously wants to impress you."

"Beth, Lauri is pregnant," Adam blurted out. "And I'm going to marry her."

Beth squashed out her cigarette and looked at the dying embers in the ashtray. She could not bring herself to look at him. "Does she want the baby?" she asked finally.

"Of course she wants the baby."

"Does she want to marry you?"

Adam did not answer.

"Well, does she?"

"I'm going to marry her because it's the right thing to do," he said with finality.

"Your chivalry is touching, even if it's misplaced," Beth said dryly.

"I'll talk to the lawyer in the morning about starting the divorce proceedings." Adam started to leave the room.

"I *asked* you for a divorce once," Beth's voice reached him. "I asked, and you refused. You're not asking me, you're *telling* me."

"That was different." Adam stopped but did not turn around. "That Bradbury guy was all wrong for you. He would have ruined your life."

"And what is my life now?" She tried to keep the panic out of her voice.

Adam shrugged his shoulders helplessly. "You're still an attractive woman. You're bright and you're worldly. You won't have any money problems. You know lots of people."

"I think you'd better go." Beth sank down in her bed and turned on her side. She could not continue the conversation.

She listened to his footsteps as he walked down the long hallway which led to the front foyer. She found herself straining to hear his footsteps on the marble floor. She heard the front door open and shut quietly.

Slowly she turned and stared at the embossed ceiling. She noticed the plaster of one of the flower shaped moldings was chipped and wondered who fixed that sort of thing these days. Getting out of bed she walked over to the terrace door, which was still open. Standing naked, she felt the cold wind caressing her body. She felt completely calm.

Part III

TOMORROW

1

Beth leaned back in the seat of her mother's limousine and looked at the Hudson River as Joseph drove down the West Side Highway on the way to New York. It was the Friday after Thanksgiving and the road was almost deserted. The large mounds of dazzling white snow resting peacefully on the side of the parkway were clear reminders of the raging snow storms that had battered the East Coast for the last few days. A feeble sun was trying to come through the overcast sky, but the icy river beyond the white-powdered dunes affirmed the below-zero temperature outside. Beth pulled the fur blanket over her knees and tried to immerse herself in the tranquil scene.

"Your visit to your mother was nice." Joseph said, and Beth looked over at him. "She misses you more than she lets on." He smiled sadly into the rearview mirror. "And having you there for three weeks was a real treat."

Beth returned his smile and closed her eyes. She felt strangely content.

Going to stay with her mother was the right choice. She knew she had to get away the morning after Adam left, and there were only three possibilities. Gillian in Darien, Ali in Northampton or Mary in Greenwich. Her feud with Gillian had ended shortly after Adam was elected to his first term in Congress, and they were closer than ever. She was sure Gillian would accept her with open arms, but also knew Gillian would suspect something was wrong and Beth was not yet ready to discuss or explain. She herself did not fully understand what had happened.

She did call Ali. Beth had never been to Ali and George's home and the noise in the background when Ali picked up the phone was horrendous.

"What's going on there?" Beth asked.

"The kids are playing in the living room. It's been snowing for days and they can't go out doors."

Beth did not even ask about going up to Northampton. Instead she invited Ali to spend Thanksgiving in Greenwich. She needed some reassurance about herself and assumed Ali would be the one to give it to her. It had even occurred to her that she might talk to Ali about Adam.

"Your grandmother would be thrilled if you came," Beth said, knowing Ali's genuine affection for Mary. "And I'm dying to see you. It's been so long."

"Oh, Mother," Ali wailed over the background noises. "George and the boys would love it if you came up here, but I can't possibly leave them. We've been planning Thanksgiving dinner for weeks. Besides, George's brother, his wife and three kids are coming up and so are his sister and her children."

"And you're going to prepare the meal for everyone?" Beth asked in disbelief.

"George is a wonderful cook, and we're doing it together." Ali sounded happy. "It's great. George has a recipe for stuffing . . ."

Beth stopped listening. Ali was no longer her little girl. She was part of a family, and it was not the Stillman family anymore. Hearing Ali's mindless chatter made the thought of confiding in her ludicrous.

"When will I see you?" Beth asked when Ali's lengthy dissertation stopped.

"We're driving into New York on Friday after Thanksgiving. George wants to take the boys on a cruise around the city and to the Statue of Liberty." She caught her breath with excitement. "We'll probably spend the night at a hotel, and then we're driving to Washington, D.C."

Beth was itching to ask them to stay at the apartment with her, but refrained. Understanding as she was about Ali's involvement with George Lothar, she had not really accepted the idea. Old-fashioned as it might be, Beth knew she would be uncomfortable at having them share a bedroom under her roof. Also, it would involve explaining Adam's absence, and she had not yet decided how she would break the news.

"How about you having lunch with me on that Friday, then?" Beth asked.

"I'd love it," Ali answered enthusiastically. "Where?"

"Le Cirque at one?"

"Super, and I can catch up with George and the boys afterward."

"Have them join us for dessert and coffee," Beth suggested.

"The kids will love that, Mother. Besides, I'm dying for you to meet them. They're super. And you've only met George once, and you don't really know him. I know you'll adore him."

Her decision to go to Greenwich turned out to be an unexpected pleasure. Mary was overjoyed at having Beth with her and behaved with exceptional warmth and graciousness. As involved as ever in herself, she was grateful to have Beth around. She was most overt in her appreciation when she found Beth waiting up for her when she arrived home in the evening after a social function or a charity affair. She also accepted Beth's explanation about Adam being busy without prying.

But it was Martha who made the visit a true delight. From the minute Beth arrived Martha treated her as though she were a child again.
She prepared dishes she knew were her favorite, made sure she had everything at her fingertips, brought breakfast to her room and sat and
reminisced about the past. Childhood events that had been forgotten
were recalled, anecdotes were retold and the world of yesteryear was
suddenly seen from a totally different vantage point. Beth was fascinated
by Martha's perception of what the Van Ess household was like. Drew,
Mary, Allen and Beth were a fairytale-like family. King, queen and
prince and princess. Allen's tragic passing brought a tear to Martha's
eyes, but as far as she was concerned, Allen's death was a dreadful accident from which the judge and his wife never truly recovered.

"Your mother pretended she got over poor Master Allen's passing, but
I know better. She cried herself to sleep every night for many months,
but on the surface she kept up appearances. She had little choice. The
judge was nearly out of his mind with grief," Martha said confidentially.

"Do you remember our moving from the house in the city to the
apartment?" Beth asked holding back her excitement. She had never
been able to recall that period, and it always bothered her.

"Of course I do." Martha squinted, trying to relive the period. "You
were sent to stay with friends in Southampton, and your mother and I
came into the city and packed. We worked for days just putting things
in cartons and trunks. Master Allen's things were all put in camphor and
are still in the attic upstairs, until this very day."

Beth was shocked at the revelation. As far as she was concerned, her
brother simply ceased to exist for everyone but her.

"And my father, where was he?"

"He stayed at the beach." Martha's voice was nearly a whisper.
"Joseph was with him all the time. The judge refused to go back to the
house in the city. Said he felt closer to Master Allen in Southampton. It
was he who refused to give up that house, although your mother
thought it would be a wise thing to do." She paused for a long minute.
"Your mother was real strong then. She needed him, but never a word of
complaint. 'He needs time alone,' she kept saying and, 'we'll manage
somehow.' And we did."

It brought Mary into focus for Beth. It suddenly occurred to her that
she had confused her mother's strength with coldness and indifference,
and for the first time in her life she actually felt close to her.

Sitting in the car, driving toward the city Beth felt her mother's loneliness and she empathized with it as never before. Unconsciously, her
hand reached over and touched the small Rockwell painting resting on
the seat beside her, which Mary had given her just as she was leaving.
She looked down at it. It was an extremely generous gift, unusually sen-

sitive, since it had been Beth's favorite since she was a child, and most unlike Mary, who cherished possessions. Did possessions fill the void that Drew and Allen left in her mother's life, Beth wondered. Would she too grow old and cling to things rather than people?

"Shall I drive you home or would you like to be dropped off somewhere?" Joseph's voice interrupted her thoughts.

Beth opened her eyes and saw that they had left the highway and were stopping for a red light on Riverside Drive and Ninety-seventh Street. The feeling of contentment which she had lulled herself into while in Greenwich was shattered and the reality of her life came back to her. She glanced at her watch. It was just noon. The trip had taken a shorter time than she anticipated.

"I guess you'd better drop me off at the apartment," she said. She was back in New York and she was aware that she had avoided thinking about walking into the apartment, which suddenly loomed empty and frightening.

Beth restrained herself from asking the doorman if Adam was in. She dared not ask the elevator man if Adam had been around while she was gone.

Once in the apartment, Beth walked directly into the library, took down the painting she had hung in place of the Rockwell and rehung the precious masterpiece where it had been years ago when she was still living with her parents. Stepping back, she looked at it for a long time. It was comforting to have it there. Feeling better she walked over to the desk and picked up the mail Lydia had stacked in the filigreed silver basket. She glanced through them hurriedly. There were several bills, quite a few envelopes obviously containing holiday greetings or invitations to parties and a letter from Jimmy Jay. She ripped the latter open with excitement.

"Beautiful Aunt: May I be presumptuous and ask you to spend Christmas in St. Moritz and New Year's Eve in London with your adoring nephew, Jimmy Jay."

The message brought tears to her eyes, and she could not decide whether she was crying because of Jimmy Jay's gracious invitation or the mention of St. Moritz. She'd never gone back there. Had never wanted to, but somehow the idea of spending Christmas, twenty-five years later, in a place where she had been young and happy and filled with dreams, was touching. She was Ali's age then. She smiled in spite of herself. They were so different. She looked back at the letter. Somehow, from all the people whom she loved and who loved her, Jimmy Jay was the one who would be most likely to understand what she was going through. The temptation to pick up the receiver, make the call and accept the invitation was great, but she knew she had to stay in town. Sarah was coming and she could not be away.

Absentmindedly, Beth started opening some envelopes. As she suspected, most of them were invitations with the usual 'request the pleasure of your company' engraved on expensive stationery with the RSVP underlined. Something about them bothered her. For no apparent reason, she picked up the phone and dialed the number of one of the invitations.

Peggy Brentwood was delighted to hear Beth's voice.

"You are coming, aren't you?" she asked immediately.

"I'd love to, but Adam is exhausted and is going away on vacation," Beth said pleasantly.

"Oh," Peggy paused. "Are you going with him?" The gracious tone changed imperceptibly.

"Of course I am," Beth answered quickly, and felt her face grow red with embarrassment. She had known instinctively what the reaction would be and was furious at herself for making the call.

"What a shame." Peggy's relief was transparent. "You know you're more than welcome to come alone. We'd love to have you."

"You're sweet, Peggy, but I'm quite tired myself. Have a wonderful holiday and we'll get together after the New Year."

Compulsively she made two more calls. The would-be hostesses were equally delighted to hear from her, but each in her own way made Beth feel the invitation was meant for Adam and his wife. Only after she assured them she too would be away, were they able to say that they would have loved to have her, anyway.

Hanging up the phone after the last call, Beth stared into space. Was that what her life would be like from now on? "We want you if you're Mrs. Adam Stillman, but just Beth is a burden." It didn't have to be, she thought angrily. She was not just Adam Stillman's wife. She had an identity of her own. She existed before she became his wife. Beth Van Ess existed. She said the name out loud. It sounded strange, yet throughout the time she spent in Greenwich she felt like Beth Van Ess. She picked up a pencil and wrote the name out. It looked foreign to her, but it was also exciting. She lifted her eyes and looked at the Rockwell again. She felt a strong presence of the past, and the feeling was reassuring.

The clock struck the half hour and Beth remembered that her date with Ali was for one o'clock. Quickly she dialed the number of the restaurant. She had forgotten to make a reservation. The line was busy. It did not matter, she was sure they'd give her a table.

She ran into her bedroom and seated herself in front of her makeup table. Applying a bit of rouge and lipstick, she ran a comb through her hair. She looked well rested and was pleased with her appearance. Just before leaving the room, she caught sight of herself in the full length mirror of the open dressing-room door. She stopped and examined herself. The three piece, light gray pin-striped pant suit showed off her tall, thin figure to perfection. She moved closer and pushed the hip length jacket aside. The trousers, tightly fitted at the waist and hips, flared out fashionably around the calf and ankles. The manly vest hugged her rib cage. The white silk shirt, open at the neck was flattering. Damn it, she thought, I look great and I'll make it, somehow. She was about to turn away when she caught sight of Adam's suits hanging neatly inside the dressing-room closet. They were all there. The sight threw her. Somehow she was sure Adam would have taken them out while she was away. Curiously she walked into the small room and pulled open the built-in drawers that contained Adam's shirts, linens and other personal effects. Everything was intact. Beth could not decide if she was relieved by the discovery.

2

The maître d' at Le Cirque rushed over to Beth the minute she walked in.

"Don't you look lovely today, Mrs. Stillman." He smiled warmly at her. "Do you have a reservation?"

"I'm sorry." Beth smiled back. "I just came in from Greenwich . . ."

"Oh dear." He looked over the reservation list in his hand. "The city is so overrun with foreigners and tourists from all over that I have a hard time taking care of my own guests."

Beth did not answer, knowing he would find her a table.

"Why don't you leave your coat with the hat-check girl and I'll work it out, somehow."

"Beth?" She heard her name called as she was handing her coat to the young girl in the cloak room and she turned around. A tall, stocky, middle-aged woman with shoulder-length streaked blond hair was smiling uncertainly at her. "It's Jody Blake." The woman identified herself.

"Jody!" Beth found her voice. "My God, it's been ages." They had not spoken since the time Jody turned her down to a party she was giving for Adam many years back, and the feelings of resentment were strangely vivid.

"I haven't changed that much, have I?" Jody laughed pleasantly.

"No," Beth lied, struggling to regain her composure. "My mind was simply preoccupied for the minute."

Now that Jody had identified herself, Beth could see a vague resemblance to the young, pug-nosed, freckle-faced girl she had known.

"How have you been?" Beth tried to match Jody's friendliness.

"I've been just fine," Jody answered, and turned to a young man who was standing next to her. "This is Beth Stillman. We went to school together." She laughed almost gaily. "It seems like it happened in another lifetime."

Beth shifted her gaze to the man and put her hand out. She felt unaccountably embarrassed by what Jody was saying. She was sure she looked much younger than Jody.

"Steve Graham," he said in a low, pleasant voice. He was quite young and looked out of place in the elegant restaurant. In a glance, Beth noticed the wrinkled sports jacket, the inexpensive turtleneck sweater and the worn raincoat flung over his shoulders. He took Beth's hand in his, and she was conscious of the delicacy of its bone structure, even though the handshake was firm. "I'm delighted to meet you." He did not take his eyes off her and an appreciative grin appeared on his face. She was flattered.

"What have you been doing with yourself?" Jody was oblivious to what was transpiring around her.

Beth turned back to Jody. "Well, being married to a New York Congressman is a full-time job." She was shocked by what she was saying but could not stop. "Between Washington and New York and the endless trips Adam has to take, I find life very hectic. That and having three children . . ."

"I thought you had two daughters," Jody said, and it surprised Beth that Jody was aware of it.

"We have two daughters, but we also have a nephew who's like a son. You may have heard of him. Jimmy Jay Faulkner. He's a rock singer."

"Jimmy Jay is your nephew?" Steve asked, obviously impressed.

"Isn't he black?" Jody asked.

"Yes he is," Beth answered, and wondered if there was veiled bigotry in the question. Suddenly she remembered Jimmy Jay's invitation to St. Moritz.

"As a matter of fact it's a real coincidence our meeting today. He's in Paris and he invited me to spend Christmas with him . . ." she stopped. It was tactless to mention St. Moritz to Jody. "In Europe," she finished lamely.

"That's sweet," Jody said, seemingly unaware of the discrepency in what Beth had said. Then turning to Steve she put her hand on his arm. "Be an angel and get my coat."

"How's John?" Beth asked, recovering from her confusion.

"He's fine. He had to go to Japan on business for the firm."

"What firm?" Beth asked, knowing full well that John Blake was president of the largest textile firm in the United States and one of the wealthiest men in the country. She knew everything about Jody's life, having followed it in endless newspaper reports, seeing pictures of the Blakes' various homes around the world, reading numerous profiles of who the Blakes were, what the Blakes did, what they wore, who they saw and where they went. Beth was aware they had moved to Alabama many years back since the main mills were in the South. She also knew they had one son and that they were the most sought after family among the wealthy, both in the United States and abroad. Beth had never coveted that life, but somehow she was envious of Jody. As youngsters, Beth was the glamorous, popular, exciting personality. By comparison, her life with Adam seemed dull and uneventful.

"Blake and Blake is a firm that deals in textiles," Jody said, and it took Beth a minute to remember what she had asked.

"If you're staying in town for a while, why don't we have lunch," Beth suggested politely.

"I'd love it, but John is meeting me and we're taking our son to St. Moritz for the holidays."

"Are you really?" Beth wanted to laugh. She was being so careful to avoid bringing back sad memories.

"Yes. As a matter of fact, we love it so that we finally bought a house there."

"How lovely," Beth mumbled. She felt like a romantic fool.

"It's a gorgeous place," Jody continued. "It belonged to an old titled French family, and we got it for a song since the owners were in the midst of an ugly divorce."

"What was their name?" Beth asked, knowing the answer before Jody said it.

"De Langue. He was a marquis or something. A dreadful man."

"I met them years ago." Beth wanted to protest. "They were charming, as I remember."

"I can't imagine anyone calling him charming. He was a fat drunk who sat at the Palace Hotel ogling the young American girls when they arrived. Everybody knew about his affairs, and finally his wife couldn't take it anymore, so she divorced him."

"How sad," Beth said keeping her voice in control. "They seemed so happy."

"How can you tell about those foreigners." Jody's tone grew prissy.

"Your table is ready." The maître d' touched Beth's arm, and she was relieved.

"Jody, it was nice seeing you. Call me when you're next in New York." She did not mean it, but it came out instinctively.

"I'd love to," Jody said, and suddenly she leaned over and kissed Beth on the cheek. "I will."

Just as she was turning away, Beth caught a glimpse of her childhood friend. It was something about the eyes which struck her, but she could not decide what it was.

Walking toward her table, Beth was preoccupied with the memory of Jean Paul of years ago and she felt heartbroken. She had not thought of him in years, but somewhere in the treasure chest of her memories he always existed. He was part of a lovely fantasy that had rested there through the years. Now it had been taken away from her.

As she was seated, Beth got a last glimpse of Jody being helped on with a luxurious mink coat and being escorted out by her young companion.

What the hell was Jody doing with someone who looked young enough to be her son, Beth thought angrily and was surprised at her reaction. She forced her mind away from Jody and glanced around the room.

She knew several of the women lunching there and wondered, for the first time, who they really were and what they did with themselves. Some were with two or three other women, some were with men, who were not their husbands. Most of them were divorced. Divorce! She was one of the few who was happily married. *Had been* happily married. It was no longer so. Jody pushed her way back into Beth's thoughts. Was Jody happily married? Was Steve her lover? She had gotten away with a love affair just before she married John Blake. Was she still having affairs? And what could someone like Steve Graham see in a woman who looked and sounded like Jody Blake.

A waiter brought over a glass of white wine, which she had not ordered and Beth was about to protest when she caught sight of Ali coming toward her. She was dressed in faded tight-fitting dungarees, heavy boots and a ridiculous raccoon Eisenhower jacket. Her blond hair was braided and she wore no makeup. In spite of the inappropriateness of the outfit, the girl's beauty was overwhelming. Beth was aware that several people turned to stare at Ali as she came toward her.

"Mother." Ali leaned over and kissed her. "You look gorgeous."

"So do you, darling," Beth said and pushed the table back allowing Ali to slip in beside her. The presence of Ali wiped away the creeping unhappiness that was beginning to gnaw at her. She put her arm around the girl's shoulder and pressed her close. "I do miss you so."

"Mother," Ali said breathlessly, "before George and the boys get here, I wonder if I could ask you a favor. George has to go to an art gallery opening of one of his old classmates, and I wondered if you could take the boys off our hands for about an hour." She paused watching Beth carefully. "George forbade me to ask you, but they would be bored stiff, and it's something George wants to do. And then George wants us to all have dinner together." She looked anxiously at Beth.

"What would I do with the boys?" Beth felt uncomfortable. It had been a long time since she had been in the presence of children.

"Well, it's cold outside, but the park is lovely at this time of year. You could take them to the zoo."

Beth lowered her eyes. Ali was being insensitive, but by the same token, it was not an unreasonable request to make of a mother. She also wondered if she had been equally insensitive to Mary's moods when she first married Adam.

"I'll be delighted to," she said finally.

"That's great." Ali sighed with relief. "And I'm famished."

They ordered lunch and Beth picked up her wine. She was trying to cut down on her drinking. She had had no need for alcohol while in Greenwich. Now she felt restless and was grateful for the waiter's thoughtfulness.

"When do you think you'll leave for Washington?" She turned to look at Ali.

"George decided it would be better if we left tonight, so he and the boys can get an early start in touring the city tomorrow."

"What a pity your father won't be there to show them around."

"He probably would have been too busy." The voice became shrewish.

"I resent that," Beth said evenly. "Your father would have been delighted to take you and the kids around." She toyed with the wine glass nervously. "Why, he was a wonderful father to you, Sarah and Jimmy Jay, and you seem to have forgotten it completely."

Ali lowered her eyes.

"You don't think so?" Beth asked.

"He had no time for anyone or anything but his work. He was never home. Whenever I needed him, he was away." Ali's eyes were still lowered.

"That's ridiculous." Beth was enraged. She was convinced the accusation was somehow directed at her as much as at Adam. "Until he was elected to Congress, he was home all the time. After that he broke his back to get to New York whenever he could." She paused and wondered at her vehemence, but her anger pushed her to continue. "He was a good and devoted father, and instead of being angry with him, you should be proud of him."

"Were you happy with him?" Ali looked up for the first time.

"Yes I was." Beth's anger abated.

"Well, I can't imagine how you could have been. You were alone so much of the time."

"That's not the criteria of what makes a good marriage," Beth countered.

"Well, it's not my idea of what a marriage should be," Ali said. "I want a man who lives with me all the time, who's around when I need him. I could never accept your type of life."

Beth felt herself tremble inwardly. Did Ali know? Was Ali aware that she had never truly accepted her life with Adam as her final goal in life? That after giving up Dan, she had never stopped looking for that elusive prince charming who would come into her life and sweep her off her feet and carry her off to a fairyland?

"Will you be content to live on a small campus? It's hardly an exciting sort of life," Beth said slowly.

"Exciting by whose standards?" Ali asked. "You and Dad had an exciting life. Are you happy? Those glamorous men and women who are photographed all over the place, smiling like hyenas but who beat each other up when they're behind closed doors and come into courts pleading cruelty, wearing dark glasses because they're too black and blue to show themselves. Is that what you call exciting? Well, I may not have that exciting life, but I'll tell you that when I walk into my home with George and we're alone behind a closed door, I'm happy and it's exciting to me."

"But you're not married," Beth said lamely.

"Good God, what has that to do with it? His wife is in a coma and has been for the last eight months. Before that she was completely burned in that freak car accident which left her in a vegetablelike state. Do you expect George to divorce her just so we can get a piece of paper that would make you and Dad more comfortable?"

Beth absorbed herself in her food and tried to remember what George looked like. She had met him only once when she went to visit Ali at college and he was her art professor. A pipe smoker, he was a tall, fair-haired man in his late thirties, with incongruously dark eyes and bushy brows, and a moustache that drooped over thin lips. Surprisingly, he had a boyish smile. The outstanding thing about him, as Beth recalled, was his completely bohemian attitude and manner.

"I'm sorry, Mother," Beth heard Ali say, and she looked over at her and smiled. She doubted if Ali meant it.

They continued to eat in silence, and then as though the solemn conversation had never taken place, Ali began talking about her life in Northampton.

Beth listened and was fascinated by Ali's total involvement in herself and her newly acquired family. Every phrase was preceeded by "George thinks," or "George says" or "George wants." It was a bore, and Beth discreetly lifted her hand to the waiter indicating she wanted another glass of wine. He brought it over and cleared the table, but it did not stop the flow of Ali's conversation. Beth settled back and stared at her daughter. She sounded like a middle-class bourgeois lady, masquerading as a young girl with pigtails and trendy clothes. Except for the way she was dressed, she reminded Beth of Mary Van Ess. It was a shocking revelation, and she wondered what George saw in her.

Suddenly Ali's face lit up, and the beautiful, lively, flirtatious girl

Beth had always known replaced the monotonous woman she had been listening to. The transformation was astounding, and Beth looked around and saw George coming toward them, followed by two tow-haired youngsters. They were equally inappropriately dressed, but it did not matter since they carried it off with aplomb and made a handsome group.

"I forgot how beautiful you are, Mrs. Stillman," George said, slipping in beside Ali, who seemed to melt into the crook of his arm as she smiled warmly at the boys who were standing at the table.

"Boys, I want you to meet my mother," Ali said, and each put out his hand in greeting. "And you remember George, don't you?" She looked at George with pride.

The subtle interplay, the texture of intimacy among the four was inescapable. Beth felt excluded and tried to concentrate on the boys who were seated across from her.

"What are your names?" she asked.

"I'm Russel and he's Andrew," the older boy said. "And I'm nine and he's six. Thank you."

They all started laughing, and the tension was broken.

"They're adorable," Beth said sincerely, "and very well mannered."

"It's Ali's doing." George pressed Ali's hand which was resting on the table. "And I also think they're awed by the elegance of the restaurant." He looked around. "This is quite a place."

"The food here is awfully good. You really should have joined us for lunch," Beth said.

"Mrs. Stillman, I'm afraid the prices here would be out of sight for an art professor," George said lightly.

"Please call me Beth." The reference to money made Beth think of Adam's accusation that George might be interested in Ali because of her inheritance. It seemed like a ridiculous assumption.

"George, Mother agreed to take the boys while we're at the gallery." Ali leaned closer to him.

"It's out of the question," George said emphatically. "I would like you to join us, though, Beth. It's a great exhibit, done by a most unusual man I know. We went to school together, and he left the art world when we graduated to become an editor for some big publishing house. Recently, the urge to paint got to him and within a year he's put together a show, and from the slides I've seen, I'd say he's one of our finer up-and-coming painters."

"May I call you Gramma?" Andrew said suddenly.

Beth felt the blood drain from her face.

"I don't blame you for wanting to be related to this beautiful lady,

Andrew," George said, and the merriment in his voice was clear. "But I'm afraid she's much too young to have you as a grandson."

"I think it would be neat," Ali laughed. "If the boys call me Mom, I don't see why . . ."

"Would you think it disrespectful if they called you Beth?" George interrupted.

"I don't think I'd mind being called Gramma." She tried to sound unruffled.

"I would," George said seriously.

Suddenly Beth could not wait for the meal to be over. She would take the children to the park, in spite of George's objection. It would all be over in a couple of hours, and she could escape to the solitude of her home. Warm and pleasant as they all were, she knew she was sinking into depression and she needed to be alone.

Standing on the corner of Madison Avenue and Sixty-fifth Street, Beth turned to Ali and George. "We'll meet at the zoo at around five."

"You're coming with us," George said firmly, slipping his arm through hers. "I really want you to." His voice was gentle but compelling. She could understand why Ali was attracted to him. Adam would actually love this man, she thought sadly.

They started down the Avenue and Beth felt Andrew put his hand in hers. The feel of the damp little palm in hers made memories of the past loom larger than life. She pressed it with affection.

The gallery was empty when they walked in.

"Steve?" George called out, and the young man who had been with Jody at the restaurant came running out of a back room.

The men hugged each other, and then George turned and introduced him to Ali and Beth.

Steve smiled mischieviously at Beth. "I knew we'd meet again, but I didn't think it would be so soon," he said, reaching out to take her hand.

For a brief moment Beth was elated. The depression that had pressed down on her seemed to evaporate. She felt like an attractive, desirable woman, being appreciated by a young man. But almost immediately she was seized by panic. Steve Graham, young as he looked, was George's age. He was no child. He was a grown man who might believe she was interested in him—might misinterpret her behavior. She wasn't prepared for a relationship with him or anyone else, for that matter. Men had a way of misunderstanding her flirtatious manner, but in the past she could retreat to being Adam's wife. Now she had no escape hatch.

"I think I'd better keep my promise to the boys and take them to the zoo." She turned to Ali and George.

"Aren't you interested in my show?" Steve asked in a mocking voice.

Beth blushed. "I really hate openings of any sort. I would like to come around in a few days and see it without distractions."

"Please let me know when you're coming, and I'll make a point of being here." There was an intimacy in the invitation.

"Of course I will."

Taking the hands of the two boys, she almost ran out of the gallery.

3

Sitting in the car next to George with Andrew nestled in her arms and Ali leaning over the back seat, Beth felt happy. The young child's tousled blond head resting on her breast, his small fingers clutching her sleeve, emphasized his need to be protected. He reminded her of Jimmy Jay, whose fear of being deserted was paramount when he was growing up. Beth looked back and saw Russel sprawled on the flat surface of the station wagon. He too was asleep.

"Is he all right back there?" she asked automatically. "I always worry when children sleep in a car without someone next to them."

"Oh Mother, you sound like you did when we used to go on drives with Dad." Ali laughed merrily.

Beth smiled and touched her daughter's head with affection.

She had fallen into the role of protective mother from the minute she arrived with the children at the park. Contrary to her expectations, she enjoyed her time with them. It brought back the years when she spent endless days with Ali, Sarah and Jimmy Jay at the zoo, the ice-skating rink, the carousel, wandering the mysterious paths that promised adventure, but led nowhere. And the memories were not accompanied by feelings of sadness or sense of loss. They simply affirmed the fact that there was a time for everything in a woman's life. She felt fortunate enough to have experienced the joy of bringing up her children, caring for them, worrying about them. Now she was ready for new experiences, a new life.

"I've never seen him take to anyone as he did to you, Beth," George said, glancing briefly at her. "He's usually shy and leery of strangers."

"He's a lovely child." Beth looked down at the boy. "They're both wonderful. As a matter of fact, a lady at the ice-skating rink thought I was their mother."

"And you quickly corrected her didn't you?" Ali said mockingly.

"No, as a matter of fact, I accepted the compliment and was very flattered." She could not hide her satisfaction.

"Well, let me tell you, you're not only a hit with the younger male generation," George said. "Steve Graham was totally captivated by you."

"He flipped for you," Ali interjected. "He didn't stop raving about the fact that I had a mother who looked as you did. I bet if you weren't married, he'd call and ask you out."

"Knowing Steve, I doubt that it will deter him." George laughed and winked at Beth.

"George!" Ali gasped.

"For a today girl, she sure is naïve." George reached back and patted Ali's arm. "We're rapidly plunging back to the Victorian age with the younger generation."

Beth listened to the banter and smiled. George, Steve and she were a generation away from Ali, and her feelings of being the interloper in a world she did not belong to disappeared.

"Wouldn't you like to spend the night at the apartment instead of driving to Washington at this hour?" Beth suggested when they reached her house. Feelings of anxiety returned when the doorman opened the car door.

"I'd rather get there and have an early start with the boys."

"I'll call you, Mother," Ali called out as the car pulled away from the curb, and Beth found herself standing alone on the curb, watching the disappearing vehicle.

As the elevator shot up to her floor, she felt anxious and nervous.

While looking for her house keys, Beth heard the elevator door shut and the quiet hissing as it started its descent. She was tempted to ring for its return, to ask the elevator man to wait while she opened the door. It was a ridiculous thought. It was not the first time she had come home to an empty apartment, but never before had she felt the fear that suddenly gripped her. She pushed the door open and the darkness within was ominous. She ran in, nearly stumbling over the suitcases which Joseph had placed in the front foyer earlier in the day, and switched on the light. Within seconds she felt better. The familiarity of the room calmed her. She was home. This was her haven, her security, her fort. Walking into the library, she turned on all the lights and threw her coat on a chair. It slipped to the floor, but she made no move to pick it up. It would bother no one. She was alone, and she was free to do as she pleased. She poured herself a stiff brandy and sipped it while taking off her shoes, leaving them lying in the middle of the room. With equal abandon she peeled off her jacket, the vest and undid the buttons of her shirt. Finishing her drink she poured herself another. She stared at it before putting it to her lips. She did not want it, but the idea that no one would be around to comment, that she could do exactly as she pleased, made her take a sip. Then placing the drink on the desk, she removed her shirt, stepped out of her slacks and took off her panty hose, remaining in her bra and bikini panties. Standing nearly naked she allowed the feelings of contentment to spring forth. Life was wonderful, she thought and started sifting through the papers on the desk. Jimmy Jay's letter caught her eye. She reread its message and for a brief moment wished Sarah was not coming home for the holidays. It would have been fun to go to St. Moritz. The chance meeting with Jody came back to her. She dismissed the verbal exchange between them but lingered on the look in Jody's eyes as they were saying good-bye. Somewhere, hidden behind that silly acquired Southern accent lay her childhood friend. She wondered if Jody would call when she returned from her vacation. She hoped she would. There was something fortuitous about the meeting. She had last seen Jody just before she married Adam. It was fitting she should meet her when the marriage was coming to an end. The last thought distressed her and she dismissed it quickly. She did not want to think of Adam. Her eyes wandered across the other papers, and she saw her scribbling of the name Beth Van Ess on a large pad.

"Beth Van Ess," she said out loud, as she had earlier in the day. It did not sound as strange as it had. "This is Beth Van Ess speaking," she continued. "Yes, the Van Esses from Greenwich." She laughed merrily. She felt like Beth Van Ess. She was Beth Van Ess.

Picking up her calendar she turned to the latter part of November. She had forgotten about the theater she and Adam were going to on the Saturday following Thanksgiving. They rarely made advance bookings, Adam's schedule being what it was. But she knew he would be home for the Thanksgiving weekend, and it was a play she wanted to see. She could go alone, she thought. It was quite acceptable these days for women to go out alone. She could even go to one of the small French restaurants on Eighth Avenue afterward. But even as the plan formulated in her mind, she knew she would not do it. She was used to being alone, but she was not used to doing things alone. With equal rapidity she dismissed the thought of calling any of her women friends. There were only three or four whom she considered truly close. Each was alone, either by design or by choice, but they were her "weekday friends." She rarely saw them on the weekends. Besides, it would involve explaining why she was alone. She could not lie to them, and knew she would end up telling them about what had happened. If only Gillian lived in New York, she thought longingly. Gillian was the only one who would not pry, and if she suspected, would not push the subject.

She would take Steve Graham. The thought came from nowhere. When Steve called she would invite him to join her. The use of the adverb "when" rather than "if" struck her and she smiled. She was sure he would call, even before George and Ali had said what they did. There had been a rapport between her and Steve from the minute they met.

Beth felt better. Throwing herself on the large sofa, she stretched out and nursing her drink allowed her mind to dwell on the meeting.

Since her breakup with Dan she had met many men either through Adam or when appearing on his behalf when he was busy. At first she was too heartbroken to pay attention to them, but even as the memory of her deep feelings for Dan began to ebb, she was nervous about getting involved, fearful of repeating the experience. She had a need to be desired, and there were occasions when she met someone to whom she was attracted—but then she would back off and start emphasizing her marital status, her maternal duties, her obligations and loyalties to her family. Vaguely she was aware that none of the men were interested enough to pursue her seriously, but she was convinced that if she wanted to get involved with someone, she could make it happen. She knew most of their friends were convinced she did sleep with men other than Adam. Her girlfriends were always dropping hints, indicating their suspicions. She neither denied nor confirmed their allusions. She suspected that even Adam thought she was unfaithful to him, but intimate matters were never discussed between them, and in a way it perpetuated an image and bolstered her ego. In recent years, she had become more reserved, more aloof. Whether it was her diminishing confidence, or whether it was an indifference to the opposite sex, she could not decide. Somehow the idea of having an affair became a burden, something requiring too much effort. She was content with the superficial admiration, the flirt, the innuendos. Her uncharacteristic self-confidence over her meeting with Steve Graham, she decided, was due to her obvious interest in him. Men must have been aware of her disinterest and reacted accordingly. Now that she was free for the first time in so many years, she must have communicated her readiness for a relationship.

Although his image was vague in her mind, she remembered the tall, thin frame, the dark smiling eyes, the unusually narrow, delicate hands. Unconsciously, she undid her bra and ran her hands over her breasts, down her stomach, touching her vagina through the thin silken fabric of her bikini panties. For a minute she felt as though it was Steve's hand stroking her body. She moved over on the couch as if to allow him to come and lie beside her. She spread her legs wide, waiting for him to start making love to her.

The sharp ringing of the phone shattered the silence. Beth reached over to pick up the receiver without opening her eyes. She groped for it blindly only to discover that she was not in her bed. She opened her eyes and realized she had fallen asleep in the library and the phone was on the desk on the other side of the room. She ran to it, aware of her nakedness and feeling chilled.

It was her mother.

"Did you just wake up?" Mary's rasping voice came through the phone. "It's nearly one in the afternoon."

Beth looked toward the windows and saw the feeble winter sun shining through the sheer curtains. She settled down in a chair, and cupping the phone between her chin and shoulder she looked around for a cigarette. It was bound to be a long conversation, filled with reprimand since Beth had forgotten to call her since she returned from Greenwich the day before.

"I'm alone," Mary wailed, "and you just don't care."

"Mother, you're not alone. You have Martha and Joseph and tons of friends," Beth said, between puffs on her cigarette.

"Friends. What are friends? Wait till you grow old and need your children to show some interest in you and realize that they are too busy with their own families to think of your needs. Just wait."

In spite of the pleasant time in Greenwich, in spite of the new revelations about her mother through Martha's stories, Beth found Mary a spoiled, petulant, self-centered woman who was terribly aggravating. Longingly, Beth thought of having a cup of coffee and wished she were in the kitchen. Instead, she picked up a pencil and paper and started making notes of chores she had to attend to during the day.

The conversation finally ended with Beth promising to call later in the day.

Hanging up, she looked down at the list she had drawn and found it pitifully small. It did not warrant being written out. Angrily she put the paper down, and picked up her clothes which were strewn around the room and went into the kitchen.

She was having her coffee when Adam called.

"How are you, Beth?" he asked politely.

"I'm fine, Adam," she answered lightly, trying to sound pleasant but distant. "Just fine, and you?"

"Everything is okay with me." He paused briefly. "I called to tell you I would be in town over the holidays so that when Sarah arrives I will be more than happy to meet her young man."

"That's wonderful," Beth countered, her brain racing furiously. He had been so evasive about his holiday plans, and she wondered what had caused him to change his schedule. "I'll leave a message with your office about dates and all. Is that all right?"

"Fine." He sounded strained.

The silence after his last answer grew long.

"Sure you're all right?" he repeated at last.

"I'm just fine, Adam," Beth said, her voice growing edgy.

Still he did not hang up.

"Adam, I've got a million things to do, so if there's nothing else you want to tell me, I must hang up."

"No, there's nothing else," he answered. "Just call me when you know Sarah's plans."

As soon as she hung up she started racing around getting ready to attend to the chores she had mentioned. Pouring herself a second cup of coffee, she hurried to the front hall and tried to lift the suitcases to take them into her bedroom. They were too heavy to carry alone. She made a mental note to ask one of the handymen to come in and help her. Flinging them open, she took out several garments and rushed to the bedroom. Showered and dressed, she put her makeup on carefully. She was surprised at the elaborateness of the job she was doing. She rarely made herself up during the weekend unless they were going out. Angrily she put down the mascara she was holding. It was Adam's sudden call that had discombobulated her and caused her to become so frantic. Although he was pleasant, it was his concern that was infuriating. Why should he be concerned? Did he really think she could not manage without him? He had said the night he left she had everything going for her.

She was putting on her coat when she decided to have another cup of coffee. It was then she remembered the theater tickets and was aware that Steve had not called. Impulsively she picked up the phone and dialed one of her friends. There was no answer. She replaced the receiver and tried another. The recorded service answered that the party was out of town and would not be back before the fifteenth of December. With greater urgency, Beth called two other women. Both were away for the weekend.

Everyone was doing something. She had to conjure up chores. She thought of Steve again. What if he called and she were not in? If he really wanted to see her, she decided, he'd call back. Unimportant as her chores were, she had to do something.

With exaggerated purposefulness she put on her coat and started out the front door. The phone rang at that moment. She raced to answer it. It turned out to be a wrong number. She sat down on the straight-backed chair which stood next to the phone and noticed that her hands were trembling. She looked at the clock. It was three in the afternoon and she was exhausted. Abandoning the idea of going out, she went into her bedroom and fully clothed she lay down on the bed and fell into a deep sleep.

She woke up at seven in the evening with a bad headache and remembered that she had not eaten all day. Preparing a sandwich she was again aware that Steve had not called. What struck her even more forcefully was that no one had called. Except for her mother and Adam and the wrong number, the phone had not rung all day. Passing the phone in the foyer, she picked up the receiver to see if it was working. The sharp dial tone mocked her. Settling herself in the library, she tried to read the newspaper. She could not concentrate. Flicking on the television set she became absorbed in a game show but grew bored within minutes. Her restlessness grew. She got up and opened a chilled bottle of wine and drank down a full glass thirstily and refilled it. She wanted to talk to someone, anyone. She picked up the phone book and looked up Steve's number. He was listed and she dialed the number. He answered immediately, but she could barely make out what he was saying since the noise in the background of laughter and music drowned out his voice. She hung up in embarrassment. She'd been a fool. Steve Graham, who was going to be her first fling as a free liberated woman, was involved in a world that didn't know she existed. Tears came to her eyes. Steve Graham probably did not even remember meeting her.

The silence which had been so soothing the night before became oppressive, and she knew she had to get out. She also knew she had nowhere to go. Pouring herself another drink she started skimming through her personal phone book. When she was through the letter W, she realized there was no one she really wanted to talk to, much less spend time with. The knowledge that the reverse was equally true did not escape her.

The ticking of the hall clock seemed to grow louder and she found herself counting the monotonous rhythmic sound. Covering her ears with her hands, she stood up and started pacing. The sound was still audible. She could escape it by going into her bedroom, but the thought of lying in bed unable to sleep was too horrendous. Getting completely drunk was the solution. The noise of the clock would disappear, thoughts would fade and sleep would follow. Opening a second bottle of wine she refilled her glass and placed the bottle beside her.

The ten o'clock news held her attention. It was followed by an old release of *Little Women*. She had seen it years back, and the sight of Katharine Hepburn as a young woman gave her a start. They were all so young, and it seemed not that long ago. She became completely involved in the trials and tribulations of the March family, and by the end she realized she was crying as she had done when she had first seen it and she herself was a very young girl. She understood her tears then, but could not figure out why she was crying now. Years back she identified with Jo and was upset at the fact that things did not work out easily for her. Who was she identifying with now? The mother? Neither Ali nor Sarah were anything like the girls in the film. Neither cared for her as the four girls did for Mrs. March. Beth's sobbing grew louder. Ali had not called her all day. She had spent a whole day alone and Ali was too involved with George and the boys to call and ask how she was. The conversation with Mary came back to her. It was different, she thought angrily. Mary was an old woman, a cantankerous, ungiving person. She had been a good and understanding mother to Ali and Sarah. But mostly to Ali. Mary would never have spent the day with two small boys she was not related to as she had done.

"Wait until you grow old . . ." Mary had said.

"But I'm not old," Beth screamed to the empty room.

Her voice sounded hoarse. If she could only talk to someone, it would bring her back to reality. If only Adam were home, she could wake him up and they would talk. He would probably have been annoyed at being awakened, and would have been angry that she had had so much to drink, but he would have listened to her. Where *was* Adam.

She dialed information and asked for Lauri Eddington's number.

It rang several times and Beth wondered if Adam and the girl were sleeping or if they were making love and were too involved with each other to bother answering the phone. A feeling akin to jealousy went through her. It was almost funny. Her physical relationship with Adam had deteriorated years back, and although they did make love on occasion, it was Adam who initiated the act. Beth tried to conjure up the appearance of the girl. She was tall, beautiful and young, but the features were blurred. Did Adam satisfy that young beauty? Did she satisfy him? It suddenly dawned on Beth that in more than a year she had not had any physical contact with Adam. The feeling of jealousy grew, and Beth felt dizzy. She was about to hang up when a sleepy answering-service voice cut into the ringing phone.

Instead of hanging up, Beth found herself asking for Miss Eddington.

"She's gone away until the fifteenth of December," the voice said. "Is there any message?"

"Where did she go?" Beth felt compelled to ask.

"I'm afraid I don't know, but she will be back after the fifteenth. Who shall I say is calling?"

"It's not important," Beth said shakily and hung up. Adam would be home over the holidays because he will be in town with his young mistress after a vacation. Adam and she were going to take a vacation together after Thanksgiving. They had planned it and she was looking forward to it. Did he take Lauri Eddington instead?

She had to steady herself by holding on to the desk. Adam had betrayed her in the most humiliating way. It was not the affair with a younger woman that was hurting, it was the idea that she was replaced. Openly, Adam had taken a woman on a trip he had planned with her. The reservations were made in the name of Mr. and Mrs. Adam Stillman. Would he register that girl as his wife? Would he dare? She tried to remember the name of the hotel they were going to. She would call them and expose the fraud. Mrs. Adam Stillman was alone in New York and the young woman with the Congressman was not his wife. It would serve him right. He had humiliated her and she was going to make him pay for it.

The need for revenge was paramount in her mind, but she knew it would be an irreversible act. As far as she knew no one was aware of what had happened between her and Adam. Calling up a hotel and informing on Adam's betrayal would expose everything in an ugly light.

Oblivious to the lateness of the hour, she picked up the phone and called Gillian. It was not the first time she had awakened Gillian when she was going through an unhappy time.

The man's voice that answered was unfamiliar.

"Let me speak to Gillian," she commanded.

"Who is this?" The voice belonged to someone young and sounded quite effeminate.

"It's Beth," she said, and wondered who the young man was. The stream of "assistants" living at Gillian's country home was constantly changing. Beth disliked them all, seeing them as pathetic little leeches who nibbled at her friend and took advantage of her.

"I don't know who the hell you are, lady, but I'm not about to wake her up."

"You do as you're told you little twerp." Beth's voice grew louder.

"You're either drunk or crazy," the voice said and hung up.

She redialed the number. It rang several times, and Beth wondered if the person who answered the phone was simply not going to pick it up.

"Is that you Beth?" Gillian's husky, sleepy voice came on.

"Gillian," Beth wailed, "Adam left me." She did not mean to say it that crudely, but the words tumbled out before she could stop herself. "He left me for some young model who's going to have his baby."

There was no reply but Beth could hear Gillian's breathing.

"Did you hear what I said?" Beth screamed.

"Yes, Beth, I heard." She sounded resigned. "I heard and I knew. I've known for quite a while, and maybe it's just as well that you finally found out about it." She paused for a long minute. "You really didn't know?"

Beth found it difficult to talk. Gillian had known about Adam and the girl for a long time and had never told her about it.

"You knew?" she whispered. "You knew and never told me?" Her voice grew firmer. "You've been my friend for so long, I trusted you, depended on your friendship. You knew . . ."

"I somehow suspected that you were aware of it and were just letting nature take its course. As a matter of fact, some of us wondered if you weren't behaving in an extremely intelligent manner."

"Some of you . . ." Beth could not believe what she was hearing. "You mean others know about it too?"

"It's been common gossip among people who know you and Adam. And in a way it's a tribute to you both that everyone thinks so highly of you that it never got into the papers."

Beth put the receiver down on the desk in a daze and went over to the bar. While pouring herself a drink she could hear Gillian's voice calling her name. She looked at the receiver lying on the desk impersonally. Gillian knew. Everyone knew. She had been the laughing stock of the whole community, and her dearest friend, Gillian, had not bothered to inform her about it so that she could protect herself from ridicule. With measured steps she walked over to the desk and replaced the receiver on its cradle, cutting off Gillian's voice.

She felt strangely calm and sober. Adam had made a fool of her, and she had no further obligation toward him or the need to protect his reputation.

Sipping her drink she sifted through the papers on the desk. She would call the hotel and tell them the truth. Somewhere among the papers she knew she would come across the name of the hotel they were registered at. Although she felt her mind was completely clear, she forgot what she was looking for when she saw Jimmy Jay's letter again. It distracted her. Jimmy Jay was in Paris. It was six hours later in Paris. She would call him and tell him she was coming to St. Moritz. She began to laugh hysterically. Of course. It would serve them all right if she were not home when they needed her. Sarah, Ali and even Adam depended on her and took her for granted. She would not even leave a message as to where she was. As soon as she made the arrangements, she would destroy Jimmy Jay's letter and they would all be in a panic.

When the overseas operator answered, Beth picked up the letter and tried to focus on the number she was trying to reach. She could not make it out. The operator kept asking for the number and became impatient.

Hanging up the phone slowly, Beth knew she was much too drunk to talk to anyone. She was tired, and all she wanted was to go to sleep.

4

Lauri stepped into her burgandy-colored leather pants and had a hard time zipping them up. Sucking in her breath, she struggled with the button at the waist. That done, she pulled on a multi-colored, bulky over-blouse which she had designed for her fall collection. She was grateful for its size and let her breath out slowly, wondering if the zipper would hold. Satisfied that it would, she ran her hands through her long hair, pinched her cheeks and walked into Stan's office.

"Sit down, Lauri, and make yourself comfortable," Stan said, not looking up, absorbed in a chart he was holding.

"I can sit down, but I doubt I'll be comfortable." Lauri laughed as she slipped stiffly into a chair opposite the doctor and stretched her legs directly in front of her, so her midriff would not press against the stiff leather waistband.

Stan looked up and smiled. "Tight?" he asked.

"Stiflingly so," Lauri nodded.

"Why the hell don't you wear something looser?"

"I've got an important appointment this morning, and I've got to look smashing."

"Nothing can be that important the day before Thanksgiving."

"This is. I've designed a whole line for spring and summer, and the Aden Girl people have agreed to a tie-in with us. I'll start wearing my designs when I do the commercials. It's all set, and this morning's meeting is simply to satisfy the chairman of the board who likes to feel he's making the decisions."

"Spring and summer?" Stan raised his brows.

"Oh we've photographed all the still shots and taped the commercials. I've just got to do the voice-overs."

"Sounds fine since I really want you to slow down a bit."

"How am I doing?" Lauri kept her voice light.

"Physically you're in perfect shape. You've barely put on any weight, which is good," Stan was watching her closely. "What about the emotional state?"

Lauri smiled feebly. "I'm confused again," she confessed. "I thought I had it all solved, but suddenly things are getting sort of blurred."

"Want to talk about it?"

"There's nothing to talk about. I obviously have to decide once and for all what I'm going to do, and every time I feel I know what my plans are, I panic." She let a sigh escape her. "I know I have to make a decision soon."

"Sooner than that," Stan said gently. "You're nearly through your eighth week, and quite soon an abortion becomes serious business—both medically and morally."

"Don't say that word," Lauri whispered.

"You ladies break me up. You fight like demons to get the law passed, and then you want it applied to everyone but yourselves."

Lauri lowered her eyes.

"Lauri, do you want the baby? It's as simple as that. I know you've thought about it a great deal, and I'm sure you know the implications. But within a very short time you'll start being visibly pregnant, and because you are so thin, the changes will be more apparent."

"Oh come off it, Stan," Lauri snapped. "I know that."

"Are you aware of the fact that you probably won't be able to do the Aden Girl commercials for very much longer?"

"Why not?" Lauri protested. "I've told you that there are enough of them done to go right straight through the summer. By then the baby will be born."

"You're incredible. Do you really think the Aden people will run those commercials when they discover that their clean-cut glamour girl is going to be a mother and an unwed one at that?" Stan said deliberately, trying to make her face the facts she was obviously trying to ignore. "Damn it, they'll pull those out of circulation so fast, your head will spin."

"They wouldn't dare." Lauri stood up angrily.

Stan stood up too. He knew he had overstepped himself. "Maybe not." He tried to look cheerful. "I don't really know about big business."

Lauri picked up her large, leather Gucci bag. It was heavy.

"What have you got in there, the family jewels?" Stan smiled, helping her on with her leather cape, which matched the trousers.

"Get off my back, Stan," she hissed. "I'm a working girl and I've got to carry my work gear with me."

Stan put his arms around her shoulders. "Relax, honey. I'm your doctor, and I've got to make sounds like one."

She smiled. "See you and Peppy at Tony's tomorrow around four?"

"We'll be there and we're bringing the baby with us, you know. Peppy is all for breast feeding, and she's not crazy about leaving him with the nurse."

"Who would have thought Peppy would be that maternal." Lauri's smile broadened.

"I did." Stan grinned. "That's why I married her."

He accompanied Lauri to the door. Before opening it, he put his hand on her arm. "Just one thing, Lauri, don't mention anything about your pregnancy or thoughts of an abortion to Peppy. She's really very open-minded about women's choices and all that, but you're her friend and . . ." He seemed embarrassed by what he was saying.

"Don't worry. I won't say a word."

The doorman of the building opened the door for Lauri and the gust of snow swept into the lobby. Before walking out, she pulled on the hood of her cape and stepped out into the storm.

Everyone is so open-minded, Lauri thought angrily as she stood at the corner of Fifth Avenue and looked for a taxi. It was the height of the morning rush hour and the cars jamming the avenue were moving at snails' pace, not only because of the density of the traffic but also because of the heavy snow that had been falling for the past few days. Lauri looked up at the street sign which was barely visible through the snow flakes. She was on Sixty-fourth Street and she had to be on Fifty-fourth Street and Park Avenue by ten o'clock. She looked at her watch. It was just past nine. Crossing the street she started walking. Although she had plenty of time, she quickened her pace and within seconds she was running. Her bag was heavy and her feet kept sinking into the deep slush. A pain started throbbing at her side and she stopped to rest. The pain persisted and she felt sick. Quickly she sank down on a snow-covered bench and leaned forward, hoping to quell the nausea.

She couldn't be sick now, she thought frantically. They had all worked too hard on getting the tie-in with the Aden Girl commercials. She and Tony had piled up the still photographs which would more than cover the ones needed by the advertising agency. All of the television commercials were shot, and although it meant a grueling schedule, they had worked for a deadline that would enable her to go ahead and have the baby if she decided she wanted it. Robbie, unaware of what the rush was all about, had put the whole workshop at her disposal, and her designs were ready for each sitting. Everything was falling into place and this morning's appointment was to get the final go-ahead.

She sat up and took a deep breath. Somehow she would make it, she thought and was relieved that the nausea had passed. She lifted her head and allowed the damp snowflakes to settle on her face. The icy drops refreshed her. It would all work out, she thought with renewed confidence. The sense of optimism that had carried her through the last few weeks returned. Now she had to think more clearly about the baby.

Stan had said that time was of the essence, and she had purposely prepared everything so as to relieve her of pressures as far as her decision was concerned.

Her thoughts turned to Adam. She was meeting him at six o'clock in the evening at the Plaza Hotel after not seeing him since the night of his election. Poor Adam. He had called her for days after that night, and although she had received all of his messages from her answering service, she had put off calling him back until she felt secure enough to talk to him without feeling hysterical. Contrary to her expectations, he was calm, extremely warm and there was no recrimination in his voice. He told her he was busy but would come to New York if she wanted him to. She knew he was itching to ask about the pregnancy, but had the tact to refrain from mentioning it. They made a date for the day before Thanksgiving. She was surprised when he suggested they meet at the Plaza rather than her apartment.

Suddenly Lauri was excited about seeing him. She missed their relationship. His understanding and kindness, his ability to make her feel secure and happy. Their physical compatibility. It would be nice to sleep with Adam again, have him hold her in his arms, make love to her.

Standing up quickly, Lauri felt the button of the waistband of her trousers pop. She looked down and saw it disappearing into the deep snow around her. The sight made her laugh.

"You can't win 'em all," she said out loud, and started walking briskly down the avenue.

The elevator shot up to the forty-ninth floor and Lauri stepped into the plush reception room of the Aden Girl offices. Her pictures were everywhere, but as always, the dominant one was the massive gilt-framed portrait of Victor Adenizzio, chairman and president of the board of the huge company. Since the first time she visited the offices, Lauri had tried to decipher the personality of the man in the painting. He was a portly, almost fatherly-looking man with a mass of gray hair and piercing dark eyes. The artist had tried to flatter him, but the expression in the eyes came close to a glare, staring down at the people as they came off the elevator.

"Good morning." Kimberly Sloan, the account executive who was responsible for hiring Lauri, came toward her. English by birth, she was a woman in her mid-forties with short-cropped red hair, warm brown eyes, sharp, long nose and thin, well-shaped lips. Extremely tall, she carried herself with assurance. A powerful force in the inner circle of the company, most people feared her. Warnings that she was not to be trusted were always circulating, but Lauri found her decent and forthright. They got on well, and Lauri respected her capabilities.

Helping Lauri off with her cape, Kim handed it to a young woman who was standing by. "Hang these up, Alice," she commanded, with traces of her British accent still discernible in her speech, and took Lauri by the arm and led her into her office.

"Coffee?" she asked.

"I don't think so," Lauri answered. She would have preferred a Coke or some ginger ale, the feeling of nausea had returned, but thought better of it. "Everything in order?" she asked instead.

"No serious problems." Kim lit a cigarette. "We're going to have a full-fledged meeting. The whole top executive is on hand, not that their opinions matter. Mr. Adenizzio might put you through the grill for a few minutes, but I don't foresee any real problems. He's simply a male chauvinist through and through and looks at us women as a lesser breed, but I believe he's really excited about the whole thing, and I'm sure it will work out."

Lauri sat down and watched Kim carefully. He's a male chauvinist, she thought wryly, but what would Kim, the liberated woman of the seventies say if she knew about the baby? Would she stand up for her? Could she confide in her? The warnings about Kim's cut-throat methods crossed Lauri's mind, and she dismissed the idea.

"You really don't have anything to worry about," Kim was saying. "You have a way of presenting yourself that is completely captivating, and you're so utterly stunning, it's sickening." She laughed pleasantly. "Somehow, you always look as though you've just stepped out of a page in *Vogue* or *Harper's*." She sighed with appreciation. "How you keep that figure I'll never know."

"The meeting is about to start." Alice appeared in the doorway. "Mr. Adenizzio is here, and they're all waiting for you."

Alice was obviously in awe of the big boss. Woman's liberation had not liberated her from fear of men, Lauri thought with amusement as she followed Kim out of the office.

The conference room was discreetly lit and the hum of muted voices was barely audible when Kim and Lauri walked in.

It was a circular-shaped room with bronzed windowpanes reaching from ceiling to floor, giving one the impression of being in a glass house floating in space. The only visible piece of furniture was a huge bronze glass table, resting on a transparent plasticlike base, and chairs made of a similar material. The plush honey-colored carpet relieved the otherwise somber room.

Lauri had never been in the inner sanctum of the Aden dynasty. Her dealings were with Kim and the ad agency people who represented the cosmetic end of the Adenizzio conglomerate whose holdings were vast and diversified. Her eyes wandered over to a group of men standing at the far end of the room, and she tried to identify the man whom she had grown to know through the portrait as Victor Adenizzio. He did not seem to be there.

The men turned and stared at the two women as they entered, but no one moved. The strained mood was evident.

"Miss Eddington?" a man of medium height, in his mid-thirties, extricated himself from the group and came toward them. "I'm Victor Adenizzio," he said, and Lauri was taken aback. There was no similarity between the man and the portrait she had grown to know as the top man of the company. Aside from being considerably younger, he had almost jet-black hair and a square dimpled chin, and although the eyes were dark, they had a much lighter hue than the eyes in the painting.

Extending her hand, Lauri was tempted to say something light about the portrait in the reception room, but then she saw the unmistakable expression of the younger man's eyes, and knew he was the son of Victor Adenizzio, Sr. The glaring, almost angry look was identical.

"I thought Mr. Galandez would be here, too," Victor said letting go of Lauri's hand and waving everyone to their seats. "I would have liked to talk directly to the designer."

"I am the designer," Lauri said coolly, sitting down in a seat opposite Victor, wanting to be as far away from him as possible.

"Miss Eddington, I know you model the clothes and do them justice and I'm fully aware that your name is used to advertise them, but we don't have to play the game here." He smiled briefly. "Your secret is safe within this room."

"Mr. Adenizzio, I designed the line we photographed, and Robbie Galandez helped with suggestions and execution. There is no secret that has to be kept. We work together, out of the same shop, but in this instance, it is completely my concept from design to color and all other details." Lauri found it difficult to keep the resentment out of her voice.

"Very well," Victor said unimpressed, a shade of mistrust still in his voice. "In that case, I suppose we can get right down to business."

Raising his hand slightly, the room grew darker and a projection light beamed onto a descending small screen exposing photographs of Lauri as the Aden Girl. There were twelve slides in all, and in each one she was dressed in a different outfit designed by Lauri Eddington.

The pictures were extraordinarily beautiful, and glancing around Lauri could see the obvious appreciation of the people watching. She dared not look at Victor. When the last photograph was shown, the screen lifted out of sight and the pleasant light returned.

"Impressive," Victor said, and there was an imperceptible sigh of relief from everyone in the room. It occurred to Lauri that she was not the only one who had held her breath throughout the brief screening.

No one spoke, and the air of anticipation grew.

"I'm particularly impressed with the way you've used the denim," Victor said thoughtfully. "You've made it versatile and that's good, since it's also practical." He was silent again and Lauri found herself waiting impatiently for his next words. "The designs are equally good and appropriate for the whole concept of our spring and summer campaign, but I would like some more shots, and I'd like them on location." He paused briefly. "Some of the colors are off, and I believe it's because the pictures were taken indoors. We'll reshoot them on location, and I'm sure we'll get what I'm looking for."

"But the weather . . ." Lauri started.

"We can shoot them in Brazil," Victor interrupted her. "We can leave for Rio on December first, and it shouldn't take more than ten days."

His self-assurance was annoying, but Lauri was too preoccupied with figuring out the dates he had mentioned to react to his tone. She would be nearing the end of her third month by then. Stan had made it clear that time was of the essence. If she was in New York, she had a solid three weeks, maybe four weeks, in which to consider her options about the forthcoming birth of the baby. In Brazil it would be different. Familiar surroundings were important to her at this moment. The only saving grace would be having Tony with her. But would Tony agree to go? Was he available? Her rage surfaced.

"Mr. Adenizzio, I can clear my calendar, but I'm not sure Mr. Abbot can clear his. I'll have to check with him."

"He'll clear his calendar," Victor said calmly, and stood up. Everyone else in the room did too. "I assume we all agree this tie-in is interesting and different. I believe it adds a dimension to the whole promotion." He looked around the room and Lauri did too. Everyone nodded their agreement, and Lauri noticed Kim for the first time since they entered the room. She did not look as aggressive as usual. She looked smaller, almost insecure. She too was nodding her consent. "I'm sure we can rely on everyone's cooperation." He smiled pleasantly, and Lauri realized he was being warm and charming. The expression in his eyes changed and his face seemed to light up. He turned to her. "I wasn't sold on the idea, you know, even though Kim was enthusiastic, but you've done an excellent job both on the designs and in achieving the carefreeness we're trying to bring to the product. I'm quite sure we're going to capture the younger age group we're after."

He turned abruptly and started toward the door, which looked like one of the windows. Everyone followed except for Lauri and Kim.

Briefly, Lauri wondered if anyone had ever mistakenly walked through a window rather than the door.

"What a dreadful man," Lauri said, leaning back in her chair.

Kim lit a cigarette, inhaled deeply and smiled.

"I almost wished he'd walked through a window rather than the door." She returned Kim's smile, when she saw the older woman's face freeze as she stared past Lauri's shoulder.

"Not very likely," Victor said, and Lauri swung around. "I purposely sit opposite the door so I know where the exit is," he smiled at her. "My father taught me that a long time ago. Always know the route of escape."

In spite of the awkward situation, Lauri felt the tension leave her.

"I came back to ask if you'd have dinner with me tonight." He was oblivious to Kim's presence.

"I'm sorry, but I've got a previous engagement," Lauri answered pleasantly.

"Break it."

"Impossible. It's an appointment I couldn't break even if I wanted to, and I don't want to." She was not rude but found herself wondering if she would have broken the date if it were not with Adam.

"Fair enough," Victor said unawed, although his eyes clouded over. "I'll be flying my plane down to Rio for the photographing session and it would please me if you and Tony would join me."

"I haven't spoken to Tony yet." Lauri felt her anger return. "I'm not sure he can make it."

"I spoke to him before the meeting started," Victor said, "and he is free. As a matter of fact, he was worried whether you were."

"And I suppose you assured him I would." Lauri had a hard time keeping the sarcasm out of her voice.

"No. I could not assure him of that. I am pleased you can, though." He bowed slightly, nodded to Kim and left as silently as he entered.

"Was his father equally obnoxious?" Lauri asked.

"Lauri, take it easy," Kim said, squashing out her cigarette.

"Well, I don't know how anyone can work under these circumstances, but I guess one can and one does."

"Don't knock it. It's one of the best run organizations in the country. They've been successful at everything they touch, and let's not kid ourselves, they aren't scared of new ideas. How many companies would have agreed to work with an unknown designer as a tie-in on a cosmetics campaign. As a matter of fact, it's a tribute to the old man to have given the Aden line to Victor, Jr., and he is allowing him to run the show as he pleases."

Lauri stood up and so did Kim. "Well, I am grateful, but I must admit that the thought of a trip to Brazil at this point isn't exactly what the doctor ordered."

"Are you ill?" Kim asked with concern as the two women started out of the room.

Lauri blushed. "It's just an expression," she said quickly. "But I better get over to Tony's and start getting everything together. I have to talk to Robbie. This trip is going to throw our whole schedule out of line."

"But you will manage it, won't you?" Kim was again the boss lady, the company woman.

"I guess so," Lauri said, but she was suddenly tired. "I was hoping for a few weeks of peace and quiet between now and New Years."

The snow was still coming down heavily, and the cold wind stung Lauri's face as she started up Central Park South toward Tony's studio. Letting herself into the apartment with a key, she was relieved to find the studio door shut, meaning Tony was working and could not be disturbed. Joey looked up from the front hall desk and handed her several messages. She scanned through them. None were important.

"I'm going up to rest, and if you can just take any other calls that come through I'd be grateful," she said wearily. "I'm not really expecting anything drastic to happen today, anyway." She was halfway up the steps to the upper level when she remembered the Thanksgiving dinner. "Do we have everything we need for tomorrow?" she asked.

"Oh sure. Mr. Abbot took care of all the food and wine. The lady who is preparing the food seems to have everything in order. I've even got the bassinet for the Blyden baby, and I must say, everyone we've invited is coming. You'd think with this storm, some of the people would have canceled."

"Maybe we'll be lucky and they'll change their minds tomorrow. The weather bureau doesn't promise a let up in its forecast."

Once in her room, Lauri undressed, slipped into a loose robe and lay down on her sofa bed. The conversation with Joey made her smile to herself. Since moving in with Tony they had become like an old married couple. Tony's housekeeper loved her, and Joey treated her like the mistress of the house as did all their mutual friends.

She closed her eyes and tried to adjust to the idea of going to Brazil. A trip to a foreign land was frightening. Aside from being away from familiar sights and people she was close to, the physical exertion would be great. Her body had not changed visibly, but she was already uncomfortable in tight-fitting clothes. She did not have time to loosen them for the new photographs. Besides, she did not dare. No one but Tony and Stan knew of her condition. The seamstresses at the shop would become suspicious. Robbie would wonder. Having Tony with her on the trip would be a saving grace. It would, however, mean being far away from Adam. Even before she called him she knew he was close by, and it gave her a sense of security. She was aware that he had left his wife, but he had changed his attitude. He never again mentioned marriage or made her feel responsible for his actions. His concern was for her welfare, and although she was sure he wanted her to have the child, he seemed to accept the fact that it would be her decision, and until such time as she made up her mind about the baby he would simply stand by. In a way he and Tony were behaving in a similar fashion. They showered her with love and attention. She felt pleasantly drowsy. If she had the baby, it would only enhance her life, give it fuller purpose, greater meaning.

Lauri was on the edge of sleep when Victor Adenizzio suddenly entered her mind. Her eyes flew open. In the brief meeting with him, he had succeeded in becoming a factor in her thoughts. She would be spending ten days with him. Ten days that were vitally important to her. In spite of the feelings of minutes before, she was still uncertain about her course of action. Victor Adenizzio had no rights in her decision making, yet he was there and he had to be considered. He was not merely the man who was going to enable her to realize her ambitions in her designing career, he was also an extremely attractive man. The fact that she was aware of it made her uncomfortable. Since meeting Adam she had never even thought of going out with another man. Victor was someone she would have gone out with. She sat up nervously. She was being fickle. She was pregnant, involved with a man whom she cared about, was thinking of having his child, and yet she found herself attracted to someone she had met briefly and had not really liked on first meeting.

A light tap on the door distracted her.

"Come in," she called. Tony walked in and threw himself on the seat next to the sofa.

"I'm bushed," he said, leaning back in the seat.

"Would you like a drink or something to eat?"

"Why don't you get Joey to bring up some salad and coffee," he answered, looking at her. "Have you eaten?"

"I'll have some tea," she said, picking up the phone and buzzing the intercom.

"How did it go?" Tony asked, when she finished giving the order.

"Adenizzio liked the whole thing," she answered. "But you knew that." She paused, "He told me he spoke to you early this morning about the reshooting of some of the photographs."

"I didn't mean the Aden meeting. You saw Stan today."

"Everything is fine." Lauri lowered her eyes. "I just have to make up my mind within a very short time."

"When?"

"By Christmas, latest."

"Would he agree to your going to Brazil?"

"I suppose so."

"That's not good enough." Tony sat up. "I won't let you go unless he gives you permission."

"Tony, stop sounding like a mother hen."

"If you want to have the baby, you've got to start treating yourself with greater respect. If you don't want it, then we're in a different ball game."

"I didn't know you knew Victor Adenizzio," Lauri changed the subject. "Where did you meet him?"

"When I was studying photography in London. He took it up as well. He's damn good."

"He spoke as though he knew what he was talking about. Do you see him socially?" she asked, and was surprised by her question.

"We play tennis every weekend. He's a great guy, and the only thing he holds against me is that I introduced him to the girl he married."

"Who is she?"

"A stunning Italian model who was working in London. She was from Naples. A primitive sort of girl, who fell into modeling accidentally. She was about sixteen when I first saw her. Victor flipped over her and saw her as a sweet Catholic girl who would be his wife and mother of his children and they would live happily ever after." He smiled. "Victor was a hot, fast twenty-year-old then."

"And?"

"She had three kids, like one after the other. They lived in a magnificent house in Oyster Bay, aside from all the houses they have all over the place, Rio, Acapulco, St. Moritz, Capri, etc., but little Felicia quickly cultivated the taste for the better things in life, and being a big fat mamma to satisfy Victor became a bore."

"Are they divorced?"

"I believe Papa Victor had the marriage annulled. As a good Catholic, he could not see his son get a divorce."

"And Victor agreed?" Lauri wanted to laugh.

"The Adenizzio family goes by the book, Sr., Jr. and everyone else."

"Sounds like the 'Godfather' scene."

"Not quite. Old man Adenizzio is a chemist by profession, and he actually developed the cosmetic line and brought it to the United States." Tony stopped and scrutinized Lauri for a long moment. "Why this interest in Victor?"

"He's a damn attractive man."

"And you're a loose woman." Tony laughed. "In your condition thinking of men as being attractive."

"I agree, and I wonder if you can get your friend to skip coming on location with us. I also wonder if you could persuade him to let us pick our own spot within the borders of the States. I'd feel much more comfortable if we were closer to home."

"I can do the latter, but I doubt I can persuade him not to come along."

Joey knocked on the door and walked in with a tray of food, interrupting the conversation.

"Are you eating in?" Joey asked. "Cook wants to know."

Tony looked over at Lauri. "I am, are you?"

"No," she said self-consciously. "I've got a dinner date."

They ate in silence for a while. "Seeing Adam tonight?" Tony asked.

"Yes, I am."

Tony continued eating, not looking up at her. "You really do make waves, don't you?" he said quietly. "I thought you were going to make up your mind without outside pressure?"

"I miss him, Tony," she said simply.

They finished eating and Tony stood up. "I'll see you tomorrow around four?"

"I'll be here," she answered.

Just before she fell asleep she decided it would probably make sense to have the abortion. She was young and there would be other opportunities to have a child. Victor's face dominated her last waking moments.

5

"Good evening, Miss Eddington," the maître d' of the Oak Room at the Plaza said as Lauri entered the elegant oak paneled bar.

Lauri looked around bewildered. She did not frequent the place and wondered how the man knew her name. Her expression made him smile.

"I recognized you from the Aden commercial that was shot here," he said. "It's a very effective piece of advertising." He took her elbow politely trying to lead her to a seat.

Lauri started after him but stopped abruptly. If she was that recognizable, her meeting with Adam could prove to be embarrassing.

"I'll be right back," she said quickly, and hurried toward the exit, hoping to catch Adam before he arrived. She had done it instinctively, but as soon as she reached the crowded main lobby of the hotel she felt silly. The bar was far more secluded than a public hotel lobby. She retraced her steps and returned to the Oak Room and allowed herself to be seated in front of the large window that faced the park and was opposite the entrance door.

"I'll have a glass of white wine," she said to the waiter, and settled back.

Not since the first time she met Adam and had a drink with him at the Regency had they met anywhere but in her apartment or at his place in Washington. It occurred to her that it had been as long since she had been out on a date of any sort. Since her affair with Adam started, she had not seen anyone socially. She had not missed it. She felt totally fulfilled. She had Adam, Tony, Robbie and her work. She still saw most of the Broadway plays and went to the opera with Tony on nights when Adam was in Washington.

Now sitting in the early evening in a bar in the middle of the city, Lauri felt she had been living in a fool's paradise. Her life for the past year had been a compromise, after all. There was something wrong in being involved with someone who could not take her out openly, introduce her to his friends and his world.

"Lauri?" Adam was standing at her table, the maître d' was beside him. Lauri looked carefully at the headwaiter trying to decipher his thoughts. His face was expressionless. She turned her eyes to Adam. The sight of him made her forget where she was. When Adam came to sit beside her, all thoughts of minutes before dissolved and were replaced by an irrepressible joy.

"I'll have a glass of wine," Adam said to the maître d', who nodded respectfully and walked away. Then turning to Lauri, he took her hand in his and pressed it with great emotion. "God, I missed you," he whispered.

Lauri could not find her voice. Just sitting next to him, having him hold her hand, feeling the warmth of his presence was intoxicating.

"Why are we here?" she finally asked.

"I thought you might want to meet on neutral grounds." He smiled. "You've been sounding so officious in recent days."

She lowered her eyes and stared at his hand in hers. She wanted to pick it up and press her lips to it. "I didn't mean to sound that way. I was just trying to put things into perspective."

"It doesn't matter. What's important is that you're here and I'm here and we're together."

The waiter arrived with their wine and each picked up their glass and toasted each other silently.

"Is it all right for you to be seen in public with a strange lady?" Lauri asked, releasing his hand and turning her body so that she faced him.

"Lauri, I told you. I've left Beth," Adam said quietly.

Lauri stiffened.

"Relax, honey," he said soothingly. "It's not something you asked me to do—forced me to do. I certainly know you did not expect it of me. It's something I wanted."

The picture of Beth Stillman the night of the election came back to Lauri, and the feelings of pity and compassion she felt for the older woman returned more forcefully. "How did she take it?" she whispered.

"Beth?" Adam laughed. "I wouldn't be surprised if she was relieved." Then becoming serious he continued, "We've lived such independent lives in recent years. She has many friends, is invited everywhere, the girls take up a great deal of her time and her thoughts. She's not been happy with me for a long time." He paused, and a far away look came into his eyes. "Not for a long time," he repeated almost to himself.

"Were you?" Lauri asked.

"I don't think I've ever thought of it in those terms, just as I'm sure Beth has not thought of it. We've been married for many years, and although God knows we're the best of friends and will always be, marriage, as such, holds no interest for either of us."

"How sad," Lauri cried out.

"I don't know that it's sad. Our marriage simply ran its course."

"But what happens to her now?" Lauri's voice was barely audible.

"Happens to her?" Adam asked incredulously. "Why nothing special. She's an extremely capable woman, knows hundreds of people. She's financially better off than I am. She'll probably meet someone who will see her values and appreciate her for the wonderful person she is . . ." He stopped briefly. "She is a remarkable person, Lauri."

"Adam, let's get out of here." Lauri was unable to listen. She wanted to be alone with Adam, wanted to erase the memory of Beth Stillman, wanted to recapture their time together as it had been before the night she met his wife. She wanted to be in her apartment with him, have him make love to her, immerse herself in the warmth and security she had always felt when they were alone.

Once in the taxi, Lauri threw herself into Adam's arms, and kissed him passionately on the mouth. She felt his tongue and bit it gently. Slipping her arm inside his jacket, she caressed his body through the thin fabric of the shirt. Her excitement rose. With great effort she pulled her face away from his and rested her head on his shoulder. Adam's arm held her close.

It had grown dark outside and the snow storm caused the taxi to drive slowly.

"Damn this weather," Lauri said breathlessly. "I wish we were home already."

Adam pressed her shoulder.

"I wish we could have met at home." Lauri pulled back and looked up at Adam who was staring out the window.

"No. It was important for you to understand that it's all going to be different from here on in," he said soberly. "I wanted you to see that I meant what I said when I last saw you." He did not shift his gaze away from the taxi window, and Lauri felt strangely uncomfortable. He sounded completely sincere, yet there was a note of reservation in his voice. She replaced her head on his shoulder and realized that he had not asked her about the baby. In her excitement at seeing Adam she had briefly forgotten about it. She felt her face grow hot with embarrassment. A life was growing inside of her, a being was forming in her womb and she had simply forgotten about it. Did she want the baby? Did she want to give birth to Adam's child? She had purposely not seen him in the last few weeks because she was going to make her decision. What was it going to be? Adam had left his wife. He was ready to marry her and be a father to the baby. But she did not want to get married. Her mind began to whirl in confusion.

The cab came to a halt and Lauri was relieved.

6

Adam was snoring quietly beside her, and it bothered her. Lauri tried to ignore the sounds, but they grew louder and more gutteral, and she turned her head to look at him. His olive-skinned face against the white frilly pillowcase was as handsome as ever, but it was the graying hair that now caught her attention. He was in a deep slumber, and she noticed the deep lines of age creasing his face, and she felt she was staring at an old man.

She turned her head away. She had wanted Adam so desperately during the period when she had not seen him. It was not until he appeared at the Oak Room that she was able to fully appreciate her great physical and emotional desire for him. Subconsciously she had fantasized the meeting, the actual lovemaking, the complete fulfillment which usually ensued. Even while in the taxi, in spite of the conversation about his wife, rational thoughts were mingled with her strong physical need to sleep with him. But it had not happened as she had visualized it.

She felt his tension as they climbed the stairs to the apartment. She had fumbled with the key and became so confused that Adam took it from her and let them in. Once in the living room, Lauri threw her arms around his neck and kissed him with abandon.

"I've missed you so, Adam. I don't know how I survived."

He returned her passionate kiss and pushed her away, flicking on the light. Then lifting her face to his he looked into her eyes. "Are you all right, my little girl?"

The wording disturbed her. "Of course I am."

"Have you been seeing the doctor regularly?"

"Regularly?" Lauri asked amazed.

"Well, under the circumstances, don't you think you should be in constant touch with him?"

"Adam, I'm pregnant, not suffering from some malignant disease."

"Lauri, don't be flip," Adam said, and sounded like an authoritarian.

She pulled away and started removing her outer garments. Her buoyant mood was ebbing quickly.

"Adam, would you make love to me?" Lauri said, her back to him. "I want you to fuck me."

The silence made her turn. Adam was in the process of taking his coat off when she had worded her thoughts. She laughed self-consciously. "Don't look so shocked. That's one of the ways people refer to making love."

"I'm just surprised to hear you speak that way," Adam said, obviously uncomfortable.

"But I do want you to fuck me," she persisted. "I want you inside me, I want to feel you, know you exist not only in my mind, but right inside where it counts."

Adam seemed upset, and Lauri was actually shocked by what she was saying.

"Lauri I want to make love to you. I want you and need you. I've thought of nothing else but you for the last three weeks. Don't spoil it with childish anger," Adam said quietly, and came over to her.

"Will you make love to me?" Lauri asked softly.

"Is it all right?"

"But why wouldn't it be?" Lauri asked incredulously.

"I don't know." His color deepened. "It just seems to me that . . . what I mean is . . ."

Without a word, Lauri took his arm and led him to the bedroom.

The lovemaking had turned out differently than what she had imagined. Adam, lying naked beside her was uncomfortable and nervous. Where Lauri was open to him, groping and anxious to please, trying to repeat their past sexual experiences, Adam seemed inhibited and frightened. She felt him touch her vagina, explore her pubic hairs, with trembling fingers, his lips hardly touching hers.

"Adam, suck my breasts," she whispered, pushing his head down as her hands reached to touch his penis. She barely felt his lips encircle her nipples, aware only that his sexual organ was soft. In great frustration, she twisted her body and was about to start making love to him when he caught her and quickly straddled her body between his thighs, forcing his faltering erection into her. Briefly her excitement rose, when she felt him reach his climax and within seconds he lay limp on top of her, gasping slightly. She dared not move. His deep breathing subsided and within seconds he withdrew from her and lay by her side.

Lauri tried to think of something to say that would relieve the embarrassment of Adam's failure, but could think of nothing. As the silence grew, her confusion mounted. She had always been sexually passive, but since her affair with Adam had started, her need for sexual gratification had become an important part of her relationship with him. Her affairs until she met Adam were pleasant, but none of her former lovers had aroused her or caused her to lose her ingrained shyness. Adam made her feel like a complete woman. His failure, therefore, was shocking. She felt sorry for him, but she felt sorrier for herself.

Abandoning the idea of saying anything, Lauri waited for him to speak. Suddenly she realized his breathing had grown steady and she knew he was asleep. The gentle snoring followed.

Fearful of waking him, Lauri moved slowly out from under Adam's arm which was slung across her breasts. The snoring stopped briefly and Lauri froze. When his breathing grew steady again, she disengaged herself and slipped out of bed. Groping for a robe in the darkness she walked hurriedly across to the living-room door, closed it behind her and flung herself on the sofa opposite the unlit fireplace.

The room grew brighter as the gray daylight seeped through the skylight and Lauri absorbed herself in the dawn. The snow was still falling and she watched the flakes hit the overhead panes, settling gently but briefly before they evaporated, leaving behind them tiny droplets. They looked like tears.

"I'm sorry, Lauri." Adam's voice reached her, and she sat up. He was standing in the doorway, dressed in a robe he kept at the apartment. It was tied loosely around his waist and Lauri could see his bare chest.

"It's all right," she said unable to take her eyes off his nakedness. The hair on his chest was gray. Adam was an old man, she thought again. Why had she not seen it before? He certainly had not aged in the last three weeks. "Would you like a coffee?" she asked, turning her head away.

Adam walked over to her and knelt down beside the couch. "You're disappointed, aren't you?"

"Not really." She tried to sound convincing.

"Poor baby." Adam started stroking her hair. "Of course you are. I've failed you, and there is no way for me to apologize or explain." He sounded sad.

She did not reply.

"What are you thinking?" Adam said after a while.

"That I've got to get ready for a trip to Rio."

"Rio de Janeiro?" Adam gasped. "Brazil?"

"We've got to reshoot some ads."

"Have you discussed it with your doctor?"

"You sound like Tony." Lauri began to smile. "No, I haven't discussed it with the doctor, and I don't really intend to."

"Lauri, it might prove dangerous for you and the baby."

It was the first direct reference to the baby and Lauri turned her face to him.

"I think I'm going to abort it," she said suddenly, and was surprised at what she was saying.

"Is that what you really want to do?" Adam asked, and Lauri could not help but feel there was a tinge of relief in his voice.

"I don't know," she shot out furiously, and stood up. "I don't know what I want to do, and I'm fed up with everyone pushing me. I'll decide what and when and where and why, and I'm not going to go on being hounded by you and Tony and Stan."

"What has Tony got to do with it?" Adam too stood up. His eyes were dark with anger.

"He has as much to do with it as you do," Lauri shouted.

"Oh?"

"It sounds different than what I mean." Lauri realized what the statement implied.

"I've never met Tony," Adam said quietly, but the hurt in his voice came through. "Have you been having an affair with him during the time we . . ." He stopped.

Lauri did not answer. It would be one way of getting Adam off the hook, she thought. It would relieve him of the responsibility she had placed on him and would clear the way for her to make whatever decision she wanted without pressures.

"Lauri, I don't believe it." Adam's pain was heartbreaking.

"Of course it's not true. But it doesn't matter whose baby I'm carrying. I told you this is my responsibility and mine alone. Please believe me when I say it."

Adam turned away and walked out of the room. Lauri did not move. She could not understand why she was being so cruel to someone she loved and had been devoted to.

Within minutes he reappeared, fully dressed.

"I'll have that coffee now," he said, his old self-assurance restored.

Sipping their coffee, Lauri watched him carefully. He looked as he had in the past. The old man, the stranger was nowhere in sight. He was an elegant, suave, handsome man.

"What would you like to do today?" Adam asked conversationally.

"Do?" Lauri was surprised by the question. She had not expected to spend the day with Adam. She had to be at Tony's at four o'clock. In fact, she had planned on being there earlier to help with the arrangements. "I have plans for later in the afternoon," she said finally. "Why?"

"It doesn't matter."

"Yes it does," Lauri persisted. "What were you planning?"

"Well, I thought we'd drive up to Montauk. It's lovely at this time of the year. And I know an inn around there that's open all year round, and we could have Thanksgiving dinner together." There was no recrimination in his voice. "As a matter of fact, I'd hoped to spend the weekend with you." He smiled wryly. "What an absurd assumption," he spoke as if to himself.

"Adam, Tony and I have spent every Thanksgiving together for years. It's become a ritual."

Adam raised his brows slightly. "I must meet the man one day."

"I hope you do. But not for the reasons you're thinking." She became defensive. "We go back to high school days. He's my closest friend. He's my family."

"Of course," Adam said, getting up. "I think I'll be on my way." He walked toward the bedroom. Lauri ran after him.

"Where are you going?" she asked, watching him collect his things from the bedside table.

"I think I'll go up to the apartment on Ninety-eighth Street and see how it's coming along." He started putting on his jacket, placing his wallet in his pocket and putting on his wristwatch. "I'm having it repainted, and I've ordered some new furniture."

She had seen him get ready to leave on numerous occasions, but she felt a difference in his manner. The idea that she would not be seeing him again frightened her. She felt as she did the night of the election, knowing that their relationship was coming to an end, but still she was unable to let go.

"Where are you living?" she asked.

"I've taken a suite at the Tuscany Hotel. Do you know it?"

She shook her head. She could not let him walk out, she thought frantically. She needed him.

"It's a lovely little old-fashioned hotel in the East Thirties. I'm staying there until the apartment is ready."

"Who will you have dinner with?"

"I usually have it with Sam Ryan." He grinned. "As a matter of fact, he was quite upset when I told him I was busy this year." The smile broadened, and he looked much younger. "I bet Sam would be shocked if he knew who his competition was."

"When will I see you?" Lauri persisted.

"I'll call you in the morning."

"If I'm not here, I'll be at Tony's."

"Lauri, you're pushing me with this Tony thing." Adam's voice was edged with annoyance.

"I'm sorry." Lauri felt contrite. "We've just been working so hard on getting a campaign going with the Aden people that it made sense for me to stay up there . . ."

"Of course." Adam started toward the living room and Lauri followed him.

"You do believe me, don't you?"

"Of course." He put on his overcoat.

"Will you call me?"

Adam turned to look at her. "Lauri, I want you to understand something very clearly." His voice was somber, and she felt like a little girl listening to a lecture from her father. "I'm not a young boy who got a girl pregnant and is trying to figure out how to get out of my obligation. I'm a grown man aware of what is happening and what my responsibilities are. You're behaving erratically and rather childishly. I can fully understand your confusion, and I'm trying my best to give you as much time as you need to decide what it is you want to do, but damn it, stop playing games with me and yourself. I'm not jealous of Tony, and I refuse to believe that you're trying to push me into making a scene." He spoke quietly, and his face was very pale.

"Did you leave your wife because of me?" Lauri asked irrationally.

"Partially," Adam said thoughtfully. "But not completely."

"Do you want me to have the baby?" Lauri asked, and regretted the question.

"You've made it quite clear that it was not my place to want it or not," he paused briefly. "In a way, I want it more than anything in the world. On the other hand . . ." He shrugged. "I've been there. I've had the diapers, the childhood diseases, the waiting for the school bus, the homework, the worry over where they are, who they're playing with, what they're thinking, how they'll grow up." He seemed to have moved far away from her. Then coming back to the present he continued. "If you want the baby, Lauri, I'll do whatever you ask of me. I want to marry you, I want to take care of you and the baby. We could build a good life together."

Lauri felt a shudder go through her. She had played with another human being's life—was still playing with it—and was too selfish to let go.

"Would you feel the same way if I was not going to have a child?" Lauri asked.

He walked over to her and put his arm around her shoulder. "But you are going to have a baby," he said. "You see, my dear, actions cause reactions. We cannot pretend you're not pregnant. We can't erase the facts. If you should stop being pregnant, it would not alter the fact that for the last three weeks my actions and behavior were motivated by what has happened between us."

"Could we ever go back to being as we were?"

He pressed her closer. "Nothing is ever repeated as it was," he said gently and kissed her hair. Then letting go of her, he put his coat on quickly and left the apartment.

7

It was nearly midnight when Peppy, Stan, Tony and Lauri stood in the small vestibule outside Tony's apartment waiting for the elevator. A portable crib holding the baby rested on the floor between its parents.

"Isn't he the most gorgeous baby you've ever seen?" Peppy asked, looking down at her son.

"Objectivity was always your strongest trait," Stan said, but the pride in his voice was clear.

"He's really quite extraordinary." Tony stooped down to look at the sleeping child. "He certainly is an easy baby. I haven't heard him cry once since you arrived."

"What's to cry about?" Stan said. "He's got a crazy mother who dotes on him, feeds him whenever he's hungry, makes sure he's never uncomfortable, spoils him to the point where I doubt he'll ever have to learn to walk or talk."

"You're exaggerating." Peppy laughed happily. "He cries sometimes. It's just that he's so small, and I don't see why he should have reason to cry."

"Crying develops the lungs and vocal chords," Stan said.

"I'm not bringing up an opera singer," Peppy chided.

"Development of vocal chords does not necessarily lead to an operatic career," Stan assured her in mock seriousness.

"Well, to each his own," Peppy countered. "I prefer to have a child who does not cry. People cry when they're unhappy, and I want my child to be completely happy." She looked over at Lauri, "Don't you agree?"

"I think I'd feel the same way," Lauri said pleasantly, wanting the elevator to arrive and end the conversation and the evening.

She had been standing slightly apart from the group, wanting to join the light banter but the turmoil within her made it difficult. Since Peppy and Stan arrived with their infant son, she felt undue resentment toward them. The baby was four months old, and Peppy was still overweight and looked unkempt. She had had a thriving theatrical career before the birth of the baby. It now appeared as though she had lost all interest in her work and was totally disinterested in anything other than her child. Although still lively and amusing, she seemed removed, aloof, satisfied. It irritated Lauri.

Tony put his arm around Lauri's shoulder, pulling her gently toward the group, as if sensing her unhappiness.

"You do make a handsome couple," Peppy said looking at Tony and Lauri. "Why don't you two get married and make beautiful babies like ours."

Lauri felt herself blush, Tony laughed uncomfortably and Stan coughed as though something got stuck in his throat.

"Okay, what have I said that I shouldn't have?" Peppy asked, looking at her three companions.

"Nothing my love," Stan said, regaining his composure. "It's just that now that you have a child, you must stop interfering in other people's lives."

"Lauri and Tony are not 'other people,'" Peppy said indignantly. She looked closely at Lauri. "Would someone kindly tell me what's going on?"

"It's really nothing," Tony intervened. "I think everyone is over-sensitive about my sexuality."

"Big deal," Peppy countered, never taking her eyes off Lauri.

"Please let's get off the subject." Lauri did not flinch, but her plea was clear.

"What are your plans for the holidays?" Tony changed the subject.

"We're staying in town. How about you?"

"We're going on location on Monday. Lauri has to reshoot some pictures in a warm climate."

Stan raised his brows. "Where are you going?"

"At the moment it's Rio, but I'll try to change it to some closer spot. Maybe Palm Springs."

Stan looked at Lauri. "Is this something sudden?" he asked noncommitally.

"Sort of." She tried to sound calm.

"How interesting. How long will it take and what will it involve?"

"About ten days," Lauri said. "And it's really a very simple assignment."

"It sounds like fun," Peppy said, but her gay mood changed and she was obviously concerned. "You don't sound excited about it." She spoke directly to Lauri.

"I am," Lauri assured her. "It's really great. What with the lousy weather we've been having . . ."

"Have lunch with me tomorrow?" Peppy interrupted. She was extremely fond of Lauri and sensed that something was wrong.

"Couldn't possibly," Lauri answered quickly. "Tony and I have so much to finish up before we leave."

"I'll ring you in the morning and let's try to get together before you leave."

"Okay," Lauri said in a resigned voice. She would have liked to confide in Peppy. It occurred to her she had no women friends to whom she could talk. Her career had taken up every spare moment, and her only close friends were the ones involved with her work.

The mood of frivolity was gone and to everyone's relief, the elevator arrived and within seconds the Blydens were gone and Lauri rushed into the apartment.

It had been a long and exhausting afternoon and evening. Her back was hurting again and she felt like crying. The studio was quite dark and she lay down on the bare floor and lifted her feet onto the low coffee table. The pain persisted and she began to cry softly.

Tony came into the studio and without a word walked over to the bar, poured some drinks and came over to her. Wiping her tears quickly, Lauri raised herself on her elbow and tried to smile. He pushed a small crystal goblet toward her.

"Drink it up, it'll do you good," he said gruffly.

She downed the drink and lay back, staring into space. The pain worsened and she shifted her position again.

"Why are you crying?" Tony asked quietly.

"I don't know," she answered. "I cry at the slightest things these days. Besides, my back is hurting." She turned on her stomach, resting her head on her hands.

Tony stooped down and started massaging her back. She felt herself relax.

"It's not unreasonable, you know," Tony said, as he continued to knead her tenseness away.

"My wanting to cry all the time, or having a pain in my back?"

"Getting married."

Lauri turned around slowly. She could see he was serious.

"Well, now I know how to go about getting a husband," she said sarcastically. "All a girl has to do is get pregnant and the offers come pouring in."

"Don't be glib, Lauri," Tony snapped angrily. "I mean it."

"So did Adam when I saw him."

"I don't give a damn about Adam. I really think we should get married and call a halt to this charade you're playing."

Lauri softened her manner. "You're sweet, Tony, but you don't really want to marry anyone."

"I don't want to marry anyone. I want to marry you."

Lauri sat up and crossed her legs in a lotus position. "You mean it, don't you?"

"You're the only woman I know to whom I'll ever propose, of that you can be sure."

"Would you want to marry me even if I wasn't pregnant?" She repeated the question she had asked Adam earlier that day, and held her breath waiting for the answer.

"I'm man enough to want to have you carry my child, and someday maybe you will. But I want to marry you so that you can decide whether you want to go through with this pregnancy. As it is now you're so confused, so scared, that there is no way you could come up with a rational decision about what you should do." He reached over and touched her face. "You're my girl and have always been, and I can't see you hurting all the time."

She leaned over to him and started sobbing out loud.

"Why didn't you ever ask me to be your girl before this whole mess happened?" she said when the sobbing subsided.

"Maybe I should have," Tony said thoughtfully. "But I guess I wasn't ready, and I suspect you weren't either."

She moved out of his embrace. "I don't know that I can do it to you."

"Do what to me?"

"Tie you into my confusion."

"I couldn't be more tied in if it was my child."

"Do I get a chance to think about it?"

"Of course you do, Lauri. The point is that you have to know that I mean it and that you've got no competition." He paused briefly. "And I can promise you one thing. I'll be a good husband and a good father because you're dearer to me than anything on earth."

8

Victor Adenizzio's private plane came to a halt and the motors were shut off.

"Happy landing," Tony said, and undid his seat belt as did Victor, Kim and Lauri.

"What a lovely flight." Lauri sighed, peering out the plane window at the palm trees swaying gracefully against the dimming evening sky. "To think that a mere six hours ago we were knee deep in snow and here we are in summer weather."

Collecting their hand luggage, the group trouped out of the plane. The dry desert heat of Palm Springs was turning cool as the evening approached and the pleasant breeze was refreshing.

"Victor," someone shouted and everyone looked over at a young black man dressed in blinding white slacks and open white shirt, running briskly toward them.

"How ya doing, Buddy boy." Victor waved to him.

"The car is over there," Buddy said pointing to a silver custom-built Lincoln Continental convertible. "I've also had a station wagon delivered so that the luggage and photographic equipment can be taken to the house."

"You do think of everything, don't you," Victor said with affection, and turned to introduce him. "This is Tony Abbot, the best photographer ever put on this earth, Lauri Eddington, the top model and on her way to being a top designer, and you know Kim. Buddy Crane, my right hand man, my confidant and friend."

Buddy smiled broadly and turned his attention to Lauri.

"You know something, when I watched you come off the plane I thought for a moment you were Felicia."

"Good God, no," Victor gasped, and looked more closely at Lauri. "Do you see a resemblance, Tony?"

"I'm hardly a judge. I've known Lauri too well for too long," he said quietly. He was about to add that his feelings for Lauri would preclude seeing her objectively, but decided against it.

"Well, I don't know Lauri well, but I do know Felicia, and although the coloring is similar, I don't see it." Victor continued to stare at her for a moment longer.

"Strangely enough, now that Buddy pointed it out, I do," Kim said, and Lauri felt an edge of hostility in the woman's voice. She had sensed the same tone in Kim throughout the trip, but had put it down to a bad mood. Now it came across more clearly.

"I'll tell you what I do see," Victor said. "There is a great resemblance between Donnatella and Lauri." He looked over at Buddy, "Don't you think?"

"Who's Donnatella?" Lauri asked, feeling strangely uncomfortable at the close scrutiny.

"My daughter," Victor said with pride. "She's a beauty, and I swear you remind me of her." His voice grew husky. "I'll show you a picture of her when we get to the house."

Driving along the wide highway with palm trees lining the road, Lauri pondered Kim's attitude. She had been her greatest backer in her efforts to get the Eddington designs incorporated into the Aden Girl commercials, but since the board meeting there had been a definite change in her manner. Throwing a sideways look at Kim, who was sitting on the other side of Tony, she could see the set, handsome features and wondered what had caused the change in her attitude. She made a mental note to discuss it with Kim and turned her attention to Victor who was seated next to Buddy. He was laughing happily as the two men exchanged opinions about various subjects. They were obviously friends, and it was not until Buddy held the door for everyone to enter the car that Lauri realized he was Victor's driver. She was amazed at the change in Victor's whole demeanor since they took off from New York. He was suddenly easy going, almost carefree.

"How about tennis doubles?" Victor turned to face the back of the car.

"Not me," Lauri said quickly. "I could use a warm bath and a short nap."

"I would love it," Kim said.

"Count me out." Tony picked up Lauri's hint. "I too would like a rest, and I've got to get the equipment sorted out so we can start out early tomorrow." Lauri was grateful. She knew he loved the game and understood he was backing off because of her.

"I don't think I'm up to playing singles. Kim's too strong a player," Victor said graciously, and smiled at Kim.

"Come to think of it, a bath sounds like a good idea," Kim conceded.

The high white-washed walls, broken by a huge wrought-iron fence, gave no indication of the magnificence of the house behind them. Lauri had been too preoccupied with her thoughts to take notice when the car turned off the highway, but it seemed a long time before they reached the gate. With graceful ease the car came to a stop and someone jumped out of a small gatekeeper's house to let them through.

"Welcome, Mr. Adenizzio," the gatekeeper called, and the car started up a long winding road. It had grown quite dark and Lauri could not make out the landscape beyond the trees, although there were occasional lights illuminating various pieces of sculpture or a spray of colorful plants and small water fountains. She was marveling at a particularly beautiful figure of the Madonna when the car came to a stop and she looked around. They were in front of a long white Spanish-style house. The front door was open and the luxury within was easily discerned.

"Home sweet home." Victor jumped over the side of the car and started helping the other occupants out. "Buddy, would you take everyone to their rooms and tell the kitchen staff we'll be down for drinks in about an hour." He looked at his guests. "Will that be all right?"

"Perfect," Tony answered for everyone, as they followed Buddy into the house.

Entering her suite of rooms, Lauri was overwhelmed. She had been to quite a few magnificent houses in her life, but the opulence, the overt luxury without ostentation, the total grandiosity was staggering. Her small living room was decorated with Italian antiques, the upholstery a melange of green flowered chintz, the floors of shiny green tiles that picked up the color of the fabric. Walking into the bedroom, she found herself thrown back in time. The white starched organdy reminded her of the room her father had decorated for her when she was a child. It stirred up strange emotions and she could not tell whether she wanted to laugh or cry. For the first time in many years she thought of her mother.

Lauri was just coming out of the shower when she heard a light knock on the door of the sitting room. Pulling on her robe which had been laid out by some mysterious being while she was in the bathroom, she went to the door. It was Tony.

"Where are we?" she asked, leading him into her bedroom.

"This is one of the little hide-aways of the Adenizzios. As a matter of fact, we are in Victor's house. Papa and Mama have a bigger one on the other side of the estate."

"It's practically obscene, but I love it," Lauri laughed softly, throwing herself on the white silk bedcover and staring up at the starched organdy canopy stretching across the four-poster bed. "You know it's almost exactly the way Papa decorated my room when I was a little girl." She looked over at Tony who was staring out the french doors, which were framed with the same starkly white organdy curtains. "It's hardly what I would do with a room today, but it's sort of pleasant to feel like a princess again."

"If you play your cards right, you can have it all over again," Tony said, without turning around.

Lauri sat up. "What's that supposed to mean?"

"I believe you've made another serious conquest." He turned to her. "I believe Victor is quite smitten."

Lauri began to laugh and threw her head back on the pillow. "You've got to be kidding. I've only met him twice, today being the second time."

"I'm not kidding. The minute Victor said you didn't remind him of Felicia but rather Donnatella, I knew he was seeing you very subjectively."

"Do I look like Felicia?"

"I suppose in a superficial sort of way you do. You know, your coloring and all that. But she was a bitch on wheels, and God knows you're not. Your personalities are so different that I certainly couldn't see it, and neither could Victor."

"Kim saw the resemblance," Lauri said almost to herself.

"It figures."

"Why?"

"Lauri, she and Victor have been having an affair for quite a while, and her liberated woman's intuition is fighting for possession."

"Oh no," Lauri groaned. "Of all the stupid things that could happen." She closed her eyes. Somewhere in the back of her mind she saw an ally in Kim—to the point of possibly confiding in her about the pregnancy if the work was too rough and Tony could not manipulate the shooting schedule. "From his behavior the first time I saw him, I would have thought he would never bother with the hired help," she said bitchily. "You could have knocked me over with a feather when I realized Buddy was his driver. I thought they were friends the way he treats him compared to the way he treated the people at his office in New York."

"Buddy is his friend, even if he is the driver," Tony said. "You see, to Victor perfection and loyalty are two of the most important components required. Talent is a third, but less important, since he himself is very talented. Buddy is super at what he does, and his loyalty to Victor and the whole Adenizzio family is complete. He'd lay his life down for Victor and, frankly, Victor would do the same for him."

"Then why is he so rotten to his staff in New York?"

"Because he thinks they're parasites, which they are."

"And Kim?"

"She's as much of a perfectionist as he is."

Lauri raised herself on her elbow. "Tony, you could be wrong, you know. Just because he doesn't see me resembling his ex-wife doesn't mean he sees me as anything other than a model of the Aden Girl commercial," she said hopefully. "I really would rather not have to compete with Kim. I need her on this assignment."

"I'm not wrong. I know Victor, and when I walked into this room, the picture fell into place. You're the pure, lovely Italian Madonna who has to be protected from the outer world of reality. You're Alice in Wonderland, all over again."

"Don't make fun of me, Tony." Lauri lay back. "I'm completely miserable now."

Tony walked over to the bed and looked down at her. With her dark hair strewn on the white pillow, the long lashes quivering over the half-closed eyes, he wanted to take her in his arms and hold her, comfort her. He held himself back. Since asking her to marry him, he had entered an unfamiliar world. The wall he had built concerning his feelings about himself and Lauri was shattered. He had not proposed impulsively. He had given it thought since she announced her pregnancy, and at first he honestly believed he was doing it for her sake. But with the passage of time, thoughts of Lauri and a child belonging to them both, a life with Lauri, a home like other people had, took on new meaning and gave him a sense of joy he never suspected he would feel. The possibility of losing her was already hurting.

"You won't leave me, will you, Tony?" Lauri reached out blindly for his hand.

He took it and sat down beside her. "Don't worry, honey. I'll be right here for as long as you want me."

Lauri opened her eyes and raising herself impulsively she kissed him on the mouth.

He did not return the kiss. Instead he pulled her toward him. "All I want you to remember, Lauri, is that you do have choices," he whispered. "And that's the most important thing at this point." Then standing up, he started out of the room. "Try to get some rest," he called out. "And if you fall asleep, I'll wake you in time for that drink with Victor before dinner."

As soon as the door shut behind Tony, Lauri jumped out of bed. She suddenly did not feel tired. She felt unaccountably excited as she started dressing. Standing back from the full-length mirror she watched herself with satisfaction. Although quite pale, her eyes were shining. She had purposely brought clothes which were easy and loose fitting. The white baggy silk pants were comfortable and the large orange overblouse made of the same soft fabric outlined her long thin torso without restricting her. She was about to slip into a pair of high-heeled sandals but changed her mind. Instead she picked them up in her hand and walked out of the room. She felt completely at ease.

Walking through massive hallways, she peered into various rooms. All were magnificently decorated, and it gave her pleasure simply to look at them. Finally she wandered into an enormous living room and stood in awe at the perfection of the decor as well as the incredible paintings lining the walls. She recognized the old masters, which were perfectly lit, giving them the full benefit of their importance. As she walked slowly from painting to painting she was almost embarrassed to be in the presence of such wealth, collected in a private home. Suddenly she stopped. A painting of a small girl was sitting on an easel. Even before walking over to it, Lauri knew it had been painted by her father. The perfect L.E. was hidden at the bottom of the painting. That the Adenizzios had a painting by Larry Eddington was not too much of a shock. He had become a well-known portrait artist. The fact that the child in the painting could have been a portrait of herself when she was a child, was staggering. The girl was about six or seven. She was dressed in a white pinafore and was barefoot. Extraordinarily pretty, it was the lost expression in the dark slanted eyes that held Lauri spellbound. Did Larry know how unhappy she had been at that age? He must have, Lauri thought sadly, or he would not have been able to recapture that look so effectively in another child.

"Isn't she the most gorgeous child you've ever seen?"

Lauri swung around and found Victor standing beside her looking at the portrait.

"The artist captured her completely," Victor said with pride, and the love in his eyes was blinding.

"Do you know him?" Lauri asked slowly.

"No. My mother had Donnatella with her this summer in Palm Beach and this artist saw the child on the beach and he asked if he could paint her. He did it in one sitting."

"How old is she?"

"Donnatella is seven."

"Where is she now?"

"With my mother in New York. They're all coming down here for Christmas."

"Does she ever see her mother?" Lauri asked, in spite of herself.

Victor's expression changed. "No," he said curtly. "She doesn't want to see the children, and I doubt they ever think of her, much less miss her."

"I wonder if that's true," Lauri whispered. The pain of her own loneliness after her mother left was rekindled.

"Of course it's true," Victor said, starting out of the room. Lauri followed him. "She just walked out and never came back."

"Women don't do that without reason," Lauri persisted, as they walked into a small wood paneled bar.

"Most women wouldn't." Victor did not pick up the bait. "Most women would be grateful for having what Felicia had, and would have done everything to live with it."

"Where is she?"

"Who knows. She's part of the glamorous set and every so often there's a picture of her in some discotheque here or abroad."

"Maybe she wanted something more out of life than just being a wife and mother."

"You mean a career?" Victor sneered, and started mixing drinks.

"Yes. There's nothing wrong with a married woman who can afford to have her children cared for properly by others, looking for further fulfillment."

"Felicia didn't want a career," Victor said in disdain. "And as far as I'm concerned, a woman who has three kids has a responsibility to them, first, second and always." He sounded as he did at their first meeting in the boardroom.

"I still don't believe a mother doesn't want to see her children or know how they are."

"You wouldn't." Victor's voice softened. "Do you see the similarity between you and Donnatella?" he asked suddenly.

"In more ways than one," Lauri said sadly. "I know her soul."

"Would you consider staying here through the holidays so you can meet her?" Victor asked hopefully.

"I would love to," Lauri said and meant it, but remembered almost with a shock, that it was totally out of the question. "But Tony and I must get back to New York," she added quickly.

"If I persuade Tony to stay, would you?"

Lauri laughed. "If you could persuade him," she said, knowing full well Tony would not do that to her.

"Is my name being used in vain?" Tony walked in looking refreshed.

"Would you consider staying here over the holidays?" Victor asked the minute he saw Tony.

Tony threw a look at Lauri, who lowered her eyes quickly but not before he saw the frantic look in her eyes.

"Not a chance. I've got several assignments I have to do before the New Year," he said lightly but convincingly.

Kim arrived at that moment and they all finished their drinks and went in to dinner. The mood changed the minute the older woman arrived, but Tony kept up the light patter during the meal and the evening passed pleasantly. Lauri was unduly conscious of Victor's presence throughout. He was overwhelmingly attractive and she could not ignore it. She knew he was equally aware of her.

When he came over to kiss her good night, she blushed and was relieved when he kissed Kim with equal warmth.

9

"I'd like another shot of Lauri on the horse," Kim said walking over to Tony.

"We've got two rolls of her getting on that fucking animal and as far as I'm concerned, that's enough," Tony said, mopping his brow.

"I know, but the light is better now," Kim said quietly, but with great determination. "We took the first shots at dawn, and I think this marvelous harsh midday light will make for a better background and give me what I'm looking for."

Tony was about to protest when Lauri walked over.

"Don't you agree that we should have another couple of shots of you in this light?" Kim turned to her.

"If you'd like," Lauri answered. She looked pale and tired. "Let me just get some water and freshen up the makeup."

Tony stalked off to reload his camera and Kim watched him go.

"Aren't you overdoing it?" Victor asked, and Kim swung around in surprise. She had not heard the car approach.

"What do you mean?" she asked pleasantly, although she knew exactly what he was talking about.

"You've worked Lauri to the bone ever since we got here, and I honestly believe you're overdoing it."

"I've never heard you complain about the way I run the photography sessions." Kim kept her voice calm, looking at Victor with simulated surprise.

"I'm not complaining, it's just that for the past ten days you've insisted on redoing shots that seemed fine to Tony and me, and I can't help but wonder what's gotten into you." He looked inquiringly at her. "This weather is quite unbearable."

"I'm not exactly in the shade." Kim was still in full control of herself. "And Lauri is not as fragile as you think."

"Fragility has nothing to do with it. She's human and a damn good sport and an unbelievable model, which makes some of your insistence on reshooting . . ."

"Victor, I know what I'm doing." Kim's voice hardened. "This is an important assignment, as you well know, and I want to make sure we have enough of each pose and outfit in case . . ." She stopped.

"In case what?" Victor asked.

"I don't really know. But as far as I'm concerned I'd rather have a good file of pictures before we wrap this thing up."

"I thought you liked her?" Victor said cautiously.

"Victor, why can't we have dinner tonight?" Kim said ignoring his question. "We haven't spent any time alone since we got here." Her voice grew husky with emotion. "And I miss being with you without people around."

Tony walked over at that moment, relieving Victor from having to answer Kim's request.

"I'm ready and so is Lauri," he said angrily.

Kim and Tony walked toward the sight where the shooting was taking place.

Victor watched Lauri mount a magnificent white horse. Tony began taking pictures, and Victor became absorbed in thoughts about Lauri which were both exciting and disturbing. Since Felicia left him he had avoided emotional involvements with women; had, in fact, vowed he would stay away from any woman who might cause him to lose his independence or take him away from his children. He was convinced that if and when he did meet someone who might be of serious interest to him, he would make it clear that his children came before anything else. He adored the boys, was devoted to his daughter and was fearful for their sake of the competition if he had any other children. Lauri, however, came into his life with an unprecedented impact. It was not only her beauty. She had a quality that blended with his inner-most feelings. She reacted to him, but did not push herself at him, as most women did. Throughout the time they'd been at Palm Springs, he watched her attitude toward her work, toward the people she worked with, was amazed at her professionalism and the innate understanding of the product she was selling. But most of all, he was touched by her reaction to Donnatella. When he found her looking at the child's picture the night they arrived he knew she would love her and give her what no other woman could.

"We're done for the day, thank God," Tony interrupted Victor's thoughts. "And some day it was."

Kim and Lauri walked over as well.

"Jump in and I'll drive us home," Victor said, getting out of the car.

"I've got to get some stuff at the drugstore," Lauri said. "Would you drive me there?" she asked, looking up at Tony.

"No problem," Tony answered. "We can take the station wagon and the equipment."

Kim walked around and got into Victor's car with an air of possession that did not escape anyone's attention. "See you at the house," she called out.

"Try not to be late," Victor shouted after them. "I've had a special dinner prepared to celebrate the end of our work."

Tony opened the car door for Lauri and helped her in. She was deathly pale as she slid down in her seat and let out a deep sigh.

"How do you feel?" Tony asked, putting the car in motion.

"I'll be fine," she said resting her head on his shoulder. He put his arm around her shoulder and she nestled up to him.

"Thank God this is over," Tony said after a while. "Now we can go back to New York and you can have that well-deserved rest."

She did not answer. Tony threw a sidelong glance at her and wondered what she was thinking. Since the day they arrived in Palm Springs he had watched Lauri and Victor carefully. It was clear that Victor was infatuated with her, but he could not figure out Lauri's attitude. She was obviously attracted to Victor, but there was a reticence on her part when it came to being alone with Victor. Never a boisterous creature, she was good company, participated in what was happening around, a good sport and fun loving. In the last ten days, however, she had become withdrawn. He attributed it to Victor and the effect he had on her.

"I think Victor is the first man you ever met who is completely right for you," Tony said testily.

"I don't know about that," Lauri replied in surprise. "God knows I've met other men who would have been equally suitable."

"Not among the guys you've introduced me to in the past few years."

"What makes him so perfect?"

"For starters, his age. Then there is the social standing, and let's not discount his unbelievable wealth."

"You have a way of boiling things down to crude basics," Lauri snapped angrily.

"Let me finish." Tony calmed her down. "He's also bright, talented, artistic and, as I told you the night we got here, he's quite smitten with you."

"He's also a tyrant and would stifle the life out of me," Lauri countered.

"In what way?"

"Tony, a woman to him is someone who takes care of his home, brings up his children, entertains his friends, travels with him and is subservient to his needs."

"What's wrong with that?"

"Nothing, if that's what a woman wants. That's not me," she broke off briefly. "Certainly not now."

"Lauri, if you weren't pregnant, could you get involved with Victor?" he asked pointedly.

"But I am," she answered, and Tony marveled at the reply. It did not sound like her.

"Have you made up your mind about what you're going to do?" he asked.

It was the first time since they arrived that the subject was brought up.

"It would make no difference," Lauri said thoughtfully. "I could hardly lie to someone like Victor, or anyone for that matter, about something as serious as being pregnant." She stopped and was deep in thought. "Don't you see, I could never be involved, seriously, with anyone who would feel differently about me if they knew I was pregnant and had an abortion, or would look at me differently if I had a child out of wedlock."

"That precludes a lot of people." Tony withdrew his arm from her shoulder and parked the car in front of the drugstore. "Are you sorry you're pregnant?" he asked, turning to face her.

"No," she answered slowly. "But what's more important, being pregnant makes Victor fall into place." She sounded relieved. "Under different circumstances, I might have gotten seriously involved with him. I might have even married him, and it would have ended badly. It would have been fun for a while, I'm sure. I might have been lulled into his type of life, had a couple of children. Then the need to be my own person would have reared its ugly head. And then what?"

"That's an awful lot of logic for someone who is trying to pretend she's not in love," Tony said, trying desperately to keep his emotions in check.

"No. That's an awful lot of logic which proves that someone is not in love." She smiled up at him. "As for the endless people my pregnancy precludes as candidates for my affections, think of how lucky I am to be able to concentrate on the ones who are still in the running." She opened the car door and ran into the store.

Tony watched her and was not convinced by what she had said.

On the way back to the house, Lauri was even more withdrawn, and a film of fine sweat covered her face.

"Have you spoken to Stan since we've been down here?" Tony asked, knowing she did not want to discuss her physical condition.

"I spoke to him this morning before we went out on location." She sounded as though she were in pain.

"What about?" he asked nonchalantly, hiding his concern.

"I shouldn't have taken this assignment," Lauri said quietly. "I've begun to bleed and although Stan doesn't think it's too serious, he wants me off my feet."

"Are you in pain?"

"Sporadically. That's why I had to go to the drugstore. Among other things, Stan gave me some medication to carry me through until we get back to New York."

"Why don't you stay in bed this evening? Victor will be disappointed, but we can say you're exhausted, and after what that bitch has put you through, it would not be unreasonable."

"No," Lauri said emphatically. "I'll be down as soon as I've had a short rest."

Tony let her out in front of the main entrance and drove to the garage. He felt his heart twist with pain at the thought of Lauri losing the baby. Walking back to the house, Tony decided to call Stan. He walked into the library and found Kim and Victor having a drink together.

"Am I interrupting anything?" he asked politely.

"Nonsense," Victor said quickly. "Want a drink?"

"Love one." Tony walked over to the bar and poured himself a martini.

"Where's Lauri?" Victor asked.

"She's gone up to rest before dinner," Tony answered.

"Did she get what she wanted at the drugstore?" Kim asked with exaggerated concern. "What was it she needed, anyway? This house is as well equipped as any drugstore in the country." She laughed pleasantly. "Unless it's a prescription, of course." She looked inquiringly at Tony. When he did not answer she continued, "She isn't ill is she?"

"No, she's just tired." Tony tried to maintain his composure. "It's been a hectic ten days."

"I think I'll go up and see if there's anything I can do for her." She walked briskly from the room.

"Don't wake her if she's asleep," Tony called out after her.

"Anything wrong?" Victor asked when they were alone.

"Nothing special," Tony answered and sat down in a lounge chair. "Thank God the photography part is over. I'll drive to L.A. tomorrow and get the negatives developed, just to make sure we don't need any more photographs. Will you come with me, or will Kim?"

"I'd rather Kim go." He hesitated for a moment. "Frankly, I'd like to spend some time alone with Lauri. She fascinates me, and I hardly know her, in spite of all the time we've spent together since we got here."

"She's quite a girl." Tony kept his voice light, but the muscles of his throat tightened.

"You've known her for a long time, haven't you?" Victor asked.

"Since she was fifteen."

"Where does she come from? Who is she? What's the family background?"

"Oh, cut it out Victor. We went through this when you met Felicia, and I always felt as though I was to blame for that misfortune. But then Felicia wasn't one of my closest friends. Lauri is. Why don't you ask her about who she is and what she's all about." His voice had risen in spite of himself.

"Take it easy, Tony." Victor laughed nervously. He paused. "She means a great deal to you, doesn't she?"

"Yes she does."

"How serious are you about her?"

"Come on, Victor," Tony stood up. "For two grown men, we sound like a couple of teenagers." Then grinning sheepishly he walked over to Victor. "She's a great kid. The greatest." And he pressed his friend's shoulder. "Do we have time for a game of tennis?" he changed the subject abruptly.

Victor did not move. "Tell me about her, Tony," he said quietly.

"What's to tell? She's bright, beautiful, talented, ambitious. She's a career-minded lady. She's a good designer and expects to get better with time." He slowed down, aware that he was being too forceful.

Victor turned away and poured himself another drink. "You know I always respect talent, and I agree that she is talented," he said with his back to Tony. Then turning around he continued, "I'm serious about her," he said with conviction. "Very serious."

"If it's my blessing you want, you've got it." Tony tried to laugh. "Have you spoken to the lady about your intentions?"

"No. But if you weren't such a sonofabitch and would have agreed to stay on here over the holidays, I'd have had a chance to really get to know her and I believe we'd get somewhere. I think she finds me quite attractive, if you must know."

"I wouldn't blame her. And although she hasn't confided in me, I think she does see your qualities and not only the obvious ones." Tony waved his hand around, "But I doubt she'd cave in just because of the external accoutrement and become just a wife and mother."

"I wouldn't expect that of Lauri," Victor said quickly. "I wouldn't want her to go on with her modeling career, but she sure as hell could continue with the designing. That can be done here, in New York, Milan, Rio, anywhere."

"You're really too much. You mean she could travel with her pencils, crayons, drawing pads and a little sewing kit?" Tony could not keep the disdain out of his voice.

"You're in love with her, aren't you?" Victor said quietly.

Tony felt torn. He wanted to say that Lauri was everything to him, he wanted to put an end to any possible relationship between her and Victor, but he could not bring himself to do it. Much as he wanted Lauri and the baby, he knew it was Lauri's life and it was she who would make the final decision.

"I think I better go up and dress before dinner." Tony stood up, avoiding answering the question.

"Sure thing," Victor answered, and Tony left the room quickly.

10

Kim dressed with great care and was dabbing perfume on her wrists when she realized her palms were wet with nerves. Putting the cologne bottle down carefully, she took a cigarette, lit it and walked out to the patio. A high-strung woman, she had taken a couple of tranquilizers, hoping to relax before going down to dinner, but even as she swallowed the pills, she knew they would not relieve her state of mind. She was frightened, and she did not like the feeling.

It was she who had chosen Lauri from the numerous candidates to be the highly publicized Aden Girl. She saw in Lauri the new working woman, one who would make an independent, successful career statement. She was bright and creative, and Kim felt they could work together. When Lauri came in with the tie-in idea of the Lauri Eddington designs, Kim was thrilled. It added a new dimension to the image she was working on. She started planning a franchising concept of the Eddington line as a company under the Adenizzio umbrella over which she would preside.

Victor's interest in Lauri after the first board meeting annoyed her. She knew Victor saw women other than herself, but it never bothered her. Theirs was a unique relationship in which the physical attachment was secondary to their work. Since arriving in Palm Springs, however, Kim's trepidations grew. Lauri seemed to fascinate Victor. She would find him staring at the girl like a moon-struck kid, and it infuriated her. She could understand Victor, she could not forgive Lauri. The girl was playing Victor to the hilt, and it came as a shock. Lauri, Kim decided, was aiming for the same thing she had worked for all her life. Pretending frailty and femininity, Lauri was trying to go beyond the simple promotional tie-in of her designs. Kim was convinced that Laurie was trying to push her way into the Adenizzio conglomerate. She recognized the cool, clever game Lauri was playing and was terrified she would succeed.

For the first time in her life Kim felt old and incapable of handling the competition. Had it been within her power, she would have fired Lauri, but the younger woman was bright and would not be pushed. In desperation she tried to break Lauri physically, making her work to a point of exhaustion, determined to prove she was nothing more than a pretty face who could not stand up to pressures. She was shocked by her behavior but could not control her actions. Lauri was not phased. If anything, she came out stronger and more forceful. At this late hour, Kim felt defeated, and decided to bring the situation to a head.

Resolutely she walked along the patio toward Lauri's room. The french doors leading into Lauri's room were open. Kim knocked on the pane and receiving no answer, she pushed the curtains aside and stepped into the room.

Lauri was just coming out of the bathroom when Kim entered her room.

"You startled me," Lauri said, hiding her annoyance at the intrusion.

"I knocked but you probably didn't hear me," Kim said. Without being asked, she sat down in a small armchair near the french doors. The room was almost in total darkness and Lauri's thin silhouette was discernible in the dim light. "Are you ill, Lauri?" she asked watching the younger woman lie down carefully on the bed.

"I'm fine." The feeble tone belied the statement.

"No you're not," Kim shot back. "There's something wrong and you're trying to keep it from me." She paused briefly. When Lauri did not answer she softened her tone, "Lauri, what's the matter?"

"I've got the curse," Lauri said with finality.

"Is that all?" Kim laughed, but something in Lauri's voice caused her not to believe her. Getting up she walked over to the bed. "I had a hysterectomy years and years ago, and I must say I forget about these female problems." She laughed again. "But if it was Tampax you needed, I'm sure there is a supply of it somewhere in that medicine chest," she continued and walked into the bathroom.

"Kim," Lauri called out. "Would you mind leaving me alone for a while. I'm really not feeling too well, and I would like to sleep for a while."

"You use sanitary pads!" Kim came out of the bathroom. "A modern working girl using those?" she said in mock dismay. "Why I thought these went out with the suffragettes."

Lauri sat up abruptly. "Let's stop playing games, Kim." Her voice was cold and she was staring at the older woman. "I'm pregnant. I'm almost at the end of my third month, and this afternoon I started bleeding." The words were spoken defiantly, and then the horror of what she had said, hit her.

"You're what?" Kim exploded in disbelief.

"You heard me." Lauri's tone changed as she got up wearily and started toward the clothes closet. She was naked except for the brief bikini underpants.

Kim watched the tall, thin girl closely. Her body was still perfectly shaped and for a moment it occurred to her that Lauri was making fun of her.

"You're not putting me on, are you?"

"Hardly." Lauri regained her composure and stepped into a long, white flowing sleeveless dinner gown. Standing in the semi-dark room, she looked like a lovely white bird in flight. Her long swanlike neck was stretched upward, recalling a porcelain stem emerging from a bud vase. With her thin arms raised over her head, twisting her dark hair into a knot, her dark eyes half shut, she was staggeringly beautiful.

"Let me get this straight," Kim came over and stood next to Lauri. "You mean you're going to have the baby?"

Lauri did not answer.

"You haven't made plans for an abortion?" Kim sounded incredulous.

Lauri looked at her. "No, I haven't."

"Well, that's what I call a royal screwing." Kim regained her equilibrium.

"In what way?" Lauri moved toward her dressing table.

"You don't really believe we can run the Aden Girl commercials with you as our representative, do you?" Her manner changed and she sounded like the executive in charge, the boss who was protecting her company.

Lauri did not answer.

"Were you pregnant when we chose you?" Kim asked suddenly.

Lauri turned around slowly. "Kim, I said I was in my third month. You and I have been talking for the past six. Even you must know it takes only nine months to have a baby."

"Don't be sarcastic with me," Kim blazed. "All I know is that we've got to scrap the whole ad campaign, and at this late stage it's a real mess and a very expensive one."

"I really don't know what you're talking about." Lauri started applying eye makeup. She had known the confrontation would come, had been warned by Tony and Stan that the Aden people might try to cancel her, but foolishly she had hoped that in the final analysis, Kim, with her genuine attitude toward working women, would side with her.

"You really believe the Aden campaign with Lauri Eddington fashions can go ahead?" Kim began to laugh. "You've got to be kidding."

"I don't see why not," Lauri said with simulated innocence. "We've got all the work done. You've got all the still photographs you need. All the TV commercials have been filmed. I'll be fine by fall, and I don't see where there's a problem. Unless you find that my being pregnant is immoral." She threw the word out quietly but with great deliberation.

"I'm not the keeper of morality, nor do I set the standards of what is moral and what is not, but there are millions of women and men out there who wouldn't look with favor—and that's putting it mildly—on our product being represented by an unwed mother."

"Wait a minute," Lauri said slowly. "Whose business is it anyway? You seem to be forgetting that I'm only a face in a photograph, a girl running across a desert in a commercial for a product called Aden. Are you telling me that all those people out there have to know about my personal life? Why?" Her voice rose. "I model and I design. If I look the part, which I obviously do, you hire me. If I design clothes that women like and buy because they are well made, I earn my keep. If I have a baby, out of wedlock, married, divorced or otherwise, I should be allowed to earn my living at what I'm best equipped to do so that I can support my child."

"That's a lovely speech, but I've got a big company to think of. I may theoretically agree with what you're saying, but I'm also not in the habit of spitting into the wind when it's blowing in my direction. We've made great strides as far as women's rights are concerned, but there are too many people who just don't see it that way. Women work, but the code of behavior is still something that must be upheld as the churches and other institutions demand."

"Would it be different if I was married?" The mockery in Lauri's voice was unmistakable and Kim turned away.

"Probably," she said. "Are you?"

"No."

"Are you planning on getting married?"

"That's immaterial," Lauri said. "What I don't understand is, who's to know about my baby? Who will know if I'm married or not?"

"These things get into the papers."

"Not unless they are deliberately and maliciously planted."

The implication was clear and Kim's face turned red with fury. "I resent that," she said through clenched teeth. "And under the circumstances, I feel I should be left out of the final decision. I think Victor should."

"Will you tell him about it?"

"No. You will."

"Victor should know what, and who's going to tell him?" Victor asked.

Lauri and Kim turned around and saw Victor standing in the doorway with Tony standing behind him. He had a bottle of champagne in one hand and a tray with glasses in the other. Both men moved into the room. Victor smiled warmly at Lauri and placing the tray on a small table he began pouring the drinks. Tony ambled over to Lauri and put his arm carelessly around her shoulder. "Anything wrong?" he asked under his breath.

"I'm not sure," she whispered, not taking her eyes off Victor. He was suddenly handsomer than ever, and it threw her off balance.

"Now for the celebration." Victor walked over with the tray. Lauri took a glass and Tony did too. When Kim got hers, Victor raised his glass. "To Kim who pulled off one of the best campaigns for Aden, to Lauri who is *the* Aden Girl and to Tony who brought her to life."

Everyone raised their glasses.

"I don't see the exuberance," Victor said, trying to ignore the solemnity around him. Everyone started sipping their drinks. "Oh, come on, you all look as if we're burying something rather than giving birth to it."

"Your metaphor is well taken," Kim said bitterly.

"What's going on here?" Victor put his glass down. When no one answered, he looked over at Tony. "Will you please tell me what's happening?"

"Victor," Lauri started haltingly, and the resignation in her voice was evident, "I'm going to have a baby, and as far as Kim is concerned, that cancels out the campaign with me as the Aden Girl."

Victor threw a look of disbelief at Lauri, then slowly he shifted his gaze to Kim and finally his eyes came to rest on Tony. "Did you know this?" he asked.

"What difference does it make as far as the commercials and ad campaign go?" Tony did not flinch.

"You know goddamned well what I'm talking about," Victor hissed.

"Yes I did," Tony answered, looking directly at Victor.

"And you let me . . ." he stopped. "And you allowed this work to be done, permitted us to be duped, watched us spend thousands of dollars, endless hours, knowing that we could never run it?"

Tony lowered his eyes. He knew that Victor was not talking about the money spent, or the time wasted, if it was wasted. He felt his friend's deep sense of having been betrayed, but his loyalties were with Lauri.

"I don't think it's that clear-cut in any direction," Tony started slowly. "You see, Lauri is carrying my child, and she's known all along that if she wants the baby we would get married." He threw a look at Kim. "A married Lauri would satisfy you wouldn't it, Kim?" He had worked with women like Kim since he started in the fashion world and knew exactly what her objections would be. Then looking back at Victor he continued, "I didn't want to push Lauri into making a decision. It is her decision to make."

"That's very sweet, Tony." Lauri was having a hard time keeping her emotions in check. "But I think it's really no one's business what you and I are thinking or planning. I personally feel that my having or not having a baby is my private affair and does not in any way—should not in any way—affect my abilities to be the Aden Girl." Then, turning to Victor she continued, "Kim feels that there is a moral factor to be considered." She waited. Victor did not react. "I personally don't look at abortions as moral or immoral, just as I don't look at unwed mothers as moral or immoral. I will do what I *feel* is right for me. You're all talking about dollars and cents, successful and unsuccessful advertising, selling or not selling a product. Well, let me tell you. I'm the best model for this campaign and my clothes are perfect for what you wanted. If I can have this baby, then I will. As for my marital status, that is really of no concern to anyone but me."

Victor regained his composure and cleared his throat. "I would like to think about this whole thing, and I'll discuss it with Kim in the morning." He looked at Lauri. "I do agree with you that this is your private affair, and this discussion has gone on too long." Then bowing to everyone, he turned and left the room.

"Damn," Kim said angrily. She felt like a fool and knew that her emotional state had brought about the unnecessary confrontation. She wanted to apologize to Lauri, but the company she worked for took priority in her thinking. "Maybe we can salvage something out of this mess," she said feebly.

"I'm going to have this baby, you know," Lauri said with determination. "Nobody's going to push me around on something as important as this."

"They're going to win," Tony said quietly. "You must know that."

"But they'll have a big fight on their hands, before they do," Lauri answered defiantly, aware that Kim was still in the room. "A big fight."

11

The horror of the nightmare would not leave Beth. Someone had tried to push a door open, and she was pressing her body against it, hoping to keep him out. It was a man, but his identity eluded her. She felt her strength giving way and she tried to scream. The muscles of her neck swelled with pain, but no sound came. Frantically she ran to her bedroom to ask Adam to help her. He was not there. She started tearing at the sheets, and she woke up.

It had been a terrifying experience, and she was drenched in perspiration.

Rolling over in her king-sized bed, Beth opened her eyes. The smooth part of the bed beside her was partially rumpled from her efforts to find Adam while she was dreaming.

Adam was gone. Adam had left her and she was alone.

Slowly her eyes wandered around the room. The shades were drawn and the curtains were pulled shut. The room was in almost total darkness, but she knew it was already light out. She looked at the digital clock with its illuminated numbers, and as she suspected, it was late; it was 11:06 A.M. Drawing the blanket over her body, she tried to recall what time she had gone to bed, but could not.

Turning on her stomach, she pulled the pillow over her head. She did not want to wake up. Her head was aching, and the taste in her mouth was vile. She thought of getting up and brushing her teeth, but that, she knew, would mean she was succumbing to the idea that her day had started and she was not ready for that. Turning on her side, she pushed the soft feather pillow under her chin, hoping for the oblivion which sleep usually afforded her. She tried to relax, force her limbs to go limp, empty her mind of thought. Maybe sleep would come again, that wonderful state that shut out the world, the cruel world that made such demands on the living. She lay very still, waiting. It was useless. The brain was awake, the thought process had started and sleep eluded her.

Resigned, Beth turned on her back and felt for a cigarette on the nightstand. Her hand brushed across a glass and she heard a dull thud as it fell. She lifted herself and even in the darkened room she could make out the stain which began to form by the liquid left in the glass, as it sank into the pale green carpet. Absently she wondered if wine stains were removable. She lit her cigarette, and the flame of the match picked up the contours of the glass lying on its side. It was not a wine glass but a tumbler. It gave her pause. When did she start drinking wine out of a water glass? It did not matter. Nothing mattered.

She lay back puffing at her cigarette and gave herself over to the state of apathy which precluded all actions and thoughts. She was nothing, she was nobody, she was nowhere. It was comfortable, and she wanted it to last forever. Memories of a similar state came back to her. It was many years ago and it lasted for a long time. Allen's youthful, delicate features took form. When Allen died she had gone through a similar state. How long did it last? She could not remember. A glimmer of longing for the happy days before Allen died took hold of her. She and Allen had been so happy when they were children. Why did her father kill him?

Tears started streaming down Beth's cheeks, wetting the thin sheet. Pulling it up she covered her face and began to sob. Finally drained, she sat up. Her eyes were burning, but the throbbing pain in her head was not as severe. She was thirsty.

Laboriously she got out of bed. She was unaccountably weak and had to hold on to the furniture as she headed toward the bathroom. Gulping down a glass of water, the memory of the nightmare returned again. She shook her head, hoping to make it disappear when she caught sight of herself in the mirror. She was shocked by her appearance. Her eyes were sunken and rimmed with dark circles, her face drawn and pinched, her hair unkempt. Picking up a washcloth, she ran cold water over it and pressed it to her face.

Returning to the darkened room she walked over to the doors leading to the terrace and pulled back the drapes. She froze with dismay as the bright sunlight poured into the room. Slowly she opened the doors and felt the pleasant spring air drift in. For a minute she thought her mind was playing tricks on her. The last clear memory she had was of heavy winter snow covering the city. She looked back into the room and wondered what month it was. She looked down at her body. She was unbearably thin, the bones of her pelvis were jutting through her thin nightgown, her arms were skeletal, her skin dry. The feeling of devastation she had felt when first waking returned more acutely and she was tempted to run back to her bed, but knew that she should not. Instead, she forced herself to stay where she was and continued to look at the splendor of the terrace with its budding plants, not yet in bloom. It seemed unreal. She was straining to recall events that would give her a clue as to where she had been since that cold winter day, when she heard a light tap on her door.

Lydia walked in before Beth could call out, followed by Dr. Slattery.

"Hi, Beth," Barry Slattery said, and she detected a note of relief in his voice. "Glad to see you're up and about." He came over to her.

She felt herself shrink inwardly. "What are you doing here?" she asked, and knew instinctively it was the wrong thing to say. With a clarity that amazed her, she was aware that he had been to see her several times recently.

"How do you feel this morning?" He took her hand and put his arm affectionately around her shoulder.

"Terrible." She tried to laugh, and looked over at Lydia. "Could I have some coffee?"

"And juice," Barry added.

As soon as Lydia walked out of the room, Beth turned toward the doctor.

"What happened?" she asked in a whisper.

"You took a dive, sweetheart, a very bad one." He led her to the bed and made her lie down.

"How long . . . ?"

"It's been about six weeks."

"What month is it?" she asked with embarrassment. Barry had been the family doctor for many years, but the idea of being exposed to his care in a state of unconsciousness was humiliating.

"It's the beginning of March," he said gently.

Beth turned her head away. "Could you tell me what happened?"

"You've had a mild nervous breakdown," Barry said quietly. "I don't know exactly when it started, but sometime around the end of January I saw you at a United Nations reception and you were boozing it up and I got worried. I'd seen you at several parties over the holidays and there was a hysteria about you that was upsetting, but that day I felt you were overdoing it. The next day, Lydia came in and couldn't wake you. She called me and I came right over." He paused briefly. "You took some pills and they knocked you out."

"You mean I tried to kill myself?"

"Not very likely. You didn't take enough medication to put most people to sleep, and besides, there were quite a few pills left in the vial." He paused briefly. "You're not the suicidal type, Beth. If you were, you would have succeeded."

"Does everyone know about it?" she asked.

"Hardly." Barry smiled. "I've known you too long to expose you that way. I didn't even have to take you to the hospital. You've been home, and I've been feeding you doses of valium, vitamins and all sorts of other garbage to get you back into shape." He stopped smiling. "And we've been keeping you away from liquor."

"Am I an alcoholic?" Beth whispered the word.

"Why don't we say that in your state of mind you shouldn't have been indulging yourself as you did."

Beth looked down at the water glass lying on the floor. It had not contained wine or liquor.

"Water doesn't leave stains on rugs, does it?" she said almost to herself.

"Not that I know of," Barry answered.

"Six weeks is a long time. Where have I been. My mother, Ali, everybody must have wondered . . ."

"Gillian instructed Lydia to say that you went on a cruise, and she obviously convinced them of it."

"Gillian!" Beth gasped. She remembered speaking to Gillian about Adam's leaving and her own fury at Gillian for knowing and not telling her.

"She called the day I was here trying to revive you, and knowing the relationship between you two, I decided to tell her what was going on. She was in town within two hours after we spoke and has come in every day since." He looked at his watch. "She'll be here shortly."

"I don't want her here."

"She's a real friend."

"As they say, with friends like that one doesn't need enemies."

"Let me reverse that. With an enemy like Gillian you don't need friends," Barry said, then taking her hand in his, he leaned over and spoke seriously. "Beth, you've not been unconscious throughout the last weeks. You've been up several times, you've talked to me, to Gillian and to Lydia. Lydia has been sleeping here, and Gillian and I relieved her for a few hours every day, so I know what I'm saying. What you're doing now is purposely blanking out everything, but if you'll let yourself think, you'll see that many things will come back. You're a big girl and you've got responsibilities. It's not the end of the world, just remember that."

He was gone before Beth could answer him.

Lydia walked in minutes after Barry left and found Beth struggling into her clothes.

"I'm damned if I'm going to let Gillian see me in that bed," she said, pulling a heavy sweater over her head.

"I've got your juice and coffee, Miss Beth." Lydia put the tray down and came over to help zip up the back of the sweater.

"You can put it on the terrace," she ordered, feeling out of breath from the effort she was exerting.

"It's still quite cold out," Lydia ventured.

"I'll put a coat on," Beth snapped, and regretted her tone. Seating herself in front of her dressing table she started putting on makeup. Lydia was standing in the middle of the room looking lost. "I'm sorry, Lydia," she softened her tone. Lydia had been with her for nearly all of her married life to Adam, knew the children, was part of the family. They were probably the same age, Beth thought, and realized that Lydia had not really changed except that her body was heavier. She wondered what sort of life Lydia led. She had been so engrossed in herself she had even neglected someone as loyal and devoted as Lydia.

"How's Suzanne?" Beth asked suddenly, turning around.

"She's just fine." Lydia's face broke into a smile. "She's got one more year of college, and then she'll be a full-fledged teacher."

"Does she have a boyfriend?"

"Sure does. I think they'll get married when she graduates."

It was so simple, so clear-cut, so uncomplicated, Beth marveled. Why was everything so confused in her life? Ali, Sarah, Adam.

"You know Mr. Stillman has left?" Beth said conversationally.

"Yes, I do." Lydia's expression became serious. "I'm sorry."

"Nothing to be sorry about." Beth tried to smile. "But what I would like you to do is clear out his clothes from the closet. Pack them up and put them . . ." She stopped and wondered where they should go. "Just pack them up, all of them. Clean out his dresser drawers as well, and make sure you take everything out of the nightstand next to his side of the bed." Her voice grew more urgent. "And the medicine chest. I want everything out." She stood up. "You can put them all in Sarah's room."

"What happens when Sarah comes home?" Lydia asked.

Sarah coming home. When was Sarah coming home? She had had a fight with Sarah at one point. It was after she called Jimmy Jay and told him she would not be coming to St. Moritz because of Sarah. That was it. She was staying in town because of her, and then Sarah called to say she would not be coming in, after all. They had a fight and Beth had told her about the separation. Sarah became distraught and hung up. Had she spoken to her since? Whom had she spoken to before she went on her so called "cruise," and what had she told them?

"Sarah can use Miss Hannah's room, and Jimmy Jay's room can be like a sitting room," Beth said, feeling guilty about her feelings toward her younger child. "It can be like a small apartment for her."

"That would be nice." Lydia warmed to the idea. "Sarah will like that."

The front doorbell chimes sounded.

"That's Miss Crane," Lydia said walking out of the room.

Beth slipped into a fur jacket and walked quickly out to the terrace. Somehow she had to remember what had gone on during the past few weeks.

"Hi there." Gillian came out to the terrace dressed in a luxurious mink coat, carrying a cup of coffee. She sat down on a lounging chair and smiled warmly at Beth. "I think I'll steal Lydia away from you. She makes the best coffee on earth."

"Fat chance." Beth's resolution to be cold and indifferent was squashed. "Lydia wouldn't be found dead in your little rat hole in Darien."

"It's no such thing. It's charming early stone age," Gillian said seriously. "And she wouldn't have to polish all those antiques like she does here."

"Try her." Beth could not help but smile.

"I did, but she's just dumb and refuses to leave you."

"That's because she feels sorry for me," Beth said quietly.

"I'm not so sure of that. I think you overpay her, and she knows where her bread is buttered," Gillian said, sipping her coffee.

"I feel sorry for me," Beth said.

"That's for sure. And if you play your cards right you might even convince me to feel sorry for you."

"Don't you?"

"No way." Gillian put her cup down. "Why should I?"

"Because I'm alone, and I don't know how to live alone."

"No one does," Gillian said, and her voice was strained.

"You do." Beth looked at Gillian with surprise and noted for the first time that she was an old woman. Her hair was dyed black, but it did not hide the gray roots. The face was completely wrinkled, the mouth, which was once full and sensuous, was thin and pinched, the eyes, always sparkling and charged with life, although still alert and knowing were clouded over by a thin film of fatigue.

"No I don't. I never did." Gillian smiled, and the image of the old woman disappeared.

"But you're surrounded by people . . ." She stopped. The endless number of faceless young men who were always milling around Gillian took on new meaning. The non-ending parties, the constant gaiety around her were suddenly falling into place. "Gillian, who was the young man who answered the phone one night when I called to tell you Adam left me?"

"I've spoken to you so many times in the past few months that it would be hard to tell, but it was either Danny, Freddy, Jimmy, Bruce, who knows." Gillian shrugged.

"Well, he was utterly obnoxious."

"I doubt it," Gillian said. "Whoever he was, he was one of the people who take care of me. It was probably late and I was asleep and he didn't want to bother me."

"I couldn't live like that," Beth said, almost apologetically.

"No you couldn't, and you shouldn't. I don't have a family, so I have to create one with people who are bright and kind and who need me as much as I need them."

"Whom do I have?"

"Why don't we start with Sarah," Gillian ventured.

"Sarah?"

"Yes, Sarah needs you. She'll be coming home soon, and she really needs help. Your help."

"What's the matter with her?" Beth asked cautiously.

"I don't quite know. She's hardly an open youngster who pours her heart out. But I told you several days ago that she called me when she couldn't find you, and she sounded unhappy."

"How the hell can I help her in this state?" Beth felt trapped. "It would be like the blind leading the blind."

"You will, because you have to."

"I can see the picture. She'll arrive and find me looking like death warmed over." She grew agitated. "I can't help myself; how the hell can I help her?"

Gillian did not answer.

"Gillian, can you help me?" Beth leaned forward. "Can you tell me what's been going on since . . ."

"You went on a wild merry-go-round for a while," Gillian said seriously. "As best I can reconstruct, what happened was that after that call to me in which you finally discovered what was going on with Adam, you started partying like it was going out of fashion. For someone who doesn't particularly like to be seen, you seemed to be at every party that was taking place in town. I knew about it from various people, from your late night phone calls when you were too drunk to know what you were saying and from various gossip columns."

"Gossip columns?" Beth was shocked. "What was I doing in the gossip columns?"

"You were the wife of a prominent Congressman, who was so happily married until the break up. It's mother's milk to the press."

"What did I say?"

"It's interesting. You told everyone who would listen that you and Adam broke up, but even in your state, you never actually destroyed him. You dug deep, but you always avoided the jugular." She smiled briefly. "You're not really a killer, I guess."

"What was Adam's reaction?"

"His press secretary simply issued a 'no comment' statement."

"How gallant," Beth said sarcastically.

"What did you want him to do? You were doing a complete job on your own."

"You're being awfully loyal to him." Beth grew angry. "It was Adam who left me, remember?" Her anger took over. "After twenty-five years of living together, he got up and left me for another woman."

"No man leaves his wife for another woman," Gillian said evenly. "Men leave their wives because of their wives."

"I resent that." Beth's voice rose. Then covering her face with her hands, she tried to get control of herself. "What am I going to do, Gillian?" she asked, when she could finally speak again. "I've got to get out of this house," she whispered. "Somehow, I've got to get away from here."

"Yes, you have to get out of the house, but not run away from it," Gillian said gently. "You've got to go out there and find a place for yourself, make use of who you are. It's time you stopped depending on Adam for everything."

"You sound like you did many years ago when I first married Adam." She smiled in spite of herself. "Then you told me to use who I was to help Adam get where he wanted to go. I did it, and look at me. I've created a Congressman, a successful man, a hero, for some other woman to enjoy."

"That was twenty-five years ago," Gillian cut in. "And that was what you wanted and needed then. Grow up." She stood up angrily. "Do you realize that since Adam's first campaign, when you worked with him and for him—and did a damn good job—you've allowed yourself to become an ornament at his side rather than an active partner? You're dressed to the hilt, you're made up to perfection, you smile on command and you're a fucking bore." She caught her breath. "Why don't you go out and find a job and start using the brain that God gave you?"

"A job?" Beth gasped. "What kind of a job? Where?"

"Just say the word and I'll call several people who will see you. I'm sure Adam would help if you asked him. Or you could call any one of the hundreds of people you know. There are several jobs you can do with your hands tied behind your back. But you have to want it."

"I wouldn't call Adam or anyone connected with him to help me," Beth hissed. "This is Mrs. Adam Stillman." She mimicked her own voice. "Can you help poor Mrs. Adam Stillman rehabilitate herself now that she's alone?"

"If it weren't so sad, it would be funny," Gillian said furiously. "You are an individual in your own right."

"No I'm not," Beth shot back. "I've submerged myself so completely that I've been erased off the face of the earth. I've been painted into a corner by everyone around me, and now I'm alone." She caught her breath. "Have you any idea how alone I've been all these years?"

"Not as alone as Adam's been," Gillian said evenly.

"Is that right?" Beth stormed. "His work became his companion along with all the people he works with from early morning to late at night. And what have I had? The crumbs of his exhaustion when he arrived home from Washington at ungodly hours or on weekends?"

"He was here when you needed him. Were you around when he needed you?" She stopped and let the words sink in. "When did you last talk to Adam except during a campaign? Do you know how lonely it is for a man to come into his home and find a sullen, angry woman whose sole preoccupation is herself?"

"I wasn't always like that," Beth began to wail. "I'm the way I am because of Adam. Had he let me go off with Dan . . ."

"Are you hearing what you're saying?" Gillian interrupted. "Are you listening to what's coming from your mouth. Had *he* let you." She laughed harshly.

"Well, it would have been different had I gone away with Dan."

Gillian did not answer.

"Did you know about Dan and me?" Beth asked.

"Not until years later, although I suspected that there was something going on between you two."

"Where is Dan?" Beth asked curiously. She did not think of him often and then only in the abstract.

"Still in Europe. Still brilliant, charming, selfish and chasing after the impossible."

"We would have had a wonderful life together," Beth said wistfully.

"Dan Bradbury would have dropped you within a year," Gillian said coldly.

"What do you mean?"

"To Dan it's the challenge and the conquest that are exciting. Not the aftermath of victory. You were both grown-up people with manners and habits. You would have become a burden to him, and you would have grown jealous of his success. He did not have Adam's kindness or understanding. He also did not know you. All he would have seen was the dependent, whimpering woman who makes demands and drains the people around her."

"If that's your opinion of me, why have you stayed my friend?" Beth was deeply hurt.

"Because I know who you are and know that there is still a great, bright, witty, charming woman behind that narcissistic facade you've created."

"Why don't you leave me alone?" Beth's voice was barely audible. She turned her head away.

"I'm a phone call away, Beth." Gillian softened her voice.

She had been much harsher than she had meant to be, but her love for Beth was akin to a mother's love, and she knew she had to shock her into the realities of what lay ahead.

Gillian's voice did not reach Beth. The phrase "narcissistic facade" kept repeating itself in her brain. Mary was a narcissist, she thought dully. That was one of the reasons she was so unbearable. And ever since she could remember, that was what she had wanted to avoid—being anything like her mother.

She looked around and realized Gillian was gone. The sun disappeared behind darkening clouds, the terrace around her looked forlorn. A gust of wind blew the curtains of the bedroom open and Beth could see her bed neatly made up, the corner of the blanket turned down, the pillows plump and inviting. The temptation to run and crawl into it was overwhelming. She got up and started toward the room but stopped. That was something her mother would have done, and somehow she had to find the inner resources not to give in to that fate.

12

With a will and determination that amazed her doctor, Beth made a miraculous physical recovery. Assiduously she followed his advice and instructions, determined to be up and about by the time Sarah came home. Her mental recuperation was more difficult. Try as she did to circumvent thoughts that caused her pain, the daily realities pushed their way back into her life.

With the end of her so-called "cruise" Beth found herself deluged with calls from people she had not heard from in a long time. Bewildered by the sudden attention, she soon realized that during her mad rampage she had contacted endless acquaintances and had given them license to behave as though they were interested parties, concerned, as they put it, with her welfare. Mainly they meted out advice about what she must do so that her financial welfare would be protected; each had a lawyer who would handle the matter and see that she was not swindled; all felt that Adam had behaved badly. Angry and hurt as she was at what Adam had done, Beth could not help but marvel at the disloyalty shown toward him.

"But we don't have that sort of relationship," she tried to explain. "We're civilized people and money will not be the issue."

"That's what they all say," came the answer. "Wait till the lawyers start talking."

Beth discounted most of what was being said, but she began to wonder if Adam had taken any steps toward their formal divorce. He had said he would speak to his lawyer when he left, but she had not been contacted by anyone. She had never needed a lawyer since Adam's office always handled their affairs. Who was their lawyer? she wondered with mounting concern. As for the financial aspect of their life together, she had taken care of the daily expenses of the house while the children were around, although in recent years, Adam's office took charge. Unhappily it dawned on her that a great portion of their income came from her inheritance and was, as such, her money. The idea was disconcerting. Her money. It seemed strange to be thinking in terms of "me," "mine" instead of "we" and "ours." She felt stupid, helpless and incompetent. She knew she needed someone on her side other than curious gossipers, or gleeful onlookers to her misery. Jimmy Jay, Ali and her mother, were the obvious candidates.

Ali was subdued when Beth called. She was pleased to hear from her, inquired about the cruise then announced that George's wife had died.

"It's for the best, of course," she said seriously, "but poor George is upset and I don't blame him."

"How are the boys?" Beth asked with mild interest. She had not known the woman and was too preoccupied with her own problems.

"They don't really understand what happened," Ali said. "I've been alone with them for several days and they seem fine."

"Ali, you are aware of the fact that your father and I . . ."

"Yes, I am," Ali interrupted. "I'm sorry it came to that. Are you all right?"

"Fine," Beth said with assurance. "I'm just fine."

"I'll call you in a couple of days," Ali said before hanging up.

No support. No anger at Adam. Complete self-involvement.

The conversation with Jimmy Jay was quite different. He had called numerous times while she was ill even though he too was told she was away. On a world tour, he had made a point of keeping in touch with Lydia, as though sensing that Beth was in need.

She reached him in Capetown, South Africa.

"Have you heard that your uncle and I are separated?" Beth asked almost immediately.

"Yes, I have," Jimmy Jay said emotionally.

"From whom?"

"Adam."

"Adam wrote to you about it?" Beth was stunned.

"We've been corresponding for quite a while now," Jimmy Jay said uncomfortably, as though he were being disloyal to her.

"I'm pleased," Beth said sincerely. "How did it come about?"

"It started after we met in Israel in 1973."

Beth stretched her memory back. She knew that Adam had gone to Israel after the Israeli-Arab war, but she was sure he had never mentioned meeting Jimmy Jay.

When did you last talk to Adam? Gillian had asked her when they had their angry exchange the day Beth came to herself. Beth dismissed the thought. She was still unable to cope with what Gillian had said.

"When are you coming home?" Beth asked anxiously. "I miss you terribly."

"I've got a grueling two months ahead in this part of the world," Jimmy Jay said, and he sounded tired. "This tour is a real bitch, and it's taking the guts out of me, but I should be back in the States around the end of June. I know I'll be on the East Coast in July. I'm going to spend part of it in Southampton."

"Southampton?" Beth was surprised. "Where will you be staying?"

He mentioned the name of a prominent author who was a highly respected member of the Southampton community, and then laughing in a strained manner he said caustically, "I'll be performing at the club on the Fourth of July."

Beth was speechless.

"We're breaking two barriers at once," Jimmy Jay said, and Beth could not decide if he was being serious or not.

"Jimmy Jay, are you sure it's all right?" Beth asked. "I don't want you to be hurt."

"They wouldn't dare hurt me physically. I'm too well known for that."

"I wasn't worried about the physical hurt," Beth said quietly.

"This South African scene is no picnic," he answered. "But enough with the serious talk. I'll call again soon, and you take care."

Warm, loving, concerned. Preoccupied with his life.

It was, however, the conversation with her mother that surprised her most. In spite of the superficial amicability that existed between Mary and Adam, Beth knew her mother had never truly accepted him.

It was ironic that after all these years it was to be her mother who might advise her as to how to deal with the practical side of her separation from Adam.

Bracing herself, Beth waited for her mother to pick up the phone and plunged quickly into a lengthy description of her cruise. Mary seemed disinterested and it occurred to Beth her mother did not believe the story. She dropped the subject and with great caution turned the conversation to her separation. The expected "I told you so" or "It's for the best" were not forthcoming.

"Try to patch it up, Beth," Mary said instead.

Beth was flabbergasted. "Why should I?" she asked angrily. The fact that it was not within her power to do, was immaterial.

"Because being alone is the most horrendous thing for a woman," Mary said quietly.

"I won't be alone," Beth answered with exaggerated bravado. "I've got tons of friends. There are hundreds of projects I want to get involved in. Do you realize how many things I've put off doing because of my stupid obligations to Adam's work? Now I'll finally have the time." The distortion of what her life was really like echoed in her ears.

"Being alone makes everything seem less important." Mary's voice came through a haze.

"I won't be alone," Beth repeated firmly.

Her mother's words haunted her. She was acutely aware that Adam was not coming home, but the full impact of what it meant was still diffused by feelings of uncontrollable anger. She refused to accept her total dependence on him. She dismissed the idea that she was useless.

Instead she focused her attention on Sarah's homecoming. As soon as Sarah arrived and was settled, Beth decided, she would embark on a more active and productive life and prove who she was. There were numerous charities that boasted her name as an honorary member. Now she would give her time and become involved. Throughout the years she had planned on taking courses toward her masters. She would do that too. As if to prove her intentions, she called Columbia, N.Y.U. and Hunter College and got their brochures. And finally, she would go out and find a job. She would not ask Adam for help, but Gillian was right. There were quite a few people who would be glad to help her. She was a capable woman and could fit into any one of several positions. Gillian knew her value and would give her a good recommendation. She would do everything as soon as Sarah arrived. Her daughter's welfare came first. Her own life would fall into place once Sarah was home.

As soon as Beth was able to get around, she threw herself into the task of creating an atmosphere of warmth and hominess which she was convinced Sarah needed. In typical fashion, she attacked the project with precision and unfaltering zest.

Within days, Hannah and Jimmy Jay's quarters were transformed into an ideal bachelor-girl's dream. The peach-colored fabrics mixed with creamy delicate lace, the small antique desk, brought down by Joseph from Mary's attic, the ancient armoire from Ali's room along with the comfortable modern chairs and sofa for the small living room, were all assembled to set off Sarah's dark loveliness.

The room was nearly completed when Sarah called collect from Omaha, Nebraska.

"What are you doing there?" Beth asked, trying to hide her shock. Somehow she assumed that Sarah's arrival was imminent.

"I'm hitchhiking," Sarah answered.

"Isn't it dangerous?"

"No." Sarah was not going to elaborate.

"Any idea when you might arrive?"

"I'll call you again," she said, and after a few inane pleasantries, she hung up.

13

Waiting for Sarah's indefinite arrival was too reminiscent of the years of waiting for Adam to come home from Washington, and Beth was forced to turn her attention to her own needs and face her situation more realistically. Although not in need financially, she wanted a paying job, a framework into which she could fit, feel needed and wanted on merit rather than as someone's wife. Although disliking the atmosphere surrounding charity work, she started contacting the wives of their various friends and offered to participate actively in their efforts. The women, who had long since given up hope of drawing Mrs. Adam Stillman into their pet projects, were delighted. Everyone was aware that she and Adam were separated, still she carried the name and was deluged with calls and invitations to attend luncheon meetings, cocktail parties, dinner dances and various other fund-raising affairs, where she was displayed on the dais with pride. Beth suffered through all the events, dropping hints, whenever possible, about her desire for work.

The first interview set up for her turned out to be with a young man who wanted to run for Congress against Adam and felt it would be a coup to have the Congressman's ex-wife working on his campaign. The second was with an elderly chairman of the board of a large clothing company who, as it turned out, did not have a position for her. During the brief meeting, Beth got the distinct feeling that she was being introduced to a lonely old man who was looking for a lady friend. The third appointment was short and quite the most painful.

Joyce Gran, an energetic, socially prominent acquaintance set it up. A Mr. Brackmore, the president of a large public relations company was looking for a liaison between his United States based office and his European clients. French was a prerequisite and a sophisticated person able to cope with the international personalities was being sought.

Beth prepared for the meeting assiduously. In spite of having an extensive wardrobe, she decided to buy a new outfit that would be suitable for the meeting. The racks at Bergdorf Goodman frightened her. Her regular saleslady was away on vacation, and for the first time in her life Beth felt incapable of making the right choice. Saks Fifth Avenue was no better. She was on her way to Bendel's when she decided to go to

Arthur's. He was her friend and would know what was right for the interview. He had always been helpful and correct about what she should buy for whatever occasion. The elegant boutique on East Sixty-first Street was pleasant, and Arthur was delighted to see her.

"I've decided to go back to work," Beth said breezily, "and I want something elegant, understated but just right," she said, the minute she walked in.

"Great idea," Arthur chirped happily, going into a small room and returning with two smartly cut French suits, a skirt and jacket and silk shirt.

"What do you think?" Beth asked standing in front of the mirrored wall, dressed in the caramel-colored pleated skirt, man-tailored white silk shirt and navy blazer.

"All three outfits are gorgeous." Arthur smiled warmly at her. "Clothes just look great on you. They always did." He came toward her and put a silk scarf around her neck, tying it expertly and standing back to observe the over-all effect. "You haven't changed in the twenty-five years I've known you," he said with affection. "If anything, you're better looking now than you were then."

Beth walked over to the mirror and observed herself closely. She wanted to believe him, felt that in a way he was possibly right, but dismissed the thought with embarrassment.

"You're just saying that," she chided. "So which should I take?" she asked again. Her indecisiveness bothered her. She had always been so sure of her taste.

"The outfit you're wearing now," Arthur said with authority. "And you can come back for the other two after you start working."

"I will get the job," she said with assurance. "I'm perfect for it."

"Sure you will," Arthur said, and hugged her. "Just have them call me and I'll give you a reference they won't be able to resist."

The day before the meeting, Beth had her hair tinted and trimmed and her nails manicured. She also bought an ounce of her favorite cologne. It was exorbitantly expensive, but she felt she deserved it. A new chapter was opening up in her life and she spared no expense on herself.

The elegant offices in the General Motors building were inviting and Beth felt comfortable. Waiting for a secretary to come out, she lit a cigarette and tried to relax. The fact that she would be working one block away from where Gillian's offices used to be was a good omen.

A young woman came out, greeted her courteously, and asked her to follow her. Beth's confidence rose as she walked along the long hallway, her heels sinking into the deep plush carpet. The textured wallpaper was rich, the paintings attractive and correct for the over-all atmosphere.

Mr. Brackmore was a tall gray-haired man with somber blue eyes who rose respectfully when Beth entered. They shook hands and he waved her to a seat across from the large mahogany desk and sat back in his leather armchair.

"What can I do for you, Mrs. Stillman?" he asked, picking up a letter which he scanned quickly.

The question and his action threw her. "I'm here about the job of liaison between your European . . ." Her voice trailed off. She was sure he was not listening.

He looked up absently. "Oh, yes. Joyce Gran mentioned you to me." He paused and seemed lost for words. "Joyce is a wonderful woman, isn't she?" he said finally.

"Yes she is." Beth's confidence disappeared almost immediately.

"Her husband and I went to school together, did you know that?" Beth did not reply.

"We had dinner together the other night." He smiled pleasantly. "She's really so energetic and takes such interest in her charity work. My wife is quite involved with it too. Are you active as well?"

Beth cleared her throat. "I am interested in a job, and Joyce mentioned that you were looking for someone who spoke French and who could deal with your European clients," Beth said forcefully. "I do charity work, but it's a job I'm after."

"Well, that specific position has been filled," he said seriously, and stood up. "I am sorry, I hope you haven't been inconvenienced, and I appreciate your coming down."

"Are there any other positions here that I might be suitable for?" Beth asked, feeling humiliated, furious for demeaning herself but unable to control the blatant plea which had crept into her voice.

A look of annoyance crossed his face, and in that instant Beth knew that he had promised to see her as a favor to Joyce without any intention of giving her a job of any sort.

"I could call the personnel department and check it out." He tried to hide his displeasure. "Or better still, why don't you ask my secretary to take you down there. We have a Mrs. Robinson who is up on all that sort of thing, and if there is anything at all, I'm sure she'll be glad to talk to you about it."

Beth walked out of the office in a daze, controlling the tears which were quite close to the surface. She barely saw the secretary who said a polite good-bye to her as she passed her desk.

Going down the elevator she got control of herself, and by the time she reached the street level she was furious. She could practically hear the conversation over dinner between Brackmore and Joyce Gran. "Help my friend, the helpless lady who needs to be rehabilitated now that her husband has left her," and Brackmore, in an expansive mood, decided to comply. The scene grew out of proportion in Beth's mind as did the anger. Fishing out a coin from her purse, she walked over to a public phone and dialed Joyce's number.

"How did it go?" Joyce asked enthusiastically.

"I can set up my own rejections, Joyce," Beth hissed into the phone. "I don't need appointments made by well-meaning friends."

"What happened?" Joyce asked in dismay.

"He didn't have a job for me. He didn't even look at me, much less ask who I was or what I could do." Beth heard her voice rise.

"But he specifically told me there was an opening . . ."

"Bullshit," Beth screamed. "What did you do, make a plea for your poor little deserted housewife friend?"

"I meant well." Joyce became defensive.

"I'm sure you did," Beth said, calming down. It was foolish to call and what she was saying made no sense. She felt spent and tired. She finished the conversation stiffly and hung up.

The interview had taken less than fifteen minutes and it was still early in the morning. Absently Beth picked up a New York *Times* and looked around for a coffee shop.

Sipping her coffee, she scanned the headlines of the paper, flipping the pages aimlessly. The news, which had been so much part of her life while she was living with Adam, held little interest for her now. The ads were equally dull. Suddenly she found herself looking at the Want Ad section. She scanned the columns and wondered if there was any position which she could fill. Accounting. Bookkeeper. Buyer, experienced. Clerk Typist. Cook. Executive Secretary. She read that list more carefully. The experience required made her look on. Girl Friday. Girl, she mused. No one asked for a Woman Friday. Suddenly her eye caught sight of a large ad under the name of the Jackson Employment Agency. It listed endless opportunities and although none were of particular interest to her, Beth took note of the address. Nothing could be worse than the meeting with Brackmore she decided. Paying the check, she walked quickly out of the coffee shop, hailed a cab and gave the driver the Forty-second Street address.

Beth sat on the hard-backed chair in the quasi-elegant reception room of the Jackson Employment Agency, staring at the application which the receptionist handed her when she walked in. She filled in the space asking for her name and address but looking down the form, she knew she could answer none of the other questions. She did not have the answers to "What was your last place of employment?" "How long were you there?" "Why did you leave?" "What position are you applying for?"

It was a mistake to come, she thought, and was tempted to tear up the card and run out, but stopped herself. She was sure that nothing would come of it, but having arrived at this point, she felt she had to go through with it. Picking up the stubby pencil that came with the application, she started scribbling furiously and handed the form to the receptionist.

Settling back she felt calmer and began to examine the decor of the room and observe the people sitting around. She did not know who they were and they were indifferent to her. That helped. The impersonal atmosphere afforded her the luxury of anonymity. No one would know of her failure.

"Ms. Van Ess?" someone called out.

"Is Beth Van Ess still here?" Beth looked up at the young man who was standing in the doorway and realized he was calling her.

"That's me." She stood up self-consciously.

"Would you come this way?" he said leading her down a long narrow hallway toward a small cubicle at the far end. The contrast between the elegant offices of the Brackmore Company were striking, and Beth was again tempted to leave, but forced herself to follow the young man. As they walked, she could see people being interviewed in various offices and marveled at the difference in attitude between the interviewers and the ones being interviewed. The former was sitting back in a relaxed fashion, while the person in need was leaning forward anxiously, talking rapidly and nervously selling himself. The sight depressed her, and she tried to think of how she must have appeared in Brackmore's office. She was determined to maintain her poise, remember who she was, keep her dignity.

"My name is Jack Davis," the young man said, waving her to a chair by his desk and sat down opposite her. "I've looked at the application here with great care, but I must say it's not quite indicative of your past experience or, I'm sure, your capabilities." He tried to smile pleasantly. "You say that you worked as a free-lance writer for Gillian Crane Public Relations." He paused, "Who is Gillian Crane?"

Beth blushed. Jack Davis was in his twenties, and until that moment it never occurred to her that he would have no way of remembering the dynamic woman who was an innovator in political campaigns, a household word in the fifties and sixties.

"You haven't worked in quite a long time, so I assume you were busy bringing up children and caring for a family." The effort to keep the boredom out of his voice was thinly disguised. "May I ask what kind of work you're looking for?"

"Well . . ." Beth started, "I do write well. I'm quite good at research. I've been in charge of an office that dealt with the public." She could not go on.

"Would you consider taking a typing test?"

"I would gladly take one, but I haven't actually typed . . ." She stopped. What was she doing there, she wondered. Getting up, she tried not to sound rude. "I'm sorry to have taken up your time," she said stiffly. "I've never filled one of these things out, and I didn't realize how truly ill-equipped I am for it."

"Please don't apologize." Jack stood up too. "And you haven't wasted my time. The point is that what you're applying for in the form of office work is rather difficult. You're simply overqualified for any of the jobs we have on file."

The phrase jarred her. Overqualified for what? she wondered.

"But if you'd consider something else, I'm sure we could help you." He seemed sincere. "Won't you sit down?" he suggested, and sat down when she did.

"What kind of work would you suggest?" Beth asked haltingly.

"Well, we're a very large agency and we deal in many fields." He sifted through a thick file of papers and pulled one out. "There is a position open at a very fine restaurant which has just opened at one of the larger hotels in the center of town. I see you live on East Seventy-second Street, and I can tell you it would be within walking distance from your home." He tried to sound convincing. "You would be ideal for it. They're a class operation, and they specifically asked for a woman with elegant bearing, someone well spoken and well dressed."

Beth lowered her eyes trying to hide her confusion.

"You're an extremely attractive woman, Ms. Van Ess, and I really believe you can get that job."

Between Arthur's dress shop, her plastic surgeon and Kenneth the hairdresser, she was doing all right, she thought and it made her smile.

"You're very kind, Mr. Davis," she looked up and said sincerely. "But I really think I'd be underqualified for the position as a hostess in any restaurant." She stood up and put out her hand. "But I do thank you for your time."

She was passing the reception desk on her way out when the young woman stopped her.

"Miss Jackson asked to see you before you leave," she said, indicating a room off the main reception area.

"See me?" Beth asked puzzled.

"You are Miss Van Ess, aren't you?"

Entering a room slightly larger than the one she had just been in, Beth found herself staring at a woman in her early forties, sitting behind a large desk piled with papers.

The woman stood up and came toward her. "I'm Maggie Jackson," she said, closing the door through which Beth had entered. "Won't you sit down."

The woman looked vaguely familiar, but Beth could not place her.

"We have a system here whereby all applications are brought to my attention, so that I know what's going on," Maggie said sitting down opposite Beth.

Beth felt herself grow impatient. She had no desire to become a statistic at the Jackson Employment Agency.

"I knew Gillian Crane many years ago," Maggie said, and Beth became alert. "I was one of her so-called disciples. I even worked for her at one point." She smiled. "And you were the lady we were all afraid of, Beth."

"Afraid of me?" Beth was too flabbergasted to be embarrassed or annoyed at having her state of anonymity unveiled. She was also trying to place the woman, but found it impossible. "Are you sure we worked there at the same time?"

"You were free-lancing and were not around all the time, but we did work together briefly. And you were fearsome."

"But why for heaven's sake?"

"For starters, you were the most elegant thing around. Your manner was slightly disdainful of us girls, but most of all, you ran the show and we were all bullshitting." Maggie began to laugh, and Beth knew she was not being put down. "We were playing at being in politics, in public relations, and you took it seriously and seemed to know what you were doing."

"Well," Beth said, and stood up, "you're obviously not bullshitting any more, and for whatever it's worth, thanks for the compliments." She started to turn away. Although Maggie was not trying to embarrass her, she wanted to get away.

"Beth, you're aware that this is the most difficult way for someone like you to get a job, aren't you?" Maggie's voice stopped her and Beth turned around. "I'm sure Jack told you you're overqualified. It's become a catch-all phrase these days, but he was right on the nose in your case."

"So what does someone like me do when they have to go to work, need a job as badly as the next person?"

"Have you tried talking to people who know you and want to help? I'm sure your husband . . ."

"Thanks, Maggie." Beth cut her short. "You're very understanding and I appreciate everything you've said."

"Why don't you try some of the smaller, more specialized agencies," Maggie suggested, walking her to the door.

"I probably will," Beth said politely.

"You're serious about all this, aren't you?" Maggie said suddenly.

"Listen, Maggie," Beth said, through clenched teeth, "Gillian always said that hungry people were the only reliable ones when it came to work. Well there are all sorts of hungers. For food, for money, for power, for position, and then there is the hunger for emotional survival. Yes, I'm hungry. Desperately hungry."

They stared at each other for a long moment.

"Thanks again for your time," Beth said icily.

"I'll call you the minute I have something I think you can do." Maggie ignored Beth's tone.

Beth could not help but smile. "Don't call me, I'll call you?" She felt better.

"You can call me anytime," Maggie said seriously. "And I mean it."

14

The meeting with Maggie Jackson helped negate some of the unhappiness caused by the disastrous interview with Brackmore, but Beth was left with the overwhelming feeling of being in limbo. She continued to call people, made dates for lunch, went shopping with the ladies who filled their days with trivialities and were delighted to have her as a companion and confidante. For the first time in her life she actually listened to what they said and was staggered at the games they played in their relationships, whether with their husbands or their lovers, without being embarrassed. The backbiting, sniping remarks, the disloyalty most of them displayed, was offensive to her. Except for the episode with Dan, which was done discreetly, her life with Adam had been a mutual effort and interest in what was happening in the world around them. Even when going through unhappy times, she never berated him or spoke against him. She was genuinely interested in what he did and said, was proud of who he was and what he had achieved.

For a while Beth was a novelty and was invited to dinners and receptions. Everyone had a man they wanted her to meet, and she found herself dating elderly men who were widowers, or younger men who were divorced. The former spent the time reminiscing about their lives, discussing their children and grandchildren, totally disinterested in who she was or what she had to say. The latter were preoccupied with anger at their former wives, the alimony they had to pay and trying to prove their masculinity. Much as she wanted to get involved with someone, she had long since forgotten the rules of dating. Few men called her for a second date. Slowly she began to withdraw into herself again and the calls dwindled. Her presence, once coveted, now seemed to embarrass her hostesses. Her status as a single woman was brought home most forcefully by the few remaining friends who still kept in touch and who treated her much as she had treated her single friends when she was still married to Adam. They would spend time with her during the day, but at a point would rush off to meet their husbands or lovers. Within a relatively short time she became the woman who was called at the last minute to attend a theater performance when someone had an extra ticket. Most upsetting was that she accepted the invitations.

Still, the days were tolerable, but the nights were unbearable. Beth's rage at Adam grew. Sitting home at night, watching television, or trying to read a book, she would find herself plotting revenge. In spite of what Gillian had said, Beth was convinced she had been a good wife, had helped Adam reach the heights he had achieved, had devoted herself to making him what he was. And in return, he deserted her at a point where she was too old to start again. How she would go about avenging her misery was unclear, but she was determined to do something as soon as summer was over.

Sarah called several times. Each call brought her closer to New York and the knowledge that she would soon be home, did bolster Beth's spirits. Sarah was her child and needed a mother who would be warm and understanding. Beth even succeeded in rationalizing that it was probably for the best that there was no job in the offing. She had neglected her younger daughter, and work would have taken too much of her time. She decided against taking the summer courses she had planned on. Instead, she would take Sarah to Southampton and they would spend time with Mary. The decision relieved some of the unhappiness. She would do everything when summer was over.

Sarah's final call came from somewhere in Maryland and Beth expected her daily after that. But it was another week before she arrived, and then it was unexpected. It was ten o'clock in the evening and Beth was on the phone with Ali when the doorman rang up. Being a new man, he sounded uncomfortable when announcing that a young woman, claiming to be Sarah Stillman, wanted to come up. Rushing back to the phone, Beth informed Ali that Sarah was on her way and suggested they speak later.

"Please come up with Sarah for a weekend, Mother," Ali said with excitement. "I'm dying to see you, and it's been so long since I've seen her that I barely remember what she looks like."

"Would you like to hang on and speak to her?" Beth asked.

"Sure, I'd love it," Ali agreed without hesitation.

The doorbell chimed and Beth ran to open it.

Sarah was standing in the tiny vestibule outside the elevator and Beth was speechless. She had a large knapsack on her back, and looked emaciated. Her long dark hair was uncombed, her eyes dull, her clothing torn and dirty.

"Hi, Mom," Sarah said, staring at her mother. Then she smiled, and in spite of her dreadful appearance, a glimmer of the old Sarah was back.

"Hi, darling," Beth said and pulled her into the apartment. "You look exhausted."

"I am tired," Sarah said unloading the knapsack off her back.

"Would you like to shower?" Beth started, and seeing a look of annoyance come to the young woman's face, she rushed on, "or would you like some food before going up to your rooms?"

"Up to my rooms?" Sarah looked inquiringly at her mother.

"I've rearranged the upstairs for you so that you have sort of a small apartment of your own up there."

"What happened to my room down here?" Sarah asked.

Beth laughed self-consciously. "I thought you'd like some privacy and space." There was no way to tell Sarah that her room had been made into a storage space for the remains of Adam's presence in the house. "You don't mind do you?" she asked anxiously.

"It makes no difference." A forelorn look came into her eyes. "I'd like to go up and go to sleep, if it's all right with you?"

The crackling of the phone reminded Beth that Ali was on the line.

"Would you like to say hello to Ali?" she asked Sarah, who was already halfway up the stairs.

"I'll call her in the morning, Mom."

Beth rushed to the phone but Ali had already hung up. She redialed the number while watching Sarah's tiny form hauling the knapsack behind her and she wondered what she could do for her child. Ali's number was busy and Beth hung up in agitation. Ali was probably not even angry, she thought, and could not help but make a mental comparison between her two children. It would have been hard to tell that Ali was the unwanted child and Sarah the one they had planned for.

Sarah needed her. That was the dominant thought in Beth's mind as she walked into the kitchen to make some coffee. Pained as she was for her younger daughter, she felt a sense of purpose as she arranged a small tray with two mugs and some cookies and carried it up to Sarah's rooms.

The lights were on in the bedroom when she got upstairs, the door slightly ajar. Beth pushed it open and found Sarah fully clothed lying on the peach-covered coverlet, fast asleep. The knapsack was flung into a corner, unopened, her sandals were carelessly thrown on the edge of the bed.

Placing the tray down quietly, Beth picked up the sandals and stared at them. They were made of inexpensive plastic and were quite worn. Beth looked at Sarah's feet. They were filthy. Slowly her eyes wandered up the young form. The dungarees were patched and dirty, the light blue T-shirt was stained. Coming closer to the bed, Beth stared at the sleeping girl. The face was deathly pale, the heavy dark lashes emphasized the white pallor. The tiny diamond earrings in the pierced ears were in complete contrast to the over-all picture of destitution. Adam and she had given Sarah the earrings as a graduation present.

Beth felt a surge of love for her daughter and leaning over, she kissed her lightly on the forehead, fearful of waking her. Sarah had been neglected too long, she decided as she turned off the light and walked out of the room. But she was home now and it would all be different.

Feeling pleasantly tired, Beth thought of having a drink but put it out of her mind immediately. In spite of Barry's assurances that she had not meant to take her life, Beth was not convinced. Her fear of a repetition of the unfortunate incident made her stay away from alcohol and continue with the medication the doctor had ordered. She did not question what it was she was taking, but knew it helped calm her and she was grateful.

Before turning in for the night, Beth tried Ali again. The phone was still busy. It did not matter. She had her two daughters close at hand, Jimmy Jay would be home soon and her life would take on a semblance of normalcy.

Sarah was sitting at a table waiting when Beth walked into the Palm Court of the hotel. The girl looked listless and unkempt, and it annoyed her. When Sarah saw her, her eyes brightened briefly and she waved. Without waiting for the waiter, Beth walked directly to the table conscious that the luncheon was a replay of her own meeting with her mother many years back. She recalled Mary's reaction to her appearance, but what came back most vividly were her thoughts while watching Mary approach. She was magnificently dressed, exquisitely put together and walked with the assurance that she was an attractive, desired woman, convinced that everyone was aware of who she was. Self-consciously Beth looked around and knew that she too was convinced of her personage, but unlike Mary before her, she knew no one was paying attention to her. She quickened her step, wanting to be seated, wanting to wipe away the reality of the passage of time.

"You look tired, honey," she said, and regretted the words. It was not what she had meant to say. She saw Sarah bristle and lower her eyes.

"I'm okay, Mom," Sarah said not looking up.

"Mrs. Stillman." The headwaiter came over to the table and was smiling down at Beth. "I didn't see you come in. I haven't seen you in ages. Have you been away?"

Beth was relieved by the interruption. "Yes, I have," she said, and turned to Sarah. "Shall we order?"

"I'll have a martini, very dry," the girl said, looking directly at the headwaiter.

"Have you had anything to eat?" Beth asked automatically.

"Oh, Mom," Sarah said impatiently.

"Will that be a vodka martini or a gin martini?" the waiter asked after a pause.

Sarah looked confused for a moment, then said with authority, "A vodka martini, please."

"I'll have a coffee, black, and I'm famished, how about you, Sarah?"

"I'll have whatever you order." Sarah settled back into her dejected mood.

Finished with the order, Beth wondered what she could talk about that would be neutral and inoffensive. Sarah had been home for over two weeks, and this was the first time Beth was able to persuade her to spend any time with her. Any hopes Beth had for a semblance of a life with Sarah were shattered the morning after she arrived. She was gone by the time Beth got up and did not return until late that night. Questioned about where she had been was followed by a screaming row, with Sarah threatening to leave if she were not left alone. Beth had no idea where she went, who she spent her time with or what she did. Instinctively, Beth felt the young man whom Sarah had wanted to bring home was behind Sarah's unhappiness, but she dared not bring up the subject.

"Have you spoken to your father since you've been back," Beth finally broke the silence.

"I called him this morning, but he was in Washington and they weren't sure when he'd be back or where he could be reached today."

"When did you speak to him last?" Beth asked curiously. Surely Adam was in town a great deal of the time, especially considering his involvement with the Eddington girl. For the first time in weeks Beth thought of Lauri consciously and wondered if she had had the baby. It startled her.

"Mother, why did you and Dad separate?" Sarah cut into Beth's thoughts.

"I think we simply ran the course of what a marriage is all about," Beth said noncommittally.

"What does that mean?" Sarah persisted.

"I guess a certain boredom took over and there was no point in going on together."

"Is it inevitable that all marriages end that way?" Sarah asked, and leaned forward.

"I don't think so," Beth said cautiously. "In our case, I believe we simply wandered away from each other."

"Will you be getting a divorce?" Sarah asked anxiously.

Beth paled. "Probably." She did not want to discuss the matter.

"Will it be messy with dirty headlines?" Sarah lowered her voice to a whisper.

"Not that I can see." Beth began to feel uncomfortable. In all of her schemes for revenge, she had never once thought of the practical end to her marriage. Now she wondered on what grounds they would get their divorce. She could sue Adam for adultery. It would be easy to prove that he had been unfaithful to her with a young woman who was carrying his child, who might have already had it. It would destroy him and his career, she thought, but it gave her no pleasure. "Why do you ask?" she said finally.

"Just wondering," Sarah said, almost indifferently.

Their food and drinks arrived. Beth watched Sarah pick her martini up and sip it. She wanted one too, but knew she had to be in total control of her faculties. Not only for her own sake, but for Sarah's.

"Sarah, whatever happened to the young man you wanted us to meet?" she asked, deciding to bring the subject out into the open. Whoever he was, he must have been important for Sarah to have asked to bring him to meet them.

"He's around," Sarah said cryptically.

"Around where?"

"In New York."

"When did he get here?"

"We came together."

"Is it serious?"

Sarah did not answer, instead tears started streaming down her face.

"Honey, talk to me," Beth said gently. "Tell me what's going on. Maybe I can help."

"We were going to get married." Sarah wiped the tears with the back of her hand. "But he changed his mind."

Beth was silent, convinced there was more to come.

"We came to New York and I met his parents and I thought they liked me. Then I was going to have him meet you and Dad." Sarah sniffed, trying to control her tears, "But you and Dad are separated . . ."

"Good God, Sarah." Beth found it hard to speak. "This is the twentieth century. Divorced parents are no novelty."

"His parents don't approve of me."

"But why?" Beth exploded. She could not bear Sarah's pain, and she could not understand why any daughter of hers would want anyone who did not want her.

"His parents are Catholic, practicing Catholics, and although Philip is not orthodox, he agrees with them that he should marry someone of his own faith."

Beth stared at Sarah. She felt like laughing, although the humor of the situation would not fall into place.

"He would marry me if I converted," Sarah said sullenly.

"And you don't want to?"

"I would if he put it on a religious basis, but he puts it on the basis of principle." Sarah was suddenly defiant.

"Have you spoken to your father about it?" Beth asked haltingly.

"Of course we have," Sarah said.

The plural reference did not escape Beth's attention, but she decided to ignore it for the moment. "And what does he say?"

"He's sort of noncommittal, although I think he agrees with me. He does say that if we're really in love we should get married and we can work it out."

"When did you two meet your father?" Beth asked cautiously.

"We spent a week with him in Washington before coming to New York. Then Dad gave us a key to a small apartment on Ninety-eighth Street. It's sort of a run-down place, but Dad had it fixed up and it's quite pleasant. And it's very convenient for Philip to get to Columbia. He wants to study law there."

Beth's hand shook as she picked up her cup and put it to her lips. With a clarity she had never felt before, she knew that Sarah was far more like her than Ali ever was. The conversation they were having would never take place with Ali. What was George's religion, she wondered absently, and did it matter to Ali?

Putting her cup down carefully and aware that Sarah was staring at her, waiting for her to speak, she cleared her throat and put her hand on Sarah's arm which was resting on the table.

"Now you listen to me," she said evenly. "I don't give a damn about why Philip wants you to convert. I wouldn't care if he was Jewish and wanted you to become Jewish, or if he were a Buddhist and asked you to take up that faith. You say you love him and want to marry him, then you're damn well going to convert, and you'll do it as he wants you to and as his parents ask." She caught her breath trying to keep her emotions in check. "So that when you have children they'll know who they are. It won't even matter if you don't practice the religion, but growing up, your children will know where they come from. What they do with their life when they grow up is immaterial. If they should want to convert for whatever reason, they at least will have a point of departure— something we did not give you." The tension as she spoke was unbearable. "And having said that, let me tell you the most important thing of all. Whatever you do, do it because you want to, because you want it more than anything else."

"Oh, Mom," Sarah whispered, and the sudden switch from depths of depression to unbelievable relief wiped away the oppressive mood.

"Do I ever get to meet him?" Beth asked.

A peel of laughter greeted the question. "Soon," Sarah said, picking up her drink. Suddenly she grew serious again and leaned forward. "I hate liquor, Mom, did you know that?"

"Then why on earth did you order it?"

"You always did, and I thought I'd impress you with how grown-up I am." She looked like a little girl. "Then you pulled that black coffee bit and I felt like a fool." She smiled happily at Beth. "Have you given up liquor?"

"I think so." Beth tried to sound nonchalant.

"I'm glad, Mom," Sarah said, and although there was no recrimination in her voice, Beth felt uncomfortable.

"How about a shopping spree this afternoon?" Beth asked, changing the subject.

"Just let me call Philip and find out what his plans are."

Beth ordered a second cup of coffee and tried to recover her equilibrium. She was pleased with the way she had handled Sarah's problem. She was part of Sarah's life, and it filled the emptiness for a while.

Sarah came back beaming. "Philip said that Dad called and suggested dinner," she said breathlessly. "Can we make it a foursome?"

Beth could not turn her down although she wanted to. "Of course we can."

15

The noise of the rock music coming from the juke box was deafening as Adam pushed open the door to the restaurant on Third Avenue in the Seventies. It was early evening and the long narrow bar was crowded with young men and women obviously on their way home from work, all talking and laughing, oblivious to the din around them. Briefly, Adam wondered if he was in the right place, and realized he probably was. Sarah had chosen it, and to her the ambiance was natural. Quiet, intimate restaurants, conducive to conversation, as he knew it, were as foreign to her as this restaurant was to him.

Resigned, Adam pushed his way through the throngs of people to the back. To his relief the dining section was still quite empty, although the music was as loud as it was up front.

An attractive young man led him to a table next to a large picture window which looked out on a pretty little garden ensconced between two tall buildings. Green ivy covered the walls of the structures, and flower pots placed attractively on the terra-cotta tiles, were lit up by colorful lights. It was like a little oasis in the city of concrete and stone, and the sight gave him pleasure. This too was New York, the city which he loved and worked for. He had not been around it enough recently, he thought sadly. Although representing the city in Washington, he was a stranger to it. His perception of Manhattan had become the highway between his hotel and the airport on his way to Washington. It had begun to narrow when he met Lauri. Their time together was confined to seeing her in her apartment, or a rare walk around the Village at night, and it made him lose touch with what was happening around. It was different when he had lived with Beth, he thought. The city was an integral part of their life. They went everywhere, the Little Italy Festival, the various ethnic parades, the restaurants, the parks, the playground openings, the various sports events, and it made him feel and know the city as few other Congressmen did. Whatever her mood, Beth was always ready to join him, discuss what was happening, participate, give her opinion, take a stand.

Thoughts of Beth and their life together made him tense up. He had not seen her in nearly eight months, and he wondered what the meeting would be like. Contrary to what people thought, he was not angry with Beth for her outrageous statements to the press. He had read the various news reports quoting the things she said, and his heart went out to her. He understood her hurt. Had he been able, he would have reached out to her, tried to comfort her, maybe even explain what had happened to their life together. His one overt attempt, right after Thanksgiving, was rejected, and then her rage exploded openly and he was rendered impotent.

He was fully aware that Beth had not gone away on a cruise even before Gillian called him. Beth, he knew, was not someone able to do things alone, just as he had grown accustomed to being with her and found it difficult living as a bachelor. Gillian's call came on the heels of his discovering that Lauri had a miscarriage, and the events of that period stood out in his mind as the darkest and yet, in a way, the most enlightening time of his life.

Adam knew his affair with Lauri was over when she did not call him before leaving New York to reshoot the pictures for her ad campaign. Hoping to hear from her, he had not gone up to Sam's for Thanksgiving. It was no longer a matter of being infatuated with the young, beautiful girl that caused him concern. It was the deep feeling of responsibility for her predicament, which he felt was his as well. He did call her during that Thanksgiving weekend and was informed she would be away until the fifteenth of December, and he left for Montauk that day.

He spent the holidays alone at an inn at Montauk Point, reevaluating his life and wondering about his future. The affair with Lauri began to fall into place. He felt genuine affection and gratitude toward her. The break up of his marriage and the possible halt to his political career were sobering facts, but having known Lauri helped put many events into perspective. His life with Beth could have gone on as it had, without his being aware that she was dying emotionally at his side. He too had begun to stagnate as a human being, juggling his emotions in a pressure cooker without an outlet, living more and more with unrealistic dreams of the past, unable to accept the present, running head on into the future, oblivious to the passage of time. The apartment on Ninety-eighth Street stood witness to his unreality. Having refurnished it, he could not bring himself to live in it. The mere idea that he wanted to marry a woman young enough to be his daughter was ludicrous. But Lauri had made it possible for him to touch the future both physically and emotionally, and because of her he was suddenly able to understand and appreciate the present.

It was a lonely time for him, and a time in which major decisions were made. He put aside the thought of running for mayor with a heavy heart. It would have meant the culmination of many dreams. Although it was not the scandal of his break up with Beth that made him come to that decision. He was coming close to leaving the Republican Party, and the idea was frightening. It was a deeply personal decision, one he could discuss with no one except Beth, and walking alone on the beach, he missed her desperately.

Returning to Washington after the first of the year, Adam was swept up in the activities of a new congressional term. In spite of all his personal problems, he had continued trying to reach Lauri to no avail. Her service said they did not know where she was. Tony Abbot's secretary was noncommittal.

It was not until the first week in February, when Adam was on his way to meet Sam at the New York Athletic Club on Central Park South, that he passed Tony's building and decided to go in and, if possible, find out if she was there.

The elevator man was genuinely distressed, describing the frantic scene of Miss Eddington being rushed to the hospital. He could not tell Adam what hospital she was in or what the matter was.

Shocked and feeling guilty, Adam entered the club to find Sam absorbed in lighting a cigar. They had not really spoken since the night of the election, and the mood was strained.

"Sam, Lauri Eddington is in the hospital," Adam said soberly, sitting opposite the older man.

"I know," Sam answered, concentrating on his cigar.

"I think you should know . . ."

"I don't want to know," Sam interrupted him with finality.

"But it's important."

"No, it's not." Sam's voice was cold, his eyes blank. "All I do know is that we must reconsider your mayoralty race."

"There's nothing to reconsider," Adam said quietly. "I put that one out of my mind a while back."

"Very wise," Sam said, and waved to a passing waiter. "Brandy?" He looked over at Adam, and for the first time the camaraderie they had shared for many years was nowhere in evidence.

"Did you know about Lauri?" Adam asked after the drinks were ordered.

"I did, and I thought you were a fool."

"Rather old-fashioned kind of thinking, wouldn't you say?"

"As you wish," Sam said dryly.

"What hospital is she in?"

"Lenox Hill."

Adam stood up. He had never mentioned Lauri's name to anyone, and for a brief moment he thought of talking to Sam about what had happened, possibly explain his strange, uncharacteristic behavior. It was useless.

"I think I'll skip the drink," he said, and nodding his head to Sam he turned and left.

Walking into Lauri's room at Lenox Hill, Adam stood at the foot of her bed and stared at the sleeping girl. She looked unbelievably young and vulnerable. The thought that it could have been Sarah lying there made Adam shudder.

"Mr. Stillman?" Adam heard his name, and he turned around startled. The room was in semi-darkness and he had not seen anyone when he entered. "I'm Tony Abbot."

Adam could not help but notice the younger man's extraordinary good looks, and briefly he wondered if Lauri had been having an affair with him while he was her lover. He felt a glimmer of jealousy and it embarrassed him.

"When did it happen?" Adam asked.

"Night before last," Tony answered and looked over at the sleeping girl. "She wanted the baby desperately and tried to hold on to the pregnancy for the last five hopeless weeks."

"Will she be all right?"

"Physically she'll be fine after a couple of weeks of rest."

Adam raised his brows.

"She's got a big battle ahead of her," Tony answered the quizzical look. "The Aden people are trying to cancel her contract because of this whole thing."

"Can I help?" Adam asked, genuinely moved.

"Hardly." Tony smiled for the first time. "She'd have a fit."

"Sam Ryan will, though," Adam said.

"She's already spoken to him, and he promised to do what he can."

At that moment Lauri opened her eyes. She looked directly at Adam, and he walked over to the side of the bed. Suddenly, he realized she was not really seeing him. Then she shifted her eyes to Tony, who rushed over to her and took her hand in his.

Adam walked out of the hospital remembering the night Beth had given birth to Ali. Hannah was with him, Beth was his wife and he had a new-born daughter. Trying as it all was, they were young and they were together, rooting for each other, caring for each other. They were a family. Now he felt deserted and forlorn.

Gillian had called him while Beth was recovering from her nervous breakdown.

"I'm being disloyal," she said seriously, "but I thought you should be aware of what's going on."

"Is she home?"

"Barry is keeping her sedated and under constant surveillance. Lydia sleeps there, and I relieve her when I can."

"What can I do?"

"Just be patient and for God's sake be around."

"In my own way, I've always been around," Adam answered.

"So has Beth, Adam," Gillian said pointedly.

"I know that." Adam paused for a moment, "Can you tell her that?"

"She won't hear it if I do." Gillian sounded sad. "What's happening with you?"

"I've made a mess of it, but I think it'll all straighten out in the end."

"Incidentally, your taste in women is as impeccable as ever. I'll say that for you." Gillian's tone changed. "In her own way, Lauri is as stunning as Beth."

"I suppose you're right, but other than external beauty, they are as different as can be in every way," Adam said with assurance.

"I don't know about that," Gillian answered thoughtfully. "The framework is different, the language and times are different, but somehow I suspect that if Beth was in her twenties in this decade, had the lingo, the options, and freedom that Lauri has, the difference you refer to would not be as clearly marked."

"You're so wrong." Adam kept the shock out of his voice.

"It's a moot point," Gillian countered, "except if you try to think of Beth as a twenty-five-year-old today and try to visualize Lauri as a fifty-year-old woman today, you just might discover I'm not far from being right."

"Do you know Lauri?" Adam asked, but the vivid image that Gillian's words evoked were racing through his head.

"The whole country knows her," Gillian said. "Her Aden commercial is the rage."

Adam had been in Washington since the day he saw Lauri in the hospital and was unaware of what had happened with Lauri's situation concerning her work. "You know she's as bright as she's beautiful," he said, genuinely pleased.

"She sure is. I've met her." Gillian concurred.

"When?"

"Sam introduced me to her. She was mapping out a whole campaign if they pulled her commercials off the air. Sam thought I could help."

"How did she appear to you?" Adam asked, in spite of himself.

"She's got everything going for her, except that she's a girl who is afraid of emotional commitments." She stopped for a minute. "Without meaning to offend, Adam, Lauri is the type of young woman who looks for the impossible relationships, the ones that are no threat, that make no permanent demands. A love affair with a married man, a deep attachment to someone like her photographer, people who represent no threat to her need for independence."

"That Abbot fellow looks like a highly respectable and eligible young man," Adam interjected.

"Tony Abbot is a homosexual and no danger to her," Gillian said dryly.

The minute the words were out of Gillian's mouth, it crossed Adam's mind that he would not have liked to have his child brought up by someone like Tony. The thought distressed him. He had been irritated by Sam's attitude toward his affair with Lauri, which he felt was old-fashioned. Now he was resorting to the same passé perceptions.

"But she wanted the baby," Adam said out loud. "That would have been permanent."

"I don't know this for a fact, but I'd venture a guess that she really decided she wanted it when she thought she was losing it."

Adam wanted to disagree, but remembering his last meeting with Lauri before Thanksgiving, her state of ambivalence toward him and toward having the child, he suspected that Gillian was probably right.

"Poor girl," Adam said with emotion. "What happens to someone like her?"

"It's not a chronic or fatal state of affairs," Gillian said with annoyance. "Lauri is fortunate to be living in an age where a woman's fight and struggle for individuality and need to express herself as a person on her own does not negate becoming seriously involved with another person." She stopped and thought for a long minute. Then as though talking to herself rather than Adam she spoke more gently. "For me and my generation it was either or. You had a career or you got married. You could not really have both. That sentiment poured over Beth's time, unfortunately. But the Lauri Eddingtons are different and in a way better off. Individual success can be achieved at an earlier age, and then she can open her mind to the realization that sharing is also important. Mind you, the scar tissue that the struggle creates, is accumulated and it hurts, but at some point she'll meet the person who will understand and accept . . ."

"Have you seen her recently?" Adam had a difficult time keeping the hurt out of his voice. Although he no longer needed or wanted Lauri, his masculine ego was still vulnerable.

"As a matter of fact I was invited by her to the reception Victor Adenizzio gave when she was made senior vice-president in charge of the Lauri Eddington designing firm that was bought by the Adenizzio people."

"Only senior vice-president?" Adam laughed self-consciously.

"Victor Adenizzio is a smart man, very smart. He made Kim Sloan president. She's older and wiser. Besides, I think Victor has other plans for Lauri."

"Victor Adenizzio is old enough to be Lauri's father." The words were out before Adam could stop himself.

"Victor, Jr., is in charge of this project." Gillian let the words sink in before continuing. "Adam, there's a younger group coming up. Old man Adenizzio was there, and very much in evidence, but Junior was running the show and Lauri was deferring to him."

"Well, it certainly fits into what Lauri was after," Adam said, trying to maintain his composure.

"Yes it fits, but somehow I don't think it's only her career she's thinking of at this moment. There was a rapport between Victor and her, an interesting interplay. I don't even know if she's aware of it, but Victor is quite a powerhouse. As a matter of fact, he had his little girl at the reception, which amused everyone, but watching Lauri with the child, I think she's just about ready to reach out and touch another human being."

"You might not believe it, Gillian," Adam said slowly, "but I'm honestly happy for her."

"I do believe it, Adam."

"You will keep me posted about Beth, won't you?" he said coming back to the present as thoughts of Lauri faded and his concern for Beth took over.

"Of course I will." Gillian assured him.

Adam was aware of Beth's recovery and knew what was going on in her life from Sarah since she arrived back in town. He wished he could sit down and talk to her about their life together, discuss Sarah's unhappy predicament, tell her that he needed her and wanted her, but until this evening it was impossible.

Now he was waiting for Beth, Sarah and Philip and he felt uncomfortable.

"May I join you?" A young girl with long dark hair, holding a drink in her hand was standing by his table, smiling down at him. "You look so serious and so sexy." She slipped into a chair opposite him.

Adam laughed self-consciously. "You're very pretty and very brave," he chided. "Hasn't your mother told you it's dangerous to pick up strangers in bars?"

"You've got a kind face." She continued to smile, sipping her drink. "I'm Sue. What's your name?"

"Adam Stillman." He looked carefully at her wondering if the name would mean anything to her.

"What do you do?" she asked innocently.

"I sell shoes," he said seriously. "And what do you do?"

"I work for an advertising agency. Receptionist, but I'm hoping to get promoted."

"To do what?"

"I don't know. When they promote me I'll tell you." She finished her drink. "May I have another?" She lifted her glass toward him.

Adam waved for the waiter and ordered a drink for her and a scotch for himself. The music seemed louder and he wished the girl would go away.

"I'm going to the movies later. Would you like to come?" Sue asked coyly. "I'll pay for myself."

"I'm busy," Adam answered politely.

"It's the *Exorcist* and it's supposed to be super, and Linda Blair is just great."

"What's the *Exorcist* and who's Linda Blair?" Adam asked.

"You're kidding!" She began to giggle.

"I'm not much of a moviegoer. The last movie I saw was . . ." he stopped unable to remember what it was. "As a matter of fact, my favorite movie star used to be Margaret Sullavan and no one has ever taken her place for me."

"Margaret who?"

Adam smiled. The generation gap never ceased to amaze him. Since his affair with Lauri had ended, he had dated several young women and although none were as young as the girl sitting opposite him, they were still light years away from him. Bright, sophisticated, ambitious working women in their late twenties, early thirties, he found their point of reference different from his. The Second World War was history to them just as the French Revolution was history to him. Truman, Roosevelt, the Depression, the McCarthy hearings, were ancient names and events. When out on a date, he often felt like a college professor, and the evenings were exhausting and in a way boring.

"Well, I see you're into children younger than your daughters." Beth was standing at the table looking down at Adam and Sue. Her voice was syrupy, but her eyes were cold.

Adam stood up quickly. "Hello, Beth," he said, trying to compose himself.

"Aren't you going to introduce me to your little friend?" She turned her eyes away from him and stared at the young woman who was looking up at Beth curiously.

"This is Sue," Adam said politely. "And this is my . . . this is Mrs. Stillman."

"How dramatic," Sue chirped.

"Sue," Adam said patiently, "Mrs. Stillman and I have very important things to discuss, so if you'll forgive us."

"Oh sure," Sue said unimpressed, and stood up. "But if you change your mind about the movies, I'll be at the bar." She looked back at Beth. "Nice meeting you." And she walked away.

Beth sat down in the seat the young girl had vacated and Adam sat down too.

"Would you like a drink?" Adam asked politely.

"I'll have a Coke, thank you," Beth said pointedly.

Adam waved to a waiter and placed the order. Then turning to Beth he looked at her closely. She was thinner than he remembered, but the innate elegance, the poise, the serene, almost regal beauty were there. "You're as beautiful as ever, Beth," he said sincerely.

"Why thank you, Adam." There was a trace of sarcasm in her voice. "Single life obviously agrees with you too."

"I don't know about that." Adam decided to ignore the jibe. "What have you been doing?"

"What I've always done. Taking care of my home, my children and keeping everything flowing as normally as possible under the circumstances." She took a deep breath. "And you? Have you become the father of a bouncing baby?"

"Lauri had a miscarriage," Adam said quietly, but he felt his jaw tighten.

"Oh dear," Beth simulated sadness. "But it's really no problem, is it? She's young and you're in your prime. I'm sure it will work out next time."

"She was very upset about it," Adam said, and wondered why he did not say that he was no longer seeing Lauri.

"That's quite natural." She picked up the Coke which the waiter brought over. "Is that why you haven't rushed to get that divorce?" Her voice grew icy. "I recall your saying you were going to speak to the lawyers the night you walked out. Or are you waiting to see the merchandise before you commit yourself."

"Beth, cut it out," Adam said angrily. "Vulgarity is not quite your style."

"I wish you would attend to the divorce." Beth ignored him. "It's really quite a bore being sort of married without actually being married. There's something uncomfortable about this state of affairs. People don't really know how to behave with me, and I don't feel completely free to do as I please."

"If it's that important to you, why don't you start the proceedings? You should have no problem, and I assure you I won't contest it."

"You won't mind my naming that girl as a corespondent?"

"You're being melodramatic," Adam said coldly. "As two adults we don't have to drag innocent people into our affair."

"Who's the innocent people?"

"You know what I mean."

"I really don't," Beth said through clenched teeth. "But if it would facilitate matters, I'll call up a lawyer and get the thing over with." She paused. "What about the financial situation?" she asked, remembering the warnings of various people.

"What financial situation?" Adam looked pained. "It's your money, all cared for and handled by the office just as it has been all through the years."

Beth became confused. She hated the reference to anything being hers, and she was talking about a subject she knew nothing about. "I think you should be responsible for Sarah's education," she said uncertainly.

"If you'd like," Adam said, wishing he could take her hand and relieve her of her discomfort. "Would you like me to pay you alimony as well?" He tried to sound serious.

"Good God, no." She looked away. "Who was that little girl you were with, anyway," she asked, watching Sue who was now seated at someone else's table.

"I hate to tell you this, but she tried to pick me up."

"I wish Sarah would get here," Beth said suddenly. "I find this whole meeting distasteful, if you must know." She bit her lip. "And that God-awful music. How do they hear themselves, much less each other with that dreadful noise blaring at them?"

"They don't." Adam kept looking at Beth carefully and wondered if she was serious about asking for the divorce. He knew her well, had always been able to read her moods and thoughts. But now her anger and pain were clouding his image of her.

"Do you really want that divorce?" he asked.

She looked back at him, and her face was serious and determined. "More than anything in the world," she said with conviction.

"Hi, Mom—hi, Dad." Sarah came bounding over with a tall, bearded, blond young man wearing rimless glasses. "This is Philip," Sarah said breathlessly, looking up at him then turning back to Beth and Adam.

"Hi, darling," Beth said, and smiled. "Hello, Philip."

Adam stood up and shook the young man's hand and kissed Sarah on the cheek.

"You sit next to Mom and I'll sit next to Philip," Sarah said with authority, leaving no place for argument.

"Why don't you move over Beth," Adam said helping Beth with her chair. "Your mother's better profile is the left one." He smiled self-consciously and looked over at Beth. She did not return his smile.

The mood at the table changed abruptly. Sarah began chatting and Beth had time to observe Philip. He looked uncomfortable and insecure. He needs a haircut, she thought, and wondered if he had a firm chin or if the beard was a camouflage for a weak one. He wasn't at all what Beth had expected. Somehow she had assumed he would be dark and good looking like Adam. Slowly she turned her eyes to look at Adam. He was talking seriously to the two younger people and held their attention completely. In spite of what she had said when she first walked in, Adam did not look well. He was much too thin for his height, his hair was graying rapidly, and although it suited him, it accentuated the sunken cheeks. She saw his face break into a smile and the creases around his eyes deepened. Beth turned her eyes back to Philip. It was unfair to compare the two men. Adam was an extraordinarily good-looking man.

"What do you think, Beth?" Adam was asking.

"I'm sorry, I wasn't listening," she answered automatically. Too quickly she had fallen back into relying on Adam to handle a situation which she was displeased with.

"Sarah is thinking of taking up social work as her major at Columbia," Adam said. "And she and Philip can go on using the apartment on Ninety-eighth Street."

Beth stiffened. "Don't you have to get your degree from Berkeley?"

"I dropped out after the first year," Sarah said candidly.

"And what have you been doing since?" Beth asked incredulously.

"Working with special children," Sarah answered softly.

Instinctively Beth reached out and pressed Sarah's hand. "That's wonderful, darling," she said with great emotion. "Really wonderful."

Sarah leaned over and kissed Beth on the cheek. "Thank you, Mom," she said.

The evening droned on, with Beth wishing it would end. Being in Adam's presence was upsetting. She wondered what Sarah saw in Philip. She also knew there was no way for her to show her displeasure without alienating her. To her great relief, Adam had to catch the last plane to Washington, and they walked out of the restaurant together. Sarah and Philip stayed on to chat with friends who had come over as the Stillmans were leaving.

"What do you think of him?" Beth asked, once they were out on the street.

"Not exactly what I would have wanted for Sarah," he said seriously.

"Yet you gave them your apartment, and from your behavior tonight, I wouldn't be surprised if Philip thinks you adore him."

"I don't think it would have served any purpose if I would have behaved differently. At this moment, Sarah thinks she's in love, and if we showed our disapproval, I think it would push her into a decision she might regret."

She did not answer, resenting his rational, controlled manner.

"What did you think?" Adam asked.

"I hated him," she said vehemently.

"Well, thank God you didn't show it."

"Don't be patronizing," Beth snapped.

"I'm not. I just think that Sarah is very much like you, and pushed into a corner would do something she'd regret later on." He paused briefly. "She's extremely sensitive, and we have to help her."

"I'll be with her, Ali and Jimmy Jay in Southampton over the Fourth of July," Beth said quietly. "Maybe with Ali and Jimmy Jay we can talk to her."

"I thought of that the minute Ali mentioned that you were going to be together."

Beth was taken aback. "When did you speak to Ali?"

"We speak all the time these days." Adam seemed self-conscious. "She's far more upset about what's happening between us than she lets on." He looked at Beth carefully. "She's worried about you."

"There's nothing to worry about," Beth said coldly.

"Beth, I'm not seeing Lauri anymore," Adam said quietly.

She did not react but Adam could see her body stiffen.

"Lauri didn't want the relationship, after all," he continued lamely.

Still not reacting, Beth turned abruptly and started walking away.

"May I drop you off in a cab?" Adam caught up with her.

"I'd rather walk."

"Sure it's safe?"

"I do it quite often these days, thank you." She did not look at him as she hurried down the Avenue.

Watching Sarah and Ali sitting beside her on the drive out to Southampton, Beth felt strangely content. Ali, blond and graceful, had her arm around Sarah, who was leaning comfortably against her sister. They did not look as though they were related, but in the time that Sarah had been home, she had come back to herself and her dark, intense beauty matched Ali's Nordic good looks. They were laughing and enjoying each other's company, and Beth was swept up by their gaiety.

"Will Grammy let Jimmy Jay into the house?" Ali asked mischievously.

"As a matter of fact, she did say she wanted us to invite him for a drink on the Fourth of July," Beth announced happily.

"How patriotic," Sarah chirped.

"It wasn't easy for her," Beth said seriously. "She's really very old and she isn't feeling well."

"I didn't mean to sound mean," Sarah apologized. "She's really quite a lady."

"Does she know about George and me?" Ali asked.

"She knows you've got a beau, as she calls him, and she's very pleased he's a professor," Beth said, with a twinkle in her eye. "She does not know you are living in sin, though."

"Don't tell her," Sarah said seriously. "I think it would hurt her."

Impulsively Beth put her arm over Ali's and they both held Sarah between them.

Martha and Joseph were waiting when the car came to a stop in front of the house.

"Where's Mother?" Beth asked with concern.

"She's lying down." Martha's voice was strained.

"Is she ill?"

"No, she's just tired." The old housekeeper tried to smile. "But now that you're all here she'll bounce right back."

"Let's all go up and see her," Beth suggested walking quickly toward the front door.

"Why don't you wait until she wakes up," Martha suggested. "She only fell asleep a few minutes ago."

A sense of foreboding took over immediately. Beth felt it and could see that both Ali and Sarah reacted as she did.

They went out to the patio and Martha came out with cold drinks and a magnificent tray of hors d'oeuvres, as Mary would have done had she been there.

"Joseph is taking your bags up to your rooms. Miss Mary specifically asked that you take the same rooms you had when you were little."

"I'd like to call her doctor," Beth said.

"He'll be here around four. Why don't you wait," Martha answered.

Beth looked at her watch. It was twelve noon.

"How about a game of tennis before lunch?" Ali asked Sarah.

"I'd rather stick around," Sarah said, looking at Beth.

"I'll go down to the club and be back by four," Ali said and left.

Finished with their drinks, Beth and Sarah went to their rooms. Beth felt restless and looked out her window at her mother's rooms which were across from hers. The sun was behind her and Mary's windows were strangely dark.

She's dying, Beth thought, and there's nothing I can do about it. She wanted to run to her, wanted to be in the room when her mother's life ended, but still she did not move. It would not be what her mother would want. Instead, Beth walked out of her room, knocked on Sarah's door and wordlessly the two walked down to the living room and sat silently waiting.

Mary Van Ess was buried next to her husband, and as at Drew's funeral, Beth was touched and amazed at the number of people who attended. The minister's eulogy referred to Mary as Drew's wife and recalled the old woman as a glorious extension of her illustrious husband. It bothered Beth that there was little reference to Mary as an individual in her own right, but she realized that in a way that was all that Mary wanted, and as such she had succeeded. Ali, dressed in black, standing next to George stood immobile and seemed removed. Sarah was also dressed in black and appeared more diminutive than ever. The sorrow was visible on her face, in her whole demeanor. Ali had been Mary's favorite yet Sarah was the one who was truly in mourning, and the closeness Beth had begun to feel for Sarah the day they waited for Mary's demise was re-inforced.

The eulogy ended. As the coffin was lowered, Beth struggled to re-etch her mother's features in her brain, tried to recall her voice. Already Mary was fading from her memory, and she was not yet covered with earth. There would be no more phone calls, no more fights, no more feelings of obligation, no more feelings of guilt. There would be no one to worry over or feel angry with, or frustrated about because there was little anyone could do to fill the loneliness of an old woman's life. There were so many questions that were left unanswered. Did Mary know about Gillian and Drew? What were her feelings if she did? Now she would never know.

Beth felt the tears trickle down her cheeks and put a handkerchief to her mouth hoping to stifle the sobs which were beginning to wrack her body. She had not cried for Allen and she had not cried for her father. Now she felt the pain of loss for them all. With the passing of her mother, the last vestige of the hopes and dreams of the Van Ess family was put to rest. She was no longer Allen's sister, no longer Mary and Drew's daughter. She was not Adam's wife and was not really Ali's mother, since Ali had moved into her own realm. For a while longer she could be Sarah's mother, but that too would end. She belonged to no one, and no one belonged to her.

Who am I? The old haunting thought returned. After all the years, there was no answer.

16

In the weeks following her mother's funeral, Beth watched herself as one would a stranger, and the picture was distasteful. Left in her parents' house in Southampton, with Martha and Joseph, she could feel herself being manipulated by unseen forces toward a life she had always loathed. With Mary gone, the two old servants, accustomed to their position in the Van Ess house, expected her to continue the traditions. She was the mistress who was to be served and protected. She fell into the role too easily, just as she had years back when she arrived with Ali and she thought her marriage was ending. But then she was Mary and Drew Van Ess's daughter. Now she was on her own, and she found herself settling into the empty chair left by her mother.

Breakfast was served in bed. The phone conversations with childhood friends followed. Luncheons were rotated among the summer habitués of yesteryear. Cocktail parties were dull but filled in the early evening hours. Dinner parties were elaborate and a waste of time. The country club atmosphere, with the aging roues and their wives, old and new, were unhappy reminders of the passing of time, although it seemed to Beth that she was the only one aware of it. The emphasis was on youth, and it dominated every conversation, every thought. Everybody played tennis, bridge, and the latest fad—backgammon. If the men looked ridiculous in their tennis outfits and their overbaked suntans, no one pointed it out to them. Their wives were hardly likely to notice since they were too involved with their diets, discussing the latest fashions, passing moral judgments about everything and wanting to be invited to the current "in" parties. Financial and social standing was still most important, and how to achieve both preoccupied them at all times. From the vantage point of wealth, their opinions on all matters were given with authority. On the rare occasion when Beth found herself involved in a discussion, pointing out a misconcept or disagreeing on a subject, the amazed disdain on the faces of her companions made her retreat without further comment.

She had been uncomfortable in the presence of the Southampton community for many years, but while married to Adam she felt immune and did not care about what they thought. Now, in spite of herself, she wanted to belong, to be accepted by them. She was searching for a niche and was reaching back to a long-forgotten time when she was part of the crowd. She hated herself for wanting attention from people who meant so little to her, but could not help herself. The women treated her pleasantly since she was no threat to them. The men were polite and indifferent. She was never fully aware of how indifferent they actually were to her during all the years when she had come to spend time with her mother. Then she was Congressman Adam Stillman's wife. She did not need them. Now she was simply an aging, about-to-be divorced lady.

In spite of her unhappiness, the summer went by quickly. She occupied her days sorting out her mother's clothes and various other mementoes. Everything had a history, but nothing seemed to be a foundation for the future.

Suddenly it was Labor Day weekend, and Beth discovered she had been left out of the gala end-of-season party at the club. In spite of her inner feelings about the people she had spent the summer with, she thought she had been accepted by them. She had even planned on seeing some of them in the city, hoping to widen her circle of friends and not be dependent solely on the relationships she and Adam had cultivated throughout the years.

Beth knew the party was being planned, heard the women discussing what they would wear with extra zeal and excitement. She was not included in the discussions, and on occassion she even felt conversation about the affair stopped when she was around, but she expected the invitation would be forthcoming. It did not happen. The day of the party, Beth wandered around the house, anguishing about what she had done to deserve the rejection. By ten o'clock that evening she could stand it no longer. She knew that if she did not leave the house, she would start drinking, and that terrified her. She could take a glass of wine if she was in the company of people; she dared not drink alone.

Putting on an oversized kelly-green T-shirt, a pair of white dungarees and an old pair of sneakers, she ran out to the garage, took her mother's car and started driving aimlessly. When she found herself passing the club, she drove into the parking lot as if possessed, and walked to the entrance of the small bar that was open to members even when private parties were in progress.

The bar was empty and Beth raised herself onto a barstool and ordered a brandy. Through the glass window, she could see the pool and the ballroom beyond. It was crowded with women wearing elaborate chiffon gowns or extremely high-fashioned evening pajamas, all by famous designers, and the diamond tiaras gleamed in the blazing lights. The men were in dinner jackets in varying colors and looked handsomer than they did in their daytime outfits. The clicking of champagne glasses mingled with gay laughter. Beth knew most of the people, and her bewilderment about her exclusion was more baffling than ever.

"Elaborate, isn't it?" the bartender said, looking at the glamorous crowd with admiration. Beth turned.

"The Blakes don't come to the Hamptons often, but when they do, it's always like that," he said in awe.

"Johnny and Jody Blake?" Beth was surprised. Throughout the years, Mary mentioned them with the same admiration and lamented the fact that Beth was no longer friendly with Jody.

"I'm as surprised as you are," the bartender continued. "I heard Mr. Blake was going to resign if that black singer was allowed to perform. But I guess he changed his mind, and frankly I'm glad he did. They add class to any place."

Beth looked at the man and wondered if he was aware of who she was and was being malicious.

"Give me two glasses and the best bottle of champagne you've got," someone said and Beth looked around. It took her a minute to realize the man was John Blake. The dim memory of the faceless boy Jody had dated was nowhere to be seen. He had grown into a heavy-set man with a mane of gray hair and a very tanned face. Standing next to him was a blond girl who was young enough to be his daughter. Suddenly he caught sight of Beth.

"Wanna join us?" he asked. "We're going to have a private party on the beach."

"Hello, John," Beth said, aware that he did not recognize her.

He came closer and peered at her. His breath smelled of liquor and he was obviously drunk.

"Well, if it isn't Beth Van Ess." He laughed unpleasantly. "Why don't you join us and try for a white, non-circumcised cock for a change." He put his hand roughly on her shoulder.

Her hand shot up and hit him across the face with a force that amazed her. "You're disgusting," she said, and wrestled herself free from his grasp.

Furiously John grabbed Beth's brandy glass from the bar counter and flung its contents in her face.

The alcohol made her eyes sting and she grabbed for a napkin blindly and started wiping her eyes. By the time she looked around, John and the girl were gone. The bartender was too stunned to move.

Beth ran to her car and sped out of the driveway and headed toward the highway. Her eyes were still smarting from the alcohol and she reached into the glove compartment and took out a pair of sunglasses. She did not know where she was going, but she wanted to be as far

away from the club as possible. A police car siren stopped her, and she
came back to herself and pulled over to the side of the road.

"You can get killed driving like that, lady," the officer said leaning
against the car window.

"I'm sorry. I didn't realize I was speeding," she answered trying to
sound calm. "Where am I, anyway?"

"You been drinking?" he asked leaning closer, and Beth was conscious of the odor of brandy still clinging to her clothes.

"I had a drink at the club," she started feebly.

"Let me see your driver's licence." His voice hardened.

She handed it to him.

"Registration?"

She fished it out of the glove compartment.

"Who's Mary Van Ess?"

"She's my mother."

"Please follow me to the station." He started toward his car.

Will this nightmare ever end? Beth thought following the police car
off the highway.

Beth watched the patrolman hand the license and registration to the
policeman sitting in the stationhouse. They both looked over at her and
she felt self-conscious, aware that she reeked of alcohol.

"Beth," the patrolman said unceremoniously, and the use of her first
name, offended her. "Could you step over here?"

She did as she was told.

"You sure you haven't been drinking?" one of the men asked.

"I told you I had a drink at the club," she said quietly.

"Now this Van Ess and Stillman thing. Is your mother home?"

"My mother is dead." Beth was getting angry. "My maiden name was
Van Ess, my married name is Stillman."

"What do you do for a living?"

Suddenly something snapped in her. "I think this has gone on long
enough," she said evenly. "What is it you want?"

"Well, I think you've been drinking, and I don't know whose car
you're driving. And I don't like your attitude." He sounded mean.

She did not flinch. She knew she could mention Adam's name and it
would make them change their attitude, but she dismissed the thought.

"And in my opinion, until we can figure out what's going on, I would
suggest you leave the car here and let the judge work this one out after
the weekend."

"I will not leave my car here," she said angrily. "I'm perfectly capable
of driving it home."

"If you push me, I'll have to lock you up, lady."

"On what charge?" She was furious, but kept her voice low.

"Drunken driving and possible car theft. You know you smell like a brewery."

Beth looked down at her stained shirt. She was not frightened and it pleased her. "I spilled some brandy on my shirt," she said, looking up. "That accounts for the odor, and if you don't believe me, you can give me an alcohol test. As for the stolen car charge. Please call my housekeeper, and she'll be happy to verify that the car is mine to drive."

The policemen looked at each other.

"And if you persist in this madness," she continued calmly, "I can assure you that the East Hampton police will be sued for false arrest, and you'll both feel like utter fools." She stopped, letting the words sink in. "Now, if I was speeding, which I assume I was, you can give me a ticket, but right now, I'm walking out of this place and I'll have my lawyer call the judge."

She turned around and started to walk out.

"Wait a minute lady," one of the policemen shouted angrily.

"She's right you know," someone said, and Beth saw an elderly man with a large Irish setter standing at the side of the entranceway. "If you think she's drunk, give her the balloon test, but I think your assumption about the car theft is rather farfetched."

Beth continued walking with great assurance, but her thighs were weak and her stomach was fluttering. Once outside, she leaned against the car briefly trying to regain her composure.

"You all right?" the man who had spoken on her behalf was standing beside her.

She smiled feebly. "I will be as soon as my stomach settles."

"You're the Congressman's wife, aren't you?"

"I'm Beth Stillman." She started opening the door of the car.

"R.B. is my name." He put his hand out. "May I buy you a drink?"

"I don't really want one."

"How about a coffee?"

"That sounds nice," Beth found herself saying, and was surprised.

"There's a little coffee shop up the road a bit."

The Irish setter got into the back seat and its owner sat down beside Beth.

"Arbee is a strange name," Beth said, once they were on their way.

"Those are my initials. R for Rajik and B for Barbacheck. Rajik Barbacheck was a bad way to present me to the world in Czechoslovakia; it was a worse choice for the United States. The kids at school had a field day with it when I was young. You wouldn't believe what they could do with it."

Beth found herself smiling. "When did you come to the States?"

"When I was two. But my proud parents would not hear of changing it."

"But when you grew up, didn't the older people accept it?"

"What are older people but youngsters grown bigger?"

He was extremely pleasant and Beth relaxed.

"What were you doing at the police station?" she asked.

"My lovely Rosie over there." He reached back and patted the dog fondly. "Runs away every weekend, and the cops pick her up and call me to come and get her. I think she does it on purpose so that I have to get out of the house and stretch my legs after a long week's work."

"What do you do?"

"I'm a composer and a concert pianist."

Beth threw him a sidelong glance. He was a slight man. His face was almost gaunt with high cheekbones, an aquiline nose, deep-set eyes behind large horn-rimmed glasses. His hair was white and very fine and came down over the gray turtleneck sweater. His lower lip protruded sensuously, and his smile was ingratiating.

"How did you get tangled up with the fearsome law enforcement of East Hampton?"

"I had a dreadful experience at the club back in Southampton, and I just had to get away. So I guess I was speeding."

"Nothing serious, I hope." He sounded genuinely distressed, and Beth found herself relating the whole episode with John Blake.

R.B. was a total stranger, and yet she felt more at home with him than she had with anyone that summer. He listened attentively, and when she finished he put his hand on hers and pressed it gently.

"What a dreadful story. What a dreadful man," he said with compassion.

"Where is that coffee shop, anyway?" Beth asked, embarrassed by her long dissertation.

"We passed it a while back, but I didn't want to interrupt you. It seemed you had to talk to someone, and it's good you got it off your chest."

"I think I'd better turn around." She stopped the car.

"We could have coffee at my place. It's on the beach, and I make a superb espresso."

She looked over at him.

"It's perfectly respectable. My daughter and my grandchild are there. My son will be coming in from the city later tonight, and it will all be above board. I promise."

The house was quite close to the water and was a strange conglomeration of structures, as though the owners had enlarged it at various times, indifferent to the traditional need for uniformity in architecture. It was shrouded in darkness and Beth felt uncomfortable.

R.B. opened the door for her and she walked in haltingly.

"Let me turn on lights before you trip." He rushed around turning on lamps.

The sight that greeted her put her at ease immediately. Although a complete shambles, the toys and child's clothing were all over the place, with books everywhere and unfinished meals still in plates on a low coffee table, the small living room looked refreshingly lived in.

"Chauncey is not the best housekeeper," R.B. said, but he did not seem embarrassed.

"Chauncey?"

"My daughter."

"And you suffered from a name like Rajik?" Beth began to laugh.

"My wife was Irish and insisted on her heritage when naming the children," he said seriously.

"And what's your son's name?"

"Casey."

"Are there any others?" Beth felt completely at ease.

"We have another daughter."

"Yes?"

"Ono."

"Who was Japanese in the family?"

"No one. But when Maureen was pregnant with the last one she wanted to name it Magillicutty, whether it was a boy or a girl. I put my foot down. I kept saying, 'Oh no!' every time she mentioned it, so that by the time she gave birth, Ono was it."

Beth was laughing merrily and so was R.B. "It's the God's honest truth though," he said finally, and started leading her toward a long glass-enclosed corridor at the end of which stood an enormous studio, with a domed skylight and a large picture window facing the ocean. The most prominent piece of furniture was a huge grand piano. Several sofas lined the walls and pillows were strewn all over them. Music sheets were lying carelessly on the floor.

"Here I must apologize for the mess myself," R.B. said, turning on a low lamp at the far end of the room. "This is my domain, and since Maureen's death, I won't have anyone come in here." He smiled sheepishly. "This house started out as a retreat for us and consisted of that living room you saw back there. Then the children arrived, and each time we added another room. But Maureen's ambition was to see me have a studio. She designed this, and supervised it's building, but she died before it was completed." His voice grew husky with emotion.

Beth walked over to the window and stared out. She was deeply moved by what she was hearing and felt like an intruder on someone's emotional property, and she wanted to give R.B. a minute to recover.

"If you'll make yourself comfortable," Beth heard him say, "I'll go make us the coffee I promised. Unless you've changed your mind and would like a drink."

"I really mustn't drink. It doesn't agree with me. So coffee would be lovely," she answered simply.

"Coming right up," he said, and a look of deep compassion came over his face.

Left alone, Beth wondered about the ease with which she said things to this stranger. She could not remember when she felt so comfortable with anyone. It was not anything he said but rather the way he looked at her when he spoke. The warmth he exuded, the understanding which she felt was in him from the minute she met him.

They were having coffee when a small redheaded child ambled in and walked sleepily toward R.B. He picked her up and cradled her in his arms.

"My granddaughter," he said with pride, kissing the child on the head.

Beth leaned back on the low sofa and felt happier than she had in a long time. She was in the presence of love and decency, and the pain she had been living with, for what seemed like an eternity, eased.

"You're quite the most beautiful woman I've ever seen," R.B. said quietly.

Beth believed he was sincere.

"But you're so unhappy."

"I'm not unhappy now," she answered solemnly.

They were silent for a long time. The sound of the waves settling on the sand dunes was soothing.

"Would you like to take a swim?" R.B. asked.

"I don't have a bathing suit."

"I'll get one of Chauncey's if you'd like."

"I'd love it."

He was a powerful swimmer, and after a few minutes Beth gave up and returned to the shore and watched him maneuvering gracefully through the choppy waters. An overwhelming physical desire for him sent a tremor through her body. Her heart began to pound and she found herself anxiously toying with the cool sand around her, as she strained to catch a closer look at him. It made no sense. R.B. was an old man. He was at least sixty years old, but even as the thought flashed through her mind, she realized he was not much older than Adam. Still, had anyone described him to her in the abstract, a gray-haired man, slightly stooped, a grandfather, over sixty, as a possible date, she would have been insulted.

R.B. was coming toward her and she still rebelled against the desire that was crowding out rational thinking. Settling himself beside Beth, he threw a large towel over her shoulders and pressed her to him. She did not resist. Instead she leaned closer and gave herself over to feelings that had been dormant in her for a long time. When he pushed her gently down and pressed his mouth to hers, she returned his kiss passionately. She felt his hand caress her body and she wanted to melt into him. Hesitantly she ran her fingers down his back. Her body felt light and graceful as she lifted herself off the sand to allow him to remove the lower part of the bathing suit. She was not conscious of his removing his bathing trunks, aware only that her body was pressing against his, and his lips were sucking her firm nipples. She was wet and pulsating when he entered her. A cry of pleasure escaped her, and briefly she opened her eyes. His face, close to hers against the backdrop of the dark, moonless sky, was beautiful, strong and filled with unhidden passion. When they were both spent, Beth curled up on her side with her back to him. She felt him cup her body with his as he held her close.

"Maureen has been dead for two years," she heard him whisper, "and you are the first woman I have desired since." He fell silent for a long time. "Thank you, Beth," he said finally.

"I wish Adam were dead," she said quietly. "It would make more sense if he were. I would be free then. I could start a life without anger or hurt. I could be sad, I could cry with justification that my marriage had ended. I could miss him, remember him as he was when we were happy."

"You don't mean that," R.B. said sadly. "I would give anything in the world to have Maureen back. But she is dead and that is final. She is gone forever. You still can hope."

"Hope for what?" Beth turned around to face him.

He sat up and hugged his knees, looking out to the horizon which could barely be seen in the darkness. "Hope to rebuild a life together again."

Beth sat up too and he put his arm around her shoulder and hugged her. "You're angry and hurt and puzzled. But you're beautiful, warm, kind and intelligent. I could love you deeply, try to make you happy, but it's Adam and the life you had together you will miss. With all its unhappiness, it was a life that grew and flourished. It doesn't get thrown away lightly."

"How do you know?" she asked.

"I feel it," he answered simply.

"Well you're wrong," Beth said, and for the first time since Adam left her she wondered if she meant what she was saying.

"May I call you when I get back to the city?" he asked. "I have a concerto to finish, but I shall be back in town around the fifteenth of September, and I would love to see you again."

"Please do," Beth said emotionally. "I'll look forward to it."

17

Martha was dozing on the little settee in the front foyer when Beth walked in. Dawn was breaking through and for a minute Beth did not see the old woman huddled in a blanket and was startled when Martha sat up.

"What are you doing up at this ungodly hour?" Beth gasped.

"I was worried about you, Miss Beth." Martha stood up stiffly.

The anger that surfaced briefly was put aside. "I'm a big girl, Martha," Beth said softly. "You can't go on treating me as though I were a child."

Martha became flustered and Beth felt sorry for her. "Why don't you go to bed now and I'll see you later," Beth said, starting toward the living room. She wanted to be alone with her thoughts.

"Would you like a coffee before I turn in?" Martha asked. "I have it all ready."

"I'll take it myself." Beth tried not to sound impatient.

Walking out onto the back patio Beth stood for a long time watching the sky grow brighter, taking on a spray of magnificent early dawn colors. Lying down on the padded hassock, she tried to evaluate what she had been through. The encounters with John Blake and the police were a nightmare, but the meeting with R.B. reduced their magnitude, almost wiping them away completely. Making love on the beach occupied her mind. It had happened so naturally, so simply. In her wildest fantasies she could not have imagined herself, at her age, lying on a beach naked with a man. She had watched television commercials of young, lithe girls and muscular young men running across sand dunes, embracing, kissing. She had sat through motion pictures where beautiful, young women and handsome, virile men made uninhibited love in glamorous settings, but it had been a long time since she had dared identify with the exuberant, voluptuous girls, laughing gaily at their companions. She could never drown out the longing for what was, but the reality of who she was, was ever present. She was a grown woman; a matron. She did not feel old, and knew she could be mistaken for someone years younger. But she was past fifty. That was an indisputable fact. Yet she had lain naked on a beach, just hours before, being made love to by a passionate, considerate lover. It was pleasurable and satisfying, and during that brief interlude she was ageless.

The sun was creeping slowly onto the patio and Beth was about to drift into an exhausted sleep when she heard someone running through the living room with Martha whispering urgently, "She's asleep, please come back later."

Beth sat up dazed, and it took her a minute to discern that the woman standing next to the hassock was Jody Blake. Beth blinked in disbelief and looked closely at Jody. She was dressed in an elaborate red chiffon creation and the ruby necklace and earrings were staggering. The opulent get up was in complete contrast to the haggard face, the smeared makeup, the messed up hair-do. Her eyes were hidden behind large gogglelike sunglasses.

"Were you with John last night?" Jody shouted hysterically.

"Was I what?" Beth was fully awake.

"He told me he saw you last night, and you spent the evening with him," Jody screamed uncontrollably.

"I did what?" Beth tried to make sense of what was being said.

"He always told me you were no good," Jody mumbled, and Beth realized she was drunk.

"Martha, would you get us some coffee." Beth stood up and moved toward the housekeeper who was standing in the doorway, a terrified look on her face.

"Where were you last night?" Jody demanded.

"I don't think it's any of your business, but if it will make you feel better, I spent it with a friend in East Hampton."

Jody sank down on the hassock and began to shake. "I'm sorry," she said, putting her hands over her face. "I should have known he was lying."

"I'll go help Martha." Beth wanted to get away from the distraught woman.

"Please don't leave me alone," Jody pleaded.

Beth stood indecisively and wondered what she should do.

Martha arrived with the coffee and when Beth began to pour it, she noticed Jody had gotten up and was at the small portable bar, pouring herself a stiff drink of gin.

"Coffee?" Beth asked politely.

Jody ignored her. She sipped her drink, staring into space.

"What was it John said, anyway?" Beth asked after a while.

"It doesn't really matter." Jody came back to herself. "It's just that every so often he comes out with these vicious stories, and after all these years, I still can't get used to it."

"After all these years?" Beth repeated the words slowly. "How long has this been going on?"

"I found John in bed with my son's governess when my baby was two years old." Jody sounded resigned and defeated. "And he's been unfaithful to me ever since."

Beth stared at Jody, finding it hard to believe that years earlier she had actually felt hurt and rejected by the Blakes.

"He's a crude, vulgar man," Jody's voice droned on. "He's petty and mean, and I can honestly say I hate him with every bit of passion in me." She removed her glasses and Beth was shocked to see one of her eyes was badly bruised.

"Why did you stay with him?" Beth found her voice.

"At first I felt guilty about my escapade in St. Moritz, and I thought I'd never find anyone who would marry me other than John."

Beth wanted to laugh. "Why? Because you weren't a virgin?"

"Twenty-five years ago I believed it, and there were extenuating circumstances."

"Who was it anyway?" Beth asked curiously.

"He was a boy I met while we were still at college. His name was Hans. He was German and he was studying at Harvard."

"Were you in love with him?"

"I think so." Jody smiled wryly.

"Why did you marry John, then?"

"Hans was a foreigner," Jody sounded as though the phrase was self-explanatory. "Besides, he had no money."

"But your parents had money, surely that couldn't have been a factor," Beth said with exasperation.

"You're so naïve, Beth." Jody stood up and walked over to the bar to refill her glass. "What we had isn't money. The *Blakes* have money."

"And you married and stayed with John because of his money?"

"It didn't start out that way," Jody said angrily. "He was understanding and considerate and then"—her face took on an expression of a poisonous snake—"he changed and I found myself married to this monstrous, boozing stranger." Her eyes narrowed. "He thinks I'll divorce him if he flaunts his little whores in my face, brings them into the house, takes them on trips with us, humiliates me in front of everyone. Well, he can forget it. I've paid too high a price and now I want my share, but more than anything, I want revenge."

"I'm sure any court would award you a sizable settlement, if what you're telling me is true," Beth ventured haltingly.

"But I'd be alone." The hysteria was back. "Look at me. I'm fifty years old and with all the face-lifts, the body surgery, the spas and injections, I'm not likely to find someone who would want me except for my money. I'm too old for a romance and not old enough to agree to support a young gigolo." She poured herself another drink. Then in a complete reversal of mood, she turned back to Beth. "Aren't you drinking?"

Beth felt uncomfortable. "I guess I'll have a glass of wine." She did not really want one, but her throat felt parched. Jody was wording thoughts she had secretly contemplated. Hearing them spoken, Beth knew they were alive in her unconscious mind. She too had thought of revenge, felt hurt at being deserted, humiliated by the fact that people knew of Adam's unfaithfulness. But, she thought defensively, her marriage, while it lasted, had been built on respect and admiration for Adam and what he did and stood for. And most important, she knew she did not hate Adam and was sure he did not hate her.

"Why didn't you leave John when you were younger?" Beth sipped her wine slowly.

"He wouldn't have given me my son, and I wouldn't have gotten a penny from him."

"How can that be?"

"The boy is not John's," Jody said in a strained voice. "I was pregnant when I married John, and he knew it."

Beth felt sick. Broadminded as she was, worldly and sophisticated, she could not accept what Jody was saying. She turned her back to Jody and wished she would leave.

"I told him about it before we were married and he accepted it," Jody was saying. "As a matter of fact, that was the reason he did not want me to see you. He felt it was all your fault."

"He didn't think I was the father?" Beth said mirthlessly.

"I told him we were with your friends . . ."

"What made him change?" Both ignored the remark.

"I think it would have been all right had we been able to have children together, but it turned out that John is sterile." Jody fell silent for a minute. "That's when it all fell apart. He became vicious. I wanted to leave him then, but he wouldn't give me my boy, and my choices were to drag him into court and expose everything or stay. A public scandal would have hurt everybody, so I stayed."

Beth regained her composure. "So you live a life of humiliation, degradation, eaten up with hate." She could not keep the disdain out of her voice. "Don't you mind everybody knowing about your twisted life with John?"

"Nobody knows about what I've told you," Jody gasped. "He'd kill me if he knew I told you."

"Which makes it even worse for you."

A garrulous laugh escaped Jody's throat. "When you have as much money as we do, it doesn't really matter. Everybody accepts us, no matter what. Didn't you know that? Everybody at the club in Southampton and everywhere else. They grovel to have us at their parties, listen to what we say, wait to serve us, be with us. We are responsible for people's livelihood, either directly or indirectly. We are the Blakes."

The "we" was emphasized and rang out clearly. Beth wanted to cover her ears.

"Jody, I've got several chores to do this morning," she said civilly.

Beth watched Jody walk shakily toward a chauffeur-driven Rolls-Royce, watched the liveried driver help his drunken mistress into the back seat and saw Jody sink down out of sight.

Walking back slowly to the patio, she poured the remains of her wine into the hedges, corked the bottle and went to look for Martha.

She left Southampton the next day.

18

"It's time to get up, love." Beth heard R.B.'s voice and opened her eyes to see him standing by the bed with a tray holding two cups of steaming coffee and a plate with fresh buns.

"What time is it?" she groaned, struggling to sit up in bed. The room was still in semi-darkness and she could hear the rain pounding on the window panes.

"Six-thirty, and it's March eighteenth and you asked me specifically to wake you early." He placed the tray down on her lap and sat down at the edge of the bed.

"How can you be so energetic so early in the morning?" she asked sleepily, glancing around the small bedroom she had grown to know intimately since they started their affair shortly after he returned from East Hampton.

"Rosie sees to that," he grinned. "You know how she is about her morning run. We've already been to the park, and I got these fresh buns for you." He pushed the plate toward her. "They're delicious."

"It's pouring outside." She picked up her cup and drank the hot brew slowly. "And I wish I didn't have to go to work."

"Who said you do?" R.B. said seriously. "Nobody forced you to get a job and as far as I'm concerned, I wish you weren't working and could go to St. Paul with me and hear the concert and then we could go to Bermuda and relax."

Beth smiled. "Some day I'll get there."

"Haven't you ever been?"

"I've been invited, mind you, but I never quite made it." She put her cup down, pushed the tray away and started out of bed. "I'd better get myself organized, and then I have to call Lenny and wake him up."

"Can't your boss afford an alarm clock?" R.B. asked.

"He sleeps through it, and today is an important day at the office." She picked up her clothes which were neatly piled on a chair in contrast to R.B.'s which were strewn around the room carelessly.

When Beth came out of the bathroom, showered and dressed, she walked over to the phone and dialed.

After several rings, Lenny came on the wire.

"Lenny, it's seven o'clock and the presentation is at ten." She heard him groan. "Now, really, Lenny, there are several things that you've got to attend to before the Pepsi people arrive. I've got everything set up, but you'll have to look over the projectors, the slides and make sure the speakers are properly synchronized." She looked around while speaking and could see the large studio through the bedroom archway and the endless sheets of music on the floor around the black grand piano. As always, she was amused and slightly distressed at the messiness. "Okay, Lenny. Now make sure you don't fall asleep again. And please call Mel and wake him."

Hanging up, Beth picked up a cigarette and lit it.

"Who works for whom in that office, anyway?" R.B. asked. "When you got the job six months ago, you didn't even know what media communication was. Now you seem to be running the whole show."

"No, I'm not," Beth laughed. "It's just that Lenny and Mel are two geniuses when it comes to putting on industrial shows but are hopeless on office procedure and the finer details. That's why I'm perfect for them. Gillian was right on when she recommended I go see them, and believe me, they were as scared of hiring me as I was of going to work for them."

"Well, as I see it, six months from now you'll be the boss and they'll be working for you."

"Not a chance," Beth said seriously, walking over to a small table she had converted into a dressing table, and started applying her makeup. "I don't want to be top man. When I was young I thought I did. I honestly believed the day would come when I could be the big executive who pulls all the strings." She moved away from the small makeup mirror and examined her handiwork. Her eyes were clear, her skin white and unblemished, the black turtleneck sweater emphasized her fair complexion, and she knew she looked well. "I don't have that killer instinct. I know where the jugular is, but I can never really dig the knife in. Lenny and Mel can and do. They aren't able to wake up in the morning, so they hire someone like me who can. But when it comes to the clinches, they're masters. When they put an industrial show together, they strangle the competition, wring everyone around them dry, and that's why they're tops in the field."

"How old are they?"

"I don't know. Late twenties, early thirties. But it has nothing to do with age. They're good at what they do, and they know it. That's why they could afford to hire me. They're not scared of me."

"Beth, why are you working?" R.B. asked, suddenly serious.

"Because I need a framework, a point of departure. I need to be part of something where I feel useful and productive and appreciated."

"I need you."

"Yes, I know you do. But in your life I come after Chauncey, Casey and Ono, not to mention your work. Just as Ali needs me after George and the kids, Sarah needs me after Philip." She smiled, "She's breaking up with him, but I'll be second in line when she meets her next love. Jimmy Jay needs me second to his latest lady love, his career and his causes. At that little office, I'm needed because I produce, and they don't and can't take me for granted." She got up and picked up her trench coat. "That's enough serious talk for one morning," she said in a change of mood. "And I do wish you'd let me send Lydia over here to clean up this shambles."

"No way," R.B. said in mock horror. "She'd make order and I'd never find anything ever again. Besides, Lydia disapproves of me."

Beth had to laugh. Lydia was shocked the time she came to work and found R.B. had spent the night there. She had never been able to be civil to R.B. after that. "I've got to run," she said, struggling into her coat. Then going over to him she leaned down and kissed him on the forehead.

He pulled her to him, almost roughly. "You've made me very happy these last few months. You know that, don't you?"

"I don't think I would have survived had I not met you," she whispered.

"Yes, you would have." He touched her face with the tips of his fingers. "That lady I met at the police station was a survivor."

She straightened up. "Thank you, R.B. But even survivors need a helping hand." Reaching the bedroom door she turned around, "Incidentally, I won't be having dinner with you this evening. Adam is coming over to discuss Ali's wedding and all that financial garbage which I've never been able to understand. Now that she's twenty-five and her inheritance goes to her, Adam wants to make sure that George understands who owns what."

"You see, you have your priorities too," R.B. said.

"Of course I do," Beth said patiently. "I wasn't complaining about your obligations. I was simply pointing them out. We're both grown-ups and we come to a relationship with baggage, be it family, habits or mannerisms we cannot and probably don't want to change. We're set; molded by our former lives. It's different when you marry young and are still able to change somewhat, are willing to learn new ways, fit into another human being's patterns."

"I adore you, Beth." R.B. looked at her tenderly. "And I wish I could say I would have liked to know you when you were young." He shrugged his shoulders helplessly, "But then I wouldn't have known Maureen, or known my children, so I guess you're right."

Beth threw him a kiss. "I'll speak to you later today."

Going down the elevator she thought of R.B.'s last remarks. It would have been nice to have known him when he was young, but then she would not have known Ali, Sarah or Jimmy Jay. Or Adam. The last thought pleased her. She had come a long way since that night when Adam had walked out of their bedroom.

The day rushed by and suddenly it was six o'clock in the evening and Beth knew she would be late getting home. Dialing her home number, she could not quell the feeling of satisfaction over the successes they had had with their presentation. Lenny and Mel were hired to do the show and their gratitude to her was genuine, and Beth knew she deserved their praise.

"Mr. Stillman will be there around six-thirty," Beth said when she heard Lydia's voice. "I'll probably be late since there won't be any cabs around, so if you'd put some soft drinks in the bar . . ."

"Mr. Stillman coming here?" Lydia could not contain her excitement. "Oh, I wish you would have told me earlier, I would have prepared some appetizers."

"You know he's not a great one for that." Beth smiled.

Hanging up, Beth was touched by Lydia's reaction. Her own automatic instructions concerning the soft drinks amused her even more. Habits, she thought, persisted no matter what.

Straightening up her desk, she made several notes on her calendar, called the telephone service to say she was leaving for the day, and put on the night alarm. Just before turning off the lights, she looked around her small office. It was her home away from home and she loved it.

As she suspected there were no cabs and she finally had to take a crosstown bus from Columbus Circle to her home.

Letting herself into the apartment, Beth could hear Lydia talking to Adam. Throwing her trench coat down on the chair, she walked into the library.

Adam stood up and came toward her. She had not seen him since the night they had dinner with Sarah and Philip, and she found herself looking at him almost objectively. She felt no anger, no hostility, no resentment. He was a handsome, elegant man, she thought almost impersonally.

"How are you Beth?" he asked.

"I'm great, Adam, simply great."

"You look sensational."

"It's been an unbelievable day at the office. We landed an incredible account, and I don't remember feeling such a sense of accomplishment since . . ." She stopped, and knew she was about to mention Adam's first campaign victory. "Since I don't know when," she finished, feeling slightly confused. Then she smiled. "Would you like a drink?"

"Let me get it," Adam said quickly, heading for the bar. "Wine?" he asked.

She was about to say yes, but changed her mind. "A Coke will be fine."

Settled on the couch, with Adam sitting in his usual chair, Beth marveled at how they had each taken their habitual place. The conversation about Ali's wedding preoccupied them, and fleetingly Beth knew that what she had said to R.B. that morning about former lives and priorities applied to her and Adam, to most people who shared a life together, who had a history together. To them their daughter's wedding, her future security and happiness was equally important. They had a past and it could not be ignored.

"You're not listening, Beth," Adam said, and Beth looked up in surprise.

"I'm sorry, my mind was elsewhere."

"How does the financial set-up seem to you?" he asked seriously.

"I guess it's fine. You know the money end of things is not my strongest point."

"You did all right after you figured out how to maneuver the bank manager that first year we were married." He smiled and winked at her. "You thought I didn't know your dealings, didn't you?"

"Well, you were completely hopeless in terms of what was important and what was not."

"Like beeswax candles and fresh-cut flowers daily when we could barely afford the rent?"

She laughed at the memory.

"Beth," Adam grew serious. "I've decided to run for the Senate, and I want you to help me."

She felt herself go tense.

"I don't think I can, Adam. I'm involved with an important project at work. They're depending on me."

"I need your help, Beth. I don't think I can do it alone."

She cleared her throat and looked at him for a long moment. "Frankly, Adam, I don't think you can afford me," she said finally.

"Oh, how much do you charge?"

"Nothing, and that's very expensive."

She stood up and so did Adam. Walking together toward the front door, Beth opened it and watched him ring for the elevator.

"What happens if I decide my campaign budget can take it?" he smiled at her.

"I'll think about it." She returned his smile.

The elevator arrived and Adam stepped into it.

Beth closed the door slowly and walked back into the library. She knew Adam would call, but resuming their life together would be her decision. Most important, she knew she had choices.